Autumn
Bridge

Also by Takashi Matsuoka

Cloud of Sparrows

Autumn Bridge

TAKASHI MATSUOKA

HUTCHINSON
LONDON

Published by Hutchinson in 2004

1 3 5 7 9 10 8 6 4 2

Copyright © Takashi Matsuoka 2004
Endpaper map by Michael Gellatly

Text design by Lynn Newmark

Takashi Matsuoka has asserted his right under the Copyright, Designs
and Patents Act, 1988 to be identified as the author of this work

First published in the United States by Bantam Dell,
a division of Random House, Inc. in 2004

The Random House Group Limited

20 Vauxhall Bridge Road, London SW1V 2SA

Random House Australia (Pty) Limited
20 Alfred Street, Milsons Point, Sydney
New South Wales 2061, Australia

Random House New Zealand Limited
18 Poland Road, Glenfield
Auckland 10, New Zealand

Random House (Pty) Limited
Endulini, 5a Jubilee Road
Parktown 2193, South Africa

The Random House Group Limited Reg. No. 954009

www.randomhouse.co.uk

A CIP catalogue record for this book is available
from the British Library

Papers used by Random House are natural, recyclable products made from wood
grown in sustainable forests. The manufacturing processes conform to the
environmental regulations of the country of origin

Printed and bound in Great Britain by
Mackays of Chatham Plc

ISBN 0-09-179498-6

For my grandmothers
Okamura Fudé, born in Wakayama in southern Kansai
Yokoyama Hanayo, born in Bingo Village in Hiroshima Prefecture

For my mother
Haruko Tokunaga, born in Hilo, Hawaii

And for my daughter
Weixin Matsuoka, born in Santa Monica, California

With gratitude and respect
For bringing me as close as I will ever be
to
Lady Shizuka

List of Characters

1281–1311

HIRONOBU:	*First Great Lord of Akaoka*
LADY SHIZUKA:	*Wife of Hironobu*
GO:	*Hironobu's bodyguard*

1796–1867

KIYORI:	*Great Lord of Akaoka, 1796–1860*
GENJI:	*Great Lord of Akaoka, from 1861*
SHIGERU:	*Son of Kiyori, Uncle of Genji*
HIDÉ:	*Genji's Chief Bodyguard from 1861, later Senior General*
TARO:	*Second in Command of Genji's army from 1861*
HEIKO:	*A geisha; Genji's lover*
HANAKO:	*A housemaid of the clan, later Hidé's wife*
EMILY GIBSON:	*A Christian missionary*
MATTHEW STARK:	*A Christian missionary, later a businessman in San Francisco*
KIMI:	*A village girl*
GORO:	*The village idiot*
LORD SAEMON:	*Rival of Lord Genji*

1882

JINTOKU:	*Abbess of Mushindo Abbey*
MAKOTO STARK:	*Matthew Stark's son*
SHIZUKA:	*Genji's daughter, namesake of the first Lady Shizuka*

Autumn
Bridge

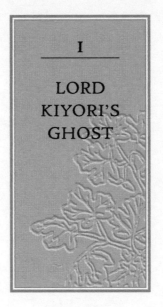

I

LORD
KIYORI'S
GHOST

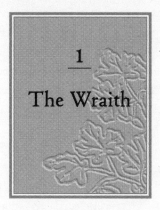

1

The Wraith

The Great Lord wields a sharp sword, rides a fierce warhorse,
commands unruly vassals. He has taken the heads of ten thousand
foes. His martial prowess is the marvel of the realm. But did he not
enter this world bawling from a woman's womb? Did he not suckle
helplessly at a woman's breast? And when the cold stars sparkle like
ice in the winter sky, and the depth of eternity chills his heart, for
what does he yearn more than a woman's embrace?

AKI-NO-HASHI

(1311)

1860, CLOUD OF SPARROWS CASTLE IN AKAOKA DOMAIN

Lady Shizuka had not changed in the slightest in all the years Lord Kiyori had known her. Her complexion was as smooth as the finest Ming porcelain, with the perfect pallor of a courtly woman of the inner chamber, unlined by the passage of time, unblemished by exposure to sunlight or hardship, without any telltale signs of inappropriate deeds, thoughts, or feelings. Her eyes, when they were not regarding him—shyly or knowingly or beguilingly, as the case may be—looked off into an imaginary distance, with an expression of imminent pleased surprise, an expression accentuated by her high, plucked eyebrows. Her hair was not arranged into a coiffure of the modern type, with its complexity of folds, stacks, waves, and accessory devices, but simply middle-parted and tied with a light blue ribbon into a loose ponytail at her shoulders, from where it continued to flow down her back in an elegance of lustrous ebony all the way to the floor. Her gowns, too, in polished and crepe silks of contrasting textures, were of the classical type, loosely fitted and layered in complementary shades of blue ranging from the brightness of a high mountain pool to the near black of the evening sky. She was the very picture of a princess of the Era of the Shining Prince. An era, he reminded himself, many centuries past.

Outside this room, the great military might of outsider nations crowded in against Japan. The gigantic steam-powered warships of America, Britain, France, and Russia now freely entered Japanese ports. Aboard those ships were cannons that could hurl explosive shells as big as men far past the shore, even beyond inland mountains and forests, and shatter armies concealed from sight before they were close enough to know who was killing them. The ocean that separated the islands of Japan from the rest of the world was no longer a defense. The navies of the outsiders had hundreds of such smoke-belching, cannon-bearing ships, and those ships could bring more than bombardment from afar. From distant shores, they could carry tens of thousands of outsider troops armed with more cannons, and with handheld firearms as well, and land them on the shores of Japan within a few months. Yet here in this room in the highest tower of Cloud of Sparrows Castle, the Japan of old lived. He could pretend, at least for a time, that this was the totality of the world.

She saw him looking at her and smiled. Her expression was simultaneously innocent and conspiratorial. How did she manage it? Even the most brilliant of geisha could rarely blend the two into a single look. Demurely, she lowered her gaze and covered her girlish smile with the wide sleeve of her antique Heian kimono.

"You are embarrassing me, my lord. Is something amiss in my appearance?"

"How can there be?" Lord Kiyori said. "You are and will always be the most perfectly beautiful being in all the realm."

A playful expression came into her eyes.

"So you say, again and again. Yet when was the last time you did me the honor of visiting me in my chambers?"

"I asked you never to speak of that again." He knew by the heat in his face that he was blushing. How shameful for a man of his dignity and years to respond like a smitten boy. "That it happened at all is a regrettable error."

"Because of the difference in our ages?"

Anyone seeing her would take her to be no more than eighteen or nineteen, in the first bloom of womanhood, a highborn lady without doubt, possibly even a virgin. Anyone looking at him would see a man of advanced years, posture unbent by age or defeat, standing in relaxed readiness, his white-streaked hair arranged in the elaborate style of a samurai lord.

The difference in their ages. Yes, there was that, too, wasn't there? It wasn't something he ever thought about anymore.

He said, "It will never happen again."

"Is that prophecy?" Her tone was mocking, but not harsh, as if she were inviting him to share in a joke rather than having one at his expense.

"You know very well it is not."

"Are you not Okumichi no kami Kiyori, Great Lord of Akaoka? Then surely you are a prophet, as is the leader of your clan in every generation."

"So people say."

"People say so because your actions are often not explicable except through foreknowledge. If you are not a prophet, then how can you know the future?"

"How indeed." He had always felt the burden of the curse of prophecy, but lately, for the first time in his life, he had begun to feel the weight of time as well. Seventy-nine years. According to the records of the ancients, men of old—heroes, sages, the blessed of the sacred gods—often lived to be a hundred and more. He couldn't imagine it for himself. Indeed, it was a marvel he had lived as long as he had, all things considered. He had acceded to the rule of the domain at fifteen, married at eighteen, had sons late, and had lost his wife at forty. During all that time, he had secretly kept company with Lady Shizuka. How long had it been? This was the fourteenth year of the Emperor Komei. They had met in the seventeenth year of the Emperor Kōkaku, whose reign had lasted thirty-eight years. After him, the Emperor Ninkō's twenty-nine years intervened before the ascension of the present sovereign. Was it sixty-four years ago? Out of habit, he double-checked himself using the outsiders' calendar. The seventeenth year of the Emperor Kōkaku was A.D. 1796. This was A.D. 1860. Yes, sixty-four years.

She had said she was sixteen when they met. She said she was nineteen now. In Kiyori's eyes, she had not changed at all. He felt a chill not brought on by the mild winter morning.

"How should I know?" Shizuka said. "You are the one with the visions, are you not?"

"Am I?"

"Surely you are not suggesting it is I who sees?"

"You have always made the claim," Kiyori said.

"And you have always denied it," Shizuka said. Concentration brought the slightest of furrows to her brow. She looked boldly into Kiyori's eyes. "Are you finally conceding the possibility?"

Kiyori was prevented from answering immediately by a voice outside the door.

"The tea is ready, my lord."

"Enter."

He distractedly watched the young housemaid, Hanako, silently slide the door open, bow, quickly survey the room, and pause. How thoughtless of him. By standing idly by the window, he gave her no point of reference. She would not know where to serve the tea. But before Kiyori could seat himself across from Lady Shizuka, Hanako went precisely where he would have guided her, at the midpoint between where he stood and where a guest would naturally seat herself in relationship to him. Hanako never ceased to impress him. From the first, when she had entered his service as a nine-year-old orphan, she had exhibited a quick intelligence and a strong intuition superior to that of most of his samurai.

"Thank you, Hanako. You may go."

"Yes, lord." Hanako bowed. Walking in reverse so as not to turn her back on the lord, she began to withdraw from the room.

"Aren't you forgetting something?" Shizuka said, her voice so faint a whisper it could have been imaginary.

"Hanako. One moment." What had he forgotten? Oh, yes. "When the courier returns to Edo tomorrow, you will accompany him. There you will join Lord Genji's household staff at Quiet Crane Palace."

"Yes, lord." Although the command had come without warning, Hanako showed no sign of surprise. She assented unquestioningly, which was exactly the correct response.

"You have served me very well, Hanako. Your parents would be proud of you." Kiyori, of course, neither made apologies nor gave explanations for sending her away with no prior notice.

"Thank you, lord. You have been very kind to put up with my failings for so long."

He ignored the formal expression of humility. "I will be very grateful if you serve my grandson as well."

"Yes, lord. I will do my best."

When she had gone, Kiyori said, "Why am I sending her to Quiet Crane?"

"Are you asking me, my lord?"

"I am only thinking out loud," Kiyori said. "A bad habit that has given me a reputation for more eccentricity than I deserve."

"It is good you have thoughts on the matter, since the decision is yours." She paused before adding, "Is it not?"

Kiyori smiled sourly. He was in the same fix he always got himself into whenever he had conversations with Shizuka. His reasoning in these matters, no matter how logical, was almost always wrong. Such was the difference between logic and prophetic guidance.

He said, "I am sending Hanako to my grandson because now that he has assumed most of the formal duties of the Great Lord of our domain, he is in greater need of reliable servants than I am. This is particularly so because three more Christian missionaries are scheduled to arrive in Edo any day now, and they will live in Japan under our protection. Their presence will trigger a crisis that will determine the future of our clan. Beyond this immediate matter, I am hoping for a mutual blossoming of affection between Hanako and Genji. She is precisely the kind of woman he needs beside him in this perilous age."

"How consistent you are, my lord. Such clarity of thought, always."

"I take it I am mistaken." Kiyori poured tea for them both, a polite formality since Shizuka, as usual, did not take hers.

"The great difference in their social status is not an impediment?"

"Because the future will bring chaos, character is far more important than status."

"How wise," Shizuka said, "how liberated from the artificial strictures of social convention, how in keeping with the times."

"You disagree?"

"Not at all. My views are antiquated, and I know so little of the outside world, yet it is clear even to one with such constricted understanding that inherent merit is now far more valuable than inherited rank."

"You agree, yet you seem amused by my words. I take it Hanako and Genji are not destined for each other."

"There is always more to know," Shizuka said. "Whether it should be known is another matter. Do you wish to know more?"

"I wish to know no more than what I must know to insure the well-being of our clan."

"Then you know enough," Shizuka said.

Kiyori sipped his tea. His expression was placid, hiding the immense irritation he felt at her failure to satisfy his obvious curiosity. Would Hanako and Genji fall in love? He could not ask her, not because the question was inappropriate—it concerned the succession of the prophetic power to the generation after Genji, a singularly important matter, and not one of mere romantic speculation—but because the asking itself raised an implication he had managed to avoid for sixty-four years. If she was going to tell him, she would have to do so without any request from him.

When it became obvious that he would not continue the conversation, a look of sadness came into Shizuka's eyes. She became very still. This happened not infrequently during their times together. In such moments of melancholy repose, her beauty was particularly ethereal. Could a man behold a vision so exquisite it alone was enough to drive him mad? If so, it would explain much, would it not? He had seen her at her most enchanting many, many times.

As he rose to leave, Shizuka surprised him. She said, "I have never asked you for a favor, my lord, nor will I ever ask another. Will you grant this one?"

"What is it?"

"If you will consent, you must do so without knowing."

To hesitate would be unmanly. "Then I consent."

Shizuka bowed deeply, her head to the floor before her. "Thank you, my lord."

Kiyori waited for her to continue. She kept her head down for a long time without speaking. When she looked up, her eyes were wet. He could not remember ever having seen her cry before.

Tears streaming, she said, "Take your evening meal here, then stay the night with me."

"This is a most unfair request," Kiyori said, genuinely aggrieved. "You have tricked me into agreeing to do what I have pledged my life and honor not to do."

"I ask only that you share my chamber, not my bed. My blood is as purely samurai as your own. I would never deceive you into violating a pledge."

Kiyori was still upset. He may not start the night in her bed, but being in the same room with her for an entire night, could he avoid ending there? Though his resolve was strong, he was a man, with all of a man's weaknesses. But there was no choice. He had already agreed. "Very well. Just this one night."

"Thank you, my lord," Shizuka said. She looked up and smiled at him through her tears.

Kiyori did not return her smile. It would be a very long night.

· · · · ·

Hanako packed her belongings for the trip to Edo. She could hear two of the younger maids chattering in the next room.

"Lord Kiyori has ordered that dinner tonight be served to him in the high tower."

"No! How many settings?"

"Two! And he specifically said there was to be no sake."

"Dinner in the high tower. And no sake. How strange. He would only have dinner there if he intended to see an important guest in private. But for such a guest, he would order sake, wouldn't he?"

"Perhaps he doesn't expect a guest of the usual kind."

"You don't mean—"

"Yes!"

"His wife, do you think, or the other?"

This had gone too far. Hanako put down her folded clothing, went to the door dividing the two rooms, and slid it open. The two maids jumped, saw who it was, and sighed in relief.

"Oh, it's you, Hanako."

"Yes, it's me, fortunately. What if it weren't? What if it had been Lord Kiyori?"

"Oh, he never comes into the maids' quarters."

"Nevertheless, stop gossiping," Hanako said. "Or, if you must, then do so more discreetly."

"Yes, you're right," one of the maids said. "Thank you for reminding us." They both bowed to her.

Hanako began to close the door between the rooms again when one of them spoke up quickly, in a loud semblance of a whisper.

"Who do you think it is, Hanako? His wife? Or the other?"

"I don't speculate about it. Nor should you." She closed the door on the wide-eyed girls. After a few moments of silence, she heard them whispering to each other again.

In truth, Hanako had an opinion, of course, though she would never speak it. It would have been less distressing if Lord Kiyori were meeting his wife, Lady Sadako. But Hanako doubted that he was. During the thirteen years she had been in the service of the Okumichi clan, she had overheard bits and pieces of Lord Kiyori's private conversations many times. When he was with his unseen visitor, he never said Lady Sadako's name. And the voice he always used then was the hushed and secretive one characteristic of clandestine lovers. He was not meeting his wife's ghost. He was meeting the other.

A chill ran through her body. It stopped under her skin just short of a shudder, and bumps rose on the skin of her arms, back, and neck as if tiny needles were poking her from within.

She wondered if Lord Genji would also meet with the other. Then she wondered whether he already had.

1311, CLOUD OF SPARROWS CASTLE

Shizuka sat in meditative silence for several minutes after Lord Kiyori left the room. Then she rose and went to the window where he had stood and looked outside. Had he seen what she now saw? The evergreen hills of Shikoku Island, the heavy gray sky, the white fringes of waves whipped to life by distant ocean storms and winter winds? She should have asked him. Perhaps tonight she would. They would stand together by this window in the high tower of their castle, and they would look out over their domain of Akaoka. It would be their last night together. They would never see each other again.

"My lady."

"Enter."

The door slid open. Her chief lady-in-waiting, Ayamé, and four other attendants bowed at the doorway. None of them bowed in the normal ladylike manner, with both hands placed on the floor and the forehead lowered gracefully nearly all the way down. Instead, they knelt on one knee only and bowed at a slight incline from the waist, the bow of warriors on the battlefield. They were dressed in trouserlike *hakama* instead of the elaborate, flowing kimonos of women of the inner chamber, and the sleeves of their abbreviated jackets were tied back out of the way, so their arms could more freely wield the long-bladed *naginata* lances they carried. In addition to the naginata, each of the attendants had a short *wakizashi* sword tucked into her sash. Ayamé alone had two swords at her waist, a long-bladed *katana* in addition to the wakizashi. Except that she was a young woman of seventeen, she was the picture of a heroic samurai. Even her hair had been cut, no longer flowing to the floor and behind her, but truncated into a ponytail that stuck out barely ten inches from her head. Man or woman, how easy it would be to fall in love with someone so handsome.

Ayamé said, "It is as you said it would be, my lady. Lord Hironobu has not returned from the hunt. No messenger has come from him. And here at the castle, none of the samurai known to be loyal to the lord and to you can be found."

"My lady," said one of the attendants behind Ayamé, "it is not too late to flee. Take a horse now and ride to Lord Hikari's castle. He will surely protect you."

"Lord Hikari is dead," Shizuka said. She went on as shocked gasps came from her ladies. "So is Lord Bandan. And their heirs and all their families. Treachery has reached almost everywhere. Tonight, their castles will go up in flames. Tomorrow night, the traitors will be here."

Ayamé bowed, again the short military bow of the battlefield, her eyes locked with Shizuka's. "We will take many of them with us, my lady."

"Yes, we will," Shizuka said. "And though we will die, they will not triumph. Lord Hironobu's line will continue long after theirs have been extinguished." She felt the child kick and placed a palm on her swollen belly. Patience, child, patience. You will enter this tragic world soon enough.

Her attendants bowed their heads and wept. Ayamé, the bravest of them, fought back her tears. They welled in her eyes, but did not fall.

It was as dramatic as a scene in one of those Kabuki plays that Lord

Kiyori sometimes mentioned. But, of course, there was no such thing now. Kabuki would not be invented for another three hundred years.

1860, CLOUD OF SPARROWS CASTLE

Shigeru alternated between great stillness and sudden movement, sliding from shadow to shadow through the corridors of his own clan's castle as stealthily as an assassin. Though the ordinary eye could apprehend him if it alighted upon him, he moved in such a way that neither servants nor samurai noticed him. If they had, they would have acknowledged his presence, greeted him respectfully, and bowed. He in turn, seeing what was not there, would draw his swords and cut them down. This was his fear and the reason for his stealth. His control was slipping and he didn't know how much he had left.

His ears resonated with a demonic cacophony. His eyes struggled to ignore transparent images of torture and slaughter. Though he could still distinguish the world he walked through from the world that emanated from his mind, he doubted that he could do so for much longer. He had not been able to sleep for days and the visions that kept him awake pushed him ever more strongly toward insanity. He was widely considered to be the greatest warrior of the present era, the only samurai in two hundred years worthy to be mentioned in the same breath as the legendary Musashi. With neither excessive pride nor false modesty, he believed his reputation was valid. But all his martial skills were useless against this enemy within.

As his malady worsened, he had resisted turning to the only person who could possibly help him. His father. As Lord Kiyori's only surviving son, Shigeru had been too ashamed to confess such weakness. In every generation of the Okumichi clan, one was born with the gift of prophecy. In the generation before, it had been his father. In the generation after his own, it was his nephew, Genji. In his, the burden had been placed on Shigeru himself. For over sixty years, Kiyori had used prescience to guide and protect the clan. How could Shigeru go crying to him the moment his own visions began?

Now, almost too late, he realized he had no choice. Visions did not come in the same way to everyone, nor could every seer cope with them on their own. He was being inundated with a hallucinatory deluge. Gigantic freakish machines resembling monsters of fable and legend writhed over the landscape, consuming passive lines of people dressed in bizarre uniform clothing. Air in colorful, putrid layers smothered the castle and the town. At night, the sky itself growled like the belly of a huge invisible beast and gave birth to a rain of fire that washed over screaming victims below.

What did this mean? If they were visions of the future, in what direction did they point him? Only someone with a similar experience could understand.

The conversations of maids told him where Lord Kiyori was. In the high tower. Because he was compelled to avoid being seen, it took Shigeru the better part of an hour to travel a distance that would normally have taken only a few minutes. But he congratulated himself on getting there undetected. No one had greeted him, so no one had died. Also, during the prolonged journey, his visions had abated. They would surely return soon enough, but the respite was welcome. He was just about to announce himself to his father when he heard him speak.

"I am sending Hanako to my grandson," Kiyori said, "because now that he has assumed most of the formal duties of the Great Lord of our domain, he is in greater need of reliable servants than I am."

Kiyori paused as if listening to a response, then spoke again. He continued in this way for some time. Outside the door, Shigeru focused his entire attention as carefully as he could, but did not succeed a single time in hearing the voice of whoever was with his father.

"Because the future will bring chaos," Kiyori said, as if answering a question, "character is far more important than status." Then after a short pause, "You disagree?" And after another pause, "You agree, yet you seem amused by my words. I take it Hanako and Genji are not destined for each other."

Hanako and Genji? Shigeru was shocked. Hanako was a maid in the castle. How could she be destined for a lord? Surely his father was not plotting some kind of devious mischief against his own grandson? Shigeru had to see Kiyori's companion. Whenever he spoke, Shigeru could tell the direction in which Kiyori faced by the waning and waxing of his voice. He waited for the appropriate moment and silently moved the sliding door enough to create a sliver of an opening. Moving across it from side to side, he scanned the room within as the conversation continued.

"I wish to know no more than what I must know to insure the well-being of our clan."

Kiyori sat in the center of the room sipping tea. The setting was for two. Another cup, filled, sat untouched across from Kiyori. Shigeru completed his survey of the room. There was no one else there. Had the person left through a secret passage unknown to Shigeru? That seemed unlikely. But he remembered that Kiyori had designed the tower himself, and no one else had seen the plans. Whoever had met with him certainly had not gone out the window. The only other way down was past Shigeru.

"What is it?" Kiyori said.

Thinking he had been seen, Shigeru went to his knees and bowed. He hesitated for a moment, not knowing what to say, and during his hesitation Kiyori spoke again.

"Then I consent."

Shigeru rose quickly. So someone was still there. Again, he looked into the room. Kiyori looked straight ahead and spoke again as if addressing someone directly in front of him.

"This is a most unfair request," Kiyori said. "You have tricked me into agreeing to do what I have pledged my life and honor not to do."

Shigeru shrank back, suddenly cold.

"Very well," he heard his father say. "Just this one night."

Shigeru retreated, moving with care at first, then he fled from the castle as swiftly as he could. His father could not help him, for he, too, was insane. Kiyori had been speaking to a woman. It might have been Lady Sadako, Kiyori's wife and Shigeru's mother. That was bad enough. Lady Sadako had died shortly after Shigeru's birth. But he didn't think the lady in question had been his late mother. Kiyori had spoken of a broken pledge in a peculiar, conspiratorial manner. He would not use such a tone with his own wife, not even the ghost of his wife.

The high tower of Cloud of Sparrows Castle, where Kiyori always spent so much time alone, had long had the reputation of being haunted. It was said the uncertain shadows of twilight there often resembled ancient bloodstains. Such stories always arose around places of ancient tragedy, and what castle in Japan had not seen its share? In this case, the tragedy had been treason, assassination, and gruesome murders that had nearly extinguished the Okumichi clan in its earliest days. That had been in the fall of the tenth year of the Emperor Go-Nijō.

The witch and princess, Lady Shizuka, had spent her last hours in that very room of the tower.

His father was consorting with a ghoul dead for more than five hundred years.

1311, CLOUD OF SPARROWS CASTLE

Shizuka and Ayamé looked out the windows of the high tower and watched the three streams of warriors moving toward Cloud of Sparrows.

"How many do you think they are?" Shizuka said.

"Six hundred from the east, three hundred from the north, another hundred from the west," Ayamé said.

"And how many are we?"

"Your sixteen ladies-in-waiting are within the tower. Thirty men, all personal retainers of Lord Chiaki, await the traitors at the gates of the castle. They came as soon as they were summoned. Messengers have been sent to find him. Perhaps he will arrive before the assault begins."

"Perhaps," Shizuka said, knowing he would not.

Ayamé said, "I find it difficult to accept that Go has betrayed Lord Hironobu and yourself. Is there no other possibility?"

"Go has arranged for Chiaki to be away from here at the critical moment," Shizuka said, "because he knows his son's loyalty is unshakable. Chiaki's absence is the proof. Go does not wish to kill him when he kills me."

"How cruel life is," Ayamé said. "Lord Hironobu would have died in childhood if not for Go. He would not have lived to become a Great Lord without Go's steadfastness and courage. And now this. Why?"

"Jealousy, greed, and fear," Shizuka said. "They can destroy heaven itself if the gods are lax for even a moment. How much more vulnerable are we here below."

They watched the enemy multitude merge and form a huge pool of warriors. Well before the sun fell behind the mountains, campfires sprang to life among them.

"Why do they wait?" Ayamé said. "They have an overwhelming advantage. One thousand against less than fifty."

Shizuka smiled. "They are afraid. Night falls. It is a time of power for witches."

Ayamé laughed. "Such fools. And they aspire to rule the world."

"Such is the aspiration of fools," Shizuka said. "Tell my attendants and Chiaki's samurai to rest. We are safe for a while."

"Yes, my lady."

"You need not return right away, Ayamé. I will be fine. Spend time with your sister."

"Are you certain, my lady? What of the child?"

"She's well," Shizuka said, "and will arrive when she should and not before."

"She?"

"She," Shizuka said.

If it was truly possible to feel great joy and great sorrow in a single moment without distinction, then perhaps Ayamé managed it then, as tears fell from her eyes and her face brightened with a perfect smile. She bowed low and departed in silence.

Shizuka composed herself and awaited Kiyori's arrival.

1860, CLOUD OF SPARROWS CASTLE

Hanako walked through the central garden of the castle. She would not usually presume to do so. The garden existed for the benefit of the lords and ladies of the clan, not for servants. But she was willing to risk censure. Tomorrow she would leave for Edo. Who knew when she would return? Perhaps never. She wanted to see the roses before she left. They blossomed here in such profusion, the castle was sometimes called Rose Garden Keep, instead of Cloud of Sparrows. She preferred the flowery name.

One blossom caught her eye. It was smaller than the rest, but fully petaled, and so red it could have been that color's definition.

Its brilliance in the fading light of day was irresistible. She reached out to touch it. An unseen thorn pricked her. When she drew her hand away, she saw a single drop of blood, the exact color of the petals, forming a tiny rosebud on her fingertip.

Hanako shuddered. Was it not an omen?

She hurried away to resume her evening duties.

· · · · ·

"What are you doing here?" Kiyori said.

Hanako and a second maid carrying the settings for dinner entered as he expected. Behind them, unannounced, came Shigeru.

Shigeru bowed at the threshold of the doorway.

"I apologize for appearing without your prior approval."

His quick survey of the room revealed no one other than his father. The dimensions of the room were unchanged, so no secret compartments had been installed since he had last been here. Yet tonight, as earlier in the day, he was sure his father had been talking to someone.

Kiyori did not like to be surprised. Hanako should have alerted him before she opened the door. He cast a disapproving look her way. But her startled expression showed that she had been unaware of Shigeru's presence. That could only mean that Shigeru had used stealth to remain undetected behind her. He noted his son's newly gaunt facial features and excessively bright eyes. Under other circumstances, his bizarre behavior and the clear outward signs of a deep inner turmoil would make Shigeru the immediate center of his focus. Tonight, however, Lady Shizuka must have his full attention. For all the years he had been seeing her, her visits had been no more often than twice a year at most. During the past week, he had seen her every day. This was surely a sign of his own mental deterioration. Okumichi prophets with rare exception were immolated by their prophetic powers at the end. Why should he be an exception? But he was determined not to shame himself and his clan. If his own time had come, and he was no longer of use to anyone, he would put an end to his own life rather than die a madman. He would have to deal with Shigeru later. If there was a later.

"Well, what is it?"

"I had hoped to speak with you on an important matter. However, I see that you are expecting a guest, so I will not intrude further. I will ask for your indulgence at another time." Shigeru bowed and departed. He had already done what was necessary earlier while the food was being prepared. He had come only to verify what he suspected. The guest was visible to no one other than his father.

· · · · ·

"The turning points of his life have already been reached," Lady Shizuka said after they were once again alone. "There is no more to do but to await the inevitable unfolding."

"That is not encouraging," Kiyori said.

"Why must you be encouraged or discouraged?" Shizuka said. "Facts are clearest when emotional qualities are not unnecessarily imposed upon them."

"Human beings," he said, "always feel emotions, though by training, inclination, or circumstance, they cannot and do not always act upon them."

"Human beings," she said. "Was it my imagination, or did you emphasize those words?"

"I did. I don't know what you truly are, but you are not human."

She raised a sleeve to cover her mouth and laughed, her eyes sparkling with an almost childish merriment.

"How alike we are, my lord, and how unalike. At the end of our time together, you have reached a conclusion similar to the one I reached at the beginning, when you first appeared to me."

It was several moments before Kiyori recovered enough to speak. "When *I* appeared to *you*?"

She rose, the silk of her layered kimonos rustling ever so slightly, the sound of wisteria leaves gently touched by a light breeze, and went to the eastern window.

"Will you indulge me, my lord?"

Kiyori, too shocked to resist, rose and stood beside her. She gestured out at the landscape.

"What do you see?"

"Night," he said.

"And what features of the night stand out?"

He struggled to center himself. Regulating his breathing, slowing his racing heart, ignoring the storm of thoughts that pressed against his eyes and temples, he concentrated on the night. At sea, a vigorous onshore wind raised whitecaps the height of a man and threw them against the rocky shore below. The same wind had blown the sky clear, and the stars sparkled unobstructed by clouds or mist. Inland, the sound of the wind in the trees drowned out the call of nightbirds.

He said, "A strong wind, a clear sky, rough seas."

She said, "It is night, but there is no wind at all. Mists roll down through the valleys, drift eastward over the campfires, and out into the ocean. In the morning, it will return to land as heavy fog. In the hour of the dragon, when the fog lifts, I will die." She smiled. "Of course, that means nothing to you, since you believe I am already dead, and have been for five hundred years."

"I see no campfires," he said.

"I know you do not," she said, "because just as I am not really there, you are not really here." She moved suddenly with unexpected speed, and before he could evade her, she touched him briefly. He felt, not the warmth of another's hand, but instead—

"A chill," she said, completing his thought, "not on the skin but deep within the bones, not like that brought by a northern wind, but sharper, as of a premonition of disaster."

"Yes," he said. "And for you?"

"The same," she said. "Listen. What do you hear?"

"The wind, rising."

"I hear a flute," she said. "Lady Ayamé, playing 'The Unseen Moon.' "

"I know the song," he said. "When Genji was a child, he played it often."

"What does it sound like?"

He felt that chill again.

He said, "The wind, rising."

"Yes," she said. "The wind, rising."

· · · · ·

Shigeru knelt before the altar of the temple in the dim light of a single candle. Only one course of action remained open to him. Had he not been so caught up in his duelist's ambition for so many years, he might have noticed that something was amiss with his father. Perhaps he would not have been so quick to ignore the rumors he had heard. Now it was too late.

He lit the first of the one hundred and eight sticks of incense he would burn during this sitting. One hundred and eight were the afflictions of man, one hundred and eight were the eons he would spend in one hundred and eight hells for the crimes he had begun to commit this night. By now, his father was already dead, poisoned by the blowfish bile Shigeru had put into his food. After his repentance ceremony was completed, he would find his wife and children. Then only his nephew, Genji, would be left. Soon the opportunity would come and Genji, too, would die. The curse of prophetic vision would end. That the Okumichi bloodline would also end was an unavoidable consequence.

With a reverent bow, Shigeru placed the incense on his father's funerary altar. "I am sorry, Father. Please forgive me."

He took a second stick and repeated the procedure.

"I am sorry, Father. Please forgive me."

The curse would end. It must.

"I am sorry, Father. Please forgive me."

The future was not meant to be known. When it was, it turned and devoured the knowers.

"I am sorry, Father. Please forgive me."

He hoped Lord Kiyori had not suffered. Before it brought death, blowfish bile induced hallucinations of the most vivid kind. Perhaps he had imagined himself in the embrace of his ghostly lover for the last time.

Shigeru lit the fifth incense stick. Smoke began to fill the small temple.

Outside, in the sky above, clouds had been blown ashore by the rising wind. The moon, full and bright an hour ago, was now hidden and unseen.

QUIET CRANE PALACE IN EDO

Okumichi no kami Genji, next in line of succession to the rule of Akaoka Domain, reclined on the floor in his usual unmartial manner, propped up on an elbow, a cup of sake in his hand, a faint smile on his lips. Most of the dozen geisha in attendance were dancing and singing and plucking out gay tunes on the strings of their *koto* and *shamisen*. One sat by his side, ready to pour should his cup need refilling.

She said, "Why have you stopped singing, my lord? Surely you know the words. 'The Abbot and the Courtesan' is one of the most popular songs of the season."

He laughed and raised his cup to her. "In a contest between singing and drinking, I fear singing must always lose." He lowered his cup after taking only the slightest of sips from it. His manner was that of an inebriated man, but his eyes, clear and bright, were not.

Genji's hair, elaborately and formally arranged as befitted that of a high lord, was in slight disarray, with a stray lock falling across his forehead. It not only emphasized his air of mild drunkenness, it also suggested a certain effeminacy, a quality suggested as well by the kimono he wore. It was much too brightly colored and intricately embroidered for a serious samurai of twenty-four, especially for one who was destined to be a Great Lord someday. In all Japan, there were only two hundred sixty of them, each an absolute ruler in his own domain. In Genji's case, the inappropriateness of his attire was further highlighted by his face, which bordered perilously on prettiness. Indeed, his smooth skin, long lashes, and delicately shaped lips would have improved the appearance of any of the geisha present. Except one. It was she who had Genji's full attention at the moment, though he disguised his interest well enough to conceal it.

Mayonaka no Heiko—Midnight Equilibrium—sat on the opposite side of the room, playing a shamisen. She was this season's most celebrated geisha. Genji had heard of her reputed perfection repeatedly during recent weeks. He had not given it much credence. Such reports were bandied about regularly every season. Last year's incomparable beauty was inevitably eclipsed by a new one this year, just as this year's would give way to yet another next year. Finally, he invited her to his palace, less out of interest than in order to maintain his reputation as the shallowest, most unserious lord in all of the Shogun's capital city of Edo. Now here she was, and to Genji's great surprise, she surpassed even the most fevered descriptions he had heard.

All true beauty transcended the merely physical. Yet her every action was so exquisite, he was not entirely sure whether he was seeing or imagining. The closing and opening of the delicate fingers of her hand, the inclination of her head in one direction or another, the slight parting of her lips as she inhaled in polite surprise at someone's supposedly clever remark, the way her smile began, not at her mouth, but in her eyes, as every sincere expression did.

This is not to say she was physically deficient in any way. Her eyes were the perfect shape of elongated almonds, her skin as unblemished as the nocturnal snow falling in the light of the full winter moon, the subtle curves of her body in her kimono an ideal complement to the fall of the silk, the small bones of her wrists suggestive of a tantalizing bodily fragility.

Genji had never seen a woman so beautiful. He had not even imagined one.

The geisha next to him sighed.

"Oh, that Heiko. Whenever she is around, it is impossible for the rest of us to keep anyone's interest. How cruel life is."

"Who are you talking about?" Genji said. "How can I see anyone else when you are so close?" His gallantry would have been more effective if he had said her name, but in truth, he could no longer remember it.

"Ah, Lord Genji, you are so very kind. But I know when I am defeated." She smiled, bowed, and made her way across the room to Heiko's side. They exchanged some words. Heiko passed her shamisen to the other geisha and came to sit beside Genji. When she crossed the room, the eyes of every man there followed her. Even Saiki, his dour Lord Chamberlain, and Kudo, the commander of his bodyguard corps, could not restrain themselves. If any of his samurai were traitors, as his grandfather suspected, now would have been the ideal moment to assassinate Genji. Except, of course, even the traitors, if there were any, were also watching Heiko. Such was the power of beauty. It overwhelmed even discipline and reason.

"I did not mean to interrupt your performance," Genji said.

Heiko bowed and sat beside him. The slight silken rustle of her kimono reminded him of the sound of waves receding gently from a distant shore.

"You have not interrupted me, my lord," Heiko said.

This was the first time he had heard her speak. It took all of his considerable self-discipline to keep from gasping in awe. Her voice had the quality of chimes, not in an exact sense, but in the way that their reverberations seemed endless even as they faded away. Now that she was close, he saw a hint of light freckles beneath her makeup. She could easily have concealed them, but she had not. The slight flaw brought to mind the necessary imperfections of life itself, its brevity and unpredictability, and imbued her beauty with a perfect hint of melancholy. Was she really so ravishing, or was his pretense of drunkenness more authentic than he had intended?

"I have interrupted you," Genji said. "You are no longer playing the shamisen."

"That is true," Heiko said, "but I am still performing."

"You are? Where is your instrument?"

She opened her empty arms as if presenting something. Her smile was as slight as it could be and still exist. She looked him directly in the eyes and did not turn away until he blinked, surprised by her words as well as her gaze.

"And what is the nature of your performance?"

"I am pretending to be a geisha who is pretending to be more interested in her guest than she really is," Heiko said. Her smile was slightly more apparent now.

"Well, that is very honest of you. No geisha I have known has ever made such a confession. Isn't it against the rules of your craft to admit even the possibility of insincerity?"

"It is only by breaking the rules that I will attain my goal, Lord Genji."

"And what is your goal?"

Above the sleeve that Heiko lifted to cover the smile on her lips, her eyes smiled brightly at Genji.

She said, "If I told you that, my lord, there would be nothing for you to discover but my body, and how long would that hold your interest, seductive and skilled though it may be?"

Genji laughed. "I have heard of your beauty. No one warned me of your intelligence."

"Beauty without intelligence in a woman is like strength without courage in a man."

"Or nobility without martial discipline in a samurai," Genji said, with a self-deprecating grin.

"How amusing it will be, if anything is to be at all," Heiko said. "I will pretend to be a geisha pretending to be more interested in her guest than she really is, and you will pretend to be a lord without martial discipline."

"If you are only pretending to be pretending, then doesn't that mean you really are interested in your guest?"

"Of course, my lord. How could I not be interested in you? I have heard so much about you. And you are so unlike other lords."

"Not so unlike all other lords," Genji said. "Many have dissipated their strength and their treasure on women, poetry, and sake."

"Ah, but none I know except you has pretended to do so," Heiko said.

Genji laughed again, though he did not feel like laughing. He took more sake to gain time to consider what she had said. Did she really see through the ruse? Or was it only a geisha's parlor game?

"Well, I can pretend to be pretending, all the while I am actually what I am pretending to be."

"Or we can drop all pretense," Heiko said, "and be with each other what we truly are."

"Impossible," Genji said, and took more sake. "I am a lord. You are a geisha. Pretense is the essence of our being. We cannot be what we truly are even when we are utterly and completely alone."

"Perhaps, as a start," Heiko said, refilling his cup, "we can pretend to be what we really are. But only when we are with each other." She raised her own cup. "Will you make the pledge with me?"

"Of course," Genji said. "It will be entertaining, while it lasts."

His grandfather had warned him that grave danger would soon come in the form of traitors. Kiyori had not warned him about overly clever geisha.

What would he make of this one? Genji would make sure the two met as soon as Kiyori arrived back in Edo after the New Year. In these uncertain times, the one thing that could be relied on completely was Kiyori's judgment. Gifted as he was with infallible prophetic powers, he could never be misled.

"What are you thinking about so seriously, my lord?" Heiko asked.

"My grandfather," Genji said.

"Liar," Heiko said.

Genji laughed. When the truth was unbelievable and lies revealed more than they concealed, what characteristics would a love affair have? It would be very entertaining indeed.

Lord Chamberlain Saiki made his way next to Genji.

"Lord, the hour grows late. It is time to send the geisha home."

"That would be cruelly inhospitable," Genji said. "Let them stay the night. We have abundant room. The south wing is vacant." Those had been the guards' quarters recently vacated by twenty of his best samurai. They, along with the cavalry commander, were presently stationed at Mushindo Monastery, pretending to be monks.

"Lord," Saiki said, grimacing most fiercely. "That would be highly imprudent. Our security would be seriously compromised. With half the household guard gone, we are dangerously shorthanded. We would not be able to watch so many people."

"What is there to watch?" Genji waved off Saiki's next objection before he could speak it. "Have we grown so weak that we must fear a dozen half-drunk women?"

Heiko said, "I am not half drunk, my lord. I am completely drunk." She turned to Saiki. "I wonder, Lord Chamberlain, does that make me doubly dangerous, or completely innocuous?"

Such an interruption from anyone else would undoubtedly have raised Saiki's ire. But though he did not smile, he did play along with her.

"Doubly dangerous, Lady Heiko, doubly dangerous. Without question. And when you are asleep, you will be even more dangerous than that. Which is why I am urging my lord to send you and your companions home."

The exchange amused Genji. Not even a samurai as deadly serious as Saiki was immune to Heiko.

Genji said, "In political matters and on the battlefield, I will always follow the advice of my Lord Chamberlain. Where geisha and sleeping arrangements are concerned, I must most humbly claim the greater expertise. Have the south wing prepared for our guests."

Saiki did not continue to protest. Like the old-school samurai that he was, once his lord made a decision, obedience was the only path.

He bowed and said, "It will be done, lord."

During Genji's brief conversation with Saiki, Heiko had emptied two more cups of sake. She had imbibed prodigiously all evening. Had he indulged as much, he would have become unconscious long ago.

She was not entirely steady as she sat on her knees in the classic posture of attendant subservience. That, and the slightly sleepy way she blinked, made her look as if she might topple over at any moment. He was ready to catch her if she did, but he doubted she would. That would be too clichéd an action. The few minutes he had known her were enough to tell him that she would never do the expected. Even the visible effects of her condition were unusual. Most women, including the most practiced geisha of the first rank, tended to become less attractive when excessively intoxicated. A certain sloppiness of appearance and behavior tended to reveal too much of the human reality beneath the fairy-tale beauty.

But wine had quite the opposite effect on Heiko. Though she swayed slightly from side to side and front to back, not a strand of her hair was out of place, and her makeup, much less heavily applied than was traditional, remained flawless. The silk of her kimono flowed over her body as perfectly as it had done when she had arrived. Her elaborate sash and bow were as elegant as ever. While many of her fellow geisha had grown much less formal in behavior as they had grown less sober, Heiko had become more prim. The neck of her kimono was more tightly closed, its skirt well tucked around her thighs and under her shins, and she continued to sit quite properly on her knees. What would a man need to do to penetrate such disciplined reserve? Large quantities of alcohol frequently gave women a bloated look. In her case, all it did was perfectly suffuse her eyelids and earlobes with a vivid blush, emphasizing the seductive, innerchamber paleness of her complexion. Inevitably, it made him wonder where else she might be blushing.

Genji did not invite Heiko to spend the night with him. He was certain she would decline. While in such a state, she was far too elegant to yield to any man, even one on the verge of becoming a Great Lord. Perhaps more to the point for him, it would have been distastefully crude to even ask it of an intoxicated woman. The potential depth of the relationship they had begun called for patience and subtlety. For the first time in the dozen years he had been pretending to be a dilettante, he was truly fascinated by a woman's character. The opportunity for a genuine exploration must not be destroyed by haste. Would he have been so interested had she not been so beautiful? He knew himself too well to imagine that. He might have had the patience of a bodhisattva, but he was far from being one.

"My lord?"

The housemaid who was preparing his bed stopped and looked at him. He had laughed out loud thinking of his motives.

"Nothing," he said.

She bowed and resumed her task. The other two housemaids continued to help him undress. When they were done, the three young women knelt at the doorway and bowed. They remained just inside the room, awaiting his further instructions. Like all the women of the inner chamber, they were very pretty. Genji was set apart from other men by being a lord of high rank and great power. But he was still a man. In addition to their mundane duties, they were to provide more intimate attention if he desired it. Tonight, he did not. His thoughts were too much with Heiko.

"Thank you," Genji said.

"Good night, Lord Genji," the senior housemaid said. The women backed out of the room on their knees. The door slid silently shut after them.

Genji went to the other side of his room and opened a door facing the inner garden. Dawn was less than an hour away. He enjoyed watching the rays of the rising sun cast their first light onto the carefully manicured foliage, produce intricate shadows in the raked patterns of the stone pool, inspire the birds into song. He sat on his knees in the *seiza* posture, placed his hands in a meditative Zen mudra, and allowed his eyes to narrow nearly to closing. He would let go of all thoughts and concerns as best he could. The sun would bring him out of meditation when it rose enough to light him.

If anyone had occasion to observe him now, they would see someone far different from the drunken idler of just a few minutes earlier. His posture was straight and firm and steady. That he was a samurai was beyond doubt. He could have been preparing for battle, or for his own ritual suicide. Such was his appearance.

Within, it was quite different. As always when beginning meditation, Genji found himself indulging in fancy and conjecture, instead of letting go of them.

His first thoughts were of Heiko, then of her present unobtainability, and quickly shifted to the three housemaids who had just departed. Umé, the chubbiest and most playful of the three, had been quite a diversion in previous encounters. Perhaps he had dismissed her too hastily.

That thought brought to mind a discussion he had recently had with a Christian missionary. The missionary had very gravely emphasized the importance of what he called "fidelity." He claimed that once married, a Christian man slept with no one but his wife. Genji was utterly astonished. It was not that he believed the missionary, for what he said was impossible. Such behavior was so unnatural, not even outsiders, strange as they were, could adhere to it. What shocked him was that the man so seriously made the claim. All men lied, of course, but only fools told lies no one would believe. What had been the missionary's motive? Genji wondered.

Guessing at motives did not trouble his grandfather. Prescient from the age of fifteen, and gifted with an amazing stream of accurate visions over the years, Kiyori was one man who knew, and did not wonder. Genji had been told by Kiyori that he himself would have three visions, and only three, during his entire life. He was also assured that these three would be enough. How three visions could enlighten an entire lifetime Genji could not imagine. But his grandfather was never wrong, so he must believe, even if he could not help being concerned. He was already twenty-four and had not yet seen a single glimpse of the future.

Ah, he was thinking, not letting go. Fortunately he had caught himself before he had gone on too long. He took a deep breath, exhaled fully, and began letting go.

An hour or a minute passed. Time had different dimensions in meditation. Genji felt the warmth of sunlight on his face. He opened his eyes. And instead of seeing the garden—

. . . . .

—Genji finds himself among a vast crowd of screaming men, all dressed in the graceless clothing of the outsiders. They wear no topknots. Instead, their hair is in the unruly confusion of madmen and prisoners. Out of habit, Genji immediately looks for weapons against which he may have to defend himself, and sees none. No one is armed. That must mean there are no samurai present. He tries to check for his own swords. But he cannot voluntarily move his head, his eyes, his hands, his feet, or any other part of his body. He walks inexorably down the long aisle, no more than a passenger in his own body. At least, he assumes he is in his own body, for he cannot see any of it except an occasional peripheral glimpse of his hands as he walks toward the podium.

There, an elderly white-haired man strikes the tabletop with a small wooden hammer.

"Order! Order! The Diet will come to order!"

His voice is lost in the torrent of warring words that come at Genji from both sides of the aisle.

"Damn you to hell!"

"*Banzai!* You've saved the nation!"

"Show honor and kill yourself!"

"May all the gods and all the Buddhas bless and protect you!"

The voices tell him he is hated and revered with almost equal ardor. The cheers come from his left, the curses from his right. He raises his hand to acknowledge the cheers. When he does, Genji the passenger can see that the hand is indeed his own, though perhaps showing more signs of the passage of time.

An instant later, a shout comes from the right.

"Long live the Emperor!"

Rushing at him from that direction is a young man. He wears a plain dark blue uniform with no emblems or insignias. His hair is cut close to the scalp. In his hands is a short-bladed wakizashi sword.

Genji tries to move defensively. His body doesn't budge. As he watches, the young man drives his sword deep into Genji's chest. Passenger or not, he feels the sudden jolt of contact and a sharp stinging sensation as if a huge venomous creature has stung him. Blood explodes into his assailant's face. It is a moment before Genji realizes the blood is his. His muscles suddenly relax and he falls to the ground.

Among the faces peering down at him is that of an unusually beautiful young woman—unusual both in the degree and quality of her beauty. Her eyes are hazel, her hair is light brown, her features are exaggerated and dramatic and reminiscent of the outsiders. She reminds him of someone he can't quite place. She kneels down and, oblivious of the blood, cradles him in her arms.

She smiles at him through her tears and says, "You will always be my Shining Prince." It is a play on his name, Genji, the same name as an ancient fictional hero.

Genji feels his body trying to speak, but no words come. He sees something sparkling at her long, smooth throat. A locket marked with a fleur-de-lis. Then he sees nothing, hears nothing, feels nothing—

· · · · ·

"Lord Genji! Lord Genji!"

He opened his eyes. The housemaid Umé knelt beside him, a worried look on her face. He raised himself up on one elbow. While unconscious, he had fallen out of his room and into the garden.

"Are you well, my lord? Forgive me for entering without permission. I was on duty outside and heard a thud, and when I called, you did not answer."

"I am well," Genji said. He leaned on her and sat down on the veranda.

"Perhaps it would be best to summon Dr. Ozawa," Umé said. "Just to be safe."

"Yes, perhaps. Send one of the others for him."

"Yes, Lord Genji." She hurried to the doorway, whispered to another maid who waited there, and hurried back.

"May I have tea brought to you, my lord?"

"No, just sit with me."

Had he had a seizure? Or was that, at last, one of the visions he had been promised? It couldn't be, could it? It made no sense. If it was a vision, it was a vision of his own death. What use was that? He felt a kind of deep, cold fear he had never experienced before. Perhaps instead of becoming a visionary, he was destined for early madness. That had happened often enough in his family. Still dizzy from the fall and the vision or dream or hallucination, he lost his balance.

Umé caught him softly with her body.

Genji leaned against her, still very afraid. He would send a message to his grandfather today asking him to hurry to Edo without delay. Only Kiyori could explain what he had experienced. Only Kiyori could find the sense in it, if sense there was.

But before his messenger left, another arrived from Cloud of Sparrows Castle.

Okumichi no kami Kiyori, warrior and prophet, the revered Great Lord of Akaoka for sixty-four years, was dead.

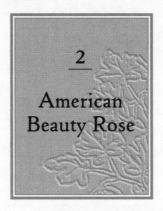

2
American
Beauty Rose

*A favorite samurai saying proclaims, "First thought on waking—
death. Last thought before sleep—death." This is the wisdom of fools
who have never given birth.*

*Instead of accepting a weakling who sees only death in blood,
find someone who sees life therein.*

First thought on waking—life!

Last thought before sleep—life!

Only such a one knows that death comes soon enough.

*Only such a one is truly capable of understanding a
woman's heart.*

AKI-NO-HASHI

(1311)

1867, QUIET CRANE PALACE, EDO

Emily Gibson's yearning was so great, she awoke every morning to the
scent of apple blossoms borne on the wind. It was no longer the
memory of the Apple Valley of her childhood that caused the painful
emptiness in her breast, nor did the imaginary wind bear that lost fragrance from an orchard on the banks of the Hudson River. She missed the
other Apple Valley, the dell that sheltered barely a hundred trees a little
more than an arrow's flight from Cloud of Sparrows Castle.

That she was able to feel nostalgic about a place in Japan was indicative of how long she had been away from America. It had been more than six years since she had left, and almost as long since she had last thought of it as home. She had been sixteen then. She was twenty-three now, and felt much older. In the years between, she had lost her fiancé, her best friend, and, perhaps most significantly, her sense of propriety. Knowing what was right and doing what was right were two very different things. Emotions were not as easily controlled as logic would dictate. She was in love, and she should not have been.

Emily rose from her bed, a canopied four-poster in what Robert Farrington, the American embassy's naval attaché, assured her was the latest style in the United States. It was on his advice that she had ordered it. Her discomfiture with discussing such an intimate article of furniture with a man not related to her was overcome by necessity. There was no one else to advise her on such matters. The wives and daughters of the few Americans in Edo avoided her company. This time, it was not because of her beauty, or, more accurately, not primarily because of it, but because of her excessively close association with an Oriental, which, Lieutenant Farrington told her, was something of a scandal in Western ambassadorial circles.

"What is there to be scandalized about?" Emily had asked. "I am a Christian missionary doing Christ's work under the protection of Lord Genji. There is nothing improper in the slightest about our relationship."

"That is one way to look at it."

"I beg your pardon, Lieutenant Farrington," Emily said, her shoulders stiffening. "I fail to see any other way."

"Please. We have agreed, have we not, that you will be Emily and I will be Robert. Lieutenant Farrington sounds so distant and, well, military."

They were in the drawing room overlooking one of the inner courtyards of Quiet Crane Palace. It had been converted to the Western style, at first to accommodate Emily, and more recently to receive Western guests.

"Is that wise, sir? Would I not expose myself to further scandal?"

"I do not give an iota of credence to the rumors," he said, "but you must admit the circumstances make such conjecture inevitable."

"What circumstances?"

"Do you not see?" Robert's handsome face squinched up in that boyish way he had of unconsciously showing anxiety.

She wanted to laugh, but of course she did not. While it was something of a struggle to maintain her serious expression, she managed to do so.

She said, "No, I do not see."

Robert stood and went to the doorway overlooking the garden. He walked with the slightest of limps. He had dismissed it as the result of an accident during the war. The ambassador, however, had told her that Robert had received the wound during naval actions on the Mississippi River, actions for which he had been awarded numerous commendations for valor. She found Robert's modesty endearing. Indeed, she found many things about him endearing, not the least of which was his ability to speak English. That was perhaps what Emily had missed most during these long years in Japan—the sound of an American voice.

Once at the doorway, Robert turned to face her. Apparently, he felt the need to stand at some remove in order to say what he had to say. His face still displayed a squinch. "You are a young unmarried woman, without the protection of father, husband, or brother, living in the palace of an Oriental despot."

"I would hardly call Lord Genji a despot, Robert. He is a nobleman, rather like a duke in European countries."

"Please. Let me continue while I have the courage to do so. As I was saying, you are a young woman, and, moreover, a very beautiful young woman. That alone would be enough to ignite gossip in any circumstance. To make matters worse, the 'duke,' as you style him, whose roof you share—"

Emily said, "I would not phrase it that way."

"—is one notorious for debauchery even among his own debauched peers. For God's sake, Emily—"

"I must ask you not to use the Lord's name in vain."

"Excuse me," he said, "I forgot myself. But surely, you can see the problem now."

"And is that how you see it?"

"I know you are a woman of impeccable virtue and utterly steadfast morality. My concern is not with your behavior. Rather, I fear for your safety in such a place. It borders on the miraculous that you have remained here unmolested for so long. Isolated this way, at the mercy of a man whose every whim is an ironclad command to his fanatic followers, anything could happen, anything, and no one could help you."

Emily smiled kindly. "I appreciate your concern. But really, your fear is entirely without foundation. Your generous characterization of my appearance is not shared by the Japanese. I am considered quite hideous, not unlike the demons that periodically appear in their fairy tales, breathing fire. No person is less likely to excite ungovernable passions in the Japanese than I, I assure you."

"It is not the generality of Japanese that concerns me," Robert said, "just one person in particular."

"Lord Genji is a true friend," Emily said, "and a gentleman who conforms to the highest standards of decency. I am safer within these walls than I would be anywhere else in Edo."

"The highest standards of decency? He consorts with prostitutes on a regular basis."

"Geisha are not prostitutes. I've explained that to you many times. You willfully refuse to understand."

"He worships golden idols."

"He does not. He expresses reverence for his teachers and ancestors by bowing to the images of Buddhas. I've explained this also."

Robert went on as if he hadn't heard her. "He has murdered dozens of innocent men, women, and children, and caused many others to be killed. He has not only condoned suicide, which is sin enough, but he has actually ordered others to commit the act. He has decapitated, or caused to be decapitated, more than a few of his political enemies, and has compounded those atrocities by actually delivering the severed heads of those unfortunates to their families and loved ones. Such cruelty is beyond belief. My God, do you call this conforming to the highest standards of decency?"

"Calm yourself. Here. Have some tea." Emily needed the pause. All of the issues he had raised were easily answerable, if not completely defensible, save one. The murder of the villagers. Perhaps if she left that aside and addressed the other issues, he would not notice.

Robert seated himself. He was breathing rather heavily, overexcited as he had been by his recitation of Genji's sins.

"I beg your pardon," he said, "but is coffee available by any chance?"

"I'm afraid not. Do you really prefer it to tea?" Coffee was apparently one of the more recent postwar fads in the United States. "I find it rather acidic, and it tends to upset my stomach."

"It's an aquired taste, I suppose. During the war, when Brazilian coffee was more readily available than English tea, I found coffee to have one great advantage. It supplies a tremendous burst of energy completely lacking in tea."

"You seem, if anything, to have an excess of energy rather than a dearth," Emily said. "Perhaps you should reduce your coffee consumption in any case."

Robert took the offered tea and smiled. "Perhaps," he said, and continued to smile at her in such a way that she knew she could lead the conversation in another direction with little effort. That direction, which Robert had attempted in several previous conversations, had dangers of its own, however, so Emily stayed with the subject at hand.

"Must I cover the subjects of geisha and Buddhism again, Robert?"

"I concede that your explanations, if true, would be valid." He held up a hand to stop the protest he knew was coming. "And further, I concede, for the sake of argument at least, that they are valid."

"Thank you. Now, as a military man yourself, you surely know that martial tradition is what sometimes compels samurai to take their own lives. By our Christian standards, this is a mortal sin. There is no question of that. But until they are converted to the true faith, we can hardly hold them to standards that are, at present, utterly repugnant to them."

"That seems an excessively flexible viewpoint for a Christian missionary, Emily."

"I do not consent. I simply understand, which is all I ask of you."

"Very well. Go on."

"As for the delivery of heads"—Emily took a deep breath and tried, without complete success, to avoid visualization. She had seen too many of them herself—"that is considered the honorable thing to do. If Lord Genji had not done so, it would have been a breach of the samurai's equivalent of the code of chivalry."

"Chivalry? How can you even think of using that word to describe wanton acts of butchery and mutilation?"

"Excuse me, Lady Emily." Hanako knelt at the doorway and bowed, her right hand to the floor, the empty sleeve on her left draped elegantly beside it. "You have another visitor. I told him you had a guest with you, but he insisted—"

"Well, well, how gratifying to see you at leisure, Admiral. But can you really afford such a luxurious expenditure of time?" Charles Smith smiled and arched an eyebrow at Robert. His Georgia drawl, Emily noticed, was highly exaggerated, as it always was in Robert's presence. "Don't you have homes to loot, cities to burn, and defenseless civilians to bombard?"

Robert shot to his feet. "I have borne the last insult I will ever bear from a traitor such as yourself, sir."

"Gentlemen, please," Emily said, but neither gave any indication that they had heard her.

Charles gave the slightest of bows to his adversary. "I am at your service, sir, at any time of your choosing. And the choice of weapons, sir, is also yours."

"Robert!" Emily said. "Charles! Stop it this instant."

"Since I have offered the challenge," Robert said, "the choice is necessarily yours, sir."

"I am compelled to decline, sir, since it would confer upon me an entirely unfair advantage," Charles said. "I would naturally choose either pistols or swords, and you and your kind, I believe, are much more comfortable with long-range mortars, flung torches, and starvation by siege."

If Emily had not flung herself bodily between the two men at that moment, there was no doubt they would have come to blows on the spot. Thankfully, they both retained enough presence of mind to halt before colliding with her.

"I am ashamed of you," she said, looking disapprovingly first at one and then at the other. "You are Christian gentlemen, and should be setting an example for our hosts. Instead, you are behaving in a barbarous manner hardly distinguishable from the worst of their own."

"Surely I have a right to respond to insult intentionally given," Robert said, still glaring at Charles, who, of course, also continued to glare at him.

"If the truth is an insult," Charles said, "then perhaps you ought to examine the heinous acts giving rise to it."

"What is more heinous than slavery?" Robert said. "We righteously put an end to it, along with your rebellion."

Charles laughed derisively. "As if you care a whit about the fate of any Negroes. That was a mendacious excuse, not a reason."

"Unless you cease this argument immediately," Emily said, "I shall be compelled to ask you both to leave. Should I learn that you have engaged in any violence against each other, I will find it impossible to see either of you again. Ever."

Robert Farrington and Charles Smith both looked as ready to kill each other as ever, and would no doubt remain ready for the foreseeable future. Emily was equally sure that they would not do so, the reason being that the quarrel between them was not really about politics generally, or even the late war specifically. For one thing, Charles's family had originally been Georgian, but that was several generations in the past. Charles himself had been born in Honolulu, in the Hawaiian Kingdom, as had both his parents. He was heir to a sugar plantation and a cattle ranch there, and had never even seen Georgia. Furthermore, Emily knew from earlier conversations that Charles had been a fervent abolitionist, and had contributed significant sums to the cause. No, in point of fact, the men's ire arose from their mutual wish to win Emily's hand in marriage.

What made a man think he could win a woman's heart with displays of murderous rage? It was as if in even the most civilized male breast, the residue of brutish prehistoric life was ever ready to resurrect itself to its former dominance. Truly, without the civilizing influence of women, even the best men of Christendom, such as Robert Farrington and Charles Smith certainly were, stood in constant danger of descending back into barbarism. For her part, she had made it eminently clear to them that any violence, even of the nonfatal kind, would immediately disqualify the perpetrator from her further consideration.

Which one to accept was not a decision easily reached, though Emily was determined to shortly accept one or the other. The reason for her newfound haste was the same as the reason for her previous disinclination to consider any proposal whatsoever. Love. Love of the deepest and most unshakable kind. But a love, unfortunately, that she did not feel for either of the two gentlemen seeking her hand.

After they departed, at an interval of fifteen minutes at her insistence, Emily went to her study to continue her translation of *Suzume-no-kumo*— "Cloud of Sparrows" in English—the secret scrolls of history and prophecy of Lord Genji's clan, the Okumichi of Akaoka Domain.

There, on her desk, was a single red rose, just as there had been every morning now since the vernal equinox. It was of the variety known to Genji's clan as American Beauty, an unexpected name for a flower which bloomed only in the inner garden of Cloud of Sparrows Castle. She brushed its soft petals gently against her lips. For love's sake, she would marry Robert or Charles, neither of whom she loved. She placed the rose in the small vase she kept handy for the purpose and put the vase on a corner of her desk.

Today, she would begin a new scroll. Because they were not numbered or marked in any way, she was sometimes well into a scroll before she knew what part of the history it covered. That the first scroll she had translated six years ago had been the first scroll, written in 1291, was purely chance. The second had been from 1641 and the third from 1436. If any two scrolls were chronologically contiguous, it was not by design. It was this way, Genji said, because as every succeeding lord read the history, he tended to reread certain scrolls more than others, and thus any order, if there had ever been an order, was lost and lost again, repeatedly through the years. At first, this lack of sequential arrangement had bothered her. But soon, she found herself enchanted by the unpredictability. It was quite like opening a Christmas present, and being pleasantly surprised each time.

This was particularly so when, as today, it was not only time for a new scroll but also time to open a new trunk. The disorganization of the clan history was consistent with its manner of storage. Varying numbers of scrolls from different decades and centuries were contained in trunks of vastly different designs and sizes. Since there was no order about which to be concerned, whenever it came time to select a trunk to open, Emily let her eyes wander over the containers grouped in the corner of her study. As always, she would let her fancy make the choice.

Would it be a large one or a small? One that showed obvious age, or a newer one? That one of European vintage, closed with a rusty iron bolt? Or the elegant black lacquerware oval from China? Or the fragrant Korean sandalwood chest? But as soon as her eyes alighted on the odd leather-covered box, she knew her curiosity would not permit her to open any other. Upon its topmost surface was a painting, faded but with its original colors still apparent, of a red dragon curling around blue mountain spires. Her study of East Asian art enabled her now to recognize the country of origin of most artifacts she saw. But she could not identify this one.

The lid had been sealed to the rest of the box with wax, which also coated the entire surface of the container. Flecks of broken wax indicated it had been opened only recently, which was somewhat strange. Genji had told her that it was the duty of every Great Lord of Akaoka to read the history in its entirety upon his ascension, so of course, it should have been opened long ago. Genji must have resealed it with wax after he had read the scrolls, then opened it again before Emily received it. She would ask him about it later.

Inside, a rough cloth covered the contents. Within this cloth was another, of embroidered silk, brilliant with color. When Emily unfolded the first flap, she saw a pattern of roses, a wild profusion of them, in red, pink, and white, against a field of billowy white clouds in a bright blue sky. Since the American Beauty rose was near to being an unofficial symbol of the clan, it was more surprising that this was the first time she had encountered it among the cloths that always wrapped the scrolls within the trunks.

She removed one and unrolled it. Unlike every other scroll she had seen so far, this one was written almost entirely in the simple native Japanese phonetic script, called *hiragana*. The others had been written primarily in *kanji*, the Chinese characters which had been adapted by the Japanese to render complex ideas in their own language. Kanji had proved difficult for Emily in her studies of Japanese, but hiragana was another matter. She read the first line with little difficulty.

Lord Narihira learned from the visitor that the arrival of American beauty—

She stopped, surprised, and reread it. Yes, she had made no mistake. There were the phonetic marks for "American"—*ah-me-li-ka-nu*. If the word was mentioned, the scroll must date from a time after the Japanese were aware of the existence of the New World. The previous scroll she had translated covered much of the late eighteenth century. Perhaps this was also from that period. She began again.

Lord Narihira learned from the visitor that the arrival of American beauty in Cloud of Sparrows Castle would signal the ultimate triumph of the Okumichi clan. Fool that he was, he caused roses to be planted in the inner garden of the castle, and named them American Beauty roses, thinking that by so doing, he was bringing the prophecy to fruition. Is this not typical of a man, to try to force the river to flow in a certain way, rather than to understand its currents, and ride it effortlessly to its natural destination? It is hard to imagine a woman so foolish, is it not? When heaven gave men command of the world, the gods above were surely displaying a most mischievous sense of humor.

The style of the narrative was quite different from the formality of the writing in the other scrolls she had translated so far. The archaic language posed a challenge, but with the help of the bilingual dictionary she and

Genji had been compiling, she was able to understand what she read with comparative ease, thanks to the absence of kanji. She continued without bothering to write down any immediate English translation. That could come later. She was too excited.

She finished the scroll just as Genji came to take his midday meal with her. By then she knew this trunkful of ancient writings contained something other than *Suzume-no-kumo*. That clan history had been written by the succeeding lords of the domain, beginning in 1291. The author of this scroll was surely a woman.

She had written her chronicle around the same time that the official one was begun.

And she told, as if from direct experience, of occurrences that spanned centuries beyond her lifetime.

1281, CLOUD OF SPARROWS CASTLE

"I don't understand this at all," Lady Kiyomi said, pouting at her husband. "Why must you help the Lord of Hakata? Has he not been an enemy of our clan for generations?"

Masamuné calmed the impatient warhorse beneath him. He wanted to sigh, but his five hundred retainers were gathered around him on their own horses, and he could hardly do something so unmartial in front of them. He should have listened to his father and married a woman less beautiful and less obstreperous.

"As I have already repeatedly explained, our sacred homeland has been invaded by the Mongol hordes."

"You have *said* repeatedly, my lord, but merely saying explains nothing. Hakata Domain is not our sacred homeland. Why should we care if Mongol hordes, whatever they are, invade Hakata? Let them destroy the place. Then we would have one enemy less, would we not?"

He turned to his chamberlain for help, but that man, being gifted with both experience and wisdom, had fixed his entire attention on the distant tree line some minutes ago.

"If the Mongols destroy Hakata, then it is only a matter of time before they come here."

She laughed. "Please be serious. Hakata is on Kyushu island and we are on Shikoku." She said it as if it clarified all that needed to be understood.

Though Kiyomi had been his wife for ten years and borne three children, she still seemed so very young to Masamuné, especially when she laughed. He could not find it within himself to be angry with her, despite her painful lack of political understanding.

He bowed in the saddle. "I will return with many Mongol heads."

"If you must bring back something of the Mongols, bring back Mongol jewels," she said. "I don't understand your fascination with heads at all."

This time, despite his every effort, Masamuné sighed before he turned his horse's head toward the castle gate. "Farewell."

When the men were gone, Lady Kiyomi's senior lady-in-waiting said, "I understand why you are behaving in such a way, my lady, but is it wise to do so? Wouldn't Lord Masamuné benefit more from your actual wisdom at such a time rather than your pretended silliness?"

Lady Kiyomi said, "If I had knowledge unavailable to him, or if I could give advice he could not get elsewhere, yes, then your concern would be well-founded. Our lord has good counselors around him. He doesn't need yet another. Better that he thinks I don't understand, then he won't worry about me worrying. When I come to mind, he will smile in amusement. Then he will focus his full attention on his task. Perhaps, in such a way, I can help him to come back."

"Surely there is no doubt of that," another of her ladies said. "Lord Masamuné is the greatest warrior of Shikoku."

"Shikoku is a speck in the sea," Lady Kiyomi said, "and the other islands of Japan just more specks. The Great Khan of the Mongol Empire commands armies numbering in the millions. He and his ancestors have conquered kingdoms many times the size of this insignificant place. Our lord is more likely to die in battle than to return."

They walked in silence to the courtyard where the children played. There they joined in the childish games and spoke no more of war.

· · · · ·

"Masamuné!" Gengyo, Lord of Hakata, was stunned to see one of his worst enemies arriving with reinforcements.

Masamuné bowed, a broad smile on his face. Gengyo's dismay alone was worth the rigors of the arduous journey. "We have come to help you expel the arrogant invaders."

"My deepest thanks to you. Unfortunately, we are not yet in a position to expel. With your help, we can perhaps hope to slow their advance until the Shogun's main armies arrive."

"Nonsense! When the Mongols came seven years ago, they broke and ran as soon as we charged." If Masamuné tried to recall the details, he would remember that this was not quite true. The fighting had been hard and bloody, and it was quite possible that had the storm not come and driven their ships away, the Mongols would have taken the field. But his perception of the first invasion had taken on an entirely different shape, thanks to exaggerated retellings of those battles.

"There are more of them this time," Gengyo said, "many more."

"What does it matter? Let us charge immediately. What barbarian can stand against an all-out samurai attack?"

Gengyo gestured for Masamuné to follow him. He led the way to earthwork walls on the rise overlooking the shoreline plain. "See for yourself."

Hakata Bay was filled with ships, hundreds of them, and hundreds more approached from the horizon. On land, Mongols were encamped in well-spaced, well-defended groups behind earthwork walls of their own. Masamuné estimated the number of Mongols he could see at twenty thousand. But their camps extended all the way down the shore and out of sight behind the western hills. If all the troops aboard the ships had come ashore, there could be as many as fifty thousand Mongols already in Japan, with many thousands more soon to land.

"Horses," Gengyo said. "See? They have horses, too. Many of them. What we heard about them, the way they conquered China and Korea, and unknown empires in the Far West, must be true. We've skirmished a few times. The way they fight from the saddle is incredible. I don't remember them fighting that way before." No doubt Gengyo, too, had done his share of reshaping memories. "Our brave sailors from Choshu and Satsuma Domains have been climbing on board the enemy ships at night and killing many of them. But for every one that's killed, ten more arrive."

"What are they unloading now?"

"Those tubes and cylinders?" Gengyo looked very worried. "I don't know. But they are pointing them in our direction."

"When will the Shogun's forces arrive?" Masamuné asked.

"Tomorrow. Or the day after. The Mongols will probably attack in force at noon."

Masamuné and Gengyo watched the Mongols for several minutes in silence. Finally, Masamuné said to his lieutenant, "Remove the horses to safety. Bring the men forward on foot with their bows." He turned to Gengyo. "They must cross a wide stretch of open terrain to reach us. We will cut them down with a barrage of arrows before they're halfway here."

· · · · ·

"You!" The Mongol brigade commander pointed at Eroghut. "Bring your troop forward. You will attack with the first wave."

Eroghut said to his brother, "Mongol dogs. They send us out to die. Then they will claim their cowardly victory riding over our bodies."

"We won't die," his brother said. "Remember what Mother said. Our blood will outlive that of Kublai the Fat. When the Mongols are gone, the Nürjhen Ordos will rise again."

Eroghut said nothing. His little brother's faith in their mother's words was touching. Like the rest of the surviving Nürjhen tribesmen, he believed her to be a sorceress in the same line as the legendary Tangolhun, who supposedly instructed Attila the Great to follow the sun westward to the destined homeland of the Huns. The same legends claimed for the Nürjhen kinship with the Huns, traditional enemies of the Mongols. All nonsense and children's fables. Eroghut didn't believe there was ever a Tangolhun or an Attila of such incredible greatness. As for the revival of the Nürjhen Ordos—from whence would it arise, when there were now barely enough of them to call a clan, much less a tribe, and an Ordos was no less than a hundred tribes? No, he and his brother and their kinsmen, the last Nürjhen warriors on earth, would die here in this wretched place called Japan. They had lost, and the hated Mongols had won. But they would not die alone.

Eroghut said, "They will send us against those fortifications on that rise above the beach. They will send the Uighurs and the Kalmuks and the Khitan along with us. Use them for cover as best you can. The Mongols will follow in our shadows like the shit-eating dogs they are. As soon as we crest the hill, turn and kill Mongols."

"But what of the Japanese?" one of his cousins asked. "As soon as we show our backs, they will attack us."

"They will not," Eroghut said, not believing his own words for a moment. "They will see we are enemies of their enemy and fight with us shoulder to shoulder."

"Eroghut, you are our clan leader, and we will obey you," another cousin said, "but these wild natives are adherents of a vicious, mindless cult of death worship. Once the bloodlust is upon them, they do not stop to think. I agree with our cousin. They will attack us as soon as we are vulnerable."

"If you must die, would you prefer to die fighting for the Mongol scavengers," Eroghut said, "or against them?" That silenced all protest. The remnants of the great Nürjhen Ordos tightened the armor on their horses, adjusted their own, and rode to the front rank of the heavy cavalry. Behind them, the Chinese artillerymen and rocketeers prepared to fire.

· · · · ·

The ground shook with the concussion of charging Mongol horsemen. They came at high speed, in ordered ranks, with lances aimed straight ahead.

"Do not shoot until they reach the base of the hill," Masamuné told his men.

An instant before they were there, flames flashed from the tubes the Mongols had set up on the beach, accompanied by smoke and a roaring like angry wind, and moments later, impossibly, stars and constellations exploded in the daytime sky above them. His men stayed where they were. Many others among the samurai ran screaming in panic.

"Shoot!" Masamuné said.

His archers felled many of the Mongols, but they were few and the Mongols were many. The samurais' defenses were breached with little effort. Just as they were on the verge of being inundated, the right flank of the charging Mongol cavalry suddenly wheeled and attacked their own men. These renegades shouted a war cry different from that of the other Mongols, words that sounded to Masamuné's ears like "Na-lu-chi-ya-oh-ho-do-su!"

This sudden treachery from within their own ranks confused the Mongols. Though they had the advantage of both numbers and position, they broke off the attack and retreated. In the lull that followed, the renegade closest to Masamuné hit his chest with his fist.

"No, Mongol," he said in rough Chinese. "Yes, Nürjhen." And so saying, he pointed at his comrades, who gestured in similar fashion and said, "Nürjhen."

Masamuné's lieutenant said, "Are they saying they are not Mongols, my lord?"

"Apparently they are"—he struggled to duplicate the tongue-twisting syllables the barbarian had uttered—"Na-lu-chi-ya."

"What is Na-lu-chi-ya?"

Directly above them, stars and constellations once again exploded in the sky. The samurai hugged the ground as tightly as they could. Masamuné spit dirt from his mouth.

"They are enemies of the Mongols," he said. "What more must you know?"

This time, the starbursts were followed by deafening roars on the beach, the sound of invisible objects flying through the air, and, moments later, horrendous explosions in their midst.

"Get up!" Gengyo yelled. "They're coming again!"

Many of the samurai who did get up did so not to man the earthworks but to turn and flee, a futile effort. The continuing rain of explosions shattered men into ragged, bloody remnants of flesh and bone no matter whether they stayed or fled.

The second Mongol charge crested the defenses once again, and the enemy was among them on horseback, killing with sword and spear. Behind the horsemen came men on foot firing strange bows that launched short bolts. One of these bolts struck Masamuné in the chest and easily penetrated his armor.

"Ah!" There was only a momentary flash of pain, then no feeling at all, just a weightless kind of dizziness. A Mongol horseman came at him with a spear to finish him off. Masamuné was too weak to raise his sword in defense. Then the Na-lu-chi-ya who had first spoken knocked aside the attacker's spear and stabbed his short two-edged sword into the man's armpit. Blood flared and the horseman fell.

His Na-lu-chi-ya savior smiled at him and said, "No fear. Live! Live!"

Masamuné lost consciousness.

When he opened his eyes again, his lieutenant was dressing his wound.

The Mongols were gone. Samurai went among the wounded rescuing their own men and killing fallen Mongols. The samurai had won, at least for the time being. He saw the Na-lu-chi-ya dead all around him. No, that one still breathed. He could see the chest move ever so slightly. One of Gengyo's men went up to him and raised his sword to stab him.

"Stop!" Masamuné said. "That is not a Mongol."

"He looks like a Mongol."

"Idiot! Are you questioning my word?"

"No, Lord Masamuné, not at all." The man bowed.

"Attend to his wounds."

"Yes, lord, but he is very badly hurt. He will probably die anyway."

"If he dies, we will pray for the peaceful repose of his spirit. But see that he does not die." The Na-lu-chi-ya had saved his life. Masamuné would return the favor if he could.

· · · · ·

Eroghut did not die, but all the others did. His brother and cousins and every last kinsman were gone. He smiled through fever and pain as the cart that carried him rocked back and forth. His mother had gained a reputation for sorcery and prophecy through a clever and fortunate combination of lucky guesses and tireless self-promotion, always off casting spells and going into trances when she should have been caring for her husband and children. Now he alone was the entirety of the Nürjhen Ordos. If it were to rise again, it would arise from him, Eroghut, son of Tanghut, of the Nürjhens of the Red Dragon River and the Blue Ice Mountains. But there was no Red Dragon River anymore, or Blue Ice Mountains. The Mongols had given them different names when they had conquered his tribe. And soon, there would be no more Nürjhens. He wished he could see his mother one last time, so he could laugh in her face.

The cart carried Eroghut to another island, which he later learned was called Shikoku. The samurai he had fought beside, Masamuné, was lord of a domain called Akaoka, and there they presently arrived. Though Masamuné comported himself no differently from a khan, his domain was hardly big enough to have a name of its own. Even a Mongol—vastly overrated horsemen, in Eroghut's opinion—could ride from one end to the other in less than a day.

In the beginning, Eroghut and his new lord spoke in pidgin Chinese.

"My name Masamuné. I lord Akaoka kingdom. You?"

"My name Eroghut. I Nürjhen country. Now Nürjhen country no more."

"Your name?" Masamuné repeated, a look of confusion on his face.

"Eroghut."

"Eh-ho-go-chu?"

"E-ro-ghut."

"Eh-lo-ku-cho?"

These Japanese were hopeless. Because their language was so simple, they could hardly form any unfamiliar words, even simple ones.

" 'Ghut," Eroghut said, shortening it the way an infant would.

"Ah," Masamuné said, looking very pleased at last. "Go."

"Yes," Eroghut said, giving up. "My name Go." And from then on it was.

Go learned the language of Japan very quickly. It was not difficult to form the words, because there were only a few sounds. The Japanese were like the Mongols in one way. They loved war. As soon as the Mongols were gone from these shores, driven away by a storm, as they had been during their first attempt at conquest, Masamuné began fighting first his eastern neighbor, then his northern one, for reasons Go did not understand. It seemed honor was at stake more than land, slaves, horses, or trade routes. There could be no other reason, since the manner in which the samurai fought—a bizarre form of mass single combat, where every warrior sought an opponent of equal rank—guaranteed that almost no battle could result in clear-cut victory for either side. Their armies were not armies in the highly organized Nürjhen sense, but rather wild, heroic, uncoordinated mobs.

When the samurai told stories of their battles, they exaggerated not only their courage but the courage of their enemies as well, and wept for the enemy dead as well as their own. In one battle, an enemy lord, a fat pimply youth of perhaps twenty, was killed by his own falling horse as he turned to flee. When the story was later told, that lord had become a youth of almost blinding beauty, his courage enough to fill the breasts of a thousand brave men, his death a tragedy of nearly unbearable sadness. Go watched as Masamuné and his samurai drank rice wine and wept at the loss of the hero. Yet these very men knew the enemy lord well, had fought against him in many previous engagements, and knew he was not beautiful, not even moderately handsome, and his courage . . . well, how much courage does it take, not to mention the level of skill, or lack thereof, to turn the horse in such a way that it would fall on the rider and break his neck?

So it was that Go came to live among these overdramatic, though unquestionably brave, barbarians, fighting alongside them in their meaningless, utterly inconclusive battles, drinking with them, singing with them, and eventually reciting the same ridiculous lies of heaven-shaking fortitude, dazzling physical beauty, and fearless and defiant death. They lived for nothing beyond war and drunkenness and the mythology of their own courage.

Go felt right at home. Before Kublai the Fat's grandfather, Genghis the Accursed, gathered together all the steppe tribes, forced them to become Mongols, and gave them the mission of world conquest, the Nürjhen had been much like these Japanese. Perhaps his mother had not been so very wrong after all. Perhaps these primitive islanders were the new Nürjhen Ordos. It was amusing to toy with the thought anyway.

Go's skill with horses was much appreciated by Lord Masamuné. Under his tutelage, the samurai of Akaoka Domain soon learned to move in rapidly shifting units, rather than as inefficient individuals, the units themselves able to join to form larger units, or split apart to form smaller ones. Signal flags were used to communicate commands over long distances during the day. At night, lamps and flaming arrows served the same purpose. These were the same tactics the Huns had used during the centuries when the steppes of East Asia were theirs to command, tactics inherited by their Nürjhen kinsmen, and the same tactics the Mongols had stolen and used against them.

In the spring of the second year of Go's life among the Japanese, the Akaoka cavalrymen he had trained so well rode like Nürjhen warriors of old against the clumsy army of the Hojo regent, an army ten times their size, and destroyed it in a great slaughter on the Shikoku shore of the Inland Sea. When they returned from battle, Masamuné gave his youngest and most beautiful concubine to Go for a wife. By the fall of the next year, Go was the father of a son, whom he named Chiaki, using the Chinese characters *chi*, "blood," for the Nürjhen blood in his veins, and *aki*, "autumn," for the season of his birth.

All was well until a second Nürjhen was born among the Japanese. Then Go had cause to remember that the blood that ran in his veins, and the veins of his two children, was also the blood of his sorceress mother and that other, Tangolhun of ancient times.

1867, QUIET CRANE PALACE

"I see you are hard at work as usual," Genji said.

Emily had been so taken by her reading, she had not noticed his arrival at the doorway. She suspected he had been there for some time, watching her, before he spoke up.

"Not working nearly hard enough," she said, rolling up the scroll as casually as possible. Her feminine intuition told her it was best, at least for the time being, not to mention the different nature of the newly opened narrative.

His appearance had undergone little change in the six years since they had met. This despite serious injuries suffered in battle, the tremendous stresses of political leadership in a time of nearly endless crisis, and involvement in an intricate web of plots and counterplots involving the Emperor in Kyoto, the Shogun in Edo, and rebellious warlords in the west and north of Japan. There was also possible foreign intervention to worry about, with the navies of England, France, Russia, and the United States always prominently in Japanese waters. If this were not complicated enough, there was also Kawakami Saemon to consider.

Saemon was a son of Genji's former nemesis, Kawakami Eiichi, who at the time of his death—under Genji's sword—had been chief of the Shogun's secret police. Saemon was Kawakami's eldest son, by a lesser concubine rather than his wife, and had supposedly hated his father. When he and Genji met shortly after the unfortunate incident, he had showed every indication of friendliness. Furthermore, he and Genji were on the same side of the restoration question. They both favored the abolition of the Shogunate and the Emperor's return to power after a thousand years of political eclipse. Genji seemed to trust the man. Emily did not.

He was too much like his father in two ways. The first was in appearance. He was handsome and vain, and Emily had little faith in men who placed excessive importance on appearances. The second, more telling, was in behavior. He always gave Emily the impression of never meaning what he said, or saying what he meant. It wasn't that he lied exactly. It was more an impression—of slipperiness, of insubstantiality, of an inclination toward treachery—than confirmable fact. Perhaps it was circumstance alone that gave rise to her doubts. She could not help but wonder whether any son could truly have kindly feelings for the man who killed his sire.

She returned Genji's smile with one of her own. His smile was as care-free as it had always been, and he still looked like a noble youth with no concern beyond the location of the evening's entertainment. It was an appearance that had deceived his enemies into taking him lightly, and that mistake had cost many of them their lives. Bloodshed seemed to occur with disturbing frequency around Genji, which was another factor that had convinced Emily that the time to leave Japan had come.

She had not yet told him of the offers of marriage she had received, nor had she given any indication of her decision to leave. She feared that if she told him prematurely, he would say or do something that would cause her fragile resolve to crumble. Love was compelling her to leave, but it could just as easily prevent her doing so. She was safe so long as Genji did not return her feelings. Life was painful, but it was pain she could bear. At least she was with him.

Then the roses began to appear. What could it mean other than that Genji was beginning to develop feelings for her, the same kind of feelings she had long had for him? Her own fate did not concern her. She was willing to commit any sin, endure any condemnation, to truly be with him, so long as her presence helped him on the path toward Christian righteousness. What she most fervently did not want was to be an instrument of his injury. If she gave in to her feelings, it would cause no end of troubles for Genji, both among his own people and among Westerners, who would be revolted by the idea of an Oriental, lord or no lord, with a white wife. It would do great damage to Genji's efforts to bring Japan into the family of civilized nations. Yet she could brush all that aside as well, if she could be certain they were part of the price paid for the salvation of his immortal soul. That was her dilemma. Would having her help save him, or push him another step toward his eternal damnation?

"I see your secret admirer has brought you his daily rose," Genji said.

"He is certainly very stealthy," Emily said. "No one has ever seen him, nor has he ever left the slightest hint of who he might be." She knew she should stop there, but she could not, and added, "It's certainly not very chivalrous of him."

"It was my understanding that such anonymous tokens of affection were considered quite proper in the West. Am I mistaken?"

"A certain period of anonymity, perhaps. Six months somewhat pushes the matter from flattering to disturbing."

"How so?"

"One begins to wonder why it has gone on so long with no indication of identity. Might there be, perhaps, a motivation that is not entirely healthy?"

"Perhaps, for good reasons, your admirer cannot openly declare himself," Genji said. "Perhaps admiring you, with no possibility of anything more, is the most he can hope for."

Before she could stop herself, she said, "If so, that is cowardly behavior."

Genji smiled. "An excess of courage, in the wrong circumstances, in the wrong place, and at the wrong time, can have far worse consequences than cowardice."

"That sounds like something quite opposite from what most samurai would say," she said, then added with emphasis, "Lord Genji."

"Yes, it is, isn't it? Perhaps I will have to give up my two swords and my topknot."

"But not today," she said.

"No, not today."

She stood and made a show of examining the sky. If she pushed him into an open declaration, any declaration, her path would be so much clearer. Was her love causing her to misinterpret what was no more than friendly regard from him? If so, the romantic crisis was imaginary, and hers alone.

Emily said, "It may rain. Shall we dine indoors?"

"As you wish."

She had prepared a variation on cucumber sandwiches, which she had recently sampled for the first time at the British embassy. She found the combination of vegetable slices, covered with a sauce of her own made of whipped egg yolks and cream, particularly refreshing in the humidity of the early Edo autumn. Genji was unusually quiet throughout the meal, which meant either that he was doing his best not to gag on food he found repulsive, or he was still thinking about the anonymous rose. To err on the side of caution, she decided to remove cucumber sandwiches from future menus.

So far, her efforts to broaden his diet to include more Western foods was a complete failure. Admittedly, she had not been any more successful in adapting herself to Japanese cuisine. So much of it involved bizarre sea

creatures, many times in uncooked form sliced right from the living animal. The mere thought of it tainted the flavor of the cucumber in her
mouth. She had to fight a wave of nausea in order to swallow, and quickly
chased it with tea.

"Is something wrong?" Genji asked.

"Not at all," Emily said, putting down her sandwich. "I'm just not very
hungry today."

"Neither am I," he said, clearly relieved to follow her lead.

They were both silent then for some time. She tried to imagine what he
might be thinking. Perhaps he was doing the same with her. It was an
amusing conceit, and no doubt entirely imaginary. There was no profit in
such fantasizing. She turned her attention to another subject, one possibly
more amenable to inquiry.

Emily said, "I have a question about the *Suzume-no-kumo* scrolls. A matter of curiosity rather than an issue relating to translation. Are the supposed visions of the future always conveyed in dreams?"

"You have read several hundred years' worth of predictions, many of
which have come to pass, and you can still refer to them as 'supposed'?"

"As I have said many times, only the prophets of the Old Testament—"

"—were able to see the future," Genji said, finishing her statement for
her. "Yes, you have indeed said so many times. I can't understand how you
reconcile that belief with what you have read in the scrolls."

"If you prefer not to answer my question, just say so," Emily said, rather
more petulantly than she had intended.

"Why would I have such a preference? The answer is yes. Every glimpse
of the future has come in a dream."

"Never brought by an unexpected visitor?"

"A visitor?" This might have been the first time Emily had seen Genji
looking baffled.

"Yes," she said. "Perhaps a messenger."

"What messenger would know anything about the future?"

"Well, he wouldn't, of course. But an otherwise mundane report might
somehow be interpreted in a special way by the visionary."

"I have read the entirety of *Suzume-no-kumo* several times," Genji said,
"and no messenger is ever mentioned."

"You're right, I'm sure," Emily said. "I'll double-check with the dictionary again."

Rapid footsteps approached their doorway. That was always a sign of trouble.

Genji's chief bodyguard, Hidé, appeared and bowed. "Lord, there has been another attack on outsiders. Englishmen."

"Fatalities?"

"Not among the outsiders. They were armed with revolvers. Five Yoshino samurai were killed. Nevertheless, the English ambassador has lodged a formal protest with both the Shogun and the Great Lord of Yoshino."

"What a fool. Does the man never learn? I thought Lord Saemon had talked him into exercising restraint until the full council can meet."

"Apparently not."

"You still have doubts about Lord Saemon's trustworthiness."

"No, my lord, I have no doubts at all," Hidé said. "I am certain he is *not* trustworthy."

"On what basis have you arrived at this conclusion?"

"He is the son of Kawakami the Sticky Eye." Hidé mouthed the name as if he would spit it out if he could. "It is not possible for the son of such a father to be a man whose word has weight."

"We must learn to transcend that kind of thinking," Genji said. "If Japan is to be accepted among the Great Powers of the world, it must abandon an overemphasis on bloodlines and concentrate on individual merit. Sons should not automatically be condemned for what their fathers were."

"Yes, lord," Hidé said, utterly without conviction. Six years ago, he had been one of the few survivors of Kawakami's treacherous ambush at Mushindo Monastery. By training and inclination, Hidé was a samurai of the old school. Revenge was the only motivation he really understood, and he assumed all samurai were the same—except Lord Genji, whom Hidé viewed as a unique and awe-inspiring prophet beyond emulation.

"We had better meet with Lord Saemon," Genji said to Hidé. "We must act quickly to keep the situation from getting out of hand. Hotheads may decide the time is ripe to begin a war against the outsiders."

"Yes, lord. I will assemble the men."

"Not necessary. It will be enough if you accompany me."

"Lord—" Hidé began, but Genji stopped him.

"We must demonstrate confidence. A lack of confidence is more dangerous now than a lack of bodyguards." Genji turned to Emily and said in English, "Did you understand?"

"The essential parts, yes," Emily said. "Please be careful."

"Always," Genji said, smiling. He bowed and was gone.

· · · · ·

Emily returned to the new scroll and went over the opening passage word by word with her dictionary. There was no question that it read, *Lord Narihira learned from the visitor that the arrival of American beauty in Cloud of Sparrows Castle would signal the ultimate triumph of the Okumichi clan.* The presence of the word *American* was what excited her attention upon first reading. But now that Genji had insisted that the visions came only in dreams, the word *visitor* was even more fascinating. Those who came to Quiet Crane Palace to see Genji were referred to as *okyaku-sama*, meaning "guest." The author of the scroll had used *hōmonsha* instead. Emily would translate it as "visitor." More literally, however, *hōmonsha* meant "one who calls upon others."

Another distinction between the two terms suddenly struck Emily and, for an unaccountable reason, chilled her.

A guest was invited, or at least expected.

A visitor was not necessarily either.

· · · · ·

All during his series of meetings with the council of Great Lords, Genji's thoughts kept slipping back to Emily.

He was the one leaving the daily rose for Emily, of course. Though nothing had been said, he assumed she knew that he was aware of her feelings. Surely she believed he felt friendship for her and nothing more. All of his behavior was of that kind. Was he assuming too much? Had Emily been Japanese, he would have felt complete confidence in his assumptions. She was very distinctly not Japanese, however, and so he was certain of nothing. Well, almost nothing. He knew she loved him. Unlike Genji, Emily was entirely incapable of convincing dissimulation.

But his performance could not continue indefinitely. Today, during their midday meal together, he had been painfully aroused by the mere sight of her eating—the movement of her mouth, the way her graceful hands held the sandwich, the way her lips parted a moment before the rim of the teacup reached them. If such mundane acts excited him so much that he could not speak, it was clear that he had reached the very limit of his self-control.

His feelings, if known to her, would inevitably free her from restraining the expression of her own. This would culminate, according to the prophetic warning he had received, in her early doom. In that dream, Genji had received a vision of Emily's death in childbirth. She would insure the survival of the clan and, in doing so, would die. Genji could not accept it. He refused to think of it as an inevitability, as every vision of his grandfather's had been, but as a warning. His grandfather had received exact premonitions. Genji chose to believe his were warnings. So he was heeding the warning. He would not allow himself to get any closer to Emily than this make-believe secret admiration.

Emily would shortly receive offers of marriage from both Lieutenant Farrington, the American naval attaché, and Charles Smith, the sugar planter and cattle rancher from the Hawaiian Kingdom. Emily did not know that Genji knew this. She did not know that he had befriended each of the men precisely because he saw that they were worthy suitors for her. He knew they in turn would find her irresistible because, with the arrival of increasing numbers of outsiders, he had discovered that Emily was considered an astonishing beauty by them, the opposite of her effect on the Japanese. How strange it was. Now that he had come to love her despite her appearance, it was her appearance that would enable her to leave that love behind. The thought of never again seeing her, even as a friend, brought him great anguish, but he preferred that to being the instrument of her death.

"Do you agree, Lord Genji?" Lord Saemon asked.

He could not admit he had heard nothing, since it would be highly insulting to Saemon and extremely embarrassing to himself. He pretended a need to hear a few more opinions before arriving at one of his own, and so managed to avoid both insult and embarrassment. Difficult though it was, for the rest of the meeting, he forced himself to think no more of Emily.

Saemon saw that Genji was distracted by other concerns but gave no indication that he had noticed. When the meeting was over, he thanked Genji for his insightful comments on the present crisis, apologized for his inability to control the impetuous Great Lord of Yoshino, and moved immediately to execute the decisions of the council with which he had been entrusted.

In the meantime, he kept his own counsel. After all, who else was there he could trust so fully, or whose judgment had been proved so sound as to be nearly prescient time after time? It was a lesson he had learned well from his father, the late Lord Kawakami, a most treacherous and deceitful man, who had commanded the most feared organ of the Shogun's government, the secret police.

Trust no one around you, Lord Kawakami had said, no matter how well you think you know them.

Being the clever boy that he was at the time, he had replied, And what if I am alone? He expected his father to respond with a jest, but his seriousness never wavered.

Lord Kawakami had said, Then regard yourself with careful suspicion, question motives, examine associations, look for potential avenues of betrayal. If you find them before your enemies do, you can conceal them or, even better, bait them as traps, and you will have gained yet more advantages from what appear to others as weaknesses.

Saemon himself was a living trap. Kawakami had arranged matters so that everyone believed the son to hate the father. Being the eldest son, Saemon would normally expect to be Kawakami's heir, and his eventual successor as Great Lord of Hino. It was a title without much substance, since Hino was one of the smallest and least important of Japan's two hundred sixty domains, but being a Great Lord conferred important rewards of prestige and honor. This would not happen, since Saemon was said to be the child of a lesser concubine rather than Kawakami's wife. He was raised in a small palace in the countryside, more of a glorified farmhouse than anything else, and received none of the pampering and privileges attained by his supposed half-brothers at the main castle. Naturally, such a son would hate his father.

Saemon, of course, was not the child of the concubine but what he was said not to be, namely, the eldest son of Kawakami's wife. From his infancy, Saemon was part of a plan of deception. He grew up well known for the murderous feelings he harbored toward his father. Those feelings being perfectly appropriate, he gained entrée into various anti-Shogunate groups. It was all quite clever, perhaps even brilliant, in his father's typical manner. The only flaw was that Saemon's pretense of hatred attained a perfection Kawakami had not anticipated.

The son actually did hate the father. And the reasons for this, too, were perfectly natural.

Because of the devious long-range plot in which he involuntarily played so vital a role, Saemon had not been raised by his kindly, highborn, and loving mother in the castle of which he was the rightful heir. Instead, he was placed in the hands of a physically beautiful, lazy, sluttish concubine who had no interest in him whatsoever. To silence the bawling infant, she inflicted the most perverted sexual practices on him, which in his later view was what had ruined him for normal behavior forever. That he poisoned her with a very painful, slow-acting Chinese toxin when he was sixteen was hardly sufficient compensation, though from time to time, he still recalled with satisfaction how she took a full month to die, the month of the perfect autumn moon, and in that brief span aged twenty years. At the end, she had not a trace of her former beauty left, and what had been one of her most attractive characteristics, her intoxicating sexual fragrance, had degenerated into a stench so foul that only the lowliest servants ever entered her presence, and they infrequently.

From his father and stepmother, Saemon had learned that only he himself had his best interests at heart. Now, in a time of crisis upon crisis, great opportunities were arising for those with clarity of vision.

And who had clearer vision than one who was not burdened with false ideas of loyalty, honor, love, respect, sincerity, tradition, or family?

Lord Saemon was certain there was no one better suited to be that exemplary expression of the man of the future than he himself.

The time to act was not yet, but it was coming, and would arrive soon. Genji had saved him the trouble of killing his father. He would eventually kill Genji, as his father had planned, but not out of animosity. Genji was one of the Great Lords who could block his own ascent when the Tokugawa Shogun's regime was finally toppled. It was a practical matter, no more.

With a view to the future—the real future, not one imagined by deluded weaklings—Saemon had begun investigating the numerous rumors that had swirled around Lord Genji from the moment of his birth. Most were the obvious stuff of fairy tales and peasant superstitions. Whenever disaster threatened, be it famine, war, plague, earthquake, or tidal wave, the desperate always sought refuge in magical intervention. They had nothing else. But two reports demanded Saemon's more serious attention.

One attributed the mysterious slaughter of an isolated village of peasants in Hino Domain some six years ago to Lord Genji. Why would a nobleman of his exalted rank and high ambition sully his own hands with so minor an undertaking? No one knew.

The second concerned the departure of Lord Genji's lover, Mayonaka no Heiko, a famous geisha in her time, to America in the same year. Some said she had run away with an American, Matthew Stark, then and now a close associate of Genji's. But Saemon knew that a large quantity of Genji's gold had gone to America with the two. That would have been impossible without his approval. Indeed, the very lives of the two could not have continued without it.

What was the truth?

Saemon was determined to find out.

The most unlikely event, the most insignificant person, could hold the key to Genji's destruction.

1862, SAN FRANCISCO

It was the same ocean, yet nothing was the same. The shoreline of San Francisco Bay did not remind Heiko of Edo Bay, nor did the penetrating chill of this California autumn evoke memories of the milder coolness of the same season in Japan.

But the waves, in their constant movement, somehow took her thoughts back to that other place, and another time, when she had been the most beautiful geisha in the great capital city of the Tokugawa Shogun. It now seemed so very long ago, especially when she thought in terms of the Japanese calendar. The eleventh month in the fourteenth year of the Emperor Komei. The words and numbers bespoke a distant, barely remembered era.

Had it really been only two years ago when she had first met Genji?

She had misjudged him terribly, as had everyone. It was an easy mistake to make. Genji displayed none of the seriousness one expected of a high-ranking samurai in a time of crisis, and there was too often a smile on his lips, even when there was no reason anyone could discern for even the slightest amusement. He also dressed in a rather dandified manner. Such clothing was entirely appropriate for an actor, and no one could deny that the young lord was handsome enough for any Kabuki stage in the land, but he was not an actor, after all. He was a lord, heir to the rule of Akaoka Domain, and, if the persistent rumors were to be believed, endowed with prophetic vision. One would expect him to be more subdued in appearance, at the very least.

Her employer, Lord Kawakami, the head of the Shogun's secret police, had described Genji as a spoiled and shallow dilettante, a wastrel interested in women and wine, and not at all in the martial traditions of the samurai. Her observations had seemed to confirm this. But once she had permitted herself to be seduced by him, she knew that Kawakami was terribly mistaken. Genji had the manner of a weakling, and dressed like one, but his body betrayed his secret. His apparent softness, when clothed, was the result of a posture of feigned laxness. Disciplined muscles and sinews knit his bones together in taut potentiality, much as the string of a bow drew an otherwise harmless curve of wood into a deadly weapon. Heiko, whose own martial training gave her an intimate knowledge of human musculature, knew from the first time they had made love that Genji had spent years training with warhorse, sword, dagger, spear, and bow and arrows. That someone as well informed as Sticky Eye Kawakami did not know this suggested a degree of secret training that led to only one conclusion; Genji's outward behavior had been intended to lead observers to the faulty conclusion that Kawakami had in fact reached.

Heiko had not reported this to Kawakami. She told herself it wasn't really valuable information. Did it mean that Genji's clan, the Okumichi, plotted treason against the Shogun? Of course, that was a given. Enmity between the Shogun's clan and those of its opponents had lasted nearly three hundred years. That those three hundred years had been three hundred years of peace mattered not at all. The plotting and counterplotting would not end until one side finally triumphed conclusively over the other. Since wars among the clans were almost never truly conclusive, it was entirely likely that the plotting and counterplotting would continue until the sun itself fell from the sky. So she had not yet really learned anything worth reporting. So she told herself. And by the time she knew the truth, she was no longer Kawakami's tool, but Genji's lover.

It seemed so long ago now. Perhaps because these months in America had been the longest months of her life. The certainty that she would soon be recalled home by Genji somehow made time pass that much more slowly.

"Heiko." Matthew Stark's gentle voice was close behind her. She had not heard him approach. Memories had dulled her sense of the present. "Fog's likely to drift in from the sea soon. We should be heading home."

"Yes, thank you, Matthew." Heiko took his offered arm and leaned heavily on him as they negotiated their way up the pathway back toward the road. The hill seemed much steeper now than it had when she was going down.

"I wish you wouldn't exert yourself so much," Stark said. "Dr. Winslow told me women in your condition should spend these last weeks in bed."

The foolishness of such a notion made Heiko feel like laughing, but she restrained herself. Though the outsiders may know much about science, their knowledge of the simplest facts of nature was often ridiculously weak. "Four weeks in bed would weaken, not strengthen, and I will need strength when the time comes."

Stark said, "Sometimes you sound more like a samurai than a woman."

She smiled as he helped her into the carriage. "I take that as a compliment, Matthew. Thank you."

"I didn't mean it as one." But he returned her smile before he snapped the reins to urge the horse forward.

Heiko told herself to stop thinking of Stark and the other Americans as outsiders. This was their country. Here, she was the outsider. But she would not be here much longer. Her gaze softened. She drowsed. She was asleep and dreaming of Cloud of Sparrows Castle long before they reached San Francisco.

1308, CLOUD OF SPARROWS CASTLE

Lady Shizuka was sixteen years old when Lord Hironobu rescued her and brought her to Cloud of Sparrows Castle as his bride. As soon as she arrived, she found her way without a single misstep through oddly angled corridors to the innermost courtyard, greatly surprising Lord Hironobu. All interior passages of the castle were intentionally confusing, to thwart any attackers who might succeed in breaching the outer defenses during a siege.

"How did you know how to get here?"

But once inside, she stood in confusion. "Where are they?"

"Where are what?"

"The flowers," Shizuka said.

"Flowers?" Hironobu laughed. "There is no place for flowers here. This is a bastion of fearsome warriors. Look, here comes one now. Go, meet my new wife. Shizuka, this is my bodyguard, Go."

Go, a large, grim-visaged man, said nothing to her, and made no gesture of greeting. He said to Hironobu, "You should not have done this, my lord."

"You are too serious. This is a matter of love, not war or politics. Stop worrying." Hironobu said to Shizuka, "He was my warrior nursemaid when I was a child. It seems sometimes he thinks he still is."

But Shizuka was not interested in Go. She went to the center of the courtyard. "They should be here, right here."

"What should be right here?" Hironobu said.

"The flowers," Shizuka said. "American Beauty roses."

"What kind of roses?"

"American Beauty roses."

"American? What is American?"

Shizuka shrugged impatiently. "Where is Lord Narihira? He must have planted them in the wrong place."

Hironobu's expression was now a seriously worried one. "Who is Lord Narihira?"

"The lord of this castle," Shizuka said.

"Shizuka, I am the lord of this castle," Hironobu said.

When she remembered this incident years later, she would reflect with some amusement on those days before she realized how different her knowledge was from that of others. But now her disappointment was too keen to bear. She had so been looking forward to seeing those splendid blossoms of red, pink, and white. Tears rolled helplessly down her cheeks.

When Hironobu tried to comfort her, all she could say was "I wouldn't have cut it from its branch. I just wanted to see it. An American Beauty rose."

3

The Mongol Trunk

"You believe knowing the future and knowing the past are opposite."

The lord of the domain said, "I do."

"In fact, they amount to the same thing."

The lord said, "Nonsense. The past is done. The future is yet to come. How can the two be the same?"

"Knowing the past, can you change it?"

"Of course not," the lord said.

"And how is knowing the inevitable any different from knowing what has already happened?"

AKI-NO-HASHI

(1311)

1867, QUIET CRANE PALACE

Hanako, looking into the study, saw that Lady Emily's desk was not occupied, and entered to tidy up. She should leave it to the maids, but today's young women were not as trustworthy as those of old. They were too curious, lacked discipline, and loved gossip far too much. Everyone knew Emily was working on an English translation of *Suzume-no-kumo*, the inner history of the Okumichi clan. If a scroll were inadvertently left open, or even tied closed but not put away, one of the maids might find the temptation to look within too much to resist. This was reason enough for her to do the work. So Hanako told herself. She knew such a menial task was not her responsibility, nor was it appropriate for one of her lofty station. She was, after all, the wife of Lord Genji's chief bodyguard, Lord Hidé, and was herself entitled to the sobriquet "lady." But old habits were hard to break. She had been born a lowly farmer's daughter in the valley below Mushindo Monastery, an ancestral outpost of the Great Lords of Akaoka for six hundred years. When she was nine years old, she had lost her parents. The kindly old abbot of the monastery, Zengen, had taken pity on her and had arranged for her to enter the household service of Lord Kiyori, Genji's grandfather and predecessor. She was twenty-two, without family, connections, or dowry, and resigned to the life of an old maid, when Lord Genji himself had arranged her marriage to Hidé, a samurai she had long admired from afar.

That such unexpected things had happened still amazed her. In her twenty-ninth year, she was the mother of a noble son, the wife of the lord's most trusted companion, and the best friend of Lady Emily, the American who had, through a strange twist of fate, become as much a member of the clan as any outsider could. How fortunate they all were that Lord Genji, unlike ordinary men, could see the future. Because of that, his judgment, even if it sometimes seemed strange, could always be trusted.

Hanako pinned back the empty left sleeve of her kimono to keep it out of the way. She never did this when others were around, since she felt it called excessive attention to the absence of her left arm. Though only six years had passed since the fight at the monastery, people already spoke of it in reverent terms as the Great Battle at Mushindo Monastery. Hanako, Hidé, Lord Genji, and Lady Emily had been among the very few who had lived through the ambush by six hundred enemy musketeers, and triumphed against seemingly impossible odds. Naturally, their exploits had been magnified in retellings by those who knew nothing, and Hanako herself had gained unwanted notoriety for courage because she had lost an arm in the fight. Because of this, any visible emphasis upon her loss, even if unintended, seemed to her to be a kind of boastful display.

Scrolls were everywhere, some opened, some not. Emily, usually so neat, had left the place in an uncharacteristic mess. Had she been called away suddenly? It was a good thing Hanako had decided to clean up. Too many scrolls were open. Only someone such as herself, someone determined not to see, could close them without recognizing a single character.

To distract herself, she tried to remember what *Suzume-no-kumo* was in English. Emily had just told her the other day. It had seemed much stranger in English than in Japanese. Now, what was it?

Hanako closed another scroll and put it next to the one she had closed before it. By maintaining the order in which the scrolls had been left, it would be relatively easy for Emily to resume where she had stopped, even if the scrolls were no longer open.

Ah, yes, Hanako remembered. *Cloud of Sparrows.* She said it aloud to practice the shapes of the words in her mouth, and to hear the sounds, the better to remember them.

"*Cloud of Sparrows,*" Hanako said, and was quite pleased with herself. She had spoken the English words very clearly, she thought.

"Hello?" Emily said, and looked up from behind a table at the far end of the room. She had apparently been seated on the floor.

"Excuse me," Hanako said. "I didn't realize you were here. You were not at your desk, so I came in to clean up." She bowed and began to leave.

"No, don't go, Hanako," Emily said. "I was about to find you anyway. Look at this." She indicated the small trunk next to her, leather-covered, with a faded painting on its topmost surface.

"Ah," Hanako said, "you have opened a new box of scrolls. How exciting for you."

"They're very different from the others. Even the trunk they came in is different. Is this a Japanese design?"

Hanako looked at the dragon curling like angry red smoke around the mountains of blue ice.

"No," she said. "It is closer to the Chinese style, but wilder, more barbaric. Perhaps it was made by the Mongols."

Emily nodded. She looked worried, or perplexed, or perhaps merely tired. Though Hanako had known her for several years, and had met other outsiders since then, she still could not always tell what emotions showed on their faces. Unlike the Japanese, outsiders often did not seek to conceal their feelings, and it was this very lack of intentional control that made their expressions so difficult for Hanako to understand. Too many facial signals appeared at the same time, among them those of an unbearably inappropriate nature. Sometimes, she would be with Emily when one of her American friends came to visit. The naval officer, Robert Farrington, or the rancher, Charles Smith. At those times, she would often see displayed on the men's faces emotions of a kind so intimate, she blushed to see them. Emily, it seemed, did not recognize the display, since she continued with the conversation as if nothing were amiss, and was neither insulted, angered, or embarrassed herself. Hanako wondered, not for the first time, if they even understood each other.

Now Emily was apparently thinking about many different things, which would account somewhat for the confusion in her facial expression, for when she next spoke it was about a different matter entirely.

She said, "Do you know about Go, Lord Hironobu's bodyguard?"

"Of course," Hanako said, relieved that Emily's attention had moved away from the scrolls. They could only be read by the Great Lord and those in the line of succession. Lord Genji had made an exception in Emily's case. She could read them. Hanako could not. "He is one of the great heroes of our clan. Without him, Lord Hironobu would have died in childhood, and there would never have been any Great Lords of Akaoka."

"Was Go a Mongol?"

"Oh, no," Hanako said, shocked at the outrageous suggestion. "I'm sure he was not."

"Where was he from?"

"From? He was from Japan."

"Where in Japan?"

Hanako thought for a moment. "I don't recall ever being told anything about his childhood. Except that he could ride a horse almost before he could walk." She smiled. "But, of course, that is what is said in fairy tales. Otherwise, he is always spoken of as Lord Hironobu's bodyguard. He was the lord's bodyguard when the lord was a child, and he was the lord's bodyguard at the end."

"The end," Emily repeated. "What was the end?"

"They died together in battle," Hanako said, "holding off a Hojo army so that the lord's infant son could escape and live to exact a just revenge." This, too, was a famous episode in clan history. "This son, Danjuro, became the second Great Lord of our domain. While barely out of boyhood, he helped destroy the Hojo regency." A chilling thought suddenly occurred to her. Before she could stop herself, she asked, "Does *Suzume-no-kumo* say otherwise?"

Emily shook her head. "No, it says exactly what you say."

"Ah." Hanako was very relieved. Not infrequently, in every clan, those above knew something other than what was told to those below. In a clan such as this one, led by generations of prophets, above and below could be very different indeed. Now that she had raised the matter of the scrolls, it would be best for her to leave before the subject came up again. She bowed to her friend. "I am sorry to disturb you, Emily. I will leave you to your work now."

"I need your help, Hanako."

Hanako hesitated. "I will be happy to do all I can, so long as I am not asked to read any scroll or hear more about what is in them."

"These are not the ones that you can't read." Emily offered the scroll in her hands to Hanako.

Hanako bowed again, but did not reach to accept it. "I cannot."

"It's not *Suzume-no-kumo*."

Emily had made great strides in her understanding of the Japanese language during her time here. Hanako, however, was far from confident that Emily could distinguish what was and what wasn't part of the secret clan history. If a scroll came from one of these trunks, how could it not be a part of this history? To refuse to take it now would be extremely impolite. Yet to accept it could mean violating a fundamental rule of the clan. It was best to avoid insult whenever possible. Hesitantly, she took the scroll. At the first indication that Emily was mistaken, she would immediately cease reading.

Her first glimpse of the flowing lines of phonetic hiragana script and the almost total absence of complex kanji ideograms told her that Emily was right. No one would write the clan history in so informal a manner. But when she read the first line, the mention of Lord Narihira and the well-known misguided prophecy of the roses made her stop.

"I cannot, Emily."

"This seems to be a kind of diary," Emily said. "Gossip, not history."

"Whatever it is, it speaks of Great Lords and prophecies," Hanako said. "It would be wrong for me to continue."

Emily smiled. "Does no one here ever speak of the prophecies? Is Lord Genji never the subject of gossip?"

Hanako returned Emily's smile. Of course, she was right. Within the Okumichi clan, prophecies and the thoughts and actions of the lord were constant subjects of conversation, argument, and speculation. This was not correct behavior. But human nature being what it was, could there be any other result? Hanako resumed reading. At the end of the first passage, she couldn't keep from laughing.

"Yes," Emily said, "I laughed there, too. I would translate it, '*When heaven gave men command of the world, the gods above were surely displaying a most mischievous sense of humor.*'"

"Yes, that is correct, I think."

"A woman wrote this," Emily said.

"Beyond any doubt," Hanako said. "The handwriting, the style, the subject matter, all are very feminine." She read a little more and smiled, at ease now that she was confident she wasn't reading any forbidden material. "She's telling about a love affair, apparently an illicit and tragic one."

"Among other things."

"I wonder how it got mixed in?"

"It wouldn't be entirely accurate to say it was mixed in." Emily opened the lid of the trunk with the red dragon and the blue mountains. "These are all in the same style."

"Then the trunk itself was placed among the others in error."

"I wonder," Emily said. She moved the layer of rough cloth aside to reveal fine silk intricately embroidered with a pattern of colorful roses against a field of billowing white clouds and a sky of the brightest blue. "Aren't these what your clansmen call American Beauty roses?"

"Yes, they appear to be," Hanako said, feeling uneasy once again. "I think they must be, since the scroll mentions them by name."

"They were originally planted by Lord Narihira," Emily said.

"Yes."

"And when was that?"

"In the eighteenth year of the Ōgimachi Emperor," Hanako said.

"What year by the Western calendar?"

Hanako calculated quickly. "I believe it would be 1575."

Emily nodded. "That's what I thought, but I was sure I had miscalculated. It's very easy for an outsider to lose track of the proper sequence of emperors in the Japanese calendar." She contemplated the picture on the trunk. "It has taken me two weeks to read it. I finished it yesterday. Since then, my mind has been on nothing else." She seemed about to say more, but remained silent.

Finally, Hanako asked, "Why did you think you had made an error in dating?"

"Because of the roses," Emily said, "in the narrative and in this cloth."

"Yes?" Hanako didn't understand why Emily seemed so perturbed. The most common symbol of the clan was the sparrow dodging arrows from the four directions. This appeared on the official Okumichi battle flags. Almost as frequently depicted during the last two hundred years were these roses. They could be found on banners, kimonos, designs on armor, on the blades and hilts of swords. There was nothing mysterious about their appearance in the writings of clansmen or clanswomen, or on a piece of silk such as this, used to wrap scrolls.

"The roses were planted in 1575," Emily said, "so it would be impossible for anyone writing before that year to speak of them."

"That is true," Hanako said.

"Yet they are prominently mentioned in these scrolls," Emily said, "which the author says she wrote in the fourth year of the Hanazono Emperor."

Hanako quickly went through her memory of Imperial chronology. She said, "That cannot be. Hanazono 4 is 1311 in the Christian calendar."

Emily said, "I must go to Cloud of Sparrows Castle."

Hanako was horrified. How could Emily even think of it? The castle was three hundred miles away. Between them was a countryside filled with increasingly violent anti-foreign samurai, chief among them the so-called Men of Virtue. Attacks against outsiders had become distressingly commonplace of late. No women had been targeted. Things had not yet deteriorated so far. But Emily was notorious as a guest of Lord Genji, and he was at the top of the Men of Virtue's list of domestic enemies.

"What reason is there for such a journey?"

Emily looked straight into Hanako's eyes. She said, "We are friends. We are true friends."

"Yes," Hanako said. "We are true friends."

Emily looked at her for several more long moments before she turned to the trunk and began removing the scrolls. When they were all out, she lifted the silk cloth from the trunk and held it up. Hanako saw that it was a kimono.

"Do you notice anything about it?" Emily asked.

"It is cut in the current style," Hanako said, which was somewhat surprising if the scrolls were as old as they seemed. Not shockingly so, however, since they might have been rewrapped in recent times.

Emily held it up against her own body. "Anything else?"

"Well, it is very fancy," Hanako said. "It would most likely be worn only on a special occasion. A celebration, a festival, something like that."

"Or a wedding?" Emily said.

"Yes, it would be suitable for a wedding. Not for a guest, of course. It is too splendid. Only the bride could wear it." She looked at the profusion of intricately embroidered roses. The bride would have to be very beautiful as well, or the kimono itself would attract all the attention. "And it would need a special *obi*."

Emily reached into the trunk once again. "Like this one?" She held up a ceremonial sash as elaborate as the kimono, in complementary colors, generously embroidered with gold and silver thread.

"Yes," Hanako said, "that is perfect." What were a wedding kimono and sash doing in a trunk filled with ancient scrolls? She felt herself growing cold.

Emily said, "This trunk was sent to me." Her voice was very faint, as if she had spoken against her will.

Hanako didn't understand her concern. Everyone knew Lord Genji had asked Emily to make an English translation of the secret history. He had ordered all scrolls to be delivered to her. Naturally, if a trunk such as this was found, it would go to Emily, as had similarly found trunks over the years since her task began. Thirty generations of Okumichi lords had read the scrolls. Across such a span of time and personalities, it was inevitable that portions of the history were occasionally misplaced. Cloud of Sparrows was a very large castle, with hidden compartments and secret passageways. There were many places where things could be concealed and forgotten. Since only the lord or those he allowed could see the scrolls, whoever found them would not dare to read them, and so could not know that these scrolls were not part of the history. (Some lords had not taken either the history or the prohibition seriously, and so there had been times when many outside the direct lineage had been given access—lovers, drinking companions, geisha, and monks among them. Thus, much of the history was common knowledge, or, perhaps more accurately, common gossip.) There was nothing mysterious about the delivery of the trunk to her. Yet Emily was clearly very disturbed.

"It was found and sent to you because Lord Genji has so ordered," Hanako said.

"No," Emily said. "That's not what I mean. It's impossible; it borders on blasphemy to even consider, yet—" Emily crumpled to the floor and sat heavily, the kimono and sash in her lap. "I must go to the castle. It's the only way to disprove it. And I must disprove it, I must."

"Disprove what?" Hanako said.

"That this trunk was sent to *me*," Emily said.

1311, THE HIGH TOWER OF CLOUD OF SPARROWS CASTLE

Lady Shizuka smiled at Ayamé, her chief lady-in-waiting, and marveled that women as young as they, barely out of childhood, should bear such weighty titles as "lady" and "lady-in-waiting." Lady Shizuka was nineteen, and she would grow no older. Ayamé was only seventeen, though her serious expression made her seem more mature.

"I beg you to reconsider, my lady," Ayamé said. She sat with her legs neatly folded under her in normal courtly fashion. She seemed very delicate despite the armor she wore, her roughly shorn hair, and the long-bladed naginata halberd at her side. "I have scouted the enemy positions myself, and it is as Fumi says: Their sentries are poorly posted, their lines are porous, and half their troops are stupefied with sake. If I create a diversion, you can easily slip through to safety."

"I cannot go," Shizuka said. Her hand was on her swollen belly, as it often was in recent days. Her flowing robes concealed her condition from the casual observer, and her face, as slender as always, did its part in hiding the truth.

"You are not due for another month and a half," Ayamé said, "and the child does not seem to be in a hurry to appear early. There will be little hardship once you have escaped the encirclement. Lord Chiaki would have received word by now, and is surely on his way back with many of our samurai. You will probably meet up with him even before you reach the cape."

"That is not why I cannot go," Shizuka said. "This is where I am meant to be."

Ayamé leaned forward, placed both her hands on the floor in front of her, and bowed low. "Lady Shizuka, forgive me, for I must speak too frankly."

"There is no such thing between us, Ayamé. You are always free to speak your thoughts to me."

"I hope you will continue to think so. Many say it is not the future you see, or spirits that you meet, but your own delusions. Lucky guesses, they say, make you seem prescient. From the day I entered your service, I have never doubted you. Whatever you say, I know you have your reasons for saying it. You are wise beyond your years and experience. It is not important whether you know what is to come or not. But, my lady, if you do not leave this place tonight, you will die here."

Shizuka placed her hands on the floor and bowed low in her turn.

"You have been steadfast and loyal, and as courageous as the samurai of legend. For this, I thank you. Now you must be braver still. You will live through this night, Ayamé, and through the darkest hours of the morning, and for many, many years thereafter. This is your future, and in time, you will know I have seen it truly. You will marry a man of much virtue and merit, and will have much joy, as well as your fair portion of sorrow. You will have five children. The eldest will marry Lord Hironobu's heir, whom I carry within me, and will rule this domain as Great Lord."

"My lady," Ayamé said, shocked. It was treasonous to even think that a son of anyone other than Hironobu would succeed him. The mere suspicion of such thoughts had led to deaths among the retainers of many clans. And here the lord's own wife was saying it.

"My daughter's name is Sen. Your son you will name—" Shizuka stopped herself. Let Ayamé decide for herself, though in the completeness of time, she had already decided to call him Danjuro. Those whose pasts were separate from their futures did not see it that way. To speak the name now would be to rob her of joy yet to come. "—you will name nobly, as he deserves. In Lord Hironobu's stead, I hereby adopt him into the clan. From the moment of his birth, he will be an Okumichi."

"Lady Shizuka, if what you say is true, and you can see what is to come, then use your vision to save yourself. It is a sin to needlessly throw away your life."

Shizuka said, "Go to that window and look to the east."

After an almost impalpable hesitation, Ayamé obeyed.

"What do you see?"

"Waves, my lady, breaking upon the shore."

"Still the waters," Shizuka said.

"My lady?"

"Stop the waves, Ayamé. Calm the ocean."

"I cannot."

"Go to the western window. Look into the farthest possible distance. What is there?"

"Clear night air," Ayamé said, "a bright moon, and in the far distance, Mount Tosa."

"Bring Mount Tosa to me."

Ayamé stared at Shizuka. Had fear and sorrow driven her mad? An expression of deep concern furrowed her brow.

"My lady, not even the greatest sorceress could move such a mountain."

"You see the waves, but you cannot stop them. You see Mount Tosa, but you cannot move it. In the same way, I can see what is to come but can neither deflect nor change it in the slightest way." Shizuka smiled. "You will live through the night, and so will I. You will live through the morning, and I will not. I speak of this as I would speak of waves turning into foam on the rocks, and Mount Tosa in moonlight. It is a description of the world, not something to be done."

"To know, yet be unable to act. What use is such a gift?"

You will never know, Shizuka thought, nor will Danjuro. But Sen will. Beneath her hand, she felt her daughter stir.

"Have the scrolls been placed as I asked?" Shizuka said.

"Yes, my lady, and as you ordered, nothing was left to mark the spot, no map drawn."

"You seem doubtful, Ayamé."

"I was careful that no one saw me," she said, "but since it is far outside our walls, the enemy may find it even if they withdraw without attacking the castle."

"They will not find it," Shizuka said.

"There is yet another problem," Ayamé said. "If the castle should fall to the enemy—"

It would fall, and within hours.

"—and none of us returns—"

None now living would return. Danjuro and Sen would recover the castle in the twelfth year of the Emperor Go-Murakami. By then Ayamé and Chiaki would both be dead.

"—how will the scrolls ever be found?"

"They will be found," Shizuka said, "when they should, and in a manner befitting their purpose." She could see that Ayamé wanted to ask the purpose, and did not. It was just as well. Shizuka trusted her and would tell her whatever she asked, but she would not have understood the answer.

Ayamé bowed and took up her weapon. "With your permission, I will return to my post, my lady."

"Good night, Ayamé."

Shizuka's visitor would not arrive until the latter half of the hour. She closed her eyes and visualized nothing. The absence was very restful.

1860, THE HIGH TOWER

Sentimental and foolish though he knew it was, Lord Kiyori had ordered delicacies for a farewell dinner with Lady Shizuka. He had not touched the food. Neither had she, but then, she never did. It was placed before her in the same way offerings were made at the ancestral altar. In one sense, this was quite fitting, since Shizuka was an ancestor. In another, it was entirely inappropriate, because this specter who appeared as Shizuka was more likely only a figment of his own diseased imagination.

"You are quiet," Shizuka said, "because you are thinking I cannot possibly be who I say I am. I must be a hallucination, or a malevolent spirit. Since you do not believe in ghosts, you tend toward the conclusion that I am, as I have always been, a sign of your impending insanity. Yet you feel you are not yet so afflicted that you are compelled to speak to your own delusion. At the same time, you have already spent many years speaking to me, so what harm is there to do so again, one last time, tonight, whether I am real or not? It would not be so very different from simply thinking out loud, would it? However, since we will not meet again, this is your last chance to treat me as the figment that I am. You cannot do so by engaging me in conversation. Such are your present thoughts. What a dilemma, my lord."

"You want me to think you are reading my mind," Kiyori said, "but I am not so easily fooled. A hallucination naturally contains thoughts of the mind from which it comes."

Shizuka smiled. "Why, my lord, you have spoken to me."

Exasperated, Kiyori slapped his thigh. He had never been a sophisticated thinker, and he could not hope to match her skill in argument. Of course, even to think that was itself quite confusing. "Habit compels me, nothing else. And as you say—or, rather, as I say—it's no different from thinking out loud."

Shizuka bowed very formally, her hands triangulated on the floor before her, her head slowly lowered to touch them.

"Since I am you," she said, "I can do nothing other than agree." An expression of seriousness appeared on her face momentarily, but she could not suppress her amusement for long. At the deepest point of her bow, she began to smile, and as she came up, she covered her mouth with her sleeve. "Please do not glare so angrily at me. Remember, I am only you."

"I wish you would stop saying that," Kiyori said, growing irritated with her despite his awareness that doing so made him feel very silly indeed since, as she said, she was he and he himself was therefore to blame for anything she did or said, since it was all his own saying and doing. Oh, what was the use of such tortured mental gyrations? Let them speak together as they always had, madman and hallucination, for one last time.

"You said you would leave tonight and never return," Kiyori said. "Is it really so?"

"Have I ever told you a lie, lord?"

"No, you have not."

"Truly remarkable, is it not? In sixty-four years, speaking through me, you have never lied to yourself. Few men can say as much. Oh, excuse me. You cannot say it either, can you, since I have said it. But wait, I am you, so indeed you can, and have."

"Please." Kiyori bowed low. "Let us say our phenomenon is a ghostly one. It is so much easier that way."

"I will agree," Shizuka said, "with one small adjustment."

"Done," Kiyori said without a pause, so eager was he to escape from his conundrum. Seeing the look in her eyes, he immediately regretted giving his consent before he had heard what she would propose.

"Let us say the ghost is you, Lord Kiyori."

"That is outrageous."

"Is it?" All merriment was gone from Shizuka. "You have studied the classics of Confucius, Buddha, and the Tao. Yet, for fifty years, you have only contemplated our relationship from one side. You have dismissed Chuang-Tze's dream, the Flower Ornament Sutra, and the great lesson of Confucius."

"Chuang-Tze had many dreams," Kiyori said, "the Flower Ornament Sutra contains seven hundred thousand ideograms, and Confucius taught more than one lesson. It would be helpful if you were more specific."

"You need go no further than the most obvious instance in each."

Kiyori waited for her to go on. She stared at him in silence. He waited longer, and she continued to stare. Kiyori was Great Lord of the domain. No one ever dared to hold his gaze, and so he was unused to such a contest. He spoke first.

"Chuang-Tze dreamed he was a butterfly. When he awoke, he was no longer sure he was a man who had dreamed, or was now a butterfly dreaming of manhood." Did she smile in satisfaction at having bested him? If so, the smile was so slight it might have existed only in his imagination. What was he thinking? Of course it was imaginary. All of this was.

She bowed and said, "And the Flower Ornament Sutra?"

He had not been a very dedicated student in his youth, and that sutra was particularly long and complicated. But one image had always stayed with him because it was at once so elegant and so impossible to comprehend.

"The sutra says the Net of Indra is composed of an infinite number of mirrors, each reflecting every other mirror, and each reflecting the complete nature of reality, which is itself infinite in extent, infinite in time, and infinitely variable."

Shizuka clapped her hands approvingly. "Very good, Lord Kiyori. So you were not always sleeping with your eyes open when the Reverend Monk Koiké gave forth with his teachings."

"No, not always." Koiké, that boring old pedant. He had not thought of him for years.

"Tell me of Confucius and you will have correctly answered three scholarly questions in a row for the very first time in your life. What an accomplishment that would be."

Indeed it would. As skillful as he had been in combat with sword, staff, and his bare hands, he had never truly mastered calligraphy, memorization, and poetic composition. Mastered? In truth, he had never moved beyond woefully deficient. Think hard. What was Confucius's one great lesson? He realized the folly of his exertions. Here he was, pushing himself to the utmost to impress someone who wasn't even there. No, consider it instead a matter of self-discipline. He was a samurai. He should be able to hone his thinking to a swordlike edge and cut through all confusion.

Confucius's great lesson. What could she mean?

Respect your elders?

Preserve the way of the ancestors?

Be an obedient son to one's father, and an exemplary father to one's son?

Emulate men of merit, eschew the company of the frivolous?

Criticize oneself, not others?

He stopped himself. Such random rambling wouldn't do. Think sharply. Like a sword. Cut through confusion.

Shizuka had mentioned Confucius as one of three. What commonality existed between his teachings, Chuang-Tze's butterfly dream, and Indra's infinity of mirrors? Between the utterly pragmatic on the one side, and the wildly speculative and fanciful on the other?

"Confucius was not concerned with dreams," Kiyori said, "nor with cosmic riddles, only with the actual behavior of men, and so created guidelines for harmonious and beneficial behavior."

"Therefore?"

Therefore—what? He was about to admit defeat when the matter suddenly clarified itself. Possibilities were infinite (Indra's mirrors), fancies could turn every answer to any question into yet another question (Chuang-Tze's butterfly), and so it was up to human beings not to continually multiply matters but to reduce them to manageable proportions (Confucius's parent-child scheme of reality). How best to put this thought into the right words? Shizuka seemed about to speak, no doubt to answer her own question.

He must beat her to it!

Quickly he said, "Therefore, what is most real is what we choose to consider real."

Her smile immediately soured his triumph.

"You tricked me into saying what you wanted me to say."

"You have only drawn the obvious conclusion," she said. "There is no trickery in that."

"I said it," Kiyori conceded, "but I don't believe it. If a sword arcs in my direction, and I neither avoid it nor block it, I will be cut, whether I choose to think it is real or not."

"Cut me with your sword, Lord Kiyori."

How did she manage to always say what most irritated him? "I cannot."

"Why?"

"You know why. Because you are not really here. The sword will move through you as if you are air."

"Because I am not here?"

"Yes."

"Again, only one possibility, my lord?"

"Of course, there is a second. That I am not here." As soon as he said it, he realized that she had tricked him again.

Shizuka bowed in assent. "And following the pathways of butterflies and mirrors, we cannot say with any certainty which is more likely or, indeed, whether one possibility excludes the other. Perhaps I am your ghost, and you are mine."

1311, THE HIGH TOWER

"The possibility that I am not here," Lord Kiyori said, "is just that. A possibility only. We can say anything—words being the untrustworthy devices that they are—but I know that I am here, and you are not. All talk of butterflies and mirrors cannot negate that."

Shizuka watched him reach for something in front of him. From the way he raised what must be in his hands, she knew it was a teacup. Nothing real for Kiyori was visible to her, except Kiyori himself, and he only as a smoky image through which the walls of the room could be seen. The structure of the room was the same for them both, but not its contents. Kiyori regularly walked through screens, flower placements, and people that did not exist in his time. Shizuka knew she must be guilty of similar behavior in his eyes.

She was glad he had not yet tasted the soup. It was poisoned with blowfish bile, the toxin placed there by his son, Shigeru. Shigeru was insane and murderous, but not cruel. The dosage of the poison was such that Kiyori would slowly grow numb before paralysis set in and death followed. There would be little pain.

Kiyori lowered the teacup and said, "Besides, even if I were a ghost without knowing I was one, how could I be your ghost? You died five hundred years before I was born."

"I expressed possibilities," Shizuka said. "I never claimed to have explanations for each of them."

"Simple logic dictates that if any ghost is here, it is you."

Kiyori rose and walked to the western window. There was strong contrast between the light within the room and the darkness of the night outside. This, combined with the position of the moon on the other side of him, made the upper half of Kiyori's body difficult to see. His face she could not see at all.

She said, "It is simpler for you to think so."

"The logical aspect deserves emphasis," Kiyori said, "rather than its simplicity. Time passes and does not return. The past precedes the future. Like a waterfall, the flow is in one direction only."

"True," Shizuka said, "for almost everyone."

"There is no use arguing the point. We will never agree." He stepped away from the window. With a solid wall behind him, she could once again see his face. He looked worried rather than angry. "It doesn't matter anyway. Hallucination or spirit, you have been the means by which I have learned of things to come. I have never had a single one of the visions with which I am credited. I have known only because you have told me. If you do not return, I will provide no further prophecies."

"Does that trouble you, my lord?"

"No. I have predicted many things, more than any other Okumichi before me. I already have far in excess of my fair share of sayings in *Suzume-no-kumo*."

"Then . . . ?"

"So far, my grandson has had no visions," he said. "I have told him—as you told me—that he will have only three in his lifetime. Will they come to him in dreams?"

Kiyori's true query was obvious to Shizuka. He wanted to know whether she would ever appear to Genji. Because his own life had been made so strange by her frequent and unpredictable manifestations, his great hope was that Genji would not suffer the same fate. She looked carefully at his face. Shadowy and transparent, insubstantial and tenuous though he was, his concern was very apparent and deeply touched her sympathies. There was no reason to burden his final hours of existence with matters about which neither he nor she could do anything.

For Kiyori, time flowed as he had said, like the waters of a stream falling from the edge of a cliff, in one direction only. It was not so for Shizuka. She had died five hundred years before Kiyori had been born— and she would die before the next sunrise. And she was here now, alive, to attend him at the end of his life.

"You are the only Okumichi to whom I have ever appeared," she said, lying to him for the first time in their years together, "and the only one to whom I will ever appear," which was her second lie. But she had truly answered his unspoken question. She would not appear to Genji.

Kiyori breathed deeply, and bowed to her. "Thank you for telling me, Lady Shizuka. I feel a great weight lifted from me. I have managed to maintain the behavior of a normal person, but only because I am a samurai of the old and outmoded kind, able to pretend that what is so is not, and that what should be is, despite all evidence to the contrary. Genji has neither the inclination nor the training to behave in that way. He examines, questions, thinks for himself—vices which are no doubt the result of excessive study of outsider ways—no matter what tradition may say. If you appeared to him, he would lose himself in that endless spiral of doubts inevitably inspired by your presence."

Shizuka returned his bow. "I tell you now, Lord Kiyori, that you have nothing to fear. Genji will live a life of unusual fullness, with clarity of thought and unshakable purpose. He will be a true samurai, and sword in hand will lead the clan in battle as in ancient times, and attain victories that will be spoken of by generations yet unborn. He will be loved by women of incomparable beauty and great courage. His descendants, too, will be heroes. Have peace in your heart, my lord, for your line will continue into time beyond even my most distant vision."

Kiyori fell to his knees. His shoulders shook, his breath came in uncontrollable gasps, he sobbed, and his tears splattered the mat before him like a sudden squall. More important than his own honor was the honor of his heirs. More important than the lives of his immediate descendants was the knowledge of the continuity of his clan. Shizuka had told him what he had most wanted to hear.

"My lady?"

Ayamé's voice came from the other side of the hallway door. Quietly, Shizuka slipped away from the weeping Kiyori and left the room.

"Yes?"

Ayamé managed to glance into the room before the door was closed. She had heard her lady speaking to someone. No one was there.

Ayamé said, "The enemy has begun to move toward the castle in battle array. A night attack. It must be Go's doing. He has always had an impatient streak. They will assault the gates and the outer wall within minutes. We are too few to keep them out. Kenji and the samurai will set traps and ambushes in the courtyards and passageways. I and your other ladies-in-waiting will greet them at the base of this tower. We will make them bleed for every upward step they take. But we are few. Eventually, they will reach this room." Her gaze went from Shizuka's face to her belly, then stared up into her eyes with a look of pleading. "You said your child will survive the attack."

"Yes, she will."

"My lady, what must we do to make it so?"

"Be brave, Ayamé, as you have always been, and do as you have said, and make the traitors bleed. Trust that what I have told you will come to pass. That is all."

"Is a 'visitor' with you, my lady?"

Shizuka smiled. "I thought you didn't believe in the visitors."

Tears sparkled in Ayamé's eyes, and sparkled on her childish cheeks as they spilled out.

"I promise to believe in anyone who will save you, my lady."

"You have been a true and loving friend, Ayamé. When I am gone, remember me, and when my daughter is old enough to know, tell her everything. Will you do that?"

"Yes," Ayamé said, emotion choking her. She bowed her head and could say no more.

Shizuka went back into the room where Lord Kiyori waited. He had regained his composure and now held something up to his lips. The distance between his hands told her it was a bowl. The soup poisoned with blow-fish bile.

From the window, thousands of voices raised in war cries flooded in from the night.

The past and the future were about to meet in death.

1867, LORD SAEMON'S PALACE

"A very curious thing happened at the meeting this morning," Lord Saemon said to his chamberlain. "Lord Genji proposed the adoption of a new law."

"Another one?" the chamberlain said. "He has clearly contracted the outsiders' disease of lawmaking. They want many laws because they have no guiding principles. Wishing so much to be like them, he has abandoned the ways of our revered ancestors."

"No doubt you are right. Quite apart from that, the law he proposed was very interesting."

"Oh?"

"He wants to abolish regulations holding down the outcast class. Moreover, he also wants to outlaw the use of the term *eta*."

"What?" The chamberlain's face grew dark, as if the pressure behind the skin had suddenly shot up.

"Yes, and replace it with the term *burakumin*. 'People of the village.' It has a quaint charm, doesn't it?"

"My lord, did he actually speak of this matter before the gathered lords?"

"He did," Lord Saemon said, recalling with satisfaction the shocked expression on every face but his own, and that only because it was his unshakable habit to always keep the look of a kind of provisional acceptance there.

"Were there no protests?"

"Lords Gaiho, Matsudaira, Fukui, and several others walked out. Lord Genji has made a few new enemies as well as insured that he will keep his old ones."

"What could have driven him to such folly? Has he gone mad at last?"

"He said, and quite convincingly, too, that the Western nations, and particularly the most powerful, England, would never accept Japan as an equal as long as it has laws against outcasts. It violates something they call 'rights.' He said the Indians are held in low esteem by the English, despite their rich and ancient culture, for just the same reason."

The chamberlain looked worried. "I hope you did not support him."

"No, of course not. As moderator, I can't take sides. I simply noted the need to properly ascertain the motives of the outsiders, including the English."

"That was very wise of you, lord."

"Did you look into the matter I asked you about?"

"Yes, lord. It is evident that, some five years ago, Lord Genji did lead a contingent of samurai into Hino Domain. There are no witnesses to an actual attack. However, after Lord Genji left, an isolated village was discovered to have been burned to the ground, and all its inhabitants slaughtered. The appropriate conclusion can be drawn. And a curious coincidence, my lord, which you may find amusing. It was an eta village."

"That is curious indeed," Lord Saemon said. Genji was proposing laws favorable to the very same people he had slaughtered so mercilessly not very long ago. It made no sense. But, somehow, the two facts had to be connected.

"Find and interrogate survivors. There is an answer here hidden so well we cannot even see the question without more information."

"Lord Saemon, there were no survivors. Every hut and shed was put to the torch. One hundred and nine corpses were recovered for funeral services. Exactly that number of people lived in the village."

"There were funeral services."

"Yes, lord."

"For—" Saemon stopped and, smiling to himself, substituted Genji's word for the one he was going to say. "There were funeral services for burakumin."

"Yes, lord."

"That means someone went through the trouble of sifting through ashes and rubble to recover the burned corpses of outcasts. Who would do such a thing? Only those who care. Such people frequently know things others do not. Find them and question them."

"Yes, lord."

"Wait. One more thing. It was reported to me by the harbor police that

Lord Genji's ship, the SS *Cape Muroto*, steamed south for Akaoka Domain yesterday morning. His outsider friend, the American woman, was on board, accompanied by Lady Hanako, Lord Taro, and a contingent of samurai. A strange trunk of ancient and foreign design, containing no one knows what, went aboard with them. Find out why they are going to Akaoka and what is so precious in that trunk. Genji may be planning something dangerous in Edo, and thus seeks to remove his outsider friend to safety."

The chamberlain said, "Perhaps he is planning to lead an uprising of burakumin."

Lord Saemon frowned. "This is not a joking matter."

"No, my lord." The chamberlain bowed. "I will proceed immediately."

When the chamerlain had gone, Lord Saemon recalled his remark and laughed out loud. An uprising of burakumin. If anyone could conceive of such a ridiculous thing, it would be Genji. How on earth had a clan led by such fools survived for so long? Perhaps they really could see the future. That would explain it. Only with an advantage so huge could they compensate for their constant political misjudgments.

Lord Saemon laughed again.

Prophetic vision. It was almost as amusing a fancy as an outcast insurrection.

THE SS *CAPE MUROTO*, OFF THE SOUTHERN COAST OF SHIKOKU ISLAND

Emily, Hanako, and Taro stood together at the starboard railing as the ship rounded the promontory. The low shoreline hills slid past and opened up into a bay, and across the water, the seven winged stories of Cloud of Sparrows Castle soared above the wooded cliffs.

When Emily had first seen it, shortly after her arrival in 1861, she had been sorely disappointed. It seemed so fragile, and far too elegant. Then, a castle had meant a heavy stone fortress of the European kind, just as a nobleman had to be a knight like Wilfred of Ivanhoe. She had been blind and foolish then. After six years in Japan, she knew that the lethal and the elegant could go together very well, as it did in Cloud of Sparrows Castle, and a knight could as well be a samurai or Great Lord as a prince or a duke or any European sir. We are often blind when we encounter the unexpected. When it happened again, as it surely would, she was determined to see.

Hanako, too, was looking at the castle, her thoughts tinged with melancholy. On every previous return to Akaoka Domain, the sight of those roofs like flocks of birds aflight lifted her spirits toward heaven. It did not do so today. Seeing the castle, she could not avoid thinking about the scrolls Emily had discovered. She had not yet read much. Emily had encouraged her to do so aboard ship, but Hanako feared that exposure to the salt air would damage the ancient paper, and had refrained. She had read enough, however, to feel an uneasiness that grew inexorably into dread as they neared the dock.

The "visitor."

The first line of the first scroll mentioned a long-ago lord's *visitor*. The use of that word instead of the more usual *guest* reminded her of the last time she had seen Lord Kiyori. It had been only hours before his death six years ago. He, too, had entertained someone, someone she neither saw nor heard, though she clearly heard Lord Kiyori speaking as if in conversation. The word in the scroll frightened her because she couldn't shake off the persistent feeling that the long-ago lord's visitor and Lord Kiyori's unseen companion were one and the same.

If that was so, then the visitor could only be one whose name was better not thought of, much less spoken aloud, and she and Emily would have been better advised to avoid this place than to seek it out.

It was widely believed that Lord Kiyori had been poisoned with blowfish bile, which his son, the mad Lord Shigeru, had put into his soup. Hanako and the other maid who had served the meal were immediately seized by the lord's bodyguards. There is no doubt they would have been tortured to death, and quite rightly, for being part of such a heinous crime, unknowingly or not. But when Lord Genji arrived, he ordered the clan physician to examine the corpse. After a brief consultation, the new Great Lord declared that his grandfather's death was caused by a heart stoppage, a not unexpected natural outcome of old age. He then took Hanako into his household service, as Lord Kiyori had intended, saving her from the ostracism that would otherwise have resulted from lingering suspicions.

The general view was that Lord Kiyori had indeed been poisoned, but that Genji, seeking to keep scandal to a minimum, wished to avoid executing his uncle for the murder of his own father. Also, knowing the maids were blameless and feeling compassion for them, he made up the story about heart failure.

For a long time, this is what Hanako also believed. But having read those lines in Emily's scrolls, she no longer did. She was sure the visitor had played a part in Lord Kiyori's death and, being immortal as well as malevolent, was very likely still lurking about in the shadowy realm between the real and the unreal, patiently waiting for the next victim, someone whose thoughts and emotions exposed exactly the right vulnerabilities.

"Was the castle always seven stories high?" Emily asked.

"It had only two levels when it was captured by Lord Masamuné, the father of our first Great Lord, Hironobu."

"Captured? I thought this was the hereditary castle of the Okumichi clan."

"It became hereditary thereafter. Everything has a beginning." And an end, Hanako thought, but did not say. "Masamuné added four more floors during his lifetime, and Hironobu the last."

"So it was Hironobu who built the high tower."

Hanako shivered. The wind moving over the water was light, a summery breeze rather than a wintry one. Perhaps she had recently grown more susceptible to chills.

Taro paid no attention to the women's conversation. Other, more serious matters weighed on him.

Assassination.

Abduction.

Treachery.

Could he commit such acts and still call himself a samurai? And if he did not act, would his betrayal be worse?

Taro had come of age in the crisis of 1861. Lord Kiyori had died suddenly, leaving the domain in the hands of his untested grandson, Lord Genji. This provided an irresistible opportunity for the clan's enemies to attempt its destruction. Having no confidence in Lord Genji, his two most important generals betrayed him. The greatest warrior in the domain, Kiyori's son and Genji's uncle, Lord Shigeru, had also chosen that most unfavorable time to go completely mad. The situation was extremely unpromising. But Taro and his good friend, Hidé, had remained true to their vows and had fought at Lord Genji's side in the epic battles of Mié Pass and Mushindo Monastery. With their help, Lord Genji triumphed over his enemies. They had both been generously rewarded, and had continued to rise steadily in prestige and prominence. Hidé was now Lord Chamberlain in addition to being chief bodyguard. Taro, at the age of only twenty-five, was commander of the clan cavalry, the most celebrated cavalry in all Japan for five hundred years.

But did any of this still have meaning? Outsiders had entered Japan with their warships and guns and science, and the world that had belonged to the samurai for ages eternal was evaporating like mist in the morning sun. The Men of Virtue said there was only one solution: Expel the barbarians and close the country once again. More and more, it seemed to Taro that they were right.

From the beginning, doubt had plagued him. He was sworn as a samurai to follow Lord Genji. Yet, Genji, the most unsamurai-like of all the lords of all the domains of the empire, had never appeared to be committed to the warrior code that was the basis of his own authority. That something had been so since the long-ago days of his ancestors was not enough for Genji. He wanted a logical basis for his actions. Logic rather than tradition. How like the outsiders he was. A true samurai did not ask why. He did as his ancestors did, and unquestioningly followed the dictates of the way of the warrior. When Taro had pointed this out, Lord Genji had laughed.

"The way of the warrior," Lord Genji had said. "*Bushido*. Surely you do not think our ancestors actually believed in such drivel?"

Taro was so shocked his mouth fell open.

"Loyalty to one's lord," Genji said, "no matter what kind of fool or scoundrel he is. Sacrifice of self, of one's wife, one's parents, even one's children, for the honor of the lord. Could such evil ever be the foundation of a noble philosophy? If ever I ask you to sacrifice your children for me, Taro, you have my permission to slay me on the spot."

"I have no children, lord."

"Then acquire some soon. My grandfather said no one without children understands anything worth understanding."

"You have no children, either, lord."

"I am thinking seriously of remedying that deficiency. Now, where was I? Oh, yes, of course, revenge. Never forget a wrong, no matter how slight, and exact vengeance, even if it takes ten generations. These are not the teachings of the ancients, Taro. These are fabrications of the Tokugawa Shoguns. They created this mythology to insure that they would remain in power forever, by insuring that no one else would think to do what they did, which is make false pledges to their lord, betray their lord's heirs, act only for their own aggrandizement, and point everyone's attention into the past, so the future would be theirs alone."

"Lord Genji," Taro said, when he recovered his voice, "you know that isn't so. Our revered ancestors—"

"—were violent, ruthless men," Genji said, "living in violent, ruthless times. Times not unlike our own. Their way was not bushido, it was *budo*, the way of war. Budo is not a matter of tradition. It is a matter of maximum efficiency. Before we knew of Western science, budo was our science. Samurai on foot were not as effective as samurai on horseback, so we became mounted warriors. The long, straight *tachi* sword proved unwieldy in such an application, so we abandoned it and switched to shorter, curved katana swords. When castles became common battlegrounds, we found that even shorter swords were required for indoor combat—often treacherous, surprise attacks, by the way—so we took to wearing a second, even shorter wakizashi sword along with our katana. For very close-quarters work—if, for example, we needed to stab someone suddenly during a meal or a tea ceremony or an orgy—we also carried a *tanto* dagger."

"That is false," Taro said, so upset by Genji's words he failed to be polite. "We have a tanto because a samurai should always be ready to kill himself if honor so demands."

Genji smiled at Taro as if he were a not very gifted, but nevertheless favored, child. "That is what the Tokugawa Shoguns wanted us to believe, so when we thought of stabbing, we would think of stabbing ourselves instead of them."

The conversation had taken place just before Taro had embarked on this journey.

"If we were truly the men our ancestors were," Genji had said, "we would learn all we could from the outsiders as fast as we could, and we would abandon without hesitation or regret everything that obstructs our progress. Everything."

Taro, too horrified and angry to trust himself to speak, had only bowed his head. Lord Genji had probably taken this as a gesture of assent. It had not been one.

Wasn't Genji's treason far worse than that which Taro was contemplating? It was treason against the way of the samurai itself. Genji was determined to remake them in the grotesque, immoral, honorless image of the outsiders. Of what use would loyalty be when the only value was profit? What use was courage when one killed enemies, not face-to-face at two-sword-blades' distance, but unseen and unseeing, from miles away, with foul and noisy explosive machinery?

Taro glanced at the two women he had been sent to protect. He was commander of the most illustrious cavalry in the realm, but how long would there be cavalry in the world Lord Genji sought to create? Hanako was his best friend Hidé's wife, but Hidé was stubbornly, blindly loyal to Lord Genji. Emily was the outsider of prophecy, whose presence had insured the victory of the Okumichi clan during the crisis, but she was just that—an outsider.

One day soon—

Taro's hand did not go to his sword. His thoughts did.

The harsh rattle of chains preceded the splash of the anchor falling into the shallows.

"We are home," Hanako said.

CLOUD OF SPARROWS CASTLE

Taro sat in a room overlooking the rose garden in the central courtyard of the castle. The maids had brought various refreshments, which he completely ignored. Lost in his thoughts, he had forgotten the architect, Tsuda, sitting across from him, until he noticed the fearful look on the man's face. They had been sitting in silence for half an hour. During that time, Taro's thoughts had undoubtedly emphasized the natural ferocity of his expression.

More to assuage the man's fears than to inform him of anything, Taro said, "Lady Hanako and Lady Emily are in the tower. You will wait for them here."

He rose to go. He would ride to the cape alone and try to order his thoughts.

"Yes, Lord Taro."

Tsuda was trying hard, without any success, to get some inkling of why this meeting was taking place. The ladies and Taro, accompanied by a contingent of samurai, had arrived without warning this morning by ship from Edo. Naturally, Tsuda's first reaction was one of abject fear. What reason was there for such a high-ranking lord as Taro to appear so suddenly?

The presence of the samurai with him, twenty men of particularly fierce and humorless demeanor, had him envisioning a wide range of punishments, including execution. Perhaps Lord Genji was displeased at the slowness of the construction project, or the increasing cost, or even the design, though he himself had approved it enthusiastically. Great Lords were extremely changeable, and when they changed, the consequences always fell on someone else. Taro had not been very informative. Though it was risky to engage in conversation with any lord, Tsuda thought it best to probe a little and try to extract some guidance.

Tsuda said, "Is Lord Genji envisioning rebuilding the tower, my lord?"

Taro frowned down at the man. What a presumptuous statement.

"Why would he do that?"

The lord's fierce glower shattered Tsuda's already overwrought nerves completely. He began to babble.

"I thought, perhaps, only because Lady Hanako and Lady Emily are in the tower, my lord, and the present construction project being inspired by Lady Emily—"

Therefore—therefore what? Hot sweat had suddenly drenched Tsuda's underwear. At least, he hoped it was sweat. Urine had a more noticeable odor, and if it was urine, and should happen to seep onto the mat—Great Compassion Bodhisattva, protect me! Why did I speak? He was about to leave and like a fool I spoke. His thoughts colliding in his head this way, no more words were able to find their way out. He felt tears welling in his eyes. In another moment, he would be weeping uncontrollably, giving rise to suspicion, if his behavior thus far had not already done so, leading inexorably to questioning, intense questioning, involving, without doubt, torture of the most crippling, mutilating, painful kind!

Confess! Confess now and beg for mercy! It had been only one ryo! A little more, perhaps, but not more than two ryo! He would repay it! What had made him overcharge Lord Genji? He must have been out of his mind. Just because the lord was not present during the construction didn't mean that his many spies were not watching over things for him. Confess now!

"You think too much, Tsuda," Taro said. "Think when you are ordered to think. Otherwise, just do as you are told. Lady Hanako and Lady Emily will have questions for you. Answer them. That is all. Do you understand?"

Tsuda pressed his face against the mat. To bow more deeply, he would have had to penetrate the woven straw with his forehead. He felt such overwhelming relief, there was now definite danger that he would urinate reflexively, if he had not already done so.

"Thank you, Lord Taro," Tsuda said. "Thank you very much. I will do so without fail." He didn't raise his head until Taro was long gone.

As he waited for the two ladies, he reflected more calmly on his reactions. He came to the conclusion that he was not in the wrong, though of course in a technical sense he had committed fraud, which like every crime against a Great Lord was punishable by torture and death. Was the true wrong not in the grotesquely low price he had been forced to agree to, which almost forced him to steal in order to make a reasonable profit? Was it wrong that he felt such terrible fear, or was the wrong in his being made to feel that fear because of the intolerable power held by the Great Lords in particular but all samurai in general? How could Japan ever progress beyond the backward state in which it was mired unless such evils were done away with? The samurai had always justified their existence as the protectors of the realm. But the arrival of the outsiders in force a little more than ten years ago put the lie to that, didn't it? These great warriors couldn't even drive away the Dutch or the Portuguese, whom Tsuda understood to be inhabitants of extremely small countries in Europe. Before the truly mighty, like England, France, Russia, and America, they quivered and shook like shrubs in a storm. They had clearly outlived their usefulness. But how to get rid of them? That was the question. They had a monopoly on weapons. Or, more accurately, they had a monopoly on the right to kill with impunity.

Tsuda himself owned a weapon, a very modern weapon, a weapon far more lethal than a sword, a weapon that would permit him, if he so chose, to kill a samurai before that worthy was close enough to even stir the air around him with his ancient, outmoded sword—a .44-caliber American Colt revolver, its six chambers filled with six deadly bullets! Of course, he didn't have the revolver with him. It was at home, under the floor in his steel Dutch safe. And even if he had it with him, would he have the courage to take it out, point it at someone like Lord Taro, and fire? As he imagined the scene, his bowels answered him with an immediate dangerous looseness.

No, no, no! Urine could be mistaken for sweat, if in fact he had leaked urine earlier as he feared he had. But fecal matter? It could not be mistaken for anything other than what it was! To be crucified for shitting in his clothing in the castle of the lord! Not only would it be physically mortifying, it would be crushingly embarrassing as well!

To keep his insides inside, he resolutely turned his thoughts to money, the one thing that, thinking of it, made him stronger than he was. Merchants and bankers had all the money, something that was becoming increasingly important. Tsuda, a merchant and banker both, was particularly well placed in that regard. He was a powerful man, not a weak one. Money was stronger than the sword.

Was it, really? A sword, with its blade so sharp the merest touch could—

"Ah, Mr. Tsuda," Lady Emily said. "How nice to see you again."

"Lady Emily," Tsuda said, roused from his reverie. "Your Japanese is better every time I see you. You must be putting much effort into your studies."

He winced within. Nothing showed on his face, which remained both blandly content and eager to please, an expression he had worked years to master, and which had proved to be the least provocative face, and thus the safest to present while doing business with samurai. He winced because he realized as soon as he spoke that he should not have said what he had. He had implied that Emily *needed* to put much effort into speaking Japanese well. While this was undeniably true, truth was not necessarily a defense.

What a fool! He had insulted Emily—that is to say, *Lady* Emily, because, due to arcane factors that escaped Tsuda entirely, this particular outsider woman was always referred to with the honorific, and if he knew what was good for him, he would never even think about her without preceding her name with it—which would be the same as insulting her patron, Okumichi no kami Genji, Great Lord of Akaoka, a man who held absolute power of life and death over every being in this very realm! How could he be so stupid? In truth, Lady Emily did speak Japanese very well now—better, in fact, than some from the country's more distant and isolated areas. There, many had fluency only in dialects that were close to being foreign languages. Tsuda was furiously trying to think of the exact words that would allow him to flatter himself out of trouble when Lady Hanako spoke.

"Where is Lord Taro?" she said.

"He departed some time ago," Tsuda said. Hanako was not her usual cheerful self. Lines of concern marked her face, and when she spoke of Taro, her eyes sharpened.

Was a plot of some kind afoot? He felt himself growing nervous again. If there was a plot, no matter whose it was, he was potentially in grave, even mortal, danger. Should any part of it unfold while they were here at the castle, suspicion would alight on everyone nearby. When that happened, torture and executions inevitably followed. Innocence was far from a certain defense, in the same way that truth was not.

Oh, no! Just when things were becoming more promising! And what had he been if not utterly loyal—to Lord Genji, to Lord Taro, and to Lady Hanako's powerful husband, Lord Hidé. No matter which of them succeeded in plotting or counterplotting, or failed, as the case may be—if indeed any of them were in any way involved, which of course he had no way of knowing—he was surely blameless! Yet it was his ruined body that would be hoisted onto a stake! It was he who would die screaming, crucified! Every member of his family would also be executed, and all his possessions confiscated. How unfair! Was there no limit to the cruel, unfettered greed of these samurai?

"Thank you for coming to see us," Lady Emily said. "I'm sure you're very busy with the construction."

"I am never too busy to be of service to you, Lady Emily. And, of course, to you, Lady Hanako. That is to say, since the service, if indeed I should prove to be of service—"

"Thank you, Tsuda," Hanako said. She knew he would go on and on about nothing at great length if she did not interrupt him. All commoners were obsequious and nervous in the presence of nobles, but none so much as those who dealt with money, like Tsuda. This was because almost all samurai, and Great Lords to the greatest extent, were in deep debt to them, and Great Lords were occasionally given to erasing their debt by erasing the appropriate merchants and moneylenders on one pretext or another. Even the Shogun himself had done so more than once.

Tsuda's nervousness in particular was enhanced because he was manipulating the accounts in such a way that he was overcharging for all work under his supervision by approximately ten percent. The poor man had no idea that, through an intricate arrangement of proxies, proxies of proxies, proxies of proxies of proxies, and so on and so forth, he was not the principal owner of his bank as he thought, but rather more akin to its manager. The real owner was, of course, Lord Genji. Thanks to visionary ancestors, the Okumichi clan had gained an understanding of money long ago, when the other clans were still thinking in terms of rice lands as a measure of wealth.

Hanako knew this because she had been assigned by Genji to assist the Lord Chamberlain with the clan's financial management, and had been doing so for the past five years.

She said, "We will not take up more of your valuable time than necessary. A few questions only, about the trunk full of scrolls recently sent to Lady Emily in Edo."

"Ah, yes, Lady Hanako, Lady Emily." Tsuda bowed to each in turn, not entirely sure whom he should be addressing. "I trust it arrived as I found it, that is to say, unopened?"

On the one hand, Lady Hanako had spoken. On the other, Lady Emily was the one who apparently had the questions. Then there was the fact that Lady Hanako was an actual Japanese lady, the wife of the clan's senior general—a most grim and frightening man, one even more intimidating than Lord Taro—while Lady Emily, though called "lady," was nevertheless indisputably an outsider. Against this had to be considered another fact: Lady Emily was a close friend of the Great Lord of the realm—perhaps a very close friend of the closest possible kind, if the rumors were to be believed, to which, of course, he did not necessarily give the slightest credence or inappropriate thought—

Emily said, "We were wondering where in the castle the trunk was found."

"Ah, please forgive me if either my explanatory letter or my messenger created the impression that the trunk was discovered in the castle. In fact, it was found in a most curious place and in a rather strange way." The two ladies exchanged what appeared to be a meaningful glance. What meaning it contained was unclear to him. It was yet another thing to worry about later, when he had time to go over the events of this encounter at leisure. "Or perhaps I should say, in a most *fortunate* place and in a *propitious* way. It is really not for me to characterize—"

"Where was it found?" Hanako said.

· · · · ·

Tsuda had difficulty keeping up with the two ladies. He was not used to being on horseback. Although he could afford a horse—or ten, for that matter—he rarely rode one. He did not wish to appear presumptuous.

Traditionally, horses carried only samurai, never peasants, and the samurai of this domain in particular had been famous for centuries as mounted warriors. He could well understand the bitterness the sight of himself on a horse could cause to a samurai, especially one afoot, and if that one also happened to be in debt to him, that bitterness could easily turn to murderous rage. There was also another less frightening but tiresome mundane consideration. Whenever he happened to pass a samurai, he would have to dismount and bow, since he could not physically be above someone he was socially below. It was easier to do what was necessary if he were already on the ground.

Both ladies had changed into the pantlike garment called hakama, and rode their horses like samurai rather than sidesaddle in the fashion of courtly women. When they left the gates of the castle, they found Lord Taro and several other mounted samurai waiting to accompany them. How had Lord Taro known they were leaving the castle? Tsuda had no idea. The way samurai anticipated things was truly nerve-racking.

As they approached the construction site on the rise above Apple Valley, Tsuda began to sweat again. He wasn't worried about it this time. However wet his clothing got, by whatever cause, he could blame the horse beneath him. Horses were by nature sweaty, smelly animals. But would they find fault with the work he had done so far? Was not enough accomplished? Had he placed it on the wrong site? Was the directional orientation not to their liking? Had he misread the plans for the building? Had he cut down too many trees? Too few?

A samurai galloped next to him and said harshly, "You! Stop dawdling! You're wasting your betters' time!" He looked like he would happily decapitate Tsuda on the spot.

"Yes, sir, excuse me, sir, I'm not used to being on horseback, horses not being appropriate for lowly—"

The samurai reached over, grabbed the reins out of his hands, kicked Tsuda's horse into a gallop, and led it to the rise where the rest of the party waited. By the time they got there, Tsuda was certain his manly parts had suffered such a battering against the hard saddle that he would not be able to attempt felicitous contact with geisha ever again.

"Dismount," Taro said. "Show Lady Hanako and Lady Emily exactly how you happened to discover the trunk."

"Yes, Lord Taro," Tsuda said, and nearly fell from the saddle in his haste to obey. Why had he even put in a bid for the project? Let someone else do it. Let someone else take the risk. That's what he should have done. "We began three weeks ago," he said.

. . . . .

"Shall we begin digging now, Mr. Tsuda?" the laborer asked. He and a hundred men with shovels, picks, and other construction equipment had been waiting for nearly an hour for the architect to give them the signal to begin. What was the delay? Why was he standing there on the crest of the hill as if in a trance? They were here to build a building, not conduct religious rites.

Tsuda could hear the impatience in the man's voice. It was understandable. He was an ignorant peasant who did not understand the mystical quality of feng shui, the art of direction and location without which an architect was not an architect but a mere assembler of wood and stone. Also, since the laborers would be paid by the work actually done and not by mere time on the site, they were naturally eager to commence. His, however, was a higher calling. The place from which the first shovelful of dirt was removed would determine the destiny of the building, and thus of those who would use it, and those who would build it. If it was off by so much as one pace, bad luck rather than good fortune might find its way there.

Of the many buildings Tsuda had designed and constructed during the ten years of his career, not one had inflicted the least harm on its owners and occupants. Indeed, two of them—a certain geisha house in Kobe, and Lord Genji's rebuilt palace in Edo—could be said to have generated especially good luck for all concerned. The geisha house had risen to considerable regional prominence in recent years, and was reputed to rival the best in Edo and Kyoto. That was certainly an overenthusiastic exaggeration. However, the mere fact that the claim could be made at all was a great honor. And as for Lord Genji, though he had far more political enemies than allies, and was an Outside Lord as well, he had since the rebuilding become both a trusted confidant of the Imperial Court in Kyoto and a respected member of the Shogun's Council of Reconciliation.

Far be it from Tsuda to claim to have had anything to do with either good result. Yet, surely Lord Genji at least recognized that some credit was due, since he had awarded Tsuda the contract to build a "chapel" here, a chapel being a kind of Christian temple. He had worked with the lord's outsider friend, Lady Emily, in the design. It seemed to him to be an unnecessarily rigid plan, with fixed rows of hardwood seats, a second raised level for a group of religious singers called a "choir" in the front, and a raised podium to the side of that, where a priest would apparently stand and address the gathered worshippers. There was a bell, as in a Buddhist temple, but here it was out of reach high in a bell tower, and had to be rung, not by being struck reverently by a priest with a consecrated mallet, but by being jerked about by ropes and pulleys from below. The actual ringing was caused by a steel mallet installed within the bell itself, which swung and struck the sides of the bell haphazardly.

"It will be time for lunch before we even start," one of the men grumbled.

Tsuda held up his hand for silence. He would not be rushed. Perhaps he was not a samurai, but he took his work every bit as seriously as they took theirs. For one week, he had come to this place to meditate during both sunrise and sunset. At home, he had consulted the I Ching, using both yarrow stick and coin methods. This was the final step. He would drop all preconceptions, fears, and desires, open himself up to the inherent nature of the place, and dig the first shovelful of dirt. At that moment, there was a slight shift in the wind. The scent of ocean was displaced by that of apple blossoms. Tsuda inhaled. When he exhaled, he opened his eyes and drove the shovel into the ground.

And immediately struck something hard, just below the surface.

· · · · ·

"The shovel actually shattered the wood of the outer box," Tsuda said. "But that box protected the inner one, the one with the most elegant painting upon it. I trust it arrived undamaged, as I found it?" He had heard that Lady Emily was prone to unpredictable and frequent fainting fits, so her sudden pallor did not surprise him. That Lady Hanako also lost all color in her face did.

She said, "Why did you think to send the trunk directly to Lady Emily?"

"I would not presume to make such a decision," Tsuda said. "Because the size and weight of the trunk suggested that it contained writings rather than goods, and knowing that an English-language translation of the clan history had been undertaken at Lord Genji's command—"

"Silence!" Taro said. "Answer the question. Why did you send the trunk to Lady Emily?"

"I did not, Lord Taro." His trembling involuntarily increased until his clothing began to flap as if being whipped by a rising wind. "I instructed my courier most clearly to deliver the trunk directly to Lord Genji. If he did otherwise, then I must—"

Taro was infuriated. "You sent the trunk to Lord Genji? Why did you not deliver it to the captain of the guard at the castle? It would be his duty to take the next step, not yours."

Tsuda pressed his forehead into the dirt of the contruction site so hard, his back muscles began to cramp. "Lord Genji specifically instructed me to communicate directly with him regarding all matters pertaining to the construction of the chapel."

"Do you take me for a fool?" Taro's hand went to his sword. "What lord would permit a peasant such access?"

"Excuse me, Lord Taro," Lady Emily said. "Mr. Tsuda is correct. I was present during the conversation."

Lady Emily's words embodied the most exquisitely beautiful spoken Japanese Tsuda had ever heard, American accent and all! She had just saved his life. He would forever be grateful to her.

"He could hardly disobey a direct order of the Great Lord," Lady Emily said.

Taro grunted. He took his hand off his sword and said, "Who was the courier? Send for him."

In a few minutes, the courier groveled in the dirt next to Tsuda, sweating profusely from the frantic run he had made in answer to the summons.

Taro said, "Why did you deliver the trunk to Lady Emily's quarters?"

"I did not, Lord Taro," the courier said. "I took it to Lord Genji as instructed by Mr. Tsuda. Lord Genji opened the trunk, saw what was within, and told me to take it to Lady Emily's study."

"And what was within?" Taro said.

"I don't know, Lord Taro," the courier said. "I was bowing the entire time I was in Lord Genji's presence. I heard the trunk open. Lord Genji said there were scrolls inside, and I heard the trunk close. Lord Genji then ordered me to take the trunk to Lady Emily's study. I obeyed. That is all."

"You may go," Taro said. To Lady Emily he said, "Do you have any further questions for Tsuda?"

"No," Emily said, "not for Mr. Tsuda."

Tsuda breathed a sigh of relief, though of course not audibly, and left counting himself a fortunate man indeed.

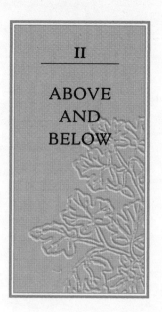

II

ABOVE
AND
BELOW

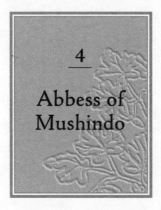

4

Abbess of Mushindo

Self-sacrificing loyalty is held to be the highest ideal of the samurai.
The reason for this is not difficult to find. The generous would call
it wishful thinking. Others would give it a harsher name.

   The true history of the clans of the realm is written in the blood
of treason. Yet, read what has been memorialized, and you will
think the great heroes of legend have come back to life again and
again.

   Is it any wonder that those who grow up listening to lies
themselves become liars?

AKI-NO-HASHI

(1311)

1882, MUSHINDO ABBEY IN THE MOUNTAINS WEST OF EDO

The Reverend Abbess of Mushindo, Jintoku, sat on her knees on the dais of the main meditation hall. She bowed low and held her bow as today's guests were led into the hall by two young women dressed in the manner of Buddhist nuns of a bygone time, their heads covered with hoods of rough brown cloth that matched their robes. The Reverend Abbess was identically attired, eschewing the more costly, more comfortable silk garb to which she was entitled by her rank. She and her acolytes wore hoods because they did not shave their heads in the usual manner of Buddhist nuns. The Reverend Abbess had discovered that nuns with long, lustrous, attractive tresses generated a noticeably lower level of donations than those who appeared more deprived. Since she had no desire to shave her own head, she would not ask her followers to do so. Her entire methodology was to lead by example. It was the only way that clearly established moral authenticity, and moral authenticity was the essential basis for her authority at Mushindo Abbey.

There were forty guests today, forty-one the day before, and thirty-seven the day before that. The women's clothing was the now standard mix of Western and Japanese popular in the cities, kimono with English hats and French shoes, with an occasional jacket of American cut as outerwear. Men tended to go in one direction, either entirely Western, from hat to boots, or stubbornly Japanese, in kimono and wooden sandals. No one wore topknots anymore, and no one wore swords. Both were forbidden. And even if they were not, who would carry them? There were no more samurai, and only samurai had been allowed swords in the past.

Attendance had steadily risen in the three years since the Abbess had thought of instituting guided tours of the temple. For this, she had the new Imperial government to thank. Traffic to the temple had increased because interest in the ancient ways of Japan had increased, coincident with the government's strenuous modernization campaign. This was not as strange as it might at first appear. While modernization meant the adoption of Western ways in industry, science, war, political form, and dress, it was accompanied by an equally energetic campaign to maintain the old cultural traditions. "Western Science, Eastern Virtue." That was the official slogan. But did anyone really know exactly what embodied Eastern Virtue?

The Reverend Abbess had her doubts. Real traditions couldn't be the ones imposed by the now discredited and overthrown regime of the Tokugawa Shoguns. For two and a half centuries, according to the new government, the Shoguns had frozen society in place, invented all manner of duplicitous fictions to maintain their control, and robbed, imprisoned, tortured, enslaved, exiled, murdered, and otherwise oppressed and terrorized all who opposed them, tactics the new government claimed to have completely eliminated. Of course, neither were all the forms and behaviors of that era to be thoughtlessly discarded, since some were true and revered traditions that had been carried over from the past and merely absorbed and used by the Shoguns. In addition to negotiating treaties, building an army and navy, confiscating the lands and wealth of the Tokugawa clan, and furiously writing new laws to satisfy the Western nations' demand for reform, the new government was also determining what was traditional and what was not. In doing so, two phrases appeared with great regularity in official pronouncements.

For ages eternal—

From time immemorial—

The Reverend Abbess knew enough about lies to recognize words designed to conceal rather than illuminate. She suspected invention rather than preservation. How much easier it was to get compliance by citing ancient precedent rather than having to convince people to risk innovation. Nevertheless, she was grateful that in designating National Historic Sites, the government had included Mushindo Abbey. It had certainly helped build interest.

"Honored guests," the Abbess said, "our deepest thanks to you for troubling to visit our isolated and simple temple."

While Mushindo was simple, it was in fact no longer isolated. The new road between the Pacific Coast and the Sea of Japan passed through the valley below. It was actually fairly easy to reach this temple, though the required travel from urban centers did give the trip a feeling of pilgrimage absent when visiting one of the more famous temples in the cities. Given the mission of Mushindo, this was more of an advantage than a disadvantage. The Abbess therefore felt it did no harm to suggest isolation.

"The world outside changes rapidly and relentlessly. Here, we live as the world-leavers of Mushindo have lived for six hundred years, following the Way of the Buddha."

Strictly speaking, Mushindo had not been continuously occupied for that entire time, but she considered that a technicality. Once a temple, always a temple.

"At the conclusion of your tour, you are most welcome to join the nuns for our midday meal if you so desire. It is a very simple meal of gruel, soy soup, and pickled vegetables."

Indeed, it was a meal very like the meal most of those in attendance had eaten on a regular basis not so very long ago, when they were mostly peasants without rights, property, or family names. With swift change came short memories.

"You will be divided into two groups. One will first tour the interior of

the temple, then the grounds. The other will follow the opposite order."
She bowed again. "Please enjoy your visit. If you have any questions, please
ask freely."

The Abbess waited while the guests left the meditation hall to begin
their tour, then she rose and went to the separate area outside the eastern
walls of the abbey. It was the only place at Mushindo where spiritual practice took place continuously, and it was the only place that was not part of
the tour. The Abbess bowed respectfully at the gate before entering the
caretaker's compound.

As always at this time of day, he tended his garden. The Abbess
thought of him privately as the Holy One—at first as a joke, later, to her
own surprise, quite seriously. The Holy One was very predictable. He followed, without deviation and without fail, the schedule set by the outsider
monk Jimbo more than twenty years ago.

Six hours of meditation before sunrise were followed by a bowl of
gruel and a single pickled vegetable, his sole nutrition for the day. How a
man so unusually big could survive on a meal so unusually small was a
mystery. Nevertheless, he did. The rest of the morning he passed in the
garden, where he was now, weeding, gently removing insects without
harming them, sweeping up dead leaves and bowing to them as he added
them to the compost heap, and picking vegetables for meals and storage.
After two hours of midday meditation in his hut, the Holy One spent the
afternoon cleaning the grounds in the rest of the abbey and making whatever repairs were needed to the buildings, walls, and walkways. Then, before his final evening ablutions, he went to the outer gate of the abbey and
gave out candies and sweet cakes to the children of nearby Yamanaka Village, with whom he was a great favorite. They were, in all likelihood, astonished that someone so huge could be so patient and gentle.

He was patient and gentle with children because Jimbo had been patient and gentle with them, and he followed the example of Jimbo in all
things. But Jimbo had not made candies or sweet cakes. The Holy One had
learned the skill somehow during his weeks of wandering twenty years
ago. That was before the Abbess became the Abbess, before he became the
Holy One, before Mushindo became an abbey, and before the Great Lords
of Western Japan overthrew the Tokugawa Shogun.

"Your garden is beautiful," the Abbess said. She always conversed with
him when she could, more out of habit than from any expectation that he

would respond in a way other than he always did. "It is such a wonder that the vegetables and flowers can thrive when you are so careful not to harm the pests that feed on them."

He looked up at her and smiled, or rather, smiled more broadly, because he almost always had a smile on his face. Then he spoke a word that was one of only two in his entire vocabulary.

"Kimi," he said.

1861, MUSHINDO MONASTERY

The village children watched from the surrounding woods. Their parents had warned them to stay away from the hundreds of the Shogun's musketeers who had occupied Mushindo Monastery. This was prudent advice, since innocent people nearby tended to die when samurai fought each other, and a fight was obviously brewing. Kimi, of course, had no intention of missing the spectacular show that was sure to come. Although she was a girl and, at eight years old, far from the oldest of the group, her intelligence and energy made her the ringleader. Also, she was the only one Goro obeyed with any regularity. Goro, the son of the village idiot woman, was a giant. He never meant anyone any harm. But he was so big and so strong, he could inadvertently hurt people, and sometimes did. All the children noticed this happened only when Kimi was not around. Surely it was mere coincidence. But children, being as they are the most superstitious of all humans, believed she had a special pacifying effect on Goro. It was a reputation that would stick with her for the rest of her life.

Goro was much bigger than any other man in the village, and even bigger than the outsider who came to live in the monastery and who became a monk, a disciple of Old Abbot Zengen. Until the outsider came, Old Zengen was the only person who lived there. The outsider had a name no one could pronounce until he became Old Zengen's disciple. Then he began to call himself Jimbo. That was easy to say. Even Goro, who had never spoken an intelligible word before, could say it, and did, all the time.

"Jimbo, Jimbo, Jimbo, Jimbo, Jimbo, Jimbo—"

"Oh, shut up, Goro," the other children would say. "He knows who he is, and he surely knows you are here."

"Jimbo, Jimbo, Jimbo—"

He would go on and on and on. Only Jimbo would not be bothered. Nothing bothered Jimbo. He was an outsider, but he was a true follower of Buddha's Way.

"That's enough, Goro," Kimi would say. "Give the others a chance to talk, too."

"Jimbo," Goro would say, one last time, and fall silent. For a while at least.

Jimbo had been away in the mountains when the musketeers came, and he still had not returned when Lord Genji arrived.

It turned out that the Shogun's force was waiting for Lord Genji. His small band of samurai was ambushed, surrounded, and trapped. Those seeking to reach the sanctuary of the monastery were blown up when gunpowder hidden there ignited. So many bullets were fired in their direction that their dead horses, which they used for cover, disintegrated into a single, massive ruin of butchered flesh. In the end, when the lord's allies arrived and destroyed the enemy, the handful of survivors were drenched in the blood of animals and men from head to foot.

Jimbo did not return until several days after the battle, and when he did, none of the children recognized him. They saw an outsider dressed like the one who had been with Lord Genji, a man who had worn guns in his belt instead of swords and, raging like a demon from the worst hell realm, had killed many men with his guns, with swords he took from men he had turned into corpses, and with his bare, bloody hands.

The children ran away from him in fear. Except for Goro.

"Jimbo, Jimbo, Jimbo," he said, and ran toward the outsider.

Kimi saw that Goro was right. This outsider was indeed Jimbo. He had discarded the Zen monk's robes he donned when he became Old Zengen's disciple and now wore the clothes he had worn when he first came to the village. He had a gun at his belt and held a long weapon with two big barrels in his hand.

"Why are you dressed like that?" Kimi asked.

"I have to do something I can't do in the other clothes," Jimbo said, looking at the ruins of the monastery. A few days later, they all learned what it was he had to do.

The other outsider came back, the demon who had been with Lord Genji. Kimi led the village children into the ruins of the meditation hall, where they hid. They watched the demon slowly slip inside the monastery walls, a gun in each hand. Jimbo stepped out of the shadows behind him, put a gun to the back of his head, and said something in English, which none of the children understood. Whatever Jimbo said, it was not the right incantation, because instead of disappearing or going away, the demon dove to one side and, twisting as he fell, fired both his guns at Jimbo. Jimbo fired, too, but only once, and too wide and too late. Just as he fired, the demon's bullets hit him and knocked him to the ground. Then the demon stood over Jimbo and emptied both his guns into Jimbo's face.

When the demon was gone, the children ran toward Jimbo. They all stopped when they saw what was left of him. Only Goro and Kimi went to his side. Goro collapsed beside Jimbo's body and wailed and moaned. Kimi put her arms around Goro and tried to comfort them both.

"Don't cry, Goro. This isn't Jimbo anymore. He's gone ahead to Sukhavati, the Pure Land. When we get there, he'll greet us, and we won't be afraid. Everything will be wonderful."

Kimi wasn't sure Goro would ever recover from the loss. But gradually, he did. He began to spend all his time in the ruins, clearing away debris, disposing of questionable fragments that might have been the charred remains of human beings, filling in the pit left by the huge explosion that had destroyed the meditation hall, raking the grounds, and collecting many of the hundreds of bullets that had been fired in the battle that had preceded Stark and Jimbo's duel. With nothing better to do, the children imitated Goro, and before they realized what they were doing, they were helping him to rebuild Mushindo.

Soon he was again saying the one word he knew.

"Jimbo."

But now he said it quietly, and only once at a time.

As the monastery reappeared from the ruins, so in a sense did Jimbo. Goro took to wearing his robes, and began following the monkly schedule Jimbo had followed. He rose in the darkest hour of morning, went to the abbot's meditation hut, and remained there until sunrise. One day, when Kimi peeked in, she saw that he was sitting very still, his legs in the lotus posture of a real monk, his eyelids lowered as Jimbo's had been when Jimbo had been deep in the *samadhi* of the Buddha. Of course, an idiot like Jimbo could not attain the perfect, blissful peace of the Enlightened One.

He was not a real follower of the Way like Jimbo. But he was doing a very good job at pretending. And it kept him quiet and happy and harmless, so Kimi did nothing to discourage him.

· · · · ·

One day, several harvests later, when Kimi was working in the village paddy with the rest of her family, a rich merchant arrived, accompanied by a band of samurai. These latter were not in the service of any lord, as were all proper samurai, but were of the masterless type known as "wave men," because like waves on the surface of the ocean, they had no roots, belonged to no one, and were without purpose, but existed nevertheless and were capable of causing great turbulence and mayhem. During recent years, as the realm was troubled by internal dissension and outsider pressure, the decay of order had produced many such men.

How much time had passed between the battle, the duel, Jimbo's death, and the arrival of this merchant, Kimi couldn't say. Every season in a farming village was much like any other. She knew more than a few seasons had passed, because much of Mushindo Monastery had been rebuilt, and her own body had begun to change, developing the embarrassing beginnings of the characteristics that would eventually lead to pregnancy, childbirth, a demanding husband, squalling children, and all the rest. She could see her future opening up before her, as vivid as a saint's mystical vision. Soon, she would be her own exhausted, prematurely aged mother, and someone else—one of her children to come—would be her brash and bratty self. This was the true meaning of reincarnation for the lowly. Perhaps Great Lords like Genji and beautiful geisha like Lady Heiko were reborn in new, exciting manifestations in exotic, distant lands. Peasants just came back as their parents and themselves, repeated what had already been done too many times before, and didn't have to pass into another life to do it.

"A new era is upon us," the merchant proclaimed from the saddle of his horse, "a new era of great and unprecedented opportunity!"

"Save your lies!" one of the farmers yelled. "We have no money. You can't trick us out of what we don't have!"

The villagers laughed. The ones closest to the farmer who had yelled out praised him enthusiastically and loudly shouted out suggestions of their own.

"Move on to Kobayashi Village! They're much richer there!"

"Yes. At least they have something to steal. We have nothing!"

The merchant smiled as the villagers laughed some more. He withdrew a large cloth bag from inside his jacket and shook it. It made a sound like heavy coins jingling together. Many heavy coins. The laughter quickly died away.

The merchant said, "Would a trickster give you his money, instead of taking yours? Would a liar take your word, instead of asking you to take his?"

"Lead will make a purse as heavy as gold," a farmer said, "and words are just words. We are not such fools not to know a thief when we see one."

One of the wave men with the merchant, apparently the leader of the group, moved his horse forward and spoke in the usual arrogant manner of samurai, masterless or not.

"Lower yourself to your proper level, peasant," he said, his hand on the hilt of his sword, "and speak respectfully to those above you."

"This is Yamanaka Village," the farmer said, not intimidated in the least. "We are subjects of Lord Hiromitsu, not homeless rabble."

The wave man drew his sword. "Lord Hiromitsu. I quiver in fear."

"Lord Hiromitsu enjoys the friendship of Genji, Great Lord of Akaoka," the farmer continued, "who crushed the Shogun's army here not so long ago. Perhaps you have heard of Mushindo Monastery?"

"Mushindo Monastery," the wave man said, lowering his sword and turning to the merchant. "I thought it was farther west."

"Turn your head," the farmer said, "and look up at that hill. There it is."

"Put away your sword," the merchant said, "and let us not speak of the past. I am here as an emissary of the future. Of the prosperous future. Will you hear me or not? If not, I will move on."

He opened the bag, reached in, removed a fistful of coins, and opened his hand. The bag did not hold lead. His palm glittered with *shu*, the rectangular gold coins with the characteristic markings of the official Tokugawa mint. Sixteen shu equaled one ryo, and one ryo was more than even the richest farmer in the village would earn from the year's harvest. If the merchant's bag was full of gold shu, he held a fortune in his hands. It was a wonder the ronin with him had not already murdered him and stolen his wealth. The presence of so much money in front of them awed the farmers into silence.

"The Shogun has recently abolished the prohibition against travel abroad," the merchant declared. "Seeing that the world will benefit from our presence, he has wisely decreed that Japanese may once again reside in foreign lands. To accommodate travelers, many new inns are being established, in Taiwan, the Philippines, Siam, Cochin China, Java, and elsewhere. Naturally, these inns must be staffed by Japanese. We cannot entrust our travelers to the care of uncivilized natives. To this end, I have been authorized to offer employment as maids, cooks, and housekeepers to the young women of your village, for a term of three years, with one shu per year paid to their families. In advance! That is three shu now, today, this very minute, for every family who will give their daughters an opportunity of a lifetime! Three gold shu!"

As soon as she heard the words *three gold shu,* Kimi knew she was as good as already in Java or the Philippines or Siam, wherever those places were. She didn't believe a word this obvious scoundrel was saying about the Shogun's proclamation or new opportunities or anything else, and doubted that anyone else in the village really did either. But there was no way impoverished peasants with too many mouths to feed could resist such an offer.

"Now, tell me the truth," the merchant said, still holding out his palm filled with gold for all to see. "Did you ever think you would live to see the day when a mere dowryless daughter would be worth so much? Truly, are we not living in wondrous times?"

Kimi's three other sisters were all married, with children too young to abandon. Kimi was the only one who could go. And go she did, that very day, along with six other girls from the village. She didn't even have time to climb the hill to Mushindo and say good-bye to Goro.

Two weeks later, she was in a warehouse on a pier in the port of Yokohama, waiting, along with a hundred other girls and young women, for a ship that would take them to someplace called Luzon. The fiction about being maids and housekeepers and cooks had been abandoned long before. Many of the older girls had already been raped by their guards, some repeatedly. Kimi and the others had escaped that fate only because the merchant repeatedly reminded the wave men that the youngest girls would bring double the price if they were still virgins when they reached their destination. In the delicate balance between lust and greed, Kimi was temporarily safe. It was, however, a safety devoid of hope. It had finally dawned on her. She had been sold. By her own parents.

For several days, the thought of escape had kept her energy and her spirits up. But that faded away soon enough. To where would she escape? If she went back to the village, the wave men would come for her, and what then would her parents do? They would give her back, because if they did not, they would have to give back the gold, and that was something Kimi could not imagine. She had seen the look in their faces as they held the coins in their hands. And if she didn't go back to the village, what would she do? How could she survive in a place like Yokohama, teeming with strangers, people as much adrift as the wave men who imprisoned her?

Hopelessness made her dull, and being dull, she lost track of time.

So this was how the rest of her life would be. Vague, hazy, numb. She would be used until she could be used no more, then she would die. What a curse to have been born a woman. If she had been a dog, even a female dog, she would at least have had the protection of the Shogun's old laws regulating their treatment. There were no laws regulating the treatment of women.

The frightened screams of the girls nearest the entry to their pen woke her up. She moved as far back into the crowd as she could. Because of her value as a virgin, she probably had nothing yet to fear, but it was better not to trust too much in greed. Those prone to vice tended to be unreliable, even in the exercise of vice. A momentary weakness, that's all it would take, and these wave men were full of weaknesses. Kimi hid.

"That's right, scream, scream," one of the guards said as the others laughed. "Frightening, isn't he? The next troublemaker who doesn't do as she's told—right away, and nicely, too—we'll give to him. How would you like that? You! Yes, you! Who will it be? Him or me?"

Kimi couldn't see what was happening, but she didn't have to see to know. She heard laughter, and frightened murmurs, the opening of the gate, the shuffling of feet. The press of the other girls' bodies against hers told her how frightened they were. They were straining to stay as far away from the gate as possible.

"We'll leave him here to watch over you," the guard said. "If you know what's good for you, you'll behave yourselves while we're gone, or else!"

The guards left with the unfortunate women they had selected for their evening entertainment, but the press of bodies against Kimi did not diminish. The new man they had left behind must truly be beastly if he compared so badly with the beasts she had already seen. She could tell he was moving along the fence, peering in at them, because the crowd of cowed women shifted first one way, then another, each time with an increased hint of panic. Some of the women had already begun to sob, in anticipation of the horror that would soon, inevitably, be visited upon them. Another shift and she caught a glimpse of him, his huge bald head towering above them. He moved this way and that along the fence, silently, his attention totally fixed on the women. He was some kind of mute, hairless monster, perhaps an outsider, brought in by the heartless wave men to terrorize them and make them obedient slaves.

The gate rattled, gently at first, then violently. The women, gasping, pressed even harder against the far wall. Something metallic snapped. Kimi could see the top of the gate swinging away. The monster was inside. The crowd of women receded as he advanced, and Kimi tried to recede with them. But she was able to do this for only so long, because they were receding away from her as well as the monster.

He was coming for her!

During the past few days, Kimi had thought about suicide, and always decided against it. Life was preferable to death. Alive, she had a chance. Dead, there was nothing at all. Also, there was the practical problem. How? Starvation wouldn't work. The guards would see what was happening and force her to eat. This had already happened to one girl. Until she saw what the guards did, she didn't know that eating could be turned into torture.

There was nothing to hang oneself from except the fence, and that was too slow a way to strangle. One of the girls had also tried this method, and only managed to damage the muscles of her neck before she gave up. Now she had a permanent tilt to her head, which lessened her value, and which would undoubtedly consign her to the worst kind of maltreatment in Luzon.

She couldn't jump from a height or slit her throat. The most she could manage would be to bash her head against the ground so hard, she would fracture her skull. She didn't think she had either the will or the strength to do that.

That left only one possibility. It was gruesome, but it was also certain death, if she had the courage to do it. She had come close a number of times and always stopped herself. Life was preferable to death. Until now.

The monster loomed ever closer. In the darkness of the pen, she couldn't make out his features, she could only see the outline of his massive body. He would tear her, he would break her, he would crush her, in the ferocity of his inhuman lust, before he left her to die in agony, wretchedly alone, here on the floor of a warehouse in Yokohama.

She turned away and knelt, her tongue stuck out as far as it would go between her teeth. She would slam her chin down on the ground, sever that mostly troublesome organ, and bleed to death. Such a life, so brief, with the only flicker of brightness brought by the outsider monk Jimbo, a time that seemed so long ago. She closed her eyes and raised her head for her final descent. Her exposed tongue was already so dry it felt parched.

"Kimi," the monster said.

1882, MUSHINDO ABBEY

"Goro," said the Reverend Abbess Jintoku.

"Kimi," the Holy One said.

"Goro."

"Kimi."

"Goro."

"Kimi."

The repetition of names could go on for a very long time. The Abbess had come to think of it as a form of chanting and on occasion, quite unintentionally and without her notice, would enter a deep state of meditation. Sometimes he would still be there when she returned to normal consciousness. At other times, he would have gone elsewhere, maintaining Jimbo's schedule without relaxation. Once, she had awakened in a pouring rain with an acolyte sheltering her with an umbrella. She had, of course, been sent there by the Holy One.

Until the day Goro found her in Yokohama, he had never spoken her name. Now, twenty years later, his vocabulary was still confined to two words. *Jimbo. Kimi.* How had he found her? She didn't know. How had he come to be employed by the wave men as a guard? She didn't know.

"Kimi," he said, and took her hand and led her out of the pen, off the pier, through Yokohama, and back to Mushindo. He was a person who regularly got lost walking from the village to the monastery, which was in plain sight. How had he traveled so far, and how did he then so easily find his way back? She didn't know.

Most of the imprisoned women were too afraid to follow, but a few did. Several of them were still at Mushindo today. There was no pursuit. Why? She didn't know. She never saw the merchant or the wave men again.

The Abbess blinked.

Goro was gone.

Ah, how long had she stood here by herself, lost in her thoughts of the past? She looked up into the sky. It was well past midday. The tour was long over, the overtly monastic meal served and eaten, the guests gone. She left the caretaker's compound and returned to the abbey, where she would tally the day's receipts. In addition to the income from donations for the tour, there were the offerings left in the meditation hall for the Buddhas, in the kitchen for the meal, and in the rectory for the holy relics of charred wood, bullets, and scroll fragments.

The charred wood came from the ruins of the meditation hall that remained after it was blown up in the famous battle. This was most popular with supplicants who believed the fragments had the power to cause a similarly explosive awakening into enlightenment. Those seeking protection from physical danger as well as the evil intentions of enemies favored the bullets as a talisman. After all, thousands had been fired at Lord Genji, and none had hit him. Surely these bullets had absorbed some of his power to ward off attack.

But the income from everything else paled in comparison to the donations the abbey received from those who must have a piece of the scrolls. Some who sought the shreds of paper were certain they were the remnants of the *Cloud of Sparrows* scrolls, the revelations by prescient Okumichi lords of things to come. Possess a piece of it, and your future would tend to attract all good and repel all evil. Others had no doubt of even greater power contained therein, the power to grant one's most deeply held desires, because the paper was the earthly remains of the *Autumn Bridge* scrolls, the collection of spells and incantations compiled by the princess witch of ancient times, Lady Shizuka.

The Abbess did not make any such claims, nor did she discourage belief in them. The bullets were in fact the bullets that had been fired in the battle and collected by Goro during the cleanup. The wood came from the ruins of the old meditation hall, as people believed. The paper fragments were pieces torn by the Abbess from ancient blank scrolls, originally twelve in number, donated to the abbey by Lady Emily some fifteen years ago. What those scrolls were supposed to be, the Abbess didn't know, and she didn't particularly care. The important thing was that Mushindo Abbey produced sufficient income to support its residents and their families. Let people believe what they would, if it gave them some measure of comfort and peace. The world had little enough of both.

She was about to remove her hood, the day being rather warm, when she saw that not all the guests had departed. One still remained, sitting quietly by himself in the central garden, a young man, unusually handsome, with very bright eyes and long, almost girlish eyelashes. His mustache fortunately saved him from an appearance of excessive prettiness. He was well dressed in the latest Western fashion, a black felt plantation hat on his head, a gray silk vest beneath his black, double-breasted woolen jacket, and dark gray woolen trousers. Only his footwear—boots of the kind worn by horsemen rather than city dwellers—seemed out of place. She bowed her head and put her hands together in the Buddhist gesture of *gassho* and made as if to continue past, but the man spoke to her before she could go on.

"Our guide gave an account of the famous battle," he said.

His pronunciation was a little odd, as if he were somewhat out of practice. Perhaps he had recently spent time abroad speaking a foreign language, and his tongue had not yet readjusted to Japanese.

"The purpose is cautionary," the Abbess said. "That such violence occurred in a holy place serves to remind us that serenity and chaos are not as far apart as we would like to think. I hope it did not disturb you too much."

"It didn't," he said, though he did in fact seem disturbed. "It's just that I've heard a different version of the story."

The way his lips formed a slight, almost mocking smile reminded her of someone she could not immediately place.

"The guide said Lord Taro led the rescue with the famous cavalrymen of Akaoka Domain," he said. "But Taro was not a lord then, and he was trapped along with Lord Genji and the others. The rescue was led by Lord Mukai, who brought his own retainers with him from the north."

"Is that so?" the Abbess said. She was surprised by the young man's knowledge. The battle had actually happened the way he said, and not the way it was told to visitors. The official story gave Taro the role played by Mukai partly to rehabilitate the former's reputation, and partly to obscure the latter. Taro had eventually come to a bad end, while unfortunate rumors about Mukai's social habits made any association potentially embarrassing to Genji. Twenty years of repetition had given the lie the weight of historical fact. There was even an altar dedicated to Lord Taro in one of the smaller temples of the abbey. Over the years, he had steadily gained popularity as a bodhisattva of rescue. Since no relics were associated with him, the Abbess did not encourage his cult. She said, "The real point of the story is not in the details of who did what. We are better served by focusing on the uncertainty of life, and the gratitude and attention each moment deserves."

"I suppose so."

He seemed very disappointed, as if it had some personal meaning for him.

"Do you have a special interest in the battle?" she asked.

"Only in the truth of it," he said. He was still smiling, and the smile still had a slight mocking quality, but now it seemed directed at himself. "I am hoping something of what I have been told is true. Anything."

"Where did you hear your version?" the Abbess asked.

"From my parents. They were there. Or so they told me."

The Abbess knew every village child who had been with her that day, watching from their hiding place in the woods. She knew everyone who had lived to become an adult, every child born to them, and every grandchild, and this young man was certainly not among them. Only eleven people on Lord Genji's side had survived the battle, four women and seven men. Three pairs of these had subsequently united in marriage, no doubt believing that fate had brought them together and caused them to survive for just that purpose. (How we loved to imbue our insignificant existences with unwarranted importance. The Abbess silently thanked Buddha for protecting her from that delusion.) The young man's parents had told him the truth about the battle but had lied to him about being there. It wasn't much of a lie, as lies go. Still, it obviously had an effect on him.

"And who are your parents?" the Abbess said.

The man then did a completely unexpected thing.

He laughed.

"That's a good question," he said, "a very good question indeed."

5

The Escape
of the
Chinatown
Bandit

Nothing in this life or the next will bring you more pain than love.
If anyone tells you otherwise, they are liars.
    Or they are still inexperienced in such matters.
    Or they have been exquisitely fortunate in their choice of lovers.
    So far.

AKI-NO-HASHI

(1311)

1882, CHINATOWN, SAN FRANCISCO

Matthew Stark paused outside the Chinese laundry at the corner of Washington and Dupont. He took a deep breath. Some people of his acquaintance liked to talk about the stench of Chinatown, as if it were the emanation of some kind of festering wound. Stark himself was comforted by the mélange of odors, not by their quantity or any particular one of them, but by the generality, the fecundity, the suggestion of vigor. It always raised hope in his heart of better things to come, no matter that he knew from experience that worse was at least as likely as better. Somehow, it also reminded him of the eventful year he had spent in Japan, now twenty years past, though there was nothing similar in the scents. Perhaps it was simply the Oriental quality of the fragrances.

Dressed as he was in a modern double-breasted wool frock coat, black with black velvet trim and fabric-covered buttons, a dark red silk brocade vest over a white silk shirt, wool trousers, and polished cotton suspenders, a felt planter's hat, a black silk cravat in a loose bow, the longish but neatly trimmed hair at his temples streaked with silver, Stark looked like any prosperous gentleman of the burgeoning city of San Francisco, except for the slight bulging of his coat at his right hip and left chest, where holsters held two .38-caliber revolvers, with five-inch and two-inch barrels respectively, the former for accuracy and the latter for compactness. These he checked before continuing on across the square in the direction of the Jade Lotus, the premier entertainment establishment in this part of the city.

Stark didn't expect any trouble, certainly not of a kind requiring the use of two firearms. But old habits were hard to break. When he was seventeen, and a runaway from an Ohio orphanage trying to be a cowboy in west Texas, Stark was almost killed by a gambler he'd caught cheating at cards. The only reason he shot the gambler instead of the other way around was because the gambler's ammunition had caused a misfire. The incident encouraged Stark to make it a habit to carry a backup himself, just in case. Since then, he'd had four occasions to fire two guns in the same encounter, all during that year in Japan. Three of those times, he was saving his own life and that of his friends. The other didn't exactly involve necessity. Stark had unloaded a .44 Colt and a .32 Smith & Wesson into a helpless man he'd already mortally wounded. It was for him the greatest irony that love can so easily drive a man to hatred, and that the resulting hatred can make a man do unreasonable things without a moment's hesitation.

Stark was going to see Wu Chun Hing, one of the richest men in San Francisco. By virtue of being Chinese, he was privileged to live in the twelve-block area around Portsmouth Square, along with some twenty thousand of his fellow Chinese, and was prudent enough not to flaunt his wealth in any way noticeable to the American residents of the city. Stark had heard that Wu was born into an influential family in China, had come to the United States as a young man to further his education, and had been marooned here when his family was annihilated during one of the rebellions that seemed to sweep through that country with tragic regularity. Whatever the truth about his past, Wu's present was as proprietor of a multitude of restaurants, bordellos, gambling houses, and opium dens. Since Stark was in entirely different lines of business, and did not avail himself of the goods and services offered by Wu, with the exception of cuisine, the two had never had any serious dealings or conflicts. He had no idea why Wu had requested the meeting.

"Please forgive me for asking you to come here," Wu said.

Stark had been led to a sitting room on the second floor. It was furnished like the small personal library one might find in the home of a college professor, complete with an abundance of books. There was nothing to suggest it belonged to anyone other than a prosperous American intellectual. This impression was completed by Wu's clothing, which resembled his guest's in taste and quality. There was not a hint of anything Oriental anywhere in sight, except in Wu's face. His hair was neatly trimmed. There was, of course, no pigtail.

"Conditions at present are such that it would not be prudent for me to venture out of my own district."

"Because of the Chinatown Bandit," Stark said.

"Yes," Wu said, looking genuinely aggrieved, "though he is not from Chinatown."

Stark said, "The newspapers say he is."

"The papers." Wu made a spitting sound. "They have two purposes only. To sell more papers, and to serve the interests of their greedy masters. Thanks to the papers, we have a Chinese Cubic Air Tax, a Chinese Miner's Tax, a Chinese Police Tax. Is this fair? There is no Mexican Cubic Air Tax, no German Miner's Tax, no Irish Police Tax, is there? And now, thanks to the hubbub about a 'Chinatown Bandit,' feelings against us are inflamed once again."

"Unfortunate, but not incomprehensible," Stark said. "All some people need is an excuse, and the Bandit's giving it to them. I would have thought you'd have put a stop to it long before now."

"I would have, if he were Chinese, because if he were Chinese, there is no way he would have remained unknown to me."

"I don't mean to be rude, Mr. Wu, but every eyewitness describes him as Chinese. They can't all be mistaken."

"They could if—" Wu began to say, then, apparently thinking better of it, began again. "This criminal accosts wealthy couples in their own neighborhoods, threatens them with a gun and a knife—"

"A meat cleaver," Stark said, "of the kind commonly found in Chinese restaurants."

"Yes. That is a fiendishly deceptive accessory. He brandishes a gun and a meat cleaver, and proceeds to take a single piece of jewelry from the woman. If the man resists, he screams out something, supposedly in Chinese, and knocks him down with a kick, or bludgeons him with the flat side of the cleaver." Wu grimaced. "Anti-Chinese sentiment grows worse by the day. I thought the looting and burning four years ago was the bottom of the pit, but the bottom is farther down than I thought, so far down I'm not sure I can see it. It was bad enough when the city and state governments passed punitive laws. Now the United States Congress is getting set to pass a Chinese Exclusion Act, and if it does, what will happen to us then? Will we be expelled? Imprisoned? Will our few poor possessions be taken from us? In this terrible situation, no Chinese would dare to worsen it by committing such crimes."

"No sane Chinese would," Stark said. "The man may not be sane."

Wu shook his head. "He is not Chinese."

Stark shrugged. "I'll take your word for it, and hope, along with you, that he is stopped before things get out of hand. Now, if you would, perhaps we can move on to the purpose of this meeting."

Wu looked quietly at Stark for a few moments before continuing. "We have been doing so, Mr. Stark."

Stark frowned. "I'm not sure I understand."

"Because of the nature of my various businesses," Wu said, "I have working relationships with a number of city police officers. From the beginning, they have sought my help, and in so doing, have shared information with me. Here are some curious facts. The Bandit knows the names of his victims. He knows where they live, and goes so far as to describe interior rooms, including, in one case, a master bedroom, suggesting he has been in the victims' houses at some point before robbing them on the street. The victims are terrified, and outraged. So far, the police have kept this from the press. If it gets out, it will not be long before a murderous mob descends on Chinatown and we have a repeat of the atrocities of '77."

"I still don't follow," Stark said. "What can I do about any of this?"

"Please permit me to continue, Mr. Stark. This is a difficult matter, requiring careful thought. So, what do we have so far? A man capable of entering houses without being detected, and without leaving any sign that he has been there. Remember, too, he commits his robberies in the very hearts of the best neighborhoods—lily-white neighborhoods, it goes without saying—yet no one has ever seen him, though because of his race he should stand out like the proverbial sore thumb."

"He may disguise himself."

"If so, we must add that ability to his formidable list of talents. And he grows ever more remarkable, because he does not steal anything from the houses he enters, though he could easily do so. This strongly suggests that he is not motivated by material gain, a very curious characteristic in a housebreaker and armed robber, is it not? The fact that he takes only a single piece of jewelry during his robberies tends to support this point."

"Let's assume you are correct," Stark said. "It still leads to no useful conclusion."

"There's more," Wu said. "My police contacts have also provided me with detailed descriptions of the jewelry taken during the robberies. From Mr. and Mrs. Dobson, a platinum brooch, six inches in diameter, containing twenty-seven diamonds with an aggregate weight of thirteen and one-half carats, thirteen sapphires with a weight of nine and three-quarter carats, and a central sapphire weighing five carats." Wu placed a brooch matching the description he had just given on his desk.

"From Mr. and Mrs. Merrill, a ring of eighteen-karat gold, with an emerald-cut diamond solitaire of three and one-half karats." He placed the ring next to the brooch.

"From Mr. and Mrs. Hart, a necklace, twenty-four inches in length, with twin chains of twenty-one-karat gold and sterling silver entwined around pearls ranging in diameter from one-quarter inch to one inch." The necklace joined the brooch and ring.

"I have not discovered the pair of matching gold and ivory bracelets contributed to the Bandit by Mr. and Mrs. Berger," Wu said. "But, of course, that was just yesterday and has not yet—how shall I say—entered the stream of events."

"I am now completely at a loss," Stark said. "If you have the proceeds of the robberies, then you must have captured the Bandit."

Wu shook his head. "I have not."

"His accomplice, then."

"No. There is no evidence that he has an accomplice."

"In that case, how is it that these jewels are in your possession?"

"They were found yesterday in a routine inspection of the women's quarters here. The women are being questioned, but everyone so far has denied any knowledge of them."

"By women's quarters, you mean the bordello."

"Yes."

"So one of them has a lover, or a patron, who is the Bandit. It should be simple enough now to discover who he is." Stark stared hard at Wu. "I fail to see why you have brought me into this."

"Because it is not so simple," Wu said. "I was hoping you would help me to solve this mystery in the least painful way for all concerned, and as quickly as possible."

"How can I do what you cannot? I know far less of this matter than you do."

"By helping me to put the facts together, and thus perhaps to reason the way to an answer. You are a man of wisdom, sir, everyone says so. Perhaps you will see what escapes the view of others. Item: The Bandit is as adept at breaking in as the best professional burglar. This means he either has training in the art, or much practice. Item: No one has ever seen him entering or leaving any of the houses. He is as stealthy as, say, one of those practitioners of the mystical secret arts of Japanese lore. What are they called?"

"Ninja," Stark said.

"Yes, ninja. I understand Mrs. Stark had such training in her homeland."

"You are certainly not suggesting that my wife is the Chinatown Bandit."

"Of course not, and I apologize most profusely if I gave that impression. I was only pointing out that whoever it is has similar skills."

"There are less than a hundred Japanese in San Francisco," Stark said. "I seriously doubt that any of them are ninja."

"Of course," Wu said. "To continue. Item: The Bandit is not motivated by material gain. This suggests he has no material needs that are unsatisfied. In short, it strongly indicates that the man is as rich as his victims, if not richer."

"That's utterly far-fetched," Stark said. Where was Wu going with this? Wherever it was, it was beginning to make him uneasy. "Why would a rich man rob anyone? He doesn't have to."

"Not out of necessity," Wu said, "but for the thrill of it. And to give impressive gifts to a pretty girl."

Stark snorted. "Who would give gifts to a prostitute?"

"Neither you nor I, of course," Wu said. "We are mature men who do not deceive ourselves about what is real and what is not. But someone with a strong romantic streak, someone very young and impressionable, perhaps, someone without much experience with women—such a young man might think it exactly the right thing to do."

"You have an idea about who it is. Are you going to tell me, or am I supposed to guess?"

Wu shrugged his shoulders. "I was hoping, Mr. Stark, that you would put the facts together and discover the culprit. Of course, if you do, and you can resolve the matter on your own, then there would be no need to involve the authorities, or to force those who may otherwise unjustly suffer injury to resort to vigilante acts. You would look for someone with ninja skills, not driven by material need, young and romantic, inexperienced in matters of love, living perhaps too sheltered a life, one giving rise to a desire for danger and adventure." Wu paused and bowed before continuing. "Also, someone who is not Chinese, but who might be mistaken for Chinese by those who don't know better."

Stark's chest tightened. The only people in the city who would be mistaken for Chinese were Japanese. And there was, to Stark's knowledge, one Japanese person who fit Wu's description exactly, and only one whom Wu would so scrupulously avoid naming in order to keep Stark from losing face. But it couldn't be, could it? Had Stark been so focused on business concerns that he had failed to see something so outrageous going on right before his eyes? It had to be. Wu was too careful a man to have this meeting with Stark if he were not sure.

"I appreciate your discretion, Mr. Wu," Stark said at last.

Wu bowed. "As far as I am concerned, Mr. Stark, this conversation never took place."

"Allow me to compensate you for the loss of business you may have suffered because of the Bandit."

"Please," Wu said, raising his hands, "that is completely unnecessary. Putting an end to these crimes is sufficient compensation." Wu did not mention the Bandit's booty, now fortuitously in his own hands. Showing the jewels to Stark was necessary to establish the facts. There was, in this particular case, no danger of loss, since Stark could not reveal his own knowledge of them without fatally betraying his own vital interests. Thus, a small fortune in precious gems and metals—for, of course, the jewelry could not remain in their present form—was Wu's. He was in fact, well compensated for his troubles, and since he had done Stark a favor—it was always useful to do favors for the rich and the powerful—Stark was now in his debt. Not that Wu would ever think to even hint at collecting it. That would be supremely déclassé. Its mere existence was sufficiently favorable.

"My thanks, then," Stark said. He paused by the door. "May I trouble you a final time before leaving?"

"Please."

"The girl's name."

· · · · ·

"When your mother and I came here in '62," Stark said, "sixty thousand people lived in San Francisco. Today, the population is a quarter of a million. This city is going to keep growing, and so are opportunities for the quick and the bold."

"Business opportunities, you mean." Makoto Stark stared out the living-room window at the city below.

"What other kinds of opportunities are there?"

Makoto looked at Stark. "That's great, Pop, for people interested in business."

"There's a lot to be interested in."

"Profits and losses, supply and demand, debits and credits," Makoto said. "Exciting stuff."

"Paperwork isn't the business," Stark said, "it's a record of the business. Do you know what the Red Hill Consolidated Company actually does?"

"Sure. Sugar, wool, mining. Some factories."

"We mine iron ore in Canada, and silver in Mexico. We have sheep ranches in California, and sugar plantations in the Hawaiian Kingdom. We operate the biggest sugar refinery in California, and we own the biggest bank in San Francisco."

Makoto shrugged.

Stark leaned back in his chair. "I've been too indulgent with you, and so has your mother." He thought of Heiko, and thinking of her, he couldn't be angry with Makoto even now.

"I've been doing exactly what you and Mom have told me to do, which is to concentrate on my studies at the university. I'm getting good reports from the professors, aren't I? Especially in English and literature."

"English and literature." Had the world changed so much in such a short time? The father a saddle tramp, the son a literary man, all in one generation? "You're going to be twenty this year. Seems you should be giving your future serious thought. How do English and literature fit in?"

Makoto smiled. "Did you have your future all mapped out at twenty?"

"Things were different then," Stark said. Robbing trading posts in Kansas, banks in Missouri. Rustling horses in Mexico, cattle in Texas. Falling in love with a whore in El Paso. Shooting men down in gunfights, nine of them before he was through. "There weren't as many opportunities for what you would call a career."

"So I guess it was a lucky thing that you happened to become partners with Mr. Okumichi."

"Yes," Stark said, "pure dumb luck." Mr. Okumichi. He still had trouble thinking of him that way. Okumichi no kami Genji, Great Lord of Akaoka, with the power of life and death over every man, woman, and child in his domain. A warlord dressed in elaborate gowns designed a thousand years ago, his hair arranged in a fancy antique style, two swords at his waist, and ten thousand utterly obedient samurai to do his bidding. Leader of a clan pledged against the Shogun for almost three centuries. All gone now. No topknots, no gown, no swords. No samurai, no domains, no Great Lords, no Shogun. They had not seen each other in twenty years, except in photographs, and their only communication had been through the letters they exchanged with faithful regularity. Stark went to Hawaii every year to check on his sugar plantations, but never went farther west. Genji had traveled to the United States last year, but he had gone by way of Europe, visited New York, Boston, Washington, and Richmond, and returned without coming to California. How could two men be trusted partners and unshakable friends without seeing each other for so long? The power of the past was great indeed. It bound them together forever, and kept them apart forever, because of all the dangers they had braved so many years ago, and of all the people they had known and loved and hated, only one mattered. Heiko. Always, there was Heiko.

Whenever he thought of her, he saw her as she was when they first met. So exquisite, so graceful, so delicate, in a silk kimono covered with a wild embroidery of wind-tossed willow trees. Her English then had been so terribly accented, he could barely understand a word. She learned fast, though, and by the time they left Japan together, she spoke it better than most of the people he'd known in Texas in his youth. He wondered, as he often did, how Genji remembered her.

He would like to tell Makoto about it, all of it, but he couldn't. He had sworn an oath of secrecy, and he would keep it.

Makoto said, "Not many Americans went to Japan in those days."

"No, not many."

"An old friend from your cattle-herding days invited you. Ethan Cruz."

"That's right," Stark said. Found what he'd left behind in the Texas hill country. Tracked him through the deserts and high plains of the West, through Mexico and California, and across the Pacific to Japan. Caught up with him in the mountains above the Kanto Plain. Put one bullet in his chest close to his heart, and the rest from both revolvers into his face. "He had some promising ideas, but took ill and died before the two of us could get started. Mr. Okumichi liked what I had to say, and went partners with me instead. I've told you the story a dozen times, at least."

"Yes, I guess you have," Makoto said. "You've told it the same way each time, too."

Stark looked at him. "Meaning?"

"Mom told me the most important thing about *ninjitsu* isn't the fighting part, or the stealth part. It's being alert to the difference between real and unreal, in word as well as deed. She said there are two ways to catch a liar. The first is easy. Most liars are stupid, and their stories keep changing, because they can't keep track of what they've been saying. The second is hard. A smart liar remembers his lies, and the story doesn't change. But that's a giveaway, too. The story stays *exactly* the same, because he's making sure he remembers *exactly* what he said."

"The truth itself stays exactly the same, too."

"The truth does, but not a true telling. Unless you have a memory like a photographic plate, the telling is a little different every time."

"Why would I lie about how the business got started?"

"I don't know," Makoto said. "Maybe there was something unsavory about it. Maybe you were smuggling contraband. Opium, or white slaves."

"I've never smuggled anything in my life," Stark said. "You're letting your imagination run away with you."

"I don't really care what happened," Makoto said. "I just think it's interesting, that's all. The only things you lie about that I can tell are your days in Texas, and your days in Japan. Makes me a little curious about what really happened."

"You're an expert on lying now?"

Makoto shrugged. "Your life's your life, Pop. You don't have to tell me anything you don't want to."

"Since we're on the subject anyway," Stark said, "tell me some lies about Siu-fong."

Makoto froze.

Stark let the moments pass as Makoto stayed silent. Stark said, "Your mom didn't tell you the third way, I guess. Which is, the liar gets so tangled up in mendacity, he can't even get a word out edgewise."

"I'm not tangled up in anything," Makoto said. "You've never asked about her before. How'd you find out?"

"I had a little conversation with Wu Chun Hing," Stark said, watching Makoto stall as he tried to figure out how much his father knew. "Siu-fong's name came up."

"She hasn't distracted me from my studies," Makoto said. "Ask any of my professors and they'll tell you my work is as excellent as it's always been."

"Such a scholar," Stark said. "I suppose the experience is solely for literary purposes. Or maybe you're teaching her English."

"It's just entertainment," Makoto said. "But every experience ultimately has possibilities in literature."

"You're going to write stories about her."

"I'm thinking about it."

"I have an idea you might like."

Makoto laughed. "You never read anything but business reports."

"If you write it, I'll read it. I even have a title for you."

"You do?"

"Yes," Stark said, "I'd call it *The Escape of the Chinatown Bandit*."

"Catchy title," Makoto said. Stark could see Makoto still wasn't sure how much he knew. "Makes you want to know what happens."

"What happens is, the Chinatown Bandit's identity is about to be exposed," Stark said. "The big surprise in the story, he's not Chinese at all."

"He's not?"

"No," Stark said, "he's not. Now, two things can happen, both bad, but one's far worse. The better possibility, he'll be arrested by the police and spend the next ten years in prison, if he manages to survive that long. I doubt there are many inside San Quentin interested in literature."

"That's the better?" Makoto said. "Sounds grim enough. What's the worse?"

"He'll be murdered by angry Tongs," Stark said, "chopped up alive with a Chinese meat cleaver, most likely, because they're none too happy with the way he's been causing trouble for them by masquerading as Chinese. The Chinese meat cleaver, that's because the Bandit's been using one in his robberies, to make sure people think he's Chinese."

With a straight face, Makoto said, "That's a nice touch, the Chinese meat cleaver. I wouldn't have thought you so imaginative."

"I have my moments."

"Your story seems headed inexorably for tragedy," Makoto said. "You should let me work on it a bit. I can probably come up with a better finale. Readers prefer happy endings."

Stark said, "Don't bother. I have the ending all worked out."

"So which is it? Prison or death?"

"Neither. Because there's another surprise. The Bandit's doting father saves his foolish son by shipping him off to Canada before the police or the Tongs can get their hands on him."

"Canada?"

"That's right, Canada," Stark said, "and not anyplace in the northland famous for its scenery, either. The Bandit spends a year in Ontario learning about iron mining firsthand."

Makoto rubbed his chin in a theatrical gesture of thought. "Mexico would be better, from a dramatic standpoint. The tropical climate is more romantic. And Mexican silver mines suggest adventures to come more than Canadian iron mines."

"The Bandit isn't going to have any more adventures," Stark said. "Once he's gone long enough to be forgotten, he'll return to San Francisco and take his proper place in the management of the Red Hill Consolidated Company. Is that understood?"

"We should consider that prospect open to discussion. The son is not always like the father." Did he flinch? Makoto thought he did, as he always seemed to do when the matter of their similarities—or, more precisely, their dissimilarities—arose.

"The matter is not presently open to discussion," Stark said. "And before you pack, bring down the gold and ivory bracelets Mrs. Berger lost."

"Yes, Father. What am I packing?"

"Whatever you want. You're leaving in one hour."

"Is such haste really necessary?"

"It most definitely is, Makoto." Stark's voice betrayed agitation for the first time. "Do you think I was joking about the police and the Tongs?"

Makoto sighed and turned to leave.

"One question," Stark said.

"Yes."

"Why?"

. . . . .

The son is not always like the father. That was an understatement, to be sure. Perhaps it would have been better to phrase it as a question. Why is the son so unlike the father? But, of course, as Professor Dykus would say, the question was clearly implied in the statement, which was just as clearly the cause of his father's unconcealable discomfiture. Involuntary reactions, his mother had told him, were also indications of truth and falsehood.

When had Makoto first noticed the dissimilarities? Late in childhood, he had recognized that he resembled his mother far more than his father.

That is because you are half Japanese, his mother had said, and our blood is strong.

He accepted the explanation because any reason was better than none, and his mother, who had begun teaching him the secrets of the arts of the real and the unreal at the age of five, had never lied to him. So far as he could tell. Lately, it had occurred to him that she was the master and he was the student, and surely she had kept some secrets of the arts to herself. If anyone was capable of escaping detection in a lie, it would be a master of lie detection, would it not?

The birth of his sister Angela Emiko when he was seven triggered his first doubts, and they were increased by the arrival two years later of his youngest sibling, Hope Naoko. Like him, they, too, were half Japanese. Yet, unlike him, they exhibited signs of his father's American half, as well as his mother's Japanese. Both Angela and Hope had medium-brown hair. Angela's eyes were light brown, and Hope's were as blue as her father's. In physical dimensions, they split the difference between their parents. In noticeable contrast, Makoto had black hair and dark-brown eyes, like his mother, and although he was considerably bigger than she was, he was nowhere near his father's size.

Blood is weaker in women than in men, his mother had said, explaining the difference.

By this time, though he saw no sign of deception, he found it difficult to completely accept his mother's answer. For one thing, he was older. For another, he knew more about the world. His science and mathematics tutor, Mr. Strauss, was an enthusiastic follower of Gregor Mendel, a scientist, monk, and fellow Austrian. What Makoto learned from him concerning Mendel's findings in plant hybridization seemed confirmed in his sisters and denied in him. Odd, at the very least. And finally, three months ago, when he met Siu-fong, unacceptable.

Siu-fong had light-brown hair and green eyes. My father Englishman, she said. Blood is weaker in women, his mother had said, and Siu-fong seemed to verify this. Her English half was as visible as her Chinese. Then he met her brother, Hsi-jian. He was a masculine version of Siu-fong. What would his mother say about this? That Chinese blood was weaker than Japanese? Mendel said otherwise.

Mr. Strauss, in discussing genetics, had cautioned him that an exact science had not yet been established, particularly as it related to more complex organisms. The matter of recessive and dominant traits, he said, became ever more difficult. Consider human beings in contrast to bean plants. The potential number of elements that play a part in determining those traits boggles the mind, does it not? Makoto agreed that it did. And yet . . .

He thought of confronting his parents, but quickly abandoned that idea. His mother's denials would be unshakable, and his father—or, perhaps more correctly, his stepfather—committed to the lie, if lie it was, would never yield the truth.

Assailed by an agony of doubt and despair, Makoto grew vengeful. But upon whom was he to wreak revenge? What was the wrong? Who were the perpetrators? And he, how had he been wronged? He was rich, perhaps the richest twenty-year-old in San Francisco. He could not deny that he was disdained to a certain extent by members of his own social class, thanks to his race, but no one insulted him to his face. The Stark fortune and Matthew Stark's political connections prevented that, and if they didn't, a more fundamental fear did.

Five years ago, a certain rival of Stark's in the burgeoning sugar business was found floating in the bay. He had been partially devoured by sharks, but enough of his upper body remained to reveal a gunshot wound in his torso that penetrated straight through his heart. Though competition from that quarter disappeared, which was to Stark's obvious advantage, there was nothing to suggest that he had anything to do with the man's unfortunate and mysterious demise. One of the city's scandal-mongering newspapers thought otherwise, and did a series of stories on other unsolved crimes linked to Stark, including some utterly laughable fabrications about gunfights in the Wild West and brutal murders in Japan. They did this without naming him, of course, but the identity was obvious. Within two weeks of the first story, the building housing the newspaper burned down, with the editor-publisher in it. There was no indication of any cause other than accident. The man was a notorious drunk. According to the fire chief, the victim had probably knocked over a kerosene lantern when he'd fallen into his usual late-night alcohol-induced stupor. The mere possibility of a more sinister cause, however, was quite enough. Everyone was always very polite, if not exactly welcoming and friendly.

Three years ago, Makoto had left his home tutors behind and matriculated at the University of California, which had in recent years moved to its new campus in the Berkeley Hills. It was his first real experience among strangers his own age. And, unfortunately, among those strangers was a beefy young man named Victor Burton, whose father was a power in the Working Man's Party, a virulently anti-Chinese group which was favored to win the governorship in the next election. Burton, who was apparently unable to distinguish Chinese from Japanese, or either from Negro, insisted on addressing Makoto alternately as "yellow nigger" and "Chink." Makoto, on his father's advice, ignored him, though Burton sometimes made it difficult. One day, Burton was absent from classes, and his fellow students all seemed unusually edgy. Makoto eventually learned that Burton had suffered an assault the previous night on his way home from a tavern, by a party or parties unknown. The assailants, whom Burton neither saw nor heard, broke his right leg at the knee, his right arm at the elbow, and his jaw in its center. The nature of his injuries made it impossible for Burton to use crutches or speak intelligibly, necessitating his withdrawal from the university.

With his departure, it could once again be said that everyone was very polite.

Makoto asked Shoji and Jiro, the two Japanese clerks in the Red Hill Consolidated Company, if they knew anything about what had happened to Burton. He asked them during their weekly training session in unarmed combat, at which both men were highly adept, having been samurai attached to Mr. Okumichi before coming to California. Makoto's conversations with them were in Japanese, as they were with his mother.

"We heard about it," Shoji said. "Bad luck, eh?"

"Bad luck," Jiro said, "but I understand the young man in question was not of good character. Bad luck tends to follow such people."

"Wait, Makoto-san, that is not the right grip." Shoji took Makoto's hand in his own. "Relax. If you tighten, I can feel you. The most effective hold is one that no one knows is there."

Makoto said, "You didn't have anything to do with it."

"With what? Burton?" Shoji looked at Jiro. Both men shrugged. "Why would we? We don't even know him."

"Look on the bright side," Jiro said. "He was not of good character. Your study environment is therefore improved by his absence."

"Attention!" Shoji said, and threw Makoto head over heels. If he hadn't pulled the throw at the last moment before impact, Makoto would have sustained a broken shoulder. As it was, he landed on the hard *tatami* mat with a thud that drove all the air from his lungs.

"You see?" Shoji said. "You didn't feel the grip, so the throw was a big surprise. Remember that, Makoto-san."

"I will," Makoto said.

So the Chinatown Bandit was born, not out of vengeance after all, but from a need to fight his own battles, on his own terms.

The housebreaking began as a way of establishing for himself how vulnerable other people were, especially people who thought their wealth and social position put them out of reach of the riffraff. Up the side of the house using clawed gloves and sandals, dressed all in black, as dark as the night. Survey the bedrooms, listen to snatches of dinner-table conversation drifting up the stairs, look through jewelry boxes, closets. He ceased these entries when he inadvertently caught a glimpse of Meg Chastain, a girl he'd known all his life, climbing out of the bath. His embarrassment was so acute, the very thought of secretly entering another house made him blush.

But once he had begun, it was difficult to stop entirely. Houses were out. That left the streets of the city. What to do there? Robin Hood? Steal from the rich and give to the poor? Stealing from the rich appealed to him. But give to what poor? Most of the poor in the city were Chinese, or white laborers who hated them. Neither seemed to offer a promising pool of charitable recipients.

Then one day, while lunching at the Jade Lotus, he caught a glimpse of a young woman who at first he almost mistook for his sister Angela, unaccountably dressed in a Chinese *cheong-sam* gown. On closer inspection, he saw the congruities were superficial and entirely due to similar mixed parentage. The attraction thereafter was not love or sex, but the implication suggested by her existence, the existence of her brother, their similarities to his own sisters, and the dissimilarities between all of them and himself. How likely was it that he was who he was told he was, namely, Matthew Stark's son? The human evidence strongly suggested that it was not very likely at all.

Siu-fong's own story was one of rejection and abuse by both English and Chinese, and sale into white slavery. It was theoretically possible for her to redeem her contract, but the amount was vast, and her debt to Wu Chun Hing grew continually. Freedom was an impossible dream.

And just like that, Makoto now had the poor to go with his Robin Hood.

He could thank his former classmate, Victor Burton, for the idea of Chinese impersonation. Burton couldn't tell the difference. With a prop or two—say, a Chinese meat cleaver and a shouted imprecation in mock Chinese—who could? Only a real Chinese, and he wasn't planning to rob any of them. The police would look for the culprit in Chinatown. No one would even think of suspecting the sheltered young man who lived among the victimized wealthy of Nob Hill.

· · · · ·

It was fun while it lasted. He stuffed random articles of clothing into a single travel bag, his thoughts elsewhere.

"I hope you will behave yourself in Canada," his mother said.

"I will have to," Makoto said. "What else is there to do at a Canadian iron mine?"

"Trouble can always be found," she said, "and it can always find you, if you are not careful. So be careful."

"I'm always careful."

"Write me often. In Japanese."

"I would have to write in *kana*," Makoto said. Kana was simple and phonetic. He had never quite mastered the two thousand pictographic kanji characters required for true basic literacy.

"You have your dictionary, don't you? A good opportunity to practice kanji."

Makoto looked at his mother and marveled as he always did at her youthful appearance, the delicacy of her features, the emotional fragility implied by her soft, almost hesitant voice. All illusions. She looked like she could be his younger sister, but she was twice his age. The daintiness of her physique belied her power. As for emotions, Makoto could not remember having seen her display fear or discouragement even once in his life. Now that he had so many questions about himself, he had begun to wonder about her as well. He knew very few details about her, even fewer than he knew about his father, and he knew very little about him.

"How old were you when you came to California?"

"Twenty. I've told you often." She looked questioningly at him.

"Were you afraid?"

She smiled as she neatly refolded a shirt he had tossed into his suitcase. "I didn't have time to be afraid. You were born almost as soon as we stepped ashore."

"Do you ever regret leaving Japan?"

"So many questions."

"Well, I'm leaving home. It's not so strange it makes me think about you leaving your home, is it? Of course, you left of your own free will, and never went back. I'm being forced to go, but I'll get to come home eventually."

"There's a famous saying," his mother said. " 'Regret is the elixir of poets.' I was never very poetic."

"Makoto-san, Mrs. Stark." Jiro bowed from the doorway. "Are you ready? I am to accompany you to Canada."

"Great," Makoto said. "I even have a nursemaid."

"Go carefully," his mother said, "and return safely."

"Don't worry. The year will pass in no time, and I'll be back before you know it."

"Take care of him, Jiro."

"Yes, Mrs. Stark."

. . . . .

But Jiro did not get the chance. Remembering his recent lessons in a grip that cannot be felt, Makoto extended the principle to being guarded at a railway station. Jiro came running breathlessly back into the house an hour after he'd left with Makoto.

"Mr. Stark! Makoto has disappeared!"

They searched the railway station, questioned everyone they could, and discovered nothing. Except for the time he had been with Jiro, no one had seen anyone fitting Makoto's description, though a young man of Japanese extraction, dressed like the wealthy collegian that he was, was bound to attract considerable attention. Stark expanded the search to other parts of the city, but he knew it was already too late.

Canada was not appealing. Makoto had a better destination in mind. Mexico seemed most likely, since he had mentioned it in their last conversation.

Jiro sat on his knees on the floor, his head bowed in shame. He had been slouched there, disconsolate, ever since he had lost Makoto at the station. Though he was dressed in modern Western clothing, his posture was entirely that of a samurai who had not fulfilled his duty. Twenty years in America and his fundamental nature was unchanged. Stark knew that if he did not handle him carefully, the man was very likely to commit suicide over what he considered his shameful failure.

"Jiro," Stark said, his voice harsh. "Why are you relaxing so leisurely? Go to the telegraph office and send a telegram to Mendoza. When you return, be ready to travel. I will count on you to catch up with Makoto. And stay with him this time."

"Yes, sir," Jiro said. The tongue-lashing energized him. Stark saw that if he felt himself sufficiently punished, and sufficiently useful still, he would live. "What should the telegram say?"

"My God, man, what do you think? Tell him Makoto is probably on his way there."

"Yes, Mr. Stark, right away." Jiro bowed and turned to go.

"Wait," Shoji said. He came into the room with a note in his hand. "From Wu Chun Hing. Urgent."

Stark knew what the note would say without reading it. The girl. He had forgotten about her. Makoto had not.

· · · · ·

The small bedroom on the bordello floor of the Jade Lotus was drenched in the blood of six bodies. Four of the men had been shot, three in the center of the torso, and one in the face. The powder burns said it was at close range. The fifth man had been gutted with a knife, probably his own, still lodged in his chest beneath the sternum. Before it burst open his heart, the knife had spilled his guts onto the floor. An angry kill. Stark looked over at the girl. The gut-spiller was probably the one who'd killed Siu-fong. She was pretty, not much older than her mid-teens, with Eurasian features. Her throat was slit deep across the line of the collarbone.

Stark said, "Makoto didn't kill her. This one did."

Wu nodded. "He came to free her, in his words. She was, ah, inadvertently injured."

"Where is he?"

"Wherever he is," Wu said, "he is doomed. There is no good alternative now." He glanced at the half dozen coppers poking around in the room. "That deputy was eating in the restaurant. He heard the gunshots. He was here an instant after Makoto got away."

"Is he wounded?"

"I don't think so. He came the closest"—Wu pointed at the corpse with the powder-burned face—"and his knife is there, bloodless. I am sorry, Mr. Stark. I had thought the problem solved. Who could have anticipated such a foolish act on his part, to risk everything for a prostitute."

Stark told himself he could have, and should have. He'd done much the same thing himself when he was Makoto's age. El Paso instead of San Francisco. Different place, same result. Because of him, she'd died, too, and in a worse way than this one. The son is not always like the father, Makoto had said. Sometimes, in some unfortunate ways, he was.

The one copper in a suit instead of in a uniform, the deputy Wu mentioned, came over and tipped his hat. "Mr. Stark," he said.

Stark had met with him on several occasions concerning thefts from the wharf. A jovial, rotund Irishman who seemed more like a friendly barkeep than a keeper of the peace. Deputy Mulligan. Ulysses Mulligan.

"Deputy Mulligan."

"What a mess," Mulligan said.

"Yes, but a fortunate mess for you," Stark said. "I understand you were the first officer on the scene."

"That's right, Mr. Stark." Mulligan looked at Stark questioningly as he spoke. "I was having a wee bit of a snack downstairs. Noodles with that red pork floating in it."

"Thank your appetite, Deputy Mulligan. You're a hero. You've caught the Chinatown Bandit and ended his reign of terror."

The deputy looked down at the dead men, from one to the other, then he looked back at Stark.

"Is one of them the Bandit, sir?"

"The one you shot in the face as he came at you with a Chinese meat cleaver."

Mulligan frowned and looked at the corpses again.

"Was it a gang, then? Shot the whole gang?"

"No, he was a daring and probably insane lone villain." Stark took the .38 revolver from his hip, flipped it around, and gave it to Mulligan handle first. "Armed with a gun and meat cleaver, as all the witnesses have described. These other poor fellows and the girl, innocent bystanders."

Mulligan took the gun and looked at it.

"All the chambers are loaded."

"I doubt they will be by the time the gun reaches the department and is entered into evidence," Stark said. "I expect you will be promoted to assistant chief for this. I'm sure Chief Winslow will say something about it to me when I have dinner with him tomorrow night."

"I don't understand, sir," Mulligan said.

"Is it necessary that you do, Assistant Chief Mulligan?"

A broad smile slowly spread across Mulligan's face until his eyes twinkled merrily.

"No, Mr. Stark, I don't guess that it is. My wife will be very happy with the raise that comes with the promotion."

"Let me be the first to congratulate you."

Stark and Mulligan shook hands.

"Ah, but if he was the Chinatown Bandit, then where are his ill-gotten gains?"

Stark looked at Wu.

Wu said, "Buried secretly who knows where?"

Stark shook his head.

"Since the Bandit has been apprehended, the victims would be extremely vexed if their jewels were not recovered. You removed them temporarily from the scene to protect them, and now you are very pleased to turn them over to Mr. Mulligan."

Wu frowned unhappily.

"I am."

"Grateful businessmen will of course be happy to pay you a reward for your part in this. Say, one thousand dollars."

"Truly grateful businessmen would be somewhat more generous, I think, considering the losses I have suffered by being a helpful citizen. Say, two thousand dollars."

"Seems only fair," Stark said. That was solved. Only one problem remained. Where was Makoto? He wouldn't go to Mexico now. Where would he go?

·　·　·　·　·

"Well, wasn't that the worst dinner ever," Hope said, when she and her older sister, Angela, were back upstairs in her bedroom. Though she was two years younger at eleven, she was the more outspoken of the two. "Whenever they address each other as 'Mr. Stark' and 'Mrs. Stark,' you know they're arguing about something."

"Makoto's in trouble," Angela said. "That's what it's about."

"He's never really in trouble," Hope said. "He's the boy, remember? So he gets away with everything."

"I heard Jiro and Shoji talking about the police. Something bad happened in Chinatown."

"The Chinatown Bandit," Hope said, suddenly alarmed. "Did he hurt Makoto?"

Angela shook her head. Hope saw that she wanted to say more, but something was making her hesitate.

"Come on, Angela, out with it."

"My Japanese is rusty," Angela said. "I must have misunderstood. And they were speaking in Akaoka dialect, which made it even harder."

"What did they say?"

Angela took a deep breath before answering.

"They were talking about Makoto as if he'd killed someone."

"What?"

Angela began to cry.

"I don't think he's ever coming home."

. . . . .

Makoto awoke aboard the SS *Hawaiian Cane*. He felt sick to his stomach. It wasn't the vast quantity of alcohol that he had consumed the previous night, though that didn't help, and it wasn't the nauseating rolling of the ship in the less-than-gentle sea, though that was certainly a contributing factor. It wasn't even the violence, or the blood, or the death, not even Siu-fong's death. It was the look of betrayal in her eyes when she stared across the room at Makoto just as the coolie cut her throat. He had promised her and she had trusted him and he had let her down. It wasn't the heroic conclusion that he had envisioned for *The Escape of the Chinatown Bandit.*

Not that he had escaped, not really. The police wouldn't be far behind, and neither would the Tongs. Matthew Stark had been wrong. There weren't two bad possibilities of one or the other, there were three, and the third was both at once. They would catch up with him eventually, and when they did, fine, there would be no escape, but there could still be a heroic, though tragic, conclusion, the Chinatown Bandit fighting to the death.

Before that happened, there was one more thing he had to do.

Makoto got up from the bunk and went out on deck. He watched the brightening sky on the line of the horizon to the east.

The land of the rising sun.

Where that was depended entirely on where you were when the sun came up. From here, it was California. He looked west, into the dark half of the sky, toward Hawaii, toward Japan.

Won't Genji be surprised to see Makoto. And if Makoto saw in him what he thought he might see, what would he say when Makoto asked him the one question he'd crossed the Pacific to ask—the same one Matthew Stark had asked Makoto in quite another context.

Why?

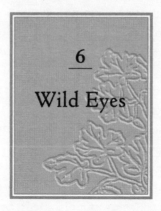

6

Wild Eyes

The lord's wife gave birth to a daughter. Years passed and no other child was born among wife or concubines. This caused much consternation among the retainers. Without a male heir, the Shogun would not fail to attempt an abolition of the clan. Yet, the lord was undisturbed until the girl, at a very early age, began to display the aspects of great beauty.

He said to his chief bodyguard, There is only one thing worse than a beautiful daughter. Can you name it?

The bodyguard replied that he could not.

An ugly one, the lord said.

The bodyguard did not know whether his lord spoke in earnest or in jest, so, neither laughing nor agreeing, he simply bowed in acknowledgment.

AKI-NO-HASHI

(1311)

1882, MUSHINDO ABBEY

A nd who are your parents?" the Reverend Abbess Jintoku asked. The young man laughed and said, "That's a good question, a very good question indeed."

"Of course it's a good question. I am Abbess here. My role in life is to ask good questions. What is your name?"

"Makoto."

That was a given name only. Very well. It was not for her to judge or demand. If he did not wish to reveal himself more fully, that was his business.

She said, "I take it, Makoto-san, that you are contemplating entering upon a renunciant's life."

"Why would you think that?" Makoto said. "It's the least likely of any possible path in my future."

"I have a talent for seeing spiritual yearning," the Abbess said. She had no such ability. What she did have was a good eye for expensive clothing, well-manicured hair, and an air of confidence that came from a lifetime of financial ease. All of these she saw very clearly in Makoto. Mushindo Abbey, like every other religious establishment, could always use another patron. A little religious flattery often went a long way. Even those who thought themselves completely devoid of belief tended to soften when told they had the calling.

"Oh, do you?" Makoto smiled at her. "You said your task is to ask questions. I always thought religious leaders answered them."

"I am not a religious leader," she said. "I am no more than a kind of janitor. I clean up and keep things in their place. Metaphorically speaking. Would you care to join me for tea? We can discuss things further."

"Thank you, Reverend Janitor," he said, bowing with his hands together in front of him in the Buddhist manner. "Perhaps some other time. Now I must return to Tokyo."

"To discover your parents," the Abbess said, "or yourself?"

"Doesn't one necessarily lead to the other?"

"A very good question, Makoto-san. Perhaps you, too, have a talent for janitorial work."

"Thank you for the compliment," he said. With a final bow, he turned and walked down the path to the gate of the abbey.

She watched him until he was out of sight. Whom did he remind her of? Oh, well, it would come to her later. Or not. It didn't matter. She was confident she would see him again. His comments about the true history of the battle indicated a degree of interest in Mushindo that exceeded the usual. Yes, Makoto-san would be back, perhaps as a generous, regular donor. She turned away from the gate and proceeded to her workshop.

Of the many tasks required by her office, the Reverend Abbess Jintoku most enjoyed the preparation of holy relics. Before they could be offered to the public, the bullets, the charred wood fragments, the remnant scraps of scrolls, all needed to be placed into vials made of hollow bamboo segments, each about the size of a little finger, and in appearance not entirely unlike the mummified remains of one, a useful reminder to temple guests of the tenuous state and eventual fate of all living beings. Once a vial was selected by a supplicant and its contents verified, a donation was gratefully accepted and the open end closed once again with a bamboo plug. In the beginning, the relics had been sold for a set price, but the Abbess, a naturally good businesswoman with a keen understanding of human nature, believed that donations would bring greater income, a belief that was quickly validated by a tenfold increase in revenue. When left to decide for themselves, those seeking material assistance from the other realm tended strongly to err on the side of generosity, lest they offend the very spirits whose help they sought.

Lately, the Abbess had begun to quarter the bullets and place ever smaller fragments of wood and scraps of scrolls into the vials. Their popularity had resulted in a noticeable diminution of what had once seemed an inexhaustible supply. Once they were actually gone, she would not hesitate to manufacture relics—it being her own firm religious conviction that sincere belief, rather than material reality, was of paramount importance—but, as a matter of simplicity, she preferred to supply the genuine article as long as possible. She saw no value in irresponsible honesty, however. If the Abbey ever ran out of relics to offer, the stream of visitors would cease, and thus so would the livelihood of a significant number of the inhabitants of Yamanaka Village. As the trusted spiritual leader of the community, she could not in good conscience allow that to happen.

This work, which the Abbess had done for so many years, had a certain natural rhythm of its own, which freed her from the burden of thought. Her left hand held a segment of bamboo, her right, a scrap of scroll; her eyes beheld both hands, the bamboo, and the paper; she heard, without fixing upon them, the sounds of her heart, her breathing, a distant childish voice laughing; she closed the vial with a suitable piece of bamboo, tightly enough that it would not fall out and displace the paper, but not too tightly that it would be difficult to remove for a supplicant's inspection prior to selection; she placed the vial in the box for vials containing pieces of scroll. Then she began the process again.

Her left hand reached for a bamboo segment, which came from the grove beside the temple.

Her right hand grasped a piece of scroll, which had been left at the temple by Lady Emily.

Her heart in her chest made the slow swooshing sound of a sea creature swimming leisurely in friendly waters.

Her breathing was very relaxed, and slowed and paused and resumed of its own accord.

The child laughed again, more distant now, moving in the direction of the valley.

The Reverend Abbess Jintoku closed the vial with a suitable piece of bamboo.

A few breaths, minutes, or hours passed in this way. Since she began anew with each vial, and attached to no thoughts as she worked, she had no consciousness of any passage of time. Only when she stopped for the day and saw the number of vials, or noticed the length of the shadows, or sometimes the almost complete absence of light, did she consider the time. Then she went into the meditation hall for her evening sitting before retiring for the night.

Today, the Reverend Abbess did not entirely lose herself in her favorite task. She kept thinking of the handsome visitor with the odd accent, and thinking of him, found herself thinking also of that long-ago visit by Lady Emily and Lady Hanako. It was during the tragic and sorrowful events of those days that the ruins of Mushindo Monastery had become Mushindo Abbey. Or had become an abbey again, for if what the two ladies had told Kimi was true, Mushindo had originally been an abbey, not a monastery. That had been almost six hundred years ago. What strange circumstances had brought the abbey into being both times. It was hard to believe, but it did explain one of the mysteries of the place, or at least its occurrence if not its precise nature.

Such an endless flow of memory and speculation naturally prevented her from slipping into the noncontemplative peace that usually accompanied her work. Thoughts, like our selves, were only bubbles in the stream, it was true. But when she so indulgently let herself focus on the bubbles, the stream could not carry her away. Sometimes, it was most appropriate to cease trying. She returned the scrolls, wood, and bullets to storage, gathered up the vials she had constructed, and proceeded to the meditation hall. Before entering, she stopped at the table that discreetly displayed the offering of holy relics and placed the vials in their appropriate places.

Evening was an entirely voluntary meditation period for the nuns of Mushindo. Participation in morning and midday sittings was required by the frequent presence of guests from the outside. It was, in a sense, a kind of performance to establish the monastic quality of the abbey. But at night, there were no guests, and thus no requirement. In the early days, no one sat then. Over the years, this had changed, and now everyone sat at night, too, at least briefly. Even those with families in the village sat before changing out of their religious garb and returning home.

Yasuko had been the first to engage in night sitting.

She said, If I am sincere and persistent, Buddha will surely answer my prayers and fix my deformity. Don't you agree, Reverend Abbess?

Yasuko had been the one who tried to hang herself when she had been a captive of the slave raiders in Yokohama, and had managed only to mangle her neck. She was desperate to return to her home village, marry, have children, and resume a normal life. But no one would ever marry a woman whose head lolled off to one side so idiotically. Thus her fervent presence in the meditation hall during every spare hour.

Buddha never fixed Yasuko's neck, but perhaps he did hear her prayers and answer them in his own way, for one day, quite suddenly it seemed, all her anguish, frustration, anger, and self-loathing disappeared, and a gentle peacefulness descended on her.

Reverend Abbess, she said, I wish to truly take holy orders.

The Abbess performed what she could remember of the initiation ceremony Old Abbot Zengen had given for Jimbo, when Jimbo had become a disciple of Buddha. The only part of it that she was entirely sure of was the repetition of the Four Great Vows, so she had Yasuko and the rest of the assembly repeat the vows one hundred and eight times, complete with a full prostration at the end of each recitation.

I vow to:

Rescue the infinity of beings—

Endlessly abjure the endless arising of desire, anger, and mistaken views—

Open my eyes to the infinite pathways of truth—

Embody the supremely benevolent Way of the Buddha.

It took the better part of a morning to complete the ceremony, and vocal and bodily fatigue, approaching a level of actual distress for some, was profound among all concerned. Thereafter, the Abbess decided that three repetitions would be sufficient for any future supplicant, and a simple bow could take the place of the prostrations. After all, was it not true that sincerity rather than form was the key to salvation?

Despite the questionable orthodoxy of the ceremony, it, like Yasuko's prayers, apparently did have an effect, for from then on, Yasuko behaved in a manner entirely consistent with her declared intent. She became as consistent in her practice as Goro was in his. Gradually, others began to follow her example.

The essentially ridiculous nature of the situation did not escape the Reverend Abbess. The true spiritual exemplars of Mushindo were a nearly mute idiot and a crippled failed suicide. Nevertheless, in time, she, too, began to engage in meditation even when it was not necessary for the sake of guests.

She silently took her place among her fellow nuns.

As she settled in, she mulled over the amount of wood fragments, bullets, and scrolls remaining, and contemplated how long they would be a source of holy relics. The scrolls were the most critical, because they would be the most difficult to replace with new material. One piece of lead looked pretty much like any other, and the same could be said for pieces of charred wood. But there was something about the look of the ancient paper that she had so far been unable to duplicate. She wondered, neither for the first time nor the last, whether they were what was left of the infamous *Aki-no-hashi* compendium of spells set down by the princess witch, Lady Shizuka, in ancient times. Not that it mattered, one way or the other. The important thing was quantity, not their nature. And that wasn't an immediate worry. There had been twelve scrolls to start with, and there were still the better part of nine left. Still, it never hurt to plan ahead. She thought about this at the start of her meditation, not so much to arrive at any solution, but simply to bring it up and set it aside.

Next, she noticed the sounds of Mushindo.

When she was young, the eerie creaking, whining, and crying had frightened her and every other child in the village. The place is haunted, they would say. Listen. Those are the voices of tortured souls and demons. When they listened, it seemed beyond doubt that they heard supernatural voices. But only if they listened. And no matter how closely they listened,

they could never quite make out what those voices were saying. Which of course only served to add more excitement to their childish fear. If they went about their business, then they heard nothing but the wind in the trees, the cries of birds and an occasional fox, the gurgling of a stream, the voices of wood-gatherers calling to each other in the distant valleys.

At the beginning of the Abbess's meditation, what she heard sounded much like the wind, animals, water, and distant voices that they most likely were, yet as her breathing slowed, and her attention clarified, it inexorably took on the demonic quality of her youthful imaginings. Was it really only because she was listening? Or were those truly the voices of denizens of other worlds calling out to her, reminding her of the evanescent nature of life in this one? Had it always been this way, or had it begun with Lady Shizuka's arrival at this very place, six hundred years ago? And if so, did it mean that Lady Shizuka had really been a witch? Or were the sounds, real or fantastic as they may be, no more than meaningless oddities of entry into meditation?

Finally, she let go of all conjecture—what use was it to cling to that which pointed at nothing real?—and flowed effortlessly through the constrictions of thought into a vibrant stillness.

1291, CLOUD OF SPARROWS CASTLE

Summer brought abysmal sorrow to Lady Kiyomi, and catastrophe to the clan. Her husband, Lord Masamuné, was trapped by an unexpectedly powerful enemy force at Cape Muroto and killed, along with her father, her two eldest sons, and almost all of their samurai. Her remaining son, Hironobu, had then become Lord of Akaoka, a hasty investiture that was to precede his first and last act as titular leader of the clan—ritual suicide in advance of the arrival of the triumphant enemy. Their leaders would, in any case, put him under the sword. With the death of his sire and his siblings, he was lord of the domain, and lords did not surrender. That he was only six years old mattered not at all. His elder brothers had been ten and eight, and their youth had not saved them. They had accompanied their father on what they thought would be a skirmish to observe combat for the first time. Instead, they had perished with him.

Now Lady Kiyomi herself had only two duties remaining in life. She would observe her youngest son's suicide—the ever-faithful bodyguard,

Go, would strike off Hironobu's head as soon as his knife's blade broke his skin—then she, too, would die by her own hand. She had no intention of remaining alive to be humiliated and abused by the usurpers. While she was not sorry for herself, she could not help feeling sorry for Hironobu. She was twenty-seven, so she had not become a grandmother. Still, she had lived a reasonably full life as lover, wife, and mother. He had become Lord of Akaoka, but he would reign for mere hours, then he would die.

But Hironobu did not die, and neither did Lady Kiyomi. At the moment before he plunged the knife into his belly, a myriad of sparrows suddenly rose from the dry streambed, the sound of their flight like that of distant waves breaking on the shore. They passed directly over Hironobu in a winged cloud. Beneath them, the flickering of light and shadow created the illusion that he himself was flickering—insubstantial, ethereal, like a ghost glimpsed out of the corner of one's eye. Everyone saw it. Several people cried out. Perhaps Lady Kiyomi was one of them.

It was an omen. The gods disapproved. This was clear to everyone. So Hironobu did not kill himself. Instead, it was decided that he would lead their handful of remaining samurai against the enemy that very night. Instead of dying by the stream, he would die on the field of battle. It was still death, but it was a bolder death, and the god of warriors, Hachiman, favored the bold. Go would insure that the boy was not captured alive by the enemy.

Kneeling as she adjusted Hironobu's child-sized armor, Lady Kiyomi was as tall as he was with his feet in his little warrior's boots and his head topped with a helmet with stylized steel horns. Lady Kiyomi barely restrained her tears. The miniature breastplate, the scaled-down swords, the lacquered gauntlets and shin guards—they were all meant for ceremonial purposes, not combat, but would soon be employed in earnest. The look of pride on Hironobu's face nearly dissolved her restraint. She spoke quickly to block her tears.

"Remember, you are now lord of this realm. Behave appropriately."

"I'll remember," he said. "How do I look, Mother? Do I look like a real samurai?"

"You are the son of Masamuné, Lord of Akaoka, who crushed the Mongol hordes of Kublai Khan at Hakata Bay. You *are* a real samurai. And a real samurai should not be so concerned with mere appearance."

"Yes, Mother, I know. But all the stories about the heroes of old tell about how splendidly they dressed. Their armor, their banners, their silk kimonos, their swords, their horses. It is said that Lord Yoshitsuné's look of warlike confidence alone broke the spirit of his enemies. It is also said that he was very handsome. These are important things for heroes."

Lady Kiyomi said, "Stories always make things up. Heroes are always handsome and victorious. Their ladies are always beautiful and faithful. That's how stories are."

"But Father was handsome and victorious," Hironobu said, "and you are beautiful and faithful. When they tell stories about us, they won't have to make things up."

She did not tell him that all little boys think their fathers are handsome and their mothers beautiful. If she spoke, she would have wept.

He thrust out his chest and put the best semblance of a warrior's scowl on his face. "Do I have a look of warlike confidence, Mother?"

"Stay close to Go," she said, "and do what he says. If it should be your fate to die, then die without hesitation, without fear, without regret."

"I will, Mother. But I don't think I will die in this battle." He reached a finger under his helmet and scratched. "One hundred years ago, at the Battle of Ichinotani, Lord Yoshitsuné had only a hundred men against thousands of foes. Like I do. One hundred twenty-one against five thousand. He won, and I will, too. Will they tell stories about me when I am gone? I think they will."

Lady Kiyomi quickly turned away and dabbed at her eyes with the soft silk of her sleeves. When she turned back, she smiled. She thought of words that would fit a fairy tale, and said them.

"When you return, I will wash the blood of our arrogant enemies from your sword."

Hironobu's face brightened. Like a warrior in combat, he dropped to one knee and gave an abbreviated battlefield bow.

"Thank you, Mother."

She placed her hands on the floor before her and bowed her head low in return.

"I know you will do your best, my lord."

"My lord," Hironobu said. "You called me 'my lord.' "

"Are you not?"

"Yes," he said, and got to his feet. They were eye to eye again. "I am."

She did not expect to see him again. When the courier brought word of his death, she would order the castle set ablaze, then she would plunge the blade of her knife into her throat. There would be no fairy-tale victory, no legends of beauty and courage. Yet they would share one quality with the heroes and ladies of those tales. They would never grow old.

A few days later, the courier did come, but he brought news not of Hironobu's death but of his victory instead. The summer that had begun in such tragedy ended in amazing triumph. Their badly outnumbered samurai had annihilated the better part of an army many times as big as their own.

· · · · ·

Word of young Lord Hironobu's impossible victory in the Muroto Woods spread very quickly. Celebrants came crowding into the domain from every direction. All had heard of the omen of the sparrows and were eager to see the favored young lord for themselves. The small castle, newly rechristened Cloud of Sparrows, became uncomfortably crowded. Near the end of the weeklong festivities, when it appeared certain that most of the visiting samurai lords would soon expire of alcohol poisoning, unpredictably shifting winds and an unusual profusion of lightning and thunder presaged the coming of an early autumn storm. Those who had been preparing to leave now prepared to remain for the foreseeable future. It seemed impossible, but everyone grew drunker. Surprisingly, no one died of it.

Go alone remained sober. Raised on *koumiss*, the strong brew made of mare's milk, he had not acquired a taste for rice wine despite ten years in Japan. When he passed by a drunken gathering, people frequently called out to him.

"Go!"

"Lord General!"

"Lord Go!"

Displaying a smile he did not feel within, Go acknowledged the cheers. Crowds in confined spaces made him uneasy. He still had the nomad's love of open space and hatred of confinement. Being among so many people within the constricting walls of a castle tightened his throat, shortened his breath, and made him sweat as if he were in the early stages of a deadly illness.

But the crowd and the walls were not the main cause of his unease. The storm troubled him even more. Never had he witnessed such horrendous violence in the sky. Not in the steppes of his homeland, not in the vast plains of China, not in the mountains and valleys of Japan. Rapid waves of lightning inflamed the sky, followed momentarily by the pounding hooves of thousands of phantom horses in stampede. In the unpredictable interval between the lightning and the accompanying thunder, Go flinched. The situation was made all the more ominous by the strange lack of turbulence on the ground. Despite the fury above, no wind, no rain, nor any other stormy effect had actually touched them. It was an omen. There could be no doubt whatsoever. But of what? It couldn't herald the approach of another Tangolhun. Go was the last of that line, and he had only one offspring, Chiaki, a son. That curse of witchery could only be empowered by a woman. His wife had given birth to a girl before Chiaki, and two girls after. Go had killed all three female infants at birth. His wife had wept, but she had not questioned him or tried to stop him. As she always promised, she put his happiness before her own. So no new Nürjhen witch had been born, or ever would be. Then why did he feel such fear with every flash of lightning and every rumble of celestial hooves?

Among the Nürjhen tribesmen, a storm after a victory was an omen of great magnitude. The Japanese did not see it that way, of course. To them, a storm was the wrath of the thunder god, a god best placated through offerings of prayers by priests, gifts of food by women and children, and heavy drinking by men. This last was highly predictable. Every event of any significance always called for the consumption of an ocean of sake, the rice wine to which apparently all samurai became addicted at a very early age. If the Nürjhen had drunk so much alcohol, they would never have conquered the rich pasturelands between the Blue Ice Mountains and the Red Dragon River. If the Mongols had, they would not have conquered the Nürjhen, and Go would still be riding with his clansmen in the vast freeness of Central Asia.

"Go! Come share sake with us!"

"Great General! Come, come!"

"Your name will live among the greatest heroes of Yamato forever!"

It was easy for the samurai to praise him lavishly. He was an outsider and would always be an outsider. Thus, he was no threat to any of them. He would never conspire against his lord, never seek dominion for himself, never lead an army to Kyoto to induce the Emperor into granting him the

Shogun's mandate. An outsider could never rule a domain, never command the loyalty of other lords, never be Shogun. That highest honor was reserved for not only samurai but those select few of Minamoto blood, the clan of the legendary Yoshitsuné. Hironobu, through his maternal grandmother, was distantly related to that great family. Perhaps one day he could think of it. But not Go. He was not even Japanese. So the samurai did not hesitate in their loud and sincere praise for him.

Go did not know what the storm portended, but he was not optimistic. He remembered what the old tribesmen said. According to them, the last time the thunder of horses' hooves had sounded so loudly in the clouds above, the greatest witch of the Nürjhen Ordos had been born.

Tangolhun of ancient times.

His mother's ancestress.

The one who told the legendary Attila to follow the sun westward. Supposedly, centuries ago, Attila had done exactly that, the Huns had followed Attila, and they had found their destined homeland at the western edge of the world, where they lived with their herds in fecund pastures to this very day, protected by a ring of mountains, and encamped on both banks of a vast river.

No matter how strongly Go had insisted that this was just a story his mother had made up to support her outrageous claims of magic, the old people could not be convinced.

The Huns of yore, they said, had not all been slaughtered by the Mongols. The ones who had followed Attila had survived to flee beyond the high Urals. One day, the Nürjhen, too, would go there.

The old, secret truths were known by witches, they said, whose spirits rode the storm, the wild herds above. One day, those who shared the secrets would also ride the storm.

His mother's prognostications, they said, were deadly accurate, and the power of her spells was beyond denial. One day, a sorceress would arise whose spells would reveal all mysteries without exception.

Go had laughed at them. His mother was a self-serving, manipulative fake, nothing more.

Now, in far Japan, with the sound of ten thousand invisible steppe ponies thundering above him, he couldn't laugh. Something was coming.

Go did not think it was a blessing.

"Oh." The whispered exclamation followed the sensation of a soft body colliding with his own. He looked down to see a woman sprawled at his feet.

"My apologies," he said, silently cursing his clumsiness. In the open, astride a horse, Go was as nimble as the dragon dancers who had spun around the flames of the Ordos campfires. Inside walls, his nimbleness was more akin to that of a harnessed ox. "I wasn't paying attention."

He reached his hand out to help her to her feet. She gasped and shied away.

She was very pretty. And very young. It was only because of what he had felt when their bodies had met that he knew she was a woman and not still a girl. But she was a woman whose first blush was not long past. By her mode of dress and the delicacy of her movements, he knew she was a noble lady, probably a daughter of one of the visiting lords. Many such were here. Hironobu's improbable triumph had suddenly made him the most eligible six-year-old lordling south of the Inland Sea.

"Are you hurt?" Go said.

The collision had not been particularly violent. No daughter of a Nürjhen khan would have fallen, much less remained on the ground for so long. They could ride and shoot as well as any man, and only a warrior who could outdo them on horseback and with a bow and arrow would dare to woo them. The wives and daughters of Japanese lords were the opposite. They gloried in their weakness. Indeed, they always pretended to be weaker than they actually were. He had once seen his own wife, who had then been a favored concubine of Lord Masamuné, Hironobu's father, break a drunken samurai's collarbone. The man, the retainer of another lord, not knowing who she was, had grabbed her wrist. She made a quick movement with her arm. The next instant, he flew head over heels into a pillar. Another inch to the right and he would have broken his neck.

How did you do that? Go had asked her.

Do what, Lord Go?

Throw the man.

Throw him? I? She covered her mouth with her sleeve and giggled. I am so small and weak, my lord, how could I throw anyone? He was drunk. He tripped. That is all.

No, that wasn't all. But she never said more, even after they were married. Even now, ten years later and after the birth of their son, Chiaki, she would never say anything about it.

It's such a secret, is it?

She laughed and said, How can anything womanly be of sufficient consequence ever to be elevated to the level of a secret?

Go said, If I tried to do something you didn't like, would you throw me?

I could never dislike anything you wished to do, my lord. You are my husband.

What if I wished to cause you pain?

Then I would be happy to feel pain.

What if only your agony could bring me joy?

Then agony would be joy, my lord.

Go laughed loudly. He couldn't help himself. He didn't really believe she would go that far, but she was so serious and so adamant, he couldn't continue with a straight face.

He said, I give up. You win.

She said, How can I win, when I yield to you in every way?

I don't know, Go said, but you always manage somehow, don't you?

She smiled. Do you mean to say I win by losing? That makes no sense, my lord.

Go wondered if this young woman also knew how to throw men. It seemed unlikely. She looked very fragile, even taking into account the way these women all exaggerated the appearance of fragility. She waited for him to step back, then got to her feet with some effort. Her right hip seemed to be injured. She took a tentative step forward, was unable to support herself, and began to fall. Go was ready. He caught her.

"Oh," she said again, as softly as before.

She held on to his arm and leaned her full weight against his chest. It was not much. Besides being very pretty and very young, she was also very light. Perhaps, unlike the others, this one was really as fragile as she seemed. Though she leaned on him out of necessity, her eyes regarded him fearfully, as if she should flee from him rather than press against him for support.

He said, "Be at ease, my lady. I am Go, Lord Hironobu's chief bodyguard. You may rely on me as you would him."

"Oh," she said yet again.

Go smiled. "You say 'oh' very sweetly, my lady. Try another word. Let us see if you can speak it as sweetly, or if your charms are limited to 'oh.' "

At this, the young woman smiled. Looking up at him shyly, she said, "I am Lord Bandan's daughter, Nowaki."

Just then, another peal of thunder echoed through the castle. Something must have shown in Go's face.

"Are you afraid of thunder?" Amusement brightened young Lady Nowaki's face. "I thought you were a mighty Mongol who feared nothing."

"I am not a Mongol at all."

"Aren't you the Go who landed at Hakata Bay with the invaders ten years ago?"

"I am. I was Nürjhen then, and I am Nürjhen now."

"Isn't that a kind of Mongol?"

"Are you a kind of Chinese?"

Lady Nowaki laughed. "No, of course not."

"Just as everyone who wears silk, drinks tea, and writes kanji is not Chinese, so, too, not everyone who rides a horse, follows the herds, and lives free is a Mongol."

"I understand, Lord Go. I will not make the mistake again." She bowed.

Since she was still holding on to him, her bow took her head to his chest, putting her hair close to his face. A most subtle fragrance arose from her abundant tresses. It reminded him of meadow flowers, lost for the year a season ago. Only someone so young would wear a spring fragrance in autumn. The childish inconsistency bespoke a refreshing guilelessness.

"May I assist you to your family's quarters?" Go said.

·　·　·　·　·

Nowaki, her head against his chest, could hear his voice above her and hear it, too, resonating within his body. She hoped he didn't feel the beating of her heart. She closed her eyes and did her best to calm her breathing. There was no reason for fear. Everything was going well. She had easily lost her nursemaid. The old woman, growing ever more vague with the years, had become easier and easier to evade. Otherwise, she would never have been able to engage in her dalliances with Nobuo or Koji earlier in the summer. They were handsome young samurai, but that's all they were. Soon, inevitably, they would grow up to be the men their fathers were. Dull, drunken, loutish, repetitious, bragging country bumpkins.

All that seemed so long ago now. Go was holding her in his arms! He hadn't noticed her following him. She'd kept her courage and took a path that crossed his, colliding with him and pretending injury. Was she brave enough to do the rest?

Ever since she was a little girl, she had heard tales of the fearsome Mongol barbarian who served Lord Masamuné. When her father was allied with Masamuné, awed voices extolled Go's limitless courage, his superhuman strength, his magical control of horses. When the two lords were relentless enemies—which seemed to be about as often as they were faithful friends—his heartless brutality, his animal cunning, and his monstrous perversity were the only things that were said about him. Both kinds of stories fascinated Nowaki. Her life in this provincial wasteland was utterly dull, with dullness her future fate as well. Her father was a country lord with painfully limited vistas. So were all the lords she knew. Her older sisters had been married off to buffoons like her father and brothers—lords of dirt, night soil, and smelly fish. None of them was more than barely literate. None was anything like the cultivated, sensitive, romantic heroes of *The Pillow Book* and *The Tale of Genji*.

Go was unlikely to resemble those heroes, either, but at least he did from afar. He had ridden across the vastness of Asia with Kublai, Great Khan of the Mongol Hordes. He had seen the jeweled cities of China, the land of the ice people in the far north, the exotic beasts of the southern jungles, the high mountains of Tibet. She had never been farther east than the Inland Sea, and no farther west than here in Akaoka Domain. If she did as she was expected to do, she would soon be betrothed to one of those bumpkin lords. Hironobu was the best candidate, and he was a snotty child of six! She would be his nursemaid for the next few years, then she would initiate him, bear his heir, and that would be it. She would spend the rest of her life listening to his drunken lies instead of her father's. Or perhaps her father's other plan would come to fruition, and she would be given away as bride or concubine to a noble of the Imperial Court in Kyoto. She had seen a noble once, a prince who had come calling on her father for help of some sort. He was a pale and powdered weakling who wore finer gowns than she did. He spoke an effeminate, lilting Japanese she could barely understand. The journey from Kyoto was so arduous, he had said, that it almost killed him. Then he'd covered his mouth with his sleeve and giggled like a girl. She would rather die

than be touched by such a degenerate, no matter how exalted his ancestors.

Then one day, early in the summer, she had gone into one of the larger
villages of her father's domain, accompanied by Nobuo and Koji, who
were serving as her bodyguards, an amusing fact considering their dangerous intimacies with her. Out of boredom, she had stopped at the hut of a
crone who was said to be a soothsayer. The old fake put on a good show.
As soon as Nowaki stepped through the doorway, the woman, who was
supposedly blind, stared openmouthed in her direction, dropped the pot
she was holding, and stumbled backward to the far wall.

It's you, the woman said.

Yes, it's me, Nowaki said, trying hard to keep from laughing, and not
quite succeeding. Do you know who I am?

I am blind, but I can see, the woman said, in her best portentous voice.

Oh? And what do you see?

Not as much as you will see.

Now she had Nowaki's full attention. Will I see much?

Much, the woman said.

What will I see? Nowaki hoped the woman would speak of faraway
places. If she did, Nowaki would eagerly believe she was a real visionary.
Tell me quickly, without delay.

You will see . . . The woman paused with her mouth still open. Her lips
trembled, her eyelids flickered, her sunken cheeks twitched.

Nowaki waited patiently. Provisionally, at least, the woman deserved
forbearance. Even if she couldn't really tell fortunes, she was at the least a
very good performer and, like all good performers, had her own sense of
timing, which must be respected. She was quite wasted in this isolated little place. If she were in Kyoto or Kobe or Edo, she would no doubt attract
quite a clientele.

The woman said, You will see what no one else has ever seen—will
ever see in your lifetime—save one.

Nowaki clapped her hands together happily. The one other the old
woman spoke of had to be Go. He was the only one she knew of who had
ever seen anything no one else had ever seen. And now she would see
those things, too!

Thank you, thank you so very much, Nowaki said, bowing deeply.
When I return to the castle, I will have rice and sake and fish sent to you.

The old woman held up her hands defensively and shook her head. She still sat on her haunches with her back to the wall where she had first fallen. No, no, you owe me nothing.

Oh, but I do, Nowaki said. You have made me very happy.

That very afternoon, she began thinking of ways to first meet Go, then to seduce him. It was true that she was very young, but she had read the classics of seduction with great care, and she had already had actual practice with Nobuo and Koji. Go would be more difficult, of course. She was confident she would find a way, if only she could also find an opportunity.

The celebration of Hironobu's victory in the Muroto Woods gave it to her.

· · · · ·

"I don't want to go where my family is," Nowaki said. "Everyone is drunk, and they keep repeating the same stupid things they always say when they're drunk."

"They are celebrating a great victory," Go said, "and so have every right to be drunk."

"You have won the victory, not them," she said, looking up at him. "With Mongol tactics and Mongol courage." Nowaki felt his body tighten. Oh, no. She'd made the mistake again and called him a Mongol. What was it he had said he was? Foreign words were very hard to remember. Na-lu-something. She was afraid she had spoiled everything by making him angry. She feigned pain and leaned more heavily against him. Her show of distress seemed to work, for when he spoke again, he didn't sound angry.

"The victory is Lord Hironobu's," Go said, holding her a little more firmly as she pretended to weaken.

"Lord Hironobu is a baby of six," she said, "barely big enough to go to the toilet alone without falling in."

Go laughed. "Nevertheless, the victory is his. And he won't be six forever. You would be wise to think of him in a different light. Soon he will be a man as well as a lord, and he will seek a worthy bride. He has been favored by a great omen carried to him on the wings of many birds."

"I don't believe in omens," Nowaki said. "Do you?"

Lightning crackled, followed by long moments of eerie silence.

A wave of brightness rolled overhead.

Daylight shadows played across the courtyard, then faded back into a darkness that seemed to rush in their direction.

At last, the sky broke apart and the gigantic sound of collapsing celestial mountains cascaded toward them from above.

· · · · ·

Within weeks after Lady Nowaki's return home from Hironobu's celebration, it became apparent that she was with child. Though she had always been a quiet and obedient daughter, she now adamantly refused to name the child's father, knowing that her father and brothers would surely kill him. When they threatened to abort the child, she promised to kill herself if they did. Lord Bandan executed the girl's nursemaid, who should have exercised more careful supervision. Still, she refused to speak. He executed two of his own men, whom he suspected of excessive fondness for his daughter. Still, Lady Nowaki remained silent.

"I am at my wit's end," Lord Bandan said.

During this crisis with his daughter, he had taken to visiting Cloud of Sparrows Castle and seeking Lady Kiyomi's advice. Though he was only a little older than she, he had spent so much of his life in military campaigns that in appearance and behavior he seemed like a grizzled old warrior of an earlier generation. His interest in women had extended only as far as the conception, birth, and nurturing of potential heirs, and thus he knew next to nothing about women beyond their basic anatomical structure. His own daughter's sudden wayward behavior and subsequent stubbornness baffled him completely. The girl's mother had died during childbirth, and there was no woman in his own castle he trusted enough to speak with so openly.

"Why won't she just tell me who the father is? That's all I want. Is that too much for me to ask?"

Lady Kiyomi said, "What will you do if she tells you?"

Lord Bandan slammed the table with his fist, causing the maids to jump forward to keep the teacups from bouncing off and spilling their contents onto the mats.

"I'll kill him," he growled, "and not slowly."

She covered her mouth with her sleeve and laughed.

"Have I made a joke?" Confusion wrinkled his brow. "I didn't intend to."

"Lord Bandan, do you really expect a young girl to reveal her lover's identity to her father so he can then torture him to death? Her child would be orphaned before it's born."

"But he has dishonored us all, whoever he is."

"Lady Nowaki is not thinking of honor. She is thinking of love. All you have done with your anger and your threats is to prevent the young man from coming forward and seeking your belated blessings."

"You know that he's a young man?"

"I know nothing at all. But your daughter is only fourteen. It is doubtful she would have fallen in love with anyone so very much older." Lady Kiyomi's expression darkened. "I hope he was not one of the two samurai you executed."

"He wasn't. She cried when I showed her their heads, but not as much as she would have cried if he had been one of them."

Lady Kiyomi blinked. "You showed her their heads?"

"Yes, to prove I did what I said. Otherwise, she might have thought I was bluffing."

"Lord Bandan, no one who knows you would ever suspect you of bluffing. It was quite unnecessary to provide such gruesome proof."

"She's not going to tell me, is she?"

"No, she's not."

"Then what should I do? The shame will be unendurable. My daughter having a child whose father is unknown to me. By all the gods and Buddhas, what wrongs did I commit in past lives to deserve such punishment? I could build a temple and have prayers said night and day, for all time. I can't think of much else that's left to do."

"That's a possible solution," Lady Kiyomi said.

Now Lord Bandan laughed. "This time I *was* joking. I am a warrior, not a priest. I don't beg heaven for favors. I solve my problems with my own hands. I'll think of something."

"You already have. Build a temple."

Lord Bandan scowled. "If the gods failed to preserve her virtue then, they are not likely to deliver up the culprit to me now, whether I build one temple or ten."

"Build a temple, not for yourself," Lady Kiyomi said, "but for Lady Nowaki. Let her enter into retreat there for, say, two years. She can have the child away from gossips, have time to regain her emotional equilibrium, and adjust to the demands of motherhood. And when she returns, she will no longer be such an object of curiosity and spiteful speculation. By that time, it is likely that the father will have made himself known, most likely by flight, thanks to your threats of torture and death. You will then—"

"—hunt him down like the dog he is and eviscerate him!" Lord Bandan proclaimed.

"—forgive him and her for their youthful transgression in full understanding of the romantic impetuosity of the young—"

"Forgive him? Never!"

"—and realizing further that only by welcoming the father into your family," Lady Kiyomi said firmly, "can embarrassment and scandal finally be left behind."

Lord Bandan had already opened his mouth to utter further protests, but stopped before any words came out. He closed his mouth and bowed.

"You are right, Lady Kiyomi. That is the only way to proceed. Thank you for so wisely guiding this ignorant warrior. I already know of a suitable site. My cousin, Lord Fumio, rules a domain in the north that will be suitable for our purposes."

· · · · ·

That winter, Lady Kiyomi began to have strange dreams. The strangest aspect of them was that she was never able to remember anything except the stunningly beautiful young woman who appeared in every one, and the way she spoke to Lady Kiyomi. She called her "Lady Mother." That was how women addressed their mothers-in-law. Convinced that she was dreaming of Hironobu's future bride, Lady Kiyomi began examining the face of every little girl she saw in an effort to recognize the woman in her dreams. Though the dreams continued, she never remembered anything more of them, no matter how hard she tried. And though she searched for the woman in every girl she saw, she did not find her.

The following spring, several weeks before his seventh birthday, Lord Hironobu won a second great victory, this time on the slopes of Mount Tosa. At the same time, in the neighboring domain, Lady Nowaki gave birth to a daughter. The child was unusually quiet—so quiet, few expected her to survive. Though she was given a name befitting her noble status, everyone called her Shizuka—Quiet.

She did not die, and she was not quiet for long. In her second week of life, she began to scream and weep almost ceaselessly. She stopped only in exhaustion, or to sleep fitfully, or to suckle with a fierce desperation, and then not for long. She was an infant, and infants cannot see, yet what she could not see terrified her. Her eyes flitted in panic in every direction.

She screamed.

She would not die and she would not stop screaming.

Now she was called Shizuka, sometimes out of hope, always out of despair, and more and more often as a curse.

· · · · ·

The next year, when Lady Kiyomi visited Mushindo Abbey, she had occasion to contemplate the recent past. The four seasons just completed had spanned the strangest, most turbulent year of her life. She understood now why people sometimes abruptly became world-leavers and entered a monastic life. If she had such an inclination, then this would be a good place for it. It was too far from home to make visitations easy, but not so far as to make them impossible. This meant that friends and relatives from the old life would not constantly appear to weaken one's dedication to holy solitude, but would also not be cut off entirely. That would not be compassionate. Leaving the world was often harder for those left behind than for those who did the leaving.

It was close enough to the northern frontier to create a sense of danger and, thus, urgency, a useful ingredient for those who sought an awakening to Buddha's Way. Yet, it was not so close to the lands of the Emishi barbarians that any attack was truly likely. The nearest habitation, Yamanaka Village, was an hour's walk away in the valley below the modest mountain upon which the abbey stood. This, too, was ideal, since its proximity allowed it to provide sustenance and labor on short notice, while its distance prevented excessive interaction, and its size was sufficient to support a small religious establishment without undue difficulty.

That an abbey had to be built at all was unfortunate; of course, worse outcomes had been possible, though perhaps not many.

From the garden of the abbey where Lady Kiyomi waited for Lady Nowaki, she could hear Hironobu's voice coming from the woods nearby, and Go's muffled replies.

Another summer had arrived and almost gone, and everything was different. Only one year ago, her husband, the Lord of Akaoka, controlled a few farms and a few fishing villages of no particular importance in a small corner of Shikoku island. Now her son Hironobu, at seven years of age, ruled territory on both sides of the Inland Sea. He had gained the sworn fealty of Lords Bandan and Hikari, and had risen to the status of Great Lord. In two lightning campaigns, her little boy's forces had so badly battered the Hojo regime that many were predicting its imminent demise.

A year ago, Lady Nowaki had been a fourteen-year-old virgin, pretty enough that her family had aspired to a link with the Imperial Family in Kyoto. Now she was the fifteen-year-old mother of an insane infant, cloistered in an abbey far from home, an abbey built especially to provide refuge for her and her unfortunate offspring. Because of the defects of the child, it was apparent that neither would ever leave the abbey.

A year ago, it had never occurred to Lady Kiyomi to travel so far to the north even once. Indeed, the only other times she had crossed the Inland Sea was when she had left her home in Kobe to marry Hironobu's father, and then on yearly visits to her family there. Now she had promised Lord Bandan she would visit his daughter twice a year, in the spring and the autumn, to see that she was well. Since she was the Great Lord's mother, and the Great Lord himself accompanied her on these visits, it was a great honor to Lord Bandan, particularly given the unpleasant circumstances. This simple act of kindness alone would bind him even more tightly to Hironobu by the demands of honor and reciprocal obligation.

As the de facto regent for her son, it was necessary for her to consider such things. The official regent, General Ryusuke, was a well-meaning incompetent. He was regent only because, as the senior surviving commander of the clan's army, it was expected of him—and because he was smart enough to know he was not smart enough to actually exercise the power of the office. Otherwise, it would have been necessary to kill him, since to pass him over would be an insult so egregious, he would have been obligated to conspire against Lady Kiyomi and Hironobu, whether he wanted to or not. She would not have done it herself, of course. Only witches killed their enemies with their own hands, usually by poisoning, or by a thin wire or a needle in the temple, under the hair, or by suffocation. The latter two methods were nearly undetectable, and therefore particularly favored by witches who slept with their victims. The thought of having to sleep with a dullard like General Ryusuke made her grimace. That alone would have been enough to stop her, even if she had been a witch. In fact, if any killing had been necessary, Go would have carried it out. Though he was a barbarian, he was as steadfastly loyal as any samurai could be. How lucky she and her son were to have him at their side.

The frantic cries of a baby came from within the abbey. Shizuka was awake.

· · · · ·

Hironobu climbed up onto a stone outcropping and said, "Go, if you had to defend this abbey from attack, how would you do it?"

Go said, "The first thing I would do is stop making myself such an easy target for enemy archers."

"There aren't any enemy archers around now," Hironobu said. "I mean 'if.'"

"You are a Great Lord," Go said. "If you are going to make assumptions about existing conditions, then you would be well advised to assume danger rather than safety."

Crestfallen, Hironobu stepped back down to the forest floor. "Must I always worry so much about being killed?"

"You should never worry about it," Go said, "but you must always be aware of the possibility. You have seized fifteen domains by force of arms, and so have made blood enemies of the former retainers and clansmen of the fifteen lords whom you have helped move on to the Pure Land."

"They have sworn to obey me in return for their lives."

"Are you really so young, my lord?"

"I am seven," Hironobu said. "That's not so young."

A high keening wail suddenly erupted from within the walls of the abbey.

Hironobu stepped close to Go. "Someone is being tortured. It's not right to do it in a holy place, is it?"

"No one is being tortured. It's a baby crying."

"A baby?" Hironobu listened again, his face doubtful. "I've heard babies cry. They don't sound like that."

"It's a baby," Go said. In the cold hollow of his chest, he could almost hear the echo of his own words. It's a baby, he said, but meant, It's a witch.

How had it happened? He wasn't sure. He had gone over that night again and again in his mind, and still he didn't know.

One moment, he was helping Lord Bandan's daughter to her quarters. The next, he was lying with her in the ruins of an old Emishi barbarian fort an hour's ride away from the castle. He had taken advantage of her youth and inexperience, he knew that much. He hadn't intended to, not at all. At first, it was only a walk, then a ride on his stallion, then shelter in those ruins from the sudden squall. Then—then it was too late to think, for what was done was done.

Go was not afraid to die. He had expected to die on the shores of Hakata Bay when he had landed with the Mongol army ten years ago, and he probably should have. Every moment since had been a gift of the gods. Now death was only a matter of time. The girl had promised not to say anything, but she was a girl, after all. Eventually, someone would hear of it, and once someone did, her father would, too. Go's head would end up on the end of a pike outside the gates of his castle. The image brought a bitter smile to his lips. At least he would have the satisfaction of knowing with certainty that his mother's bloodline died with him. Witches must span time in unbroken generations. If none was born to Go, it did not matter how many daughters were born to Chiaki or his descendants. The spell would be broken.

But weeks passed and no messenger came from Lord Bandan to Lord Hironobu demanding Go's head. Perhaps Nowaki was more resolute than he gave her credit for. Unlikely as it seemed, she was keeping the secret. If she continued to do so, no harm would come of his folly. When a messenger finally came, he wasn't an official courier but a gossip, and he brought something worse than Go's death warrant. Lady Nowaki was pregnant. He knew right away what had happened. Somehow, his mother had won. She had used him one last time from the grave to open a pathway for another of her kind.

He had to kill the witch. The safest way was to kill Nowaki, so the witch would die in the womb. Once born, witches were very hard to kill, even as infants. People around them unwittingly did their bidding, compelled by unknown forces to obey unspoken commands. His grandfather and his father, both mighty warriors, had been reduced to dried-up husks of their former selves by the demands of the one who was the daughter of the first, and the wife of the second. All his life, as boy, youth, and man, Go had been shamed by the taunts of his tribesmen. Witch's boy. Woman's dog. Eunuch's spawn. Yet in front of his mother, they were cowed, respectful, submissive. They hated her, and despised her kin. But when she spoke of the future, they listened, and brought offerings. When she cast spells, the sick were healed, the healthy died, the deaf could hear, and her enemies all went blind. Or so it often seemed. Often enough, his mother liked to remind him, to keep their campfire burning, their horses fed and watered, and their own bellies full.

How to kill Nowaki. It was a difficult problem. She was the daughter of a lord confined to the innermost part of a castle unfamiliar to him. Stealth would be the best way to approach. Unfortunately, stealth was not a skill he possessed. His way was the way of the horseman. Attack mounted, at full stride, from an unexpected direction. Not a tactic suitable for the women's quarters of a castle. He waited for a chance, any chance, and got none. Two months before it was due, the child was born.

It was, as he knew and feared it would be, a girl.

· · · · ·

"It's a baby," Go said.

"Are you sure?" Hironobu said, his expression still highly doubtful.

"Yes."

"Have you seen it?"

"No."

"I haven't, either," Hironobu said. "Neither has my mother. Nobody has. That's odd, don't you think?"

Go shook his head. "There is something wrong with the child, so the family is not eager to display it. That's quite natural."

That piqued Hironobu's interest. "Do you think it's deformed? That would really be terrible, wouldn't it?"

"It's not deformed." The infant was insane, a fact that gave Go hope. All witches were fundamentally insane, of course, but one who displayed it so obviously would have less power to manipulate, trick, and confuse. In that way, insanity was better than deformity. A witch could get away with ugliness. It was expected of them. His mother, however, had not been ugly. Quite the opposite, and it had given her even more opportunities to deceive.

"You had better go see your mother, lord. Her visit with Lady Nowaki will begin soon, I think."

"Why must I?" Hironobu scowled. "I'm not interested in babies, deformed or not, though maybe if it were deformed, I might be a little curious, at least. And I don't want to hear any mother talk, either. That's all the two of them are going to do: Talk about babies and motherhood."

"Lord Bandan is your most powerful vassal," Go said. "You honor him by visiting his afflicted offspring and showing compassion for them. Thus his debt of honor to you grows ever greater, binding him to you more strongly. This is a matter of wise command, not motherhood and babies."

"So you say. You're not the one who has to sit there through it." But Hironobu did as he was told, and went to join the two ladies. At the gate to the temple he turned back and called out to Go, "Why don't you come, too?"

"I am not permitted," Go said. "Lady Nowaki is in retreat."

"Then why am I permitted? Because I'm just a child?"

"You are permitted because you are Great Lord of the domain."

The answer, which he had not expected, pleased him greatly. He was smiling when he entered the gate.

"Here he is now," Lady Kiyomi said.

He saw his mother and Lady Nowaki sitting in an open room overlooking the courtyard garden. Lady Nowaki was the same No-chan of summers past who flew kites with him, and played hide-and-seek, and told ghost stories when they should have been asleep. That was before he became Great Lord. And that was before she grew up so suddenly. She looked very different from the girl he remembered. It wasn't so much her clothing, though her drab gray nun's robes contrasted sharply with the colorful kimono she used to wear. Her face, framed by the hood of the surplice, was that of a beautiful woman.

Lady Nowaki bowed to him. "I regret I have caused you inconvenience, my lord."

Hironobu returned her bow. "I am happy to see you again, Lady Nowaki." He tried to think of more to say, but nothing came to him. She smiled at him, and he felt himself blushing. When had she become so beautiful?

Lady Nowaki said, "My, my, how he has grown in such a brief time."

"Yes," Lady Kiyomi said, "children—" She stopped abruptly as soon as she said the word, then went on rather too quickly. "Children grow at an astonishing rate."

"You have much to look forward to," Lady Nowaki said. "The young lord's future is very bright." Her eyes watered, but she smiled and no tears fell.

Hironobu didn't hear the baby screaming. It must be asleep. He'd overheard two of his maids talking just before he and his mother had departed for the abbey. One of the maids said she had heard from one of Lord Bandan's maids that the only time it didn't scream was when it was asleep. The other maid said she had heard from the sister of one of Lord Bandan's grooms that when it screamed, the horses panicked and tried to kick down the stable doors. Neither maid knew anyone who knew anyone who had claimed to have actually seen it, but both were nevertheless certain it was frightening to behold.

While his mother and Nowaki talked, he peeked into the room as inconspicuously as he could. He thought the sleeping baby might be behind Lady Nowaki somewhere, but it wasn't. That was a disappointment. He was very curious. Go said the baby wasn't deformed, but Hironobu didn't believe him. A normal baby didn't have that kind of weird, animal voice, and it couldn't scream so loudly. A normal baby wouldn't make horses panic, either, especially those of the fierce warlike kind ridden by Lord Bandan and his samurai.

What did it really look like? He was sure it had a big mouth, and maybe even a snout, like a bear. Sharp teeth, too. Well, it was too young to have teeth yet, but when it did, they would be sharp. Maybe in several rows, like a shark. Did it have unblinking eyes, like a snake? Thick fur like a badger, or the harsh, bristly hair of a wild boar? A long tail that thought for itself, like a cat's? It must be a horrible little monster! No wonder Lord Bandan had exiled his daughter so far away from home. And who was the father?

Before the baby was born, the maids had mentioned the names of many samurai as possibilities, samurai in the service of Lord Bandan, Lord Hikari, and even Hironobu. But no one thought that anymore, the maids said. Everyone was now sure a demon or a ghost had been at work. It might have used a man's body, but the man was just a tool; his identity wasn't important. The important thing was, which demon, which ghost?

In order for the right prayers to be said, the exorcists needed to know the specific malevolent spirit responsible. Incantations that served to drive one away could easily have the reverse effect on another, and make it stronger and more horrible than ever. It was, the maids agreed, a very tragic and dangerous situation, and everyone was much better off with the mother and child far away in an abbey to the north, since the evil entity would likely follow them there.

"Hironobu, what do you think you're doing?" His mother's words startled him. He hadn't thought she was paying any attention to him. "You're acting like a prowling thief."

"I'm not doing anything, Mother. I'm just here with you, because Go said I should be."

"I'm sure Go didn't mean that you should stay. Now that you have paid your respects to Lady Nowaki, you may rejoin Go outside."

Hironobu, a stubborn look on his face, made no move to obey her. He stood where he was, frowned, and said, "That won't do. I'm being sent hither and thither by bodyguard and mother, which is not appropriate for a Great Lord."

Lady Kiyomi smiled. "You are quite right as far as it goes. But it is entirely appropriate for a seven-year-old. Please act in that capacity and do as you are told." She bowed, but it was the shallow bow of a mother bowing to her child, and not that of a lady bowing to her lord.

"The two are not compatible," Hironobu said. "If I am Great Lord, then I am Great Lord. If I'm just a little boy, then that's all I am."

"Your two roles are not compatible, it is true," Lady Kiyomi said. "Please reconcile them nonetheless. In the future, when you are leader of the clan in fact as well as in name, you will sometimes have to do two, three, even four or more things at once, and not one of them will be compatible with any other. If you cannot do these things, and bring them into harmony even if harmony seems impossible, then you will never truly be Great Lord. You will only have the name." His mother bowed again, this time deeply, and held the bow. "I hope my lord finds my words not entirely without value."

Hironobu returned her bow with one of appropriate depth, and also held it. He said, with equal formality, "Your words have much merit. I thank you for them."

As he left the compound to return to Go, he heard Nowaki say, "You have done a splendid job. He is more little man than little boy."

He was smiling even more broadly when he left the temple than he had been when he entered it. He hadn't managed to see the baby as he had hoped. No matter. There would be other opportunities in the future. One day he would see. He promised himself he would. Maybe he could even clip off a bit of its fur to show to his companions back at the castle.

· · · · ·

Go had just completed a careful circuit of the temple perimeter when he saw Hironobu returning. He had been seeking a weak point where he might be able to enter unobserved during some future night and had found none. Lord Bandan had built Mushindo Abbey like a small fortress. Go knew that the nuns who lived there had until recently been servants in Lady Nowaki's inner chamber, which meant they were skilled with weapons like the long-bladed spear, the short sword, and the dagger. They were also likely to know how to cripple and throw attackers, too, and maybe worse. He did not recognize the three men of military bearing who occupied the groundskeeper's hut outside the walls, but they were obviously samurai, not gardeners.

"I didn't get to see the baby," Hironobu said.

"As I told you," Go said. "Lady Nowaki and the baby were sent here to be hidden, not displayed."

"I still think it's deformed," Hironobu said. "What are you doing?"

"Walking. What does it look like I'm doing?"

"I don't know. More than just walking."

Go smiled. Hironobu noticed things most boys his age did not. That was promising. Perhaps one day he would grow to fill the reputation created by two strange flights of birds and a string of unexpected battlefield victories.

"Go?"

"Yes, my lord."

"What is the difference between a ghost and a demon?"

"Why do you ask?"

"Because it might help to know which fathered Nowaki's child."

Go stopped and stared at Hironobu. "Who says either did?"

"Everyone," Hironobu said, "but they can't decide which. What's the difference? Aren't both supernatural beings?"

"A demon is a creature with origins in another realm," Go said. "A ghost is the spirit of a being who once lived here on earth."

"Which is more likely to enter a man and use his body?"

"What?"

"I think a ghost," Hironobu said. "A creature from another realm would just kill the man and do as he wished with the lady. But a ghost, a ghost has no body, and so has to use one that's already here. That makes sense, doesn't it?" He waited for Go to answer, but his bodyguard just kept staring at him in silence. He looked afraid, which was impossible. Go feared nothing.

· · · · ·

Lady Nowaki's sorrowful look touched Lady Kiyomi deeply. Losing children in violent death, as she had, was tragic, but it did not compare to the agony of having a living defective child. It was the great gift of the gods that inconceivable wellsprings of love began to flow in every mother as her baby grew within her. Thus, every hardship, every burden, every pain of maternity could be borne without complaint, and when the child arrived, it found a home in the bosom of an all-embracing, inexhaustible love. But where was that love to go, and to whom was it of even the least benefit, when the child was as Lady Nowaki's? How unbearably sad to experience such crushing disappointment after waiting with such hope and happiness for so many months. And now, of course, the child's father would never come forward, so Lady Nowaki's situation was all the more lonely. She would have to suffer alone. The tears in Lady Nowaki's eyes, which she was struggling so hard to contain, brought tears of her own to Lady Kiyomi. She raised the sleeve of her kimono to absorb them.

She said, "How the dust does get in one's eyes here. It must be because the abbey is on a mountain, and lacks the protection of dense foliage."

"So true," Lady Nowaki said, using her sleeves as Lady Kiyomi did. She was deeply grateful to her for the excuse to do so, though of course she could not say anything of it. "And, unfortunately, winds so often raise the dust of mountains."

As Lady Kiyomi and the unfortunate young mother wept together while pretending not to do so, Lady Kiyomi's thoughts went to the child. She prayed to the gods and Buddhas to take the little girl to their realm very soon and grant her peace, a peace she would surely never find on earth.

1308, MUSHINDO ABBEY

By the time the great change occurred in her life, only the Reverend Abbess Suku still spoke of her as Shizuka. Out of the Abbess's presence, everyone else called her Wild Eyes, a reference to her most noticeable characteristic, the rapid changes in direction, awareness, and expression that kept her eyes in constant movement—except when they stared relentlessly at a sight only she could see. Her penchant for screaming was not as pronounced as it had been in her infancy, though occasionally the sound of her agonized voice would echo through the temple without end for days at a time. So disruptive was her presence, refuge at Mushindo Abbey was sought only by nuns who were earnest, dedicated, not easily distracted seekers of the Way, despite the generous patronage of Lady Kiyomi and Lord Bandan, which made conditions there considerably less austere than at most places of religious discipline. One of the nuns, noticing that the eyes of dreamers moved about in similar fashion beneath closed eyelids, expressed the view that the girl was never completely awake or completely asleep. Eventually, the other nuns came around to this point of view, since it would explain why she seemed to see things that were not there when her eyes were open and never displayed any evidence of restful repose when they were closed. She twitched and shifted and cried and mouthed senseless words almost as much in either case. It was even possible she was more peaceful when she was awake, for there were long spells when she would stand or sit or lie inert, her eyes staring, as if frozen in place by what she saw.

When the change occurred, it came utterly without warning.

The two nuns responsible that day for cleaning and feeding the girl had decided to delay their tasks. The canine wail, interspersed with sobs, indicated to them that proceeding now would be futile. They were debating whether it would be better to ask the Abbess's permission or act on their own initiative when the cries suddenly ceased. They were used to hearing the crazed, sorrowful voice slowly, fitfully choke and gasp into silence, as if by strangulation. Never before had they heard it end so abruptly.

"Something has happened," the first nun said.

"She has died," said the second.

The first nodded. Truth be told, it was entirely unexpected—it would not be appropriate in these circumstances to refer to it as miraculous—that she had survived this long. So extensive, relentless, and profound was the madness that possessed her, it limited her ability to perform the most fundamental survival tasks, even with the assistance of compassionate followers of the Way. What might be considered the minimum acceptable levels of nutrition, rest, and cleanliness often could not be met. It seemed likely that the girl's time had come at last.

They rushed to her cell, expecting to find her body sprawled on the floor. At first glance, they saw what they expected. She sat slumped against a wall in the farthest corner of the cell, motionless. Steeling themselves against the stench, the two unlocked the door and entered.

"We should call the Reverend Abbess."

"It would be better to confirm her condition first."

"Very well. Then let us attend to the body."

The two put their hands together in gassho, the Buddhist gesture of respect and acceptance, and moved deeper into the cell.

"Wait," said the first nun.

She need not have spoken. The second nun had already stopped. They had both noticed the same thing. The girl's eyes were not flitting around in their usual mad manner, but neither did they have the typical appearance of the eyes of the dead. They were sparkling brightly. And they seemed to be looking straight at the two nuns.

"How unnerving."

"I thought for a moment—"

"Yes, so did I. But it isn't so. The dead can't see. Look. There is blood on the floor around her."

"She has suffered a fatal hemorrhage."

"The mind and body can endure only so much."

"Let us proceed."

They continued forward, though somewhat more slowly than before. Then another unprecedented event occurred.

Shizuka smiled.

The first nun would have fallen if the second, who was directly behind her, had not caught her.

"Call the Abbess," the first nun said.

· · · · ·

The instant before the change, the voices wailing in Shizuka's ears were so loud and so many, she hardly knew she was wailing herself. Then the dreadful noise diminished drastically in volume, but took on an even more disturbing quality. She had never heard anything like it before. It was several moments before she realized what it was.

The sound of her own voice.

Never before had she heard it unaccompanied by the cacophony of the other voices that filled her aural world. Its solitary nature so shocked her, she stopped screaming. When she did, she experienced something even more strange.

Silence.

There were no voices screaming, laughing, crying, begging, cursing, talking. There was none of the noise of the vast machines that sometimes roared through her cell, or the herds of gigantic animals, or the crowds in uniforms or in rags, in ranks and files, or in riotous mobs.

All at once, not only her hearing but her every sense attained a singularity it had never before possessed. All at once, moments were sequential, discrete, without the slightest evidence of simultaneity, passing in orderly fashion one after the other, from past to future, and never the other way. Myriad people had always been with her: transparent or substantial in appearance; happy, sad, indifferent; aware or oblivious; young, old, skeletal, unborn; dead or alive. These constant companions were gone.

She was alone.

At first, the clarity, so sudden, so unfamiliar, only added to her confusion.

A terrible stench permeated the air, what she later learned were the foul emanations of her own unwashed sweat, feces, urine, and regurgitated food. She noticed this, not because of its unpleasantness, but because of its uniqueness; always before, odors of every kind from every source were so commingled, she could not distinguish one from the other, a result not very different from having no sense of smell at all.

After her ears and her nose, it was the turn of her eyes. It would have been her eyes first, had they been open at the time, but they were closed, as they often were. There was no particular purpose to having open eyes when what she saw was the same as when they were closed. Now she was fascinated by the sight of four walls, one ceiling, and one floor in all their solidity, unpenetrated by and not coexistent with any other object, natural and otherwise, as they had always been before.

As strange and as terrifying as these experiences were, they did not compare to the one that now seized her entire attention.

Something huge was clutching her.

She tried to get away from it, but when she moved, it moved, too.

When she realized it was inside her clothing with her, she almost began screaming again, which would have returned her to the only way she had engaged the world thus far in her life. But she didn't scream, because when she opened her mouth she felt it on her face as well and, putting her hand to her face, understood what was clinging to her.

Her own skin.

Her hands touched it, tentatively at first, then with increasing excitement. That which her hands touched and the hands that did the touching were the same. Her skin described the totality of the outer surface of her body, forming something she did not until then know existed.

A limit to her being. Separation between herself and everything else.

It was a liberating revelation.

She and the universe were not one.

Now something else moved, this time within her torso, forcing the bones of her ribs outward to an alarming extent. Just as she began to fear it would do her serious harm, it escaped out of her, and her chest became still once again. She looked around her cell but could see nothing. Had the curse of multiple vision been lifted from her only to be replaced by one of partial blindness? Then somehow, without her noticing it, it got back inside her and began forcing her ribs outward again.

"Ahhh—" she said, and found that air came out of her as her lungs contracted.

She was breathing.

Surely, she had been breathing all along. In the wild riot of everything possible happening at once, she had never noticed. For several moments, she closed her eyes and simply followed the air in and out of her body. Her breathing slowed, her chest moved less and her abdomen more, and she grew calmer. Air, within and without, gave her an intimate connection with all else.

So her skin was not an absolute boundary. She was apart, but not entirely apart.

The sound of wood creaking made her open her eyes. She was horrified to see a section of the wall moving slowly inward. She froze. Had she somehow, unknowingly, found clarity only to lose it so soon? Was she already slipping back into multiplicity, simultaneity, and chaos?

Two beings came through the opening in the wall. Their appearance was substantial enough that she could not see through them. This happened sometimes, though not often. Usually, the beings she saw possessed a vaguer presence. Those of this kind were much rarer. This was no comfort. Solid or amorphous, they would arrive in impossible numbers again, and crowd out her new clarity.

"Wait," the first being said. The two stopped and stared at her.

"How unnerving," the second being said.

Shizuka listened to them talk, not daring to move. At any moment, she expected more voices to emanate from every direction, until, in a reflexive effort to block them out, she herself would begin screaming again. But she heard only the voices of the two beings in front of her. As they moved slowly toward her, she saw twin darknesses on the floor of the cell moving with them. They were casting shadows. As she was. They were not hallucinations but actual people, present in this cell. She was not losing her clarity. Indeed, it was growing ever stronger.

Shizuka smiled.

Both beings staggered backward. The one in front almost knocked the other one down as she retreated hastily.

"Call the Abbess," the first one said.

Shizuka wondered why they were so afraid.

Did they see the terrifying sights she no longer saw?

. . . . .

Shizuka's newfound clarity did not last. Within three days, she began to hear disembodied voices again, see what was not there, experience the flow of events against the actual passage of time, observe multiple objects and entities occupying the same space and penetrating each other. By the end of a week, she was lost again in chaos.

With the next cycle of the moon, clarity returned. Were these new periods of quiet as random as the madness? No, for something was different. The second time, as the first, her breasts grew tender and swollen, and there was an outward flow of her life's blood, which she knew signaled the passage of a season of her own body. It was this blood that temporarily stilled the visions. It had to be, for there was nothing else that could account for it so perfectly.

In the ensuing quietude, which she knew would end as surely as had the first, she carefully examined her every action. What did she experience that encouraged chaotic thoughts and imaginings? That enhanced the quiet, and stilled distraction?

Of the first, chief were emotions, particularly those of anger, fear, and greed.

Of the second, the most reliable was the simple act of breathing, with awareness, but without forced control.

There were certain to be many more actions in each category. In the short time she had during her second cycle, these were the ones she found. When chaos returned, she breathed into it, and this time she had moments of clarity even during the madness. They were brief instants only, but they were there and they had never been before.

Shizuka was learning. Until now, chaos had controlled her. If she learned to control chaos instead, she would be free.

The moon made another passage and the blood tide rose in her again. She practiced what she had learned. With every succeeding moon, she did better than the time before. When the bleeding ended, and the visions began, she stayed with her breath, she was not angry or afraid, she did not desire, and the visions were not as overwhelming as they had been. She was not able to suppress them entirely. But she was able to keep them in the background for longer periods.

She began to think she could soon escape entirely.

Until, in the midst of her eighth tide, one of her visions, as vague and as wispy as smoke, saw her and spoke to her.

1867, THE RUINS OF MUSHINDO MONASTERY

Kimi led the way to the newly rebuilt abbot's meditation hut and proudly opened the door for Lady Hanako and Lady Emily.

"It's just as it was before the explosion, isn't it?" she said.

"I was never inside this hut," Hanako said. "The first and only time I ever saw Mushindo was during the battle."

"Oh," Kimi said. That was too bad. Since her rescue in Yokohama, she had devoted herself to the rebuilding, along with Goro and the women who had remained with them. Doing Buddha's work was reward in itself, of course. Yet it would have been nice if someone acknowledged their efforts.

The two ladies had a brief conversation in the outsider language. Then Hanako turned to Kimi and said, "Have you been following a floor plan during the rebuilding?"

"No, my lady," Kimi said. "We've been following Goro's memory. It's quite remarkable."

Hanako said some outsider words to Emily, who nodded and looked disappointed.

"Thank you, Kimi," Hanako said. "If you are sure it is appropriate, we will spend the night here."

"Oh, of course, Lady Hanako. This isn't really used as a meditation hut anymore. We just rebuilt it because, well, because it had been here before. I only regret that so little of the monastery has been restored. The old monks' quarters would have been more spacious and more comfortable for you."

"We will be very comfortable here, Kimi. Thank you very much."

"You are very welcome, Lady Hanako, Lady Emily."

After Kimi departed, Emily said, "It would have been easier to verify or disprove some of what is in the scrolls if we knew where the old buildings stood. The cell, for example. The writer claims to have left a sign of her former presence there."

"Even a floor plan might not help," Hanako said. "The building that contained the cell might have been destroyed centuries ago."

"Then, with a plan, we could find where it had been, and finding no sign such as that she mentioned, we would know the scrolls are not to be believed." She paused and added, "I don't believe them anyway."

Emily opened her valise and took out one of the scrolls. She and Hanako sat on their knees on the floor and examined it together. Over the years, Emily had learned to sit with reasonable comfort in the Japanese fashion. She could not do so for hours. But for several minutes at a time, it was quite bearable.

"Perhaps we have misread this passage," Emily said.

"There's no mistake," Hanako said. She read from the scroll. "*We will meet in Mushindo Abbey, when you enter my cell. You will speak, and I will not.*

When you look for me, you will not find me. How is this possible? You will not know until the child appears, then you will know without doubt."

"Then it is a prediction," Emily said, "which can only be false."

"To us, it would so appear. But the writer recorded it as having already occurred. As history."

Emily shook her head doubtfully. "How can someone who supposedly died six hundred years ago speak of something in the future as if it were in the past? I do not believe this was written in ancient times. I believe it is a forgery specifically intended to cause mischief."

Hanako smiled. "You are beginning to think like us, Emily."

"Well, I suppose that is inevitable to a certain degree," Emily said. "These are tumultuous times, and Lord Genji has many enemies. I suppose some of them are completely without conscience, and would resort to any measure to undermine him."

"I would like to agree with you, but I cannot," Hanako said. "Such a plot as you describe would not be carried out this way. First, the scrolls were brought to you, a person known to be completely loyal to Lord Genji. Second, because they are in the Japanese language, it is to be expected that you would consult with another, and I am known to be your closest friend. My loyalty to Lord Genji is also beyond question. Thus there could be no expectation that the contents of these scrolls would become public knowledge, and without that, what purpose can they serve in any plot?"

"You don't mean to say you think these scrolls are genuine?"

Hanako said, "I think we should not have come to Mushindo."

"We had to come," Emily said, a stubborn set to her mouth, "to disprove what is written here. Surely you are not afraid?"

Hanako said again, "We should not have come."

Taro's voice came from the other side of the door. "Lady Hanako, I have stationed men within and without as you have ordered. I myself will patrol the inner courtyard tonight."

Emily said, "Please come in, Taro."

The door slid back. Taro remained outside as he bowed. "I must see to the men, Lady Emily. If the need should arise, call out, and someone will come right away."

"Thank you, Taro," Emily said.

Hanako said, "The last time we were here, we were all soaked in horses' blood."

"That seems so long ago," Taro said. "So much has changed since then."

"And more changes will come," Hanako said. "We must all be steadfast."

Taro bowed and said, "Indeed."

After he closed the door, Hanako listened as his footsteps receded.

"What is it?" Emily said.

"Nothing," Hanako said. There was no need to worry Emily with her concerns, which were probably unfounded. During the entire trip, Taro's demeanor had not been as it usually was. There was nothing specific that bothered Hanako. It was just slight differences in the look in his eyes, his posture, the tone of his voice. Most likely, he was disturbed by the unsettled state of the nation, as they all were. But a more sinister explanation was possible. She had noticed that all the men Taro had brought with him were his personal retainers. None of her husband Hidé's samurai was among them. Ordinarily, this would not even have come to her attention. Only that slight, undefined change in Taro troubled her enough to make her look for other possible discrepancies.

Emily read the passage again.

"We will meet in Mushindo Abbey, when you enter my cell. You will speak, and I will not. When you look for me, you will not find me. How is this possible? You will not know until the child appears, then you will know without doubt."

Hanako felt very cold.

"It doesn't make much sense," Emily said. "What child? And who is the 'you' she mentions? There is no cell anywhere on the grounds, and Mushindo is a monastery, not an abbey."

Hanako said, "When Mushindo was built in 1292, it was an abbey, not a monastery."

"What?" Emily could feel the blood leaving her face.

"Before it became a ruin in the battle Lord Genji fought here, it had been a ruin before, in the civil war between our clan founder, Lord Hironobu, and the traitors who murdered him. At the same time, they burned Mushindo Abbey to the ground, with everyone still in it. It remained abandoned for centuries. Old Abbot Zengen, who died just before you arrived in Japan, rebuilt it with his own hands. He was the one who made it a monastery."

Emily struggled against what she had heard. "That still doesn't answer the other questions."

"No," Hanako agreed, "but it is not difficult to guess at them."

"I cannot. Can you?"

Hanako hesitated. She did not wish to say it, but she now believed words could do no harm. A feeling of inevitability had been growing ever since she had first seen Emily reading the scrolls back at Quiet Crane Palace in Edo. She knew whatever was to happen could not be avoided.

"The birth to which the scrolls refer," Hanako said, "must be the birth of the heir who will continue the lineage. The 'you' is the person for whom the scrolls were written."

Emily stared at her. "Hanako, you surely don't mean *me*?"

"We are here," Hanako said, "so we will soon see."

"Or we will not," Emily said with somewhat more emphasis than she had intended. "This Shizuka may have been very clever, but she was certainly no witch with supernatural powers. There is no such thing as a witch."

"I wish you would not speak her name," Hanako said, and did her best not to tremble.

· · · · ·

The two women spent the night in fitful sleep, in fearful expectation of what one thought was unavoidable and one knew to be impossible. When dawn came, and they had experienced no visitation, they were both much more cheerful than they had been the previous day. Indeed, for the first time during the journey, Hanako felt a lightness of spirit. Even her suspicion of Taro vanished.

"I am glad you were right," Hanako said. "We Japanese are too superstitious. We have heard so many old stories, we begin to believe in them despite our better judgment."

"That will change," Emily said. "Japan is on the verge of joining the community of civilized nations. One day, and that day is not far off, Japan will be as modern and as scientific as the United States, Great Britain, and the other great nations of the world. Logic, and not fairy tales, will guide us all."

That afternoon, Hanako went with Kimi to admire the garden Goro cultivated. In addition to the usual vegetables, Kimi said, Goro grew edible flowers. He had learned about them by observing the wildflowers the outsider monk Jimbo collected.

"It's such a beautiful day," Emily said, "I think I'll take a turn in the meadow there."

She strolled into the woods not far outside the temple wall. The two samurai assigned by Taro followed her at a discreet distance. This was not the side of the temple that was the site of the battle. Though six years had passed, Emily had no wish to tread upon the ground where so many had died. The memory was painful to her still. Distracted by these thoughts, she had almost passed the stand of pines when she noticed the woman in its shadows, watching her. The contrast between the sunlight in which Emily stood and the shadows that cloaked the woman made her seem ephemeral. That, and the way she stood so still, had made her easy to miss.

The woman was very young, for her hair was not arranged in the style of an adult but was tied in a girl's long ponytail. She was also exceptionally pretty, with delicate features combined with eyes less narrow than was common among the Japanese. Emily thought she must be one of the women who came back from Yokohama with Kimi and Goro. The young woman was looking at her with a mildly amused expression. She had probably never seen an outsider at so close a distance. This was a good opportunity for Emily to practice speaking Japanese with someone who would not make allowances for her accent.

"Good afternoon," Emily said, and followed the words of Japanese with an appropriate bow in the fashion of the country. She did not get the response she expected. Instead of returning the bow and polite greeting, the woman said nothing, while her face crumpled into a look of terror.

"I am a visitor from afar," Emily said. "My name is Emily."

"Lady Emily." She heard Taro's voice behind her. "Is everything in order?"

"I was just practicing my Japanese," Emily said. "Without much success." She turned back toward the young woman and found that she had fled. She smiled. "It seems my Japanese is so bad, it terrifies strangers. You are very kind not to react that way. Did you see where she went?"

Taro looked at the two samurai who had been following Emily. They both shrugged.

"No," Taro said, "I'm sorry."

"She's probably gone back to the monastery," Emily said. "I'll have Kimi introduce us properly, and show her she has nothing to fear from me."

Taro said to the two samurai, "Did you see the woman?"

"No, Lord Taro."

"You should pay closer attention," Taro said. "What use are body-guards who fail to see a potential assassin?"

"We saw no one, lord," the other samurai said. He looked at his companion in some confusion.

"That is precisely my point, isn't it?" Taro said sharply. He did not like hearing excuses.

Emily caught her shoe on something concealed by the grass. She had to lean against a pine to keep from falling. She bent down to look. It was a large flat rock, half buried in the dirt.

"Foundation stone," Taro said.

"I beg your pardon?" Emily, confused, reverted to English.

Taro was no linguist, but his English had improved almost as much as Emily's Japanese. He said, "It is an old foundation stone. Before, there was a building here, probably. With destruction and reconstruction, buildings are sometimes moved. Intentionally, to change the karma of the place. And unintentionally, because no one remembers where the old building was."

"A building?" Emily said.

"Yes," Taro said, looking in the grass. "Not a big one. See? Here is another foundation stone. It was a very small building."

"A cell," Emily said, and fainted dead away.

When she opened her eyes again, she saw Hanako looking at her with much concern, and Kimi behind her.

"She's awake," Kimi said.

"Are you well?" Hanako asked.

"Yes, yes," Emily said, sitting up. "I overexerted myself slightly. Nothing serious." She looked around and saw nearly a dozen women gathered around them. She did not see the young woman from the woods. "Are these all of the residents?"

"All but one," Kimi said. "She went to the village on an errand. Sometimes, she takes an indirect route, and ends up wandering about in the woods."

Emily sighed with relief. "So that's who I saw." She smiled at Hanako. "My imagination ran away with me. I saw the girl, then I didn't see her. I tripped on the stone. I thought of the scrolls, and I thought it was"—she remembered Hanako's request that she not say the name—"the one I expected to see." She said to Kimi, "Is she very shy?"

"Yes," Kimi said, "very, very shy."

"The prettiest girls sometimes are," Emily said.

"The prettiest?" Kimi looked puzzled.

"Here she comes now," one of the women said. "Yasuko! Come here! The lady wants to meet you. You shouldn't have run away."

Emily watched the stocky, big-boned young woman approach. She would have looked clumsy enough even if her head didn't hang off so strangely to one side, a defect made more prominent by the way her hair was bound in the usual tight coiffure. There was nothing graceful, beautiful, or even slightly ephemeral about her.

"In Yokohama, she hurt her neck," Kimi said. "Now her head won't stay up right."

Emily grew dizzy again, but this time she didn't faint. "Mushindo Abbey," she whispered.

"She is delirious," Taro said.

"I fear she is not," Hanako said.

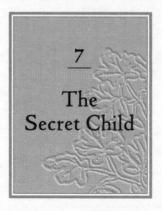

7

The
Secret Child

*An old saying has it that a man is courage, a woman kindness. This
has a certain pleasing blend of symmetry and contrast, and, like
many things that are pleasing, is quite false.*

    Courage and kindness are inseparable.

    If one seems to exist without the other, beware.

    You are in the presence of cowardice and cruelty disguised.

AKI-NO-HASHI

(1311)

1867, THE RUINS OF MUSHINDO MONASTERY

The men Taro had assigned to guard Emily during her afternoon walk were the two least reliable in the bodyguard contingent. He had brought them from Edo precisely for that attribute. They could be counted on to fail to perform their duties, which is precisely what they did, choosing instead to indulge in idle chatter with each other. Neither came close to spotting him hidden among the trees, though stealth was not one of his salient military attributes.

Like all true samurai, he disdained subterfuge and concealment, preferring to stand out in the open in a posture declarative of his intentions. The way in which he was executing his treason pained him nearly as much as the treason itself. But Lord Saemon had convinced him that this was not the time for traditional bravado. It was necessary for Taro to conceal his changed loyalties until the proper moment. He would therefore not only kill a woman and one he was pledged to protect, but he would kill her from hiding, tripling the shame he felt. He was acting to protect the ancient traditions of honor and courage that Lord Genji was so ready to abandon. Was it not strange that his first overt act in that cause should be so grotesquely cowardly? Yet it was consistent with all the other contradictions caused by the presence of the outsiders. Were he a man better able to appreciate how ridiculous life could be, he would surely be laughing at himself at this very moment.

He was one of Lord Genji's two most trusted retainers, second-in-command of the clan army, a man who had on several occasions risked his own life to defend Genji's. The son of a samurai of humble origins, he had been elevated by Genji to the rank of landed lord. No one had honored him more than Genji. No one was more deserving of his faithful allegiance, his gratitude, his reverence. And Taro was turning his back on him to serve Lord Saemon, a man perhaps even more detestable than Lord Saemon's late father, Kawakami the Sticky Eye, who had been the Shogun's secret-police commander.

The Sticky Eye had received his just reward—decapitation—in a battle at this very place. Taro and Emily had both been among the handful of survivors at Lord Genji's side. *Mushindo veteran.* He had heard the words spoken in awe many times over the years, and it had always made him proud. In a few moments, the words would have such different meaning. Better he had died then in honor. Though his cause was just, he knew the anguish of betrayal would make every one of his remaining days joyless, be they many or few.

Lady Hanako, whom he was also betraying, had lost her left arm in the battle defending her husband, Hidé, Taro's best friend, now a lord in his own right and the senior general of the clan. He hoped there would be no fatal consequences in this case. He intended Hanako no harm. He would only hold her hostage until he could convince Hidé to join him. Surely even someone as stubborn and as blindly loyal as Hidé would accept the necessity and righteousness of these actions once he was forced to stop and consider them.

He stood in the shadows, in the dense foliage, with the light coming from the trees behind him. The angle of the sun was such that anyone looking in his direction would have their vision significantly impaired.

Emily strolled leisurely toward a stand of pines. When she reached it, she would be approximately fifty arrow-lengths away. Even an archer as mediocre as himself could hit such a slow-moving target at that range. A rifle would be surer, but it couldn't be used, for practical and political reasons. The noise and smoke would mark his position too clearly, in the first instance. In the second, the use of bow and arrow—traditional weapons having nothing to do with the outsiders—made a point of its own.

Emily's death would have several immediate good results. It would trigger a violent response by the outsider nations, and if that response was like their previous ones, it would be ill-focused and excessive, increasing already feverish anti-foreign sentiment. It would also draw attention to Lord Genji's inappropriate friendship with an outsider woman, further weakening his position, which was not strong to begin with. Then the required execution of the two failed bodyguards would aggravate the divided loyalties of the clan's samurai, increasing the likelihood that fewer would remain loyal to Lord Genji as the crisis deepened. Finally, the unknown nature of the assailant, who would escape unseen, would enhance fear and suspicion, and fearful, suspicious people tended to make more mistakes than those who were not.

The scene was just as he had envisioned it. The two guards were too busy chatting to see him. Emily was walking so slowly, motion did not present any difficulty. Taro drew his bow. The bowstring in his fingers was on the verge of release when Emily stopped and began talking in her badly accented Japanese. Who was there? He could not fire without knowing. The person was well back in the trees because, try as he might, he caught sight of no one.

The moment had passed. He knew better than to press forward without auspicious circumstances. Another opportunity would come. He put the bow down in the brush and stepped out toward Emily. Though he was soon nearly at her shoulder, he still did not see anyone else. She appeared to be exchanging pleasantries with a pine tree.

"Lady Emily," Taro said. "Is everything in order?"

Apparently everything was not, for after a few innocuous words about a pair of old foundation stones half hidden in the grass, Emily suddenly collapsed, unconscious. Wasn't it bad enough that his lord had such a close friendship with an outsider woman? Did it have to be with one who was also prone to hallucinations and falling fits? It was yet another indication to Taro that he had made the right decision, difficult and rife with evil though it was. He fully accepted responsibility for the actions to which he had committed himself. At the same time, was it not undeniable that Lord Genji had made it impossible to do otherwise?

Last month, at a meeting with Hidé and Taro, Lord Genji had finally gone too far.

· · · · ·

"All our samurai now have guns," Genji said. "Soon, every troop will also have cannons on wheels that can go anywhere they go."

"Yes, lord," Hidé said, "and not many of them are happy about it."

"About the cannons?" Genji asked.

"The guns as well, my lord."

"They are not happy with the guns?" Genji seemed surprised. "Surely they are not expecting to fight future wars with swords?"

Hidé said, "It is not a practical matter. They do not believe guns properly express the spirit of samurai."

"They can express their spirit as much as they wish," Genji said, "but on the battlefield, spiritual expression is of little consequence without physical might."

Taro said, "There is a combat aspect as well, my lord. The men point to the battle at Mushindo Monastery as an example of the continuing value of the sword."

"How so? The outcome was determined by guns. What did swords do except demonstrate their complete inefficacy?"

"When the enemy stormed our position," Taro said, "we fought them with our swords, and we defeated them."

"Your memory seems to have deserted you entirely. Do you recall burrowing into the gory mud to escape the bullets? Do you remember hiding behind the spilled guts of our horses?"

Hidé said, "Taro is not entirely wrong, lord."

"I must have been in a different battle. Please describe yours."

"All the thousands of bullets they fired did not kill us," Hidé said. "In the end, they had to come at us with swords."

"You were there, yet you can mouth such nonsense? You are demonstrating precisely why the time of the samurai has passed away. It is not so much the swords in your sash that are the problem, but the swords in your heads."

"Samurai have protected Japan for a thousand years," Taro said.

"I would say ravaged, not protected."

"Lord," Taro said, "that is a poor jest."

"A jest? Hardly. For a thousand years, we have excelled at slaughtering and enslaving those who are supposed to be in our care. If the murdered dead could stand alongside their slayers, who would be more numerous?"

"We have fought each other," Taro said. "We have not waged war on peasants."

"Oh, really? For every samurai who has fallen in battle, how many peasants have been trampled, starved, speared, beheaded, or simply worked to death? Five? Ten? More likely a hundred, or two hundred. We have done all the sword-wielding. They have done most of the dying."

"That is the fate of peasants," Hidé said. "They must accept theirs as we accept ours."

"I wonder. The French peasants did not. They rose up and beheaded their nobles." Genji smiled as if enjoying the thought.

"That could not happen here," Taro said. "We are a civilized nation. Even our peasants are of a higher order. They would not even think of it."

"Yes, I suppose you're right. That's rather sad in a way, isn't it?"

"It is a matter for pride rather than sorrow," Taro said.

"Perhaps. Perhaps not. Instead of waiting for our own Reign of Terror, it would be wise of us to innovate boldly and simply abolish ourselves, our domains, and the entire ancient order of lords and retainers."

"Lord!" Hidé and Taro exclaimed in unison.

Genji laughed. "There's an outsider expression: 'Food for thought.' Less worry and more nourishment would serve the both of you better."

His words were poison, not nourishment. He had laughed, but Taro knew Genji meant what he said.

Now, when he looked back, Taro knew that was the very moment when he ceased being Lord Genji's loyal vassal.

His first attempt at killing Emily had failed. His second would not.

· · · · ·

"Are you sure you are well enough to sit up?" Hanako asked.

"Quite," Emily said. Now that she was back in the restored abbot's hut, she felt rather silly at having fainted that way. There had been no reason for such a reaction. Just because the beautiful young woman she had seen in the woods was not one of those who lived at the temple didn't mean she had seen a ghost. The woman could have been from the village, though she had seemed far too well-dressed for a peasant. Perhaps she had been a passerby, temporarily separated from the rest of her company.

"Thank you." Emily took the tea Hanako offered. "As I was saying, she was unusually beautiful," Emily said. "Her eyes were particularly striking. They were more Western than Oriental. I suppose that is not all that remarkable. We are all human, after all, and not so very different."

"You said her hair was very long," Hanako said, "reaching all the way to the ground."

"Yes, so far as I could tell. She was in shadow and I was in sunlight. It was hard to see her."

"She appeared—" Hanako searched for the right word. "She appeared dim?"

"Not dim, exactly. Shadows often play tricks on the eyes. And the pattern of her kimono made it even more difficult."

"The pattern of her kimono?"

"Yes." Emily appreciated Hanako's concern for her welfare. Still, the direction of her questioning and the detail into which she went were a trifle odd. "The pattern was very similar to the foliage in which she stood. The lack of contrast made her fade into the background rather easily."

Hanako grew pale. Her eyes lost their focus, and her body wavered. For a moment, Emily thought Hanako, too, was about to faint. She did not, though she put her hand on the floor in front of her to keep herself from falling.

"What is it?" Emily said.

Hanako did not answer right away. She didn't know what to say. Was it better for Emily to know or not? She was convinced Emily had seen Lady Shizuka, the princess witch who had either saved the clan in its earliest days, or laid a curse upon it that continued to the present. Or perhaps both. The large eyes, the long hair, the transparency of her person—for that is what Emily mistook for the pattern of her kimono. She was seeing through her. It had happened exactly as the scrolls had predicted—at Mushindo Abbey, in the old cell that had been her home in her childhood. Then perhaps all the other predictions in them were also true.

Only those of Okumichi blood ever saw Lady Shizuka. If Emily had seen her, then there was only one possibility, unlikely though it seemed.

"The day Lady Heiko left," Hanako said. "Six years ago."

"I remember it well," Emily said. It had been the last time she had seen Heiko and Matthew Stark. Their ship had sailed for California on the outgoing tide.

"Lady Heiko told me something I did not believe." Hanako hesitated. "I believe it now."

· · · · ·

It was New Year's Day by the Japanese calendar, the first new moon after the winter solstice, in the sixteenth year of the Emperor Komei. Heiko doubted she would ever see another in her homeland.

"May a bold tide bear you forth," Genji said, "and the tide of remembrance bring you home." He looked straight into her eyes as he spoke.

The six friends gathered together before the sailing of the *Star of Bethlehem*. Genji, Heiko, Hidé, Hanako, Emily, and Stark bowed and emptied the small ceremonial cups of sake. Much had changed during the swift passage of a single year.

Hidé, the wastrel, gambler, and ne'er-do-well, had become the lord's chief bodyguard. He had demonstrated his courage in fierce battles at the Mié Pass and outside the walls of Mushindo Monastery. No one had seen such potential hidden within the lazy mediocrity he had been. No one except Genji, who had unexpectedly raised Hidé from the ranks.

"*Lord* Hidé," Genji said. "That has a good sound, doesn't it?" Hidé's elevation to chief bodyguard had brought with it a simultaneous elevation to landed status. Thus, he now had to be addressed with the noble sobriquet.

Hidé's face grew as crimson as the hindquarters of a mountain monkey. "I cannot become accustomed to it, lord. I feel like an impostor."

The others laughed good-naturedly, but Genji did not. He spoke in a quiet voice that only served to emphasize the seriousness of his words. "An impostor you most definitely are not. I know no one in this life more genuine than you, Lord Hidé. In the life to come, I expect to meet no one who exceeds you in that regard, except perhaps the Buddhas and the gods."

The color instantly fled from Hidé's face as his eyes watered and his shoulders bunched. Fearlessly stolid in battle, he was so prone to tears in emotional situations, his nickname among the men was "Captain Kabuki."

Hanako quickly interceded to prevent the imminent flood. A house-maid then, she was now Hidé's wife and the mother of their infant son, Iwao. She had lost an arm at Mushindo, but none of her grace or charm. If the little boy grew up to attain a fair portion of his father's strength and his mother's wisdom, he would be an exceptional man indeed. Who could have seen what a perfect match the two would be? Who if not Genji, who had arranged the marriage himself?

Heiko could not keep from seeing a certain bitter irony in this. He could bring together two people who had never even thought of each other, but with Heiko, the best he could do was send her away.

Hanako said, "Instead of giving him a title, Lord Genji, you should have given him a theater. My talented husband cries more easily than the most skilled heroines of the stage." All Kabuki actors were male. Thus the heroines were female impersonators, and they were considered the highest exemplar of the art.

"Hidé as a geisha!" Genji said. "What do you say to that, Heiko?"

By now, everyone was laughing, including Hidé, his tears forgotten in the hilarity of the image called up by their lord.

"You're a good friend, Hidé," Matthew Stark said, "but I have to tell you, I've seen cows in the Panhandle that would dress up prettier than you."

Stark was the Christian missionary who had come to kill, had killed, and was returning to his homeland in the same ship that was taking Heiko away from hers. Had vengeance cured the pain of his loss? Had it brought him peace? The anguish that showed in his eyes every time he heard a child laugh or saw a child smile said it had not. His loss, whatever it had been, had been so great that he heard the voices of the dead, and saw their faces, more clearly than those of the living. Even when he laughed, as he did now, Heiko could see a man more dead than alive despite the heart that beat so stubbornly in his breast. Such a man would not live long. Anyone could see it. Anyone but Genji, who had entrusted him with the task of protecting a fortune in gold he was sending to America with Stark's commission as his trading agent there.

There was a perfect, sad balance in Heiko's relationship with Stark, was there not? He had lost everything that truly mattered to him, and she was about to have the same experience.

"If there is a market for pretty cows," Genji said, "perhaps you should look into it."

"Maybe I should," Stark said, "if I have the time."

Genji said, "We will be partners for many years to come. We will have time for many things. Perhaps one day we will even speak each other's language as easily as we speak our own."

Stark's lips curved up in a smile below those sorrowful eyes. "Truth be told, I don't speak my own language all that well. Too many years in the saddle, too few among people who knew how to talk right."

And what of Heiko herself? In her twentieth year, she was more beautiful than she had ever been, the most acclaimed geisha in the Shogun's capital city of Edo, an already storied heroine whom people spoke of in the same way they did the fabled courtesans, princesses, and noble ladies of legend. Her reputation for courage, the visible proof of her extraordinary physical perfection, her exquisite subtlety of demeanor, the gracefulness of even her most mundane actions, and, perhaps most surprising, the absence of that artificial haughtiness affected by lesser beauties—all these combined to make her irresistible to almost everyone. Everyone, that is, except Genji, who was sending her away to America with Stark, supposedly to establish a base there for the domain, but in reality simply to send her away.

Why?

Heiko didn't know. She knew he loved her. He showed it in the softness of his every glance, the gentle lingering of every touch, the caress in the tone of every word, the desperate yearning with which he surrendered himself to her in their every act of passion. Yet he was sending her away.

Something had changed at Mushindo. When Genji came back from that last meeting with Kawakami the Sticky Eye, something in his attitude toward her was different. It was not that he was colder or more distant. The change was not of a gross kind that could so easily be detected and labeled. No, it was almost imperceptible. Only because she was so skilled a practitioner of the arts of the nearly imperceptible was Heiko able to sense it. It was not a lessening of love, for if anything, their love had increased over the year just past. The current was stronger, but it was no longer sweeping them along together. Instead, it was pulling them apart.

Why? Genji knew. He knew so much that no one else did. But he said nothing. Every time she asked, he said there was nothing to say.

Liar.

Great Lord, hero, prophet, lover, liar.

And liar most of all.

We will be together again, in America, he said.

Liar.

The world was changing rapidly, and Heiko could imagine many things that had been unimaginable only a short time ago, but she could not see Genji in America. He was a Great Lord of the realm. More than that, he was a Great Lord poised on the verge of a historic triumph, the overthrow of his hereditary enemy, the Tokugawa Shogun, who grew weaker with every passing day. No one knew who would take power, but the possibilities were many, and Genji was among them. No Great Lord would choose this time to leave Japan for America.

She was going. Genji was not, not now or ever. She would leave and she would never see him again.

Why?

Heiko didn't know. She had looked into the matter as closely as she could and found nothing informative. Some weeks after Mushindo, Genji had led a raid into Kawakami's old domain of Hino. He was said to be seeking something—an amulet, a scroll, a person—the possibilities offered were various. There were further rumors that an isolated village of peasants had been slaughtered, but that seemed unlikely. Genji had probably attacked the remnants of Kawakami's die-hard retainers who had gone into hiding, which was only prudent. Beyond that, nothing unusual had occurred. So, at the end, she knew no more than she had at the beginning. Kawakami had said something, something destructive, and for some reason Genji had believed him.

"After a lifetime governed by obligations," Genji said, "you will find the freedom of America exhilarating, I am sure."

Heiko bowed. "I am relieved that one of us has that confidence, my lord." She said it in a cheerful manner, with a smile she did not feel. If Genji saw through it, he gave no sign. He smiled, too. They played the game for the last time.

When the party ended, she went to her quarters to retrieve her travel kit.

Hanako arrived soon after. "Lady Heiko, you sent for me?"

"Thank you, Hanako. Please enter." She closed the door after her. Heiko had thought about this for a long time. She had no right to tell Hanako anything, since the secret was Genji's, not hers. But since she was leaving, and would likely never return, someone had to know so that proper precautions could be taken.

"Last spring," Heiko said, "you will recall that Lord Genji fell unconscious in the rose garden at Cloud of Sparrows Castle."

"Yes, I remember it well. He had not fully recovered from his wounds, and overexerted himself."

"Injury was not the cause. He had a vision."

"Ah," Hanako said. She knew this, of course. Everyone did. Servants were better at discovering information than any system of spies the Shogun had ever devised. Having been one herself until very recently, she was still privileged to be the recipient of the most interesting gossip. What the vision was, none among the servants knew, of course.

"Lord Genji shared his vision with me," Heiko said. "Emily will bear his child."

Hanako was shocked. "He predicted it?"

"Not in so many words. The portents were obvious."

"Perhaps not so obvious," Hanako said. "If he did not actually make a prediction, you must have misunderstood what he said. Emily is an outsider."

"Emily is a woman," Heiko said, "like any other. She is as capable of bearing children as you or I."

"A Great Lord cannot have a child with an outsider. His retainers would not accept it. If he had any retainers left."

"So it would seem. But that is what the vision portends. Would you ignore it?"

Hanako calmed herself. She could not let herself be distracted by her own thoughts. Heiko must be wrong about the vision. But what if she were right?

"No," Hanako said, "the vision cannot be ignored."

"Good. Then I can trust you to watch over Emily?"

"It would be helpful if I can enlist the aid of others."

"And what others do you know who can accept this knowledge with equanimity?"

There was her husband, Hidé, an entirely reliable man. One prone to confusion when faced with unusual circumstances, however. When confused, he was far from his best. It may do more harm than good to tell him something so shocking.

Taro, her husband's closest friend, had similar strengths and weaknesses. And if she did not tell her husband, how could she confide in another man?

All the women who were close to her were servants at the palace in Edo and the castle in Akaoka Domain. The best of them could be counted on to watch over Emily with great care. But servants gossiped ceaselessly. Once one knew, all would know, and if all knew, it was only a matter of time before others did, including enemies of Lord Genji.

There was no one else to help her.

Hanako bowed. "I will do my best."

"Thank you. Now I can leave with a peaceful heart."

"We all look forward to your speedy return."

"I will not return," Heiko said.

"Of course you will, Lady Heiko. Our lord will not endure your absence for long. His feelings for you are obvious."

Heiko's eyes teared. Her formal seated posture dissolved and she dropped a hand to the mat on one side as she leaned to support herself.

"I have done something to displease him," Heiko said, "and I don't know what it is. Do you know what it might be?"

"No, my lady," Hanako said. "You must be mistaken."

"You have heard nothing from the servants?"

"About you, only praise. In fact, many are speculating about when Lord Genji will formally take you into his household. Really, Lady Heiko, you are sure to return. Most think in the spring, because that is a season of beginnings. I myself believe it will be in the autumn, because when the days grow cold, passion burns with the greatest heat."

Heiko laughed, as Hanako hoped she would.

"Do the servants really talk of it?"

"Yes, my lady. The only uncertainty is timing. They are guessing about everything. The year you will give birth, for example. Everyone favors the year immediately after your return. That would be two years from now, since no one believes Lord Genji can endure more than a year without you. There is also much speculation about the heir's name."

"Oh, my, the heir? Has talk gone that far?" A happy lilt had returned to Heiko's voice.

"Oh, yes. One of the maids—Mitsuko, do you know her?—even consulted a fortune-teller in Yokohama."

The two friends covered their mouths and laughed. The silliness of consulting a street-corner fraud about the destiny of a lord who could himself see the future was really too much.

"And what did the visionary say?" Heiko asked.

"She didn't actually say anything at all," Hanako said, trying hard to keep laughter from stopping her words. "She was an outsider who couldn't speak Japanese. She used strange cards with pictures on them. Mitsuko said she pointed to two of them and nodded her head, yes. A handsome prince and a beautiful princess, which Mitsuko took for Lord Genji and yourself. Then she closed her eyes, went into a trance—"

"A trance!" Heiko was laughing so hard, she could no longer sit up straight. Tears of merriment rolled down her cheeks.

"—opened a book of kanji, and pointed first to the character *ko*, for 'child,' then *makoto*, for 'truth.' "

When the friends finally stopped laughing, they called a maid, who brought tea. The sparkle in the maid's eyes told them she had overheard the recent part of their conversation and had shared in their laughter.

"If even outsider card readers agree," Hanako said, "then your separation is surely a temporary thing. Lord Genji will recall you as soon as your task is accomplished. You are leaving, not because he wishes to be rid of you, but because he trusts you as he trusts few others."

"It is nice to believe so, isn't it?" Heiko said, sipping her tea.

"It is much easier to believe you will return soon," Hanako said, "than to believe Emily will bear our lord's child."

"You will watch over her nonetheless?"

"Without fail." Yet even as Hanako said these words, her thoughts were for Heiko's child-to-be, not Emily's. While she had laughed over the fortune-teller's prediction, she had not doubted its accuracy. Those whom the gods gifted were not always as one expected them to be. Lord Genji himself was an example. Could not the foreign card reader in Yokohama be one as well? Hanako was confident she would welcome her friend back to Japan before many seasons had passed. After that, how long could it be before the arrival of the heir everyone expected? If it was more than a year, Hanako would be very surprised indeed.

· · · · ·

After Hanako finished speaking, Emily was silent for a long time.

Finally, she said, "I did not appear in Genji's dream."

She could not bring herself to say vision, so suggestive as it was of blasphemy. No one since the prophets of the Old Testament had seen the shape of things to come. By believing that Genji had done so, Hanako was committing a heretical act of damnation. Now was not the time to fix upon doctrinal matters, however, no matter how significant. That would have to wait.

"Yes," Hanako said.

"Then how does anyone leap to the conclusion that I am involved in any way?"

"Because of the locket you wear around your neck. The one with the fleur-de-lis. In the vision, Genji sees it around the neck of his child."

"That's hardly proof." Emily touched the locket tucked away beneath her blouse. "It might not be the same locket. And even if it was, there are any number of ways it could get to a child other than mine."

"What are those ways?" Hanako asked.

"Well, for one, I might give it to Genji, and he then would give it to his child."

"Will you give it to him?"

"I must admit, I hadn't planned on it."

"But it's possible?"

Inside the heart-shaped droplet of gold was a miniature portrait of a beautiful young woman with ringlets of golden hair. She was Emily's grandmother, whom Emily had never met. Everyone who saw it thought it greatly resembled Emily herself, though whenever Emily looked at it— and she did at least once a day when she said her evening prayers—it reminded her of her mother. She had died tragically when Emily was fourteen. There were only two things she kept after her mother's death. A copy of her mother's favorite novel, *Ivanhoe*, and the locket with the miniature within the golden heart. They were all she had to remember her by.

"No," Emily admitted. "It is very precious to me. I cannot imagine giving it away to anyone. In any case, it seems a rather flimsy thing upon which to base such a profound conclusion."

"It isn't just the locket," Hanako said. "It is the locket and the other vision."

"The other vision?"

"Yes," Hanako said. "Yours."

"That was no vision," Emily said. "The young woman was there."

"And, by coincidence, the manner of her appearance matches exactly the prediction in the scroll?" Hanako opened the scroll and read aloud. *"We will meet in Mushindo Abbey, when you enter my cell. You will speak, and I will not. When you look for me, you will not find me.* Did it not happen exactly that way?"

"We have not found her *yet,*" Emily said. "But then, we have not looked very hard. Tomorrow, we will have Taro help us investigate in the village."

Hanako continued reading. *"When you look for me, you will not find me. How is this possible? You will not know until the child appears, then you will know without doubt."*

Emily shook her head. "That makes no sense. The references must be to two unrelated events."

"I disagree," Hanako said. "She is saying, 'How is it possible that you two will meet?' And she answers, 'You will know how it was possible when the child appears.' "

"By that you mean when I supposedly give birth?"

"Sooner, I think. You measure the age of a child from the time of birth. We consider the child one year of age when it is born, counting the year it is carried by the mother."

"Oh. Still, how would I see what is not there merely by being with child?"

"Throughout the centuries, the lady has been rumored to appear many times. But only to those of her lineage."

"There," Emily said. "You are contradicting yourself now. If that is so, then it is impossible for me to have seen her today, or to see her ever. No matter what happens in the future, I will never be her descendant. I will live and die a Gibson."

She felt great relief. Though she had been insisting that she had seen a real person, she had been, until this moment, quite unsure. It had been unsettling to see a woman in a way that so closely matched what the scrolls predicted.

To her surprise, Hanako did not share her relief. Instead, she looked more worried than ever.

"If the child is Lord Genji's," Hanako said, "then it is of Okumichi blood. While you are carrying the child, the lady's blood is within you."

Emily's cheeks colored. "I am not with child, Genji's or anyone else's."

"No, you are not," Hanako said. "Not yet."

· · · · ·

Kimi was so excited by what she heard, she wanted to go and tell the other girls right away. The present position of the guards made immediate departure impossible. She would have to wait where she was until they moved on. The floor of the abbot's hut creaked above her as the two ladies moved about. She could hear bedding being laid out. The day had been a strenuous one for them. Not surprisingly, they had decided on an early night.

Except when she had been flustered, Lady Emily had spoken in Japanese. Her grammar and vocabulary were excellent, much better than Kimi's, which was to be expected. Kimi spoke Japanese like an unschooled peasant, which she was. Lady Emily had learned the language in palaces and castles through conversations with noble lords and ladies. Her American accent was noticeable, but not severe. Fortunately, only a small portion of her words had been incomprehensible.

There. The guards were continuing their patrol along the inner wall. Kimi waited for another minute after they were out of sight, then she crawled out from the space beneath the hut, crept in careful silence until she was far enough away, then ran to find her friends.

"Are you sure they said Lady Emily would have Lord Genji's child?" one of the girls asked.

"Yes," Kimi said, "I'm sure."

"Because Shizuka predicted it?"

"Shhh!" said several of the girls at once. "If you say her name, she'll think you're calling her, and she'll come!" Everyone huddled a little closer together in the hut they shared.

"No she won't," Kimi said, pushing the nearest girl away from her. "Unless you are an Okumichi, and if you are, what are you doing in this wretched village? Go home to Cloud of Sparrows, where you belong."

"Kimi's right. Everyone knows she only appears to her descendants."

"I heard Crazy Odo saw the lady so often, that's why she became insane. Crazy Odo is no noblewoman."

"If you grew up in this village like I did," Kimi said, "you would know why Crazy Odo saw what she did. Her mother was seduced by one of Lord Genji's ancestors. His great-grandfather, I think it was. My grandmother knows, or used to. She's senile now and doesn't even know herself."

"So she is an Okumichi, too."

"I don't believe it. Why would a samurai who can sleep with beautiful ladies want a dirty little peasant?"

Kimi said, "What makes you think a samurai is any better than a farmer at keeping his silly little plow in only the right furrows?"

The girls all laughed merrily.

"Shh," Kimi said. "The guards will hear us."

"If Crazy Odo is an Okumichi, then any of us could be, too. We had better not say the lady's name."

"Shizuka, Shizuka, Shizuka," Kimi said. "Shizuka, Shizuka, Shizuka."

"Stop, Kimi!"

"Shizuka, Shizuka," Kimi said. "Shizuka, Shizuka, Shizuka—"

Everyone held their breath.

"You see?" Kimi said. "It's fun to dream of being a lady instead of a farm girl, but we are what we are, aren't we? Lord Genji isn't going to come and take us away with him because we're his cousins."

"Exactly," one of the girls said, regaining her confidence.

"Ha! You were as afraid of saying the witch's name as the rest of us."

Kimi said, "Do you want to hear what I have to tell you or not?"

"We do, we do!"

When Kimi finished relating all that she had heard, one of the girls said, "I don't understand. Is Lady Emily pregnant or not?"

"Haven't you been paying attention? She's going to sleep with Lord Genji. She hasn't yet."

"Then there's no baby in her stomach?"

"That's what it means when you're not pregnant. There's no baby in there."

"But if there's no baby, then there's no Okumichi blood inside, either. If only those of the blood can see the lady, how did Lady Emily see her?"

"For Shizuka, where the blood will be," Kimi said, "it already is."

"I don't understand. How can something that is going to happen in the future already have happened six hundred years ago, and also happen now? That makes no sense at all."

Kimi said, "Just because you don't understand something doesn't mean it doesn't make sense. Do you understand all the words of the Buddha? All the sayings of the Zen Patriarchs? Or even one word of them?"

The girls laughed. One said, "The Zen Patriarchs always spoke in puzzles. How could we understand anything they said?"

"Just so," Kimi said, "life itself is a puzzle for us below. Only those above, like Lord Genji, understand everything." She had everyone's attention now. She paused dramatically, then said, "Time is a prison for us. Not for Shizuka. The past and future are all the same to her. So if something is going to happen, then it has as good as happened for her."

"I told you she was a witch!"

"She wasn't a witch," Kimi said. "She was a princess. A beautiful princess from a kingdom on the other side of China. She knew the magic that princesses there all know." She remembered the place the two ladies had mentioned. It had such a beautiful, faraway sound.

"The Kingdom of the Blue Ice Mountains and the Red Dragon River," Kimi said.

1308, MUSHINDO ABBEY

Shizuka ran from her cell as fast as she could. Since she had been behaving herself more or less like a normal person for more than a month, the Reverend Abbess Suku had ordered that her door no longer be locked. That was extremely fortunate, for if she could not have gotten away from the ghostly demon who spoke to her, she would surely have returned to her former state of madness. Oh, no. What if it had followed her? She was afraid to look.

She was more afraid not to look. She turned. And, to her great relief, saw no one.

This demon, like a fair number of the specters who appeared, had eyes and hair different from those of the nuns around her, and more exaggerated contours of face and form. She had come to understand that these were visitations of a distant time, either past or future, but not the present. Such people were not here now. She had learned to suppress the actual from the possible. She thought she had learned how to do it perfectly well.

But this one had seen her!

This one had spoken to her!

What did it mean? Her thoughts and emotions were too stirred up to permit clarity. She needed to immerse herself in meditative calm. Her cell frightened her too much. She proceeded to the main meditation hall and took a place close to the altar, where the Buddha's protection was thought to be strongest.

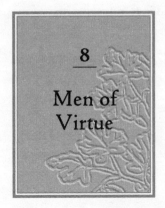

8

Men of Virtue

The most fiendish of men, the most cowardly, the most treacherous, none of them think of themselves as villains. They believe themselves to be heroes accomplishing impossible tasks against overwhelming opposition.

They convince themselves of this by seeing only what they wish to see, robbing words of their meaning, forgetting the real and remembering the false. In this way, they are not so very different from true heroes.

What is the difference?

True heroes are on our side.

Fiendish, cowardly, treacherous villains are the heroes of our enemies.

AKI-NO-HASHI

(1311)

1867, LORD SAEMON'S PALACE IN EDO

Saemon, whose self-opinion was always high, was even more pleased with himself than usual. His subversion of Taro would cripple Genji whether or not Emily Gibson was killed. The key was Taro's treason itself. Taro didn't realize this, of course. Primitive traditionalist that he was, he thought the outsider woman's death was of great importance. Taro and others like him, caught in the useless mythology of the past, believed that by stopping modernizers like Genji, they could preserve the Japan they had always known. In fact, that Japan was already mortally wounded. It would stagger to its death in the next year or two, and a new Japan, much along the lines Genji envisioned, would take its place. Survival was not possible otherwise.

The English, the Americans, the Russians, the French, the Spanish, the Portuguese, and the Dutch had gone everywhere, and everywhere the result was the same. What had happened to the Africans? They had been made into slaves. The great khanates of Central Asia were now to be found under the boot of the Czar. The rajahs of India bent their knees to the English sovereign, a woman! Was there any reason to believe these same outsiders would not try to do to Japan exactly what had worked so well for them elsewhere? Of course not. Had they not already begun the butchering and looting of China?

Genji's determination to modernize was entirely sensible. Saemon knew as well as Genji that there was no other way for Japan to survive the onslaught that the outsiders were bound to launch sooner or later. But he would never say so. Let Genji and others like him take the necessary steps and absorb all the hatred. When such idealists were gone, then realists like himself would step forward and take over. Tradition was doomed, but in the meantime, Saemon saw great usefulness in those who still claimed to adhere to it.

It was truly laughable. Samurai pride in their traditions of loyalty and honor were little more than fairy tales, much like the outsiders' fairy tales of Christian virtues. A great Commandment of their God was: Thou shalt not kill. They had slaughtered and ravaged their way across five continents under that banner for a thousand years. He did not condemn the outsiders for this. Hypocrisy was the essential nature of all modes of human control. The brilliant few did as they wished, while convincing the gullible many to follow rules they themselves disdained. In the same way as the Commandments did for Christian kings and lords, the mythology of loyalty and sacrifice cloaked a centuries-old tradition of self-aggrandizement and treachery for the samurai.

A genuine samurai was not blindly loyal, eagerly self-sacrificing, and bound by honor above all else, but rather a pragmatic, manipulative, and deceitful political genius—in other words, a man very much like Saemon himself.

Taro was only one part of Saemon's secret campaign against Genji. There was also the matter of the law Genji had proposed, a proclamation of the equality of all, including the abolition of what he called "burakumin," whom everyone called "eta." The law itself was necessary, since Japan was required to at least put on a show of subscribing to the strange outsider beliefs of "liberty" and "equality." But persistent reports told of Genji's active participation in the destruction of an eta village in Hino Domain some years ago. Was that not a curious coincidence? Saemon believed Taro knew something about it, although he had not yet revealed anything. There was surely a way to induce him to do so. The trick, as always, was how.

There was no hurry. Saemon was a master at discovering the appropriate device for the appropriate person. He would find the one that suited Taro. In the meantime, he had already sent agents to California to investigate yet another strange report he had received. It was rumor more than information, but what a tantalizing rumor.

It was said that the geisha Mayonaka no Heiko, a famed beauty known to have been Genji's lover at the time of the Mushindo battle, had been sent away to California shortly thereafter, and had given birth to a son a few months later. Exactly how many months later had not been established. His sources were also unable to confirm the identity of the father. Matthew Stark, Genji's former American comrade-in-arms and current business partner, was considered the most likely. But—and this was the tantalizing part—Genji was also a possibility.

If Genji was the boy's father, then what was the boy doing still in California? Even if he was the child of a geisha, he was a qualified male heir, and Genji had no other at present. This was especially baffling given Heiko's background. A woman of her reputed talents and beauty would be a perfectly acceptable mother for an heir. She would not necessarily have become Genji's wife, but she would certainly have been an excellent concubine. This had not happened. Why?

Was there some connection between Genji's proposals regarding the abolition of the domains, the law regarding the outcasts, and the exile of a beautiful geisha who might be the mother of his only child? Saemon could think of no possible link that made any sense. Experience had taught him, however, that his inability to see an immediate connection between disparate elements did not mean that none existed.

Continued speculation was useless. The only way to find the truth was to investigate thoroughly—in this case, to investigate the past. The geisha Heiko had never returned. If anything had been concealed, it had been done in America, and that is where it would be uncovered. Saemon had already sent two of his best agents to San Francisco. In the meantime, he had set Taro in motion. One approach or the other, or perhaps even both, would eventually bear bitter fruit for Lord Genji.

MUSHINDO MONASTERY

"Lord Taro, we should not delay any longer."

"We are not delaying," Taro said. "We are accompanying Lady Hanako and Lady Emily. As long as they choose to stay, we stay as well."

His lieutenant leaned closer and spoke in a low voice. "The men grow nervous, and nervous men lack resolve. Lord, let us finish our accompanying and get on with our real mission."

"What is there to be nervous about?"

Taro was irritated in the extreme by the mere fact that this conversation was taking place at all. What had happened to the great samurai virtue of unquestioning obedience? These young men were not like those of his youth. How different he and Hidé had been when they were this one's age! No stream of questions, no unasked-for suggestions, no jittery impatience. Yes, lord, I hear and obey. That was it, no more, no less. What would old Lord Chamberlain Saiki have done if Taro or Hidé had told him what to do? Strike them with the flat of his sword, no doubt. That Taro would never think of doing this to his lieutenant showed how soft they had all become in a few short years.

"Mushindo itself, lord, makes them uneasy."

"Uneasy? They should be honored to stand where our clan achieved one of its greatest victories."

"They are honored, Lord Taro. I do not mean to suggest they are not. The problem is all the old rumors."

"What rumors?"

"About ghosts and demons."

Taro closed his eyes. He took a deep, calm breath, in and out, and another, to keep from shouting in anger, before he opened his eyes again. He spoke very softly, as he always did when he was enraged.

"When we return to Edo," Taro said, "remind me to recruit real samurai, and let these disguised little girls return to their mothers."

"Lord," the lieutenant said. He bowed apologetically, which somewhat concealed the backward shuffling of his knees that increased the distance between them. "It is foolish, I know. But there are more than rumors. Strange noises emanate from the buildings, the woods, and it seems the ground itself. It is hard to blame the men."

"The sounds come from underground streams," Taro said. "Lord Shigeru once told me they sometimes well up in temporary hot springs. Very refreshing, he said they were."

"Lord Shigeru," the lieutenant said.

Taro took another deep breath. Very calmly, he said, "I am sure you will not tell me they are afraid of Lord Shigeru, too?"

"The villagers say he is seen in the woods from time to time. In the company of a little boy. With a kite in the form of a sparrow."

"Do we live in an age so degenerate, samurai listen to the babbling of ignorant peasants? Lord Shigeru is dead. I saw his head with my own eyes, six years ago, not a hundred paces from where we now sit. I attended his cremation ceremony. When his ashes were placed in the columbarium at Cloud of Sparrows, I was there."

"Yes, lord. I should have spoken more clearly. It isn't a living Lord Shigeru the villagers claim to see."

"Ah," Taro said, exasperation drawing a sigh from his lungs. "His ghost."

"Yes, lord."

"Leave me," Taro said, his patience at an end. He kept his eyes shut until the door closed behind his lieutenant. If these men were the most stalwart warriors he could find—and they were—how could samurai stand against the outsider armies? Ghosts, demons, disembodied voices. What foolishness.

There was one thing the lieutenant said that did bother him, albeit only slightly. He said the villagers saw the ghost of Shigeru accompanied by a little boy with a sparrow kite. The last time he had seen Shigeru with his son, the little boy was flying a kite Lord Genji had made for him.

A kite shaped like a sparrow.

How did the villagers know about that? The boy had never been to Mushindo. Undoubtedly, gossip of every kind spread far and wide in the mysterious way of gossip. No matter. What was important was the mission. The lieutenant was right about that. Taro needed a new plan, and he needed to carry it out soon. Before his men panicked, and before the two women decided to return to Edo.

Tomorrow. He would act tomorrow. Tonight, he would think of what to do.

. . . . .

Emily claimed to give no credence whatsoever to the prophecies contained in the scrolls, but it took her a long time to fall asleep, despite her exhaustion. Hanako would have spared her the worry if sparing her would make her safe. It would not. It was better that she knew the truth, and accepted it. When Emily's breathing deepened and slowed, Hanako went to the door and opened it to reveal a sliver of the night outside. She could see one of the so-called guards in the shadow of the wall. She heard another cough on the other side of the hut. These would be better men than the ones Taro had assigned to protect Emily this afternoon, since their task was genuine. She would get past them the same way the rascal girl Kimi had.

The moon in its last phase was the merest suggestion of a curved edge in the sky, its light weak, the shadows it created faint. When a cloud obscured it, Hanako slipped through the door and into the shallow space beneath the hut. Here she waited, as Kimi had waited earlier. Thoughts of the girl made Hanako smile. She was really too bold for her own good. The trait would have been fine in a boy, because boys were supposed to be bold. A girl needed more restraint. Yin and yang. The balance of man and woman.

That Kimi had overheard much of her conversation with Emily was not entirely harmless. She would not be able to keep from sharing such tantalizing information with her friends, and it would quickly enter the realm of gossip and myth that constantly swirled around every Great Lord of Akaoka. Still, her presence under the hut also served a useful purpose. It insured that no one else was there at the same time. What she and Emily had to say could be overheard without serious danger by gossiping girls, but not by Lord Genji's enemies, and they were everywhere. Even among his bodyguard corps. Or so she suspected.

Escape would be difficult. She could slip away. Emily could not, and

Emily was the important one. How strange. Heiko had been right. Emily and Lord Genji were destined for each other, and contrary to every indication, Heiko and Lord Genji had not been. She had not returned to Japan from California. Neither had her son. That had to mean the boy was not Genji's, since if he were, Genji would surely have called him to his side, even if, for reasons known only to himself, he intended to discard Heiko. Is that what had happened? Would she ever know?

Hanako knew that Emily was in love with Genji, of course, and had been for many years now. That was obvious to everyone. Emily was blind to the fact that her secret love was a secret only for her. The way she looked at him, the slight but consistent shift in her posture toward him whenever he was in her company, the change in the tone of her voice, not only when she spoke to him, but whenever she said his name. If all outsiders were as transparent, then every one of their affairs must be carried out like performances on a public stage. What must that be like, such a wanton disregard for the privacy of one's emotions?

There was nothing in Lord Genji's behavior that gave the slightest hint of affection beyond friendship. Since he was a master at concealing his inner self, this was not definitive. Still, it was very unlikely that he returned Emily's feelings. He was possessed of highly refined tastes, even for a lord, and a foreign woman of Emily's limited intimate understanding could have little appeal for him. If the prophecy of the scrolls was to come true, it must do so in a most unexpected way.

Hanako heard the murmur of voices. The two guards were together in one place now. She crawled away on the other side of the hut and made her way into the woods undetected.

She found the two foundation stones without difficulty. She could never remember the famous poems that other women recited so easily. But her memory of a place once seen was flawless. She felt along the edges of the first stone, found nothing, and moved on to the second. She didn't know what she was looking for, but whatever it was, she was sure it was here. In the scrolls, Shizuka had said she would leave a sign of her presence for Emily. At first, Hanako had assumed that was a reference to the foundation stones themselves. But what did they signify except the existence of the cell in olden times? That had already been spoken of in the scrolls. There had to be something else. The second was like the first, no more than a flat, heavy stone stuck in the ground. She stepped slowly through the grass toward where she thought the third stone would be. And there it was. Again, nothing. Following the line of the wall she visualized, she came to the fourth stone. Unlike the others, it was loose. Six hundred years ago, this had been flat ground. Since then, the shifting of earth in the mountainside had caused a winter stream to flow in this direction, where it had eroded the ground.

She reached under the stone. There was nothing immediately available to the touch except dirt and small stones. She kept feeling under it but found nothing. It was too dark for her eyes to be of any help.

Hanako froze when she heard stealthy footsteps nearby. Someone was moving in a heavily wooded area about a hundred paces distant. The samurai—she could tell he was a samurai by the topknot of his silhouette—bent down and picked something up out of the brush. When he stood, he turned his profile to Hanako. He had retrieved a bow and arrow. She couldn't see him well enough to recognize him. When he returned toward Mushindo, she followed him. It was late, so few lights burned within the monastery. There was only the single sentry lantern at the gate. The man avoided this and climbed nimbly over a dark part of the wall. When he did, his face was briefly illuminated.

Taro.

Hanako thought back to the afternoon. Emily had seen Shizuka in a clearing close by. Taro had retrieved his weapon from a spot that would have given him both concealment and an easy shot, even for an archer of his limited skills. He had been prevented from killing Emily only by her baffling behavior.

Hanako hurried back to the hut where Emily slept. This was not the time to worry about messages from ghosts. If Taro had tried once, he would try again, and almost certainly before they left Mushindo. He was playing the part of an anonymous assassin, which gave some small advantage to the two women. How could she make the best use of it?

· · · · ·

By morning, Taro decided he would act as soon as they were on the road to Edo. His men would first seize and bind Hanako in order to prevent her from attempting to defend Emily. If they killed Hanako, Hidé would never join them against Lord Genji, no matter what he thought about the right-eousness of their cause. Taro had given up any attempt at secrecy. He would kill Emily in the open, with his sword.

"Lady Hanako, Lady Emily." He stood outside the door of the abbot's hut. "We are ready to proceed as soon as you—"

He felt the bullet split open his brow before he heard the explosion of gunpowder.

"Traitor!" Hanako yelled through the closed door. She had used Taro's voice as her guide and aimed her shot where she thought his head would be. She doubted she had hit him. That would be impossibly good luck.

Taro scrambled backward as quickly as he could on his hands and knees, the pouring blood half blinding him. Had she shot out his eye? He didn't even know she had a gun.

"Lady Hanako!" he said. "What are you doing? It's me, Taro."

"I know who you are," she said, "and I know what you are." Before dawn, she had gone to the girls' hut and told Kimi to send a message to Edo as quickly as she could. They were surrounded by traitors.

I will go myself, Kimi said. I am the fastest runner here.

You can't run all the way to Edo, Hanako said.

I don't have to. Lord Hiromitsu is Lord Genji's friend. One of his senior retainers has an estate not far from here. He'll help.

The rascally girl was now their only hope. If she failed to bring rein-forcements soon, Taro and his men would storm the hut and kill Emily. Besides the gun—a silver-plated .32-caliber revolver that had come from California as a gift from Stark—she had another trick she could use. But it was risky and she preferred not to resort to it unless forced to do so.

"Hanako, are you sure you're right?" Emily said. "Taro has put himself in harm's way for my sake many times. I can't believe he would ever hurt me."

"There is no other explanation for the bow and arrow." She began shifting one of the mats from the floor. Emily helped her stand it against the door. "It won't stop them, but it will slow them. Perhaps enough."

"He might have been hunting," Emily said.

"At night? Hunting what? Owls?"

"Perhaps he hunted during the day, was distracted by my fainting spell, and forgot the bow and arrow there."

"A samurai forgetting his weapon?" Hanako said. It was unthinkable. They moved another mat and placed it against the first.

· · · · ·

The lieutenant said to Taro, "You have lost a part of your brow."

Taro pushed his hand away and held the cloth to the wound himself. "Bring the girl."

He and his men had retreated fifty paces from the abbot's hut. It would be best if Hanako could be convinced to surrender. Otherwise, it would be necessary to storm the hut. He didn't know how well Hanako could shoot. He had never seen her practicing, so she was probably not very good, despite having drawn blood with her first shot. Still, at close range, in a confined space, with the determination that Hanako had, the situation would be very dangerous. He was not concerned about casualties among his men, or even of being killed himself. His fear was that she would fight to the death to protect Emily. It was to avoid just such a tactic that he had planned to take her by surprise as soon as they were traveling once again. Unfortunately, she had somehow anticipated danger.

"Here she is." The lieutenant roughly pushed Kimi forward. Her arms were bound tightly behind her.

"You are doomed," Kimi said. "Surrender now and you may be pardoned."

"Silence!" The lieutenant slapped her hard with the back of his hand, knocking her to the ground. He jerked her back onto her feet with the rope and made to strike her again.

Taro held up his hand. The girl was woozy from the blow, and blood dripped from her nose and mouth, but she appeared completely unafraid. She was either very brave or a complete idiot, like the huge monk who wandered silently about Mushindo, always smiling.

"Are you a princess in disguise," Taro said, "that you have the power to grant us pardon?"

"The pardon would come from Lord Genji, of course," Kimi said. "He is well known for his soft heart."

"You brazen brat!" The lieutenant drew his sword.

"Stop," Taro said. "Her head is more useful where it is. For now." He would show Hanako that her hope of rescue was a false one. The girl had failed to get past his sentries.

"You can't succeed," Kimi said.

"I see," Taro said. "You are not a princess, you are a prophetess."

"Not me," Kimi said, jutting her chin forward defiantly, "Lady Shizuka."

The derisive mumbling among the men instantly evaporated. The bizarre night sounds of Mushindo had taken a toll. As the lieutenant had said, the men were nervous, and the mention of that witch's name was decidedly unhelpful.

"She is long dead," Taro said, "and the dead do not come back to life."

"Perhaps," Kimi said, "but her prophecies live. Or have you not heard of *Autumn Bridge*?"

"There is no such thing," Taro said. "A tale to frighten children, nothing more."

"Then what are those scrolls Lady Hanako and Lady Emily have been reading?"

Taro laughed. "Emily is translating the inner history of our clan. Even a peasant like you must know of it."

"Does your history predict the meeting of Lady Emily and Lady Shizuka? Does it say, *We will meet at Mushindo, where my little abode once stood. Only you will see me. When others look, they will not find me. But I will be there.*" Kimi didn't remember the exact words. That was close enough. Better than close enough, judging by the way several of the samurai were looking over their shoulders. "Didn't you yourself find the old foundation?"

"How do you know what it says? Can you even read?"

"I have ears," Kimi said. "I listened to them talking."

"Enough!" The lieutenant pulled the rope, knocking Kimi off her feet. He dragged her into the open and toward the abbot's hut. "Lady Hanako! Your messenger failed! Surrender is your only choice! No harm will come to you! You have my word!"

"What weight has a traitor's word?" Hanako answered. "Less than the downy fluff of a cygnet." And she fired a second shot. Taro had never seen her practice. Apparently she had been doing so in secret. A bright blossom of blood erupted in the center of the lieutenant's back a moment before he dropped dead. Kimi got to her feet and took off toward the hut, the rope trailing behind her.

"Take Lady Hanako without harm," Taro said. "Leave Emily to me." They drew their swords and rushed forward. Four more gunshots rang out. Two of his men fell. Taro threw himself at the door.

And found himself in a fiery explosion. Hanako had set the hut ablaze. Taro leaped out and rolled on the ground to extinguish the flames that had ignited his clothing.

"Don't stand there staring!" he said to his men. "Find them!" Several men started toward the door of the burning hut. "Not there, idiot!" Hanako might immolate herself. She would never let Emily die. "The other side!"

. . . . .

"This way!" Kimi said to Hanako and Emily. "Quickly!" Once they were in the woods, they could take any of a hundred hidden trails away from Mushindo and into the surrounding valleys and mountains. They would be safe.

But Emily slowed them too much. Taro's men cut them off before they were anywhere near the closest tree. Hanako drew her short sword and stood in front of her friend.

"Fool," she said to Taro. "You of all people should know better."

"The future of our nation is more important than any one person," Taro said. Could he disarm her without killing her? It would be difficult. He had seen Hanako in combat at this very place. She was better with her sword than many of his men were with theirs.

"The future is a mystery," Hanako said, "to you, to me, to everyone. Everyone except Lord Genji. How can you presume to act against him?"

"The time has come to make history," Taro said, "not recite fairy tales." He feinted to the left, then to the right. If he could kill Emily first, then, there being no reason to continue fighting, Hanako might surrender.

Hanako ignored Taro's first feint, but moved to intercept his second as if she thought he was making a committed attack. Two of his men, seeing the opening she wanted them to see, rushed in to grab her from behind. She promptly spun in their direction, cut down the first with an upward slash of her blade, and the second with its descent. Hanako could not have defeated two samurai intending to use their swords. Two trying to take hold of her rather than cut her down were much less of a challenge. This gave Taro his chance, however. Her back was now toward him. He leaped forward and wrapped his arms tightly around her.

"Stop struggling," he said to her. "It's over."

His men surrounded Emily but stopped short of seizing her. His orders had been to take Hanako without harm and leave Emily to him. Because he himself had taken Hanako and had done nothing about Emily, his men could not do as he had said. Without specific orders, they were befuddled by the changed circumstances. They had been trained since childhood to obey without question. Little emphasis had been put on taking the initiative, which implied a lack of competence on the part of the leader who had issued orders incapable of fulfillment.

Their hesitation was compounded by Emily's status. Until a few minutes ago, they had been treating her with the greatest deference because of her long-standing relationship with Lord Genji and the role she had played in the fulfillment of earlier prophecies. The sudden shift to thinking of her as an outsider who had to be sacrificed was far too abrupt for them. The unsettled night they had spent at Mushindo did not help. The eerie sounds, compounded by the numerous rumors and legends associated with the place, had more than a few of them seeing and hearing things that were not there. No one wanted to be the one to strike Emily down. It was up to Taro.

He said, "Here, hold Lady Hanako." As his men moved to obey, a large rock slammed down onto Taro's right foot. The sudden pain made him lean out of balance just as Hanako tried to twist out of his grasp. He fell, still holding on to her. The brat, Kimi, raised the rock to strike again, but had to dive away when one of his men slashed at her. The first cut barely missed her. The second did nothing but mow down tall grass. She was gone.

The fall loosened Taro's grip just enough. Hanako's sword was still in her hand. She shifted her angle just enough and thrust the sword backward as hard as she could into Taro's torso. The blade went in deep beneath the floating rib.

"Ah!" Taro drew back from her.

Hanako pulled the blade out of Taro, thrust it into the man nearest her, and slashed her way toward Emily. Since the men had been ordered not to harm Hanako, they could do nothing but retreat as she advanced.

"Lord!" His men moved to assist him.

"Stand away!" Taro said.

His blood drenched his clothing. He pressed his hand against the wound. His internal injuries were serious, but he was able to stanch the outward flow of blood. They were back where they had started, surrounding Emily and Hanako, with Hanako, sword in hand, ready to kill and die. Except that in a few minutes, he had lost lost six men. To an opposing force composed of an outsider woman, a brat, and the one-armed wife of his best friend.

Enough.

Taro got back to his feet.

He ignored the intense pain. His injury could well be mortal. If he fell without killing Emily, the entire plan would fail before it began. She had to die, no matter what the cost. He stepped toward the two women.

"Lady Hanako," he said, "do not sacrifice yourself for nothing. What will your son do without his mother?" He hoped his words would distract her enough for his men to surprise her. He knew nothing he said would weaken her resolve.

Hanako held her sword with the point aimed straight at Taro's eyes. She said, "He will be a loyal samurai, like his father, and he will die an honorable death. A reward you have denied yourself." Emily could not be hurt! Lady Shizuka had prophesied that she would bear Lord Genji's child. If this did not happen in the proper way, who knew what tragic consequences would result? Hanako shifted constantly from left to right, trying to keep all of her opponents within her field of vision.

With a cry of surprise, one of Taro's men dropped to his knees. He put his hand to his head. It came away bloody. He was having trouble focusing his eyes.

A second flung stone split the flesh of a second samurai's cheek.

The third barely missed Taro himself.

· · · · ·

"Very good, Goro," Kimi said, "very good."

"Kimi," Goro said, picking up another stone.

"Remember, if they chase us, run as fast as you can for the Mushroom Hot Spring," she said. "Don't worry about me. I'm small. I can hide in the grass."

"Kimi," Goro said.

"Goro," Kimi said.

Goro threw the stone. He was amazingly accurate at the range of fifty paces. In the days before he began imitating monkish ways, he used to kill rabbits for his mother. She was an idiot, too, like Goro. That was the only reason the fervent Buddhists in the village didn't ostracize them for killing fellow sentient beings, which violated Buddha's Law. Since they were idiots, they had already been ostracized. There was one thing Goro's mother could do better than normal people, though. Cook. Her rabbit stew in particular was incredibly delicious. Now that he was pretending to be a monk, Goro didn't kill anything anymore. Since his mother died, nobody made rabbit stew, either. Not that there was anyone bringing a whole lot of rabbits into the village since Goro stopped stoning them, anyway.

Now that the traitorous samurai saw Goro, they were ducking out of the way. The stone throwing was still a good tactic, since it kept them from continuing their advance on the two ladies. How could they turn against Lord Genji? When Kimi was a little girl, she and all the other children in the village had watched the famous battle. Hundreds of musketeers surrounded him and fired hundreds and hundreds of bullets at him, bullets that were still found in abundance all over the ruins of Mushindo. Not one hit him. Of course not. How could a bullet hit a lord who knew the future? He would simply not be where the bullets would go.

Kimi would ordinarily never dare to talk back to samurai, much less clout them with rocks. But this was different. She was helping Lord Genji. Lord Genji always won. He could see the future, so no one could ever defeat him. No doubt he had foreseen this treachery and had already taken steps to crush the traitors. He might arrive at any time at the head of a column of his famous cavalry, banners flying, the blades of the long lances sparkling, loyal samurai calling out his name as a battle cry. What a splendid sight that would be.

Of course, Lord Genji's triumph might occur in a completely different way, a way she could never imagine. How did that famous saying go? The old folk in the village always repeated it when they were trying to seem wise. Ah, yes.

Lord Genji said, The foreseen always occurs in unforeseen ways.

The old folk claimed to have heard him say it after the battle, when his few had defeated the Sticky Eye's many. She wondered if that was true. Unlike most in the village, Kimi had actually seen Lord Genji up close, and she had heard him speak. It was just casual conversation she'd eavesdropped on, nothing deep and profound. But personal experience had given her some insight into his character. She thought it more likely that he would have smiled that odd little smile of his and said something funny, nothing so weighty and old-folksy as the words attributed to him.

"Aim for that one holding his side," Kimi said.

"Kimi," Goro said.

"Goro," she said.

"Kimi," he said, and threw the stone.

· · · · ·

"Stop dodging about like fools," Taro said. "Use your bows. You—shoot down that stone-throwing idiot. And the brat. You—kill the outsider woman." He would have shot Emily himself, if the wound in his side had not made it impossible. "Take care not to hit Lady Hanako by mistake."

"Lord," the two men said. They pulled arrows from their quivers, nocked them, and drew their bows.

QUIET CRANE PALACE, EDO

Several samurai were waiting outside the gates when Charles Smith arrived. He was on horseback, since Genji had suggested a morning ride. All of the men bowed deeply to him as he dismounted. One of them took his reins and, still bowing, said something in Japanese, which Smith took to be an assurance that his mount would be looked after with great care.

"Thank you," Smith said, bowing in return. He did not know much about Japan or the Japanese, but he assumed that courtesy would always be understood, even when words were not. The secondary gate was opened and the samurai bowed again, their leader indicating to Smith that he should proceed first. The main gate was used only when Lord Genji arrived and departed, or when lords of high rank visited him. Smith took no offense. Ancient cultures tended to be rigidly attached to their traditional practices. When those practices were destroyed or abandoned, the culture, too, inevitably succumbed.

It had happened to the Aztecs of Mexico and the Incas of Peru when the Spanish arrived. When the English and the French reached North America, it had happened to the Huron and the Mohegan and the Cherokee, and was happening even now to the Sioux and the Cheyenne and the Apache. When his own ancestors arrived in the Hawaiian Islands at the turn of the century, there were a million Hawaiians harvesting rich crops of taro, fishing in abundant seas, and practicing a religion of gods and taboos that dictated a balance and harmony between nature and society.

Today, they were barely a tenth that number, decimated by diseases brought by Americans and Europeans, demoralized by the failure of their gods, and near extinction and annexation. What was happening in the New World was happening in the Old as well. The Russian army was crushing the Tartars and the Kazakhs, the last remnants of a Mongol empire that once ruled the better part of two continents, from the Pacific Ocean to the Baltic and the Black Seas. The British and the French, and even the Dutch, were carving Africa into their imperial possessions. In Asia, India was inexorably being absorbed into the British Empire. Britain, France, and Russia all had their eyes on China. And after China, could Japan be far behind? The Japanese were a warrior society, but so, too, had been the Incas and the Aztecs, and they had fallen. The Japanese were a great population, upwards of forty million, but India and China were far greater, and they were falling. The Japanese were not susceptible to unfamiliar diseases the way the Hawaiians were, but they were armed with swords and spears and a few old muskets, while the Western Powers possessed an abundance of the deadliest weaponry science could produce. For the Japanese, modern warfare would be as deadly as a pestilence against which they had no resistance.

The natural law that Charles Darwin had discovered applied to men and nations as well as jungle animals. Only the fittest survive.

Smith knew this. He knew the Japanese were doomed, so he was not offended by their overweening pride or their unconcealed disdain. It was no more than the ignorance and conceit of ghosts who did not yet realize they had already passed away.

Their demise was as inevitable as the rising of the sun. The civilizations of the East had unquestionably been great in their day. To know this, one had only to look upon the Taj Mahal, or the Great Wall of China, or the towering Golden Buddha at Kamakura. Smith had seen each of these places with his own eyes, and so he knew. But that day of Eastern greatness was long past. India, China, Japan, and all the rest were static societies, intent on an unchanging stability, the great ideal of the East. They had no concept of progress, and thus would be swept away by it. It was not really a matter of steam power, cannons, armies, or armadas. It was, as in everything human, a matter of belief. The West believed the golden age of mankind lay ahead. The East believed it lay in the past. That made all the difference.

He felt no particular antagonism toward the Japanese, despite the virulently anti-Western attitude of most of their leaders. They could not escape the embrace of a stagnation and degeneracy that had been tightening for centuries. It would be more accurate to say rather that, in addition to a natural sense of superiority, he felt sympathy, as any civilized man must for those facing extinction. And of course he had no antagonism toward Genji personally. Indeed, he rather liked the man. He did not relish the fact that Genji was doomed in the long run. He simply saw reality and accepted it. It was quite poignant, because Genji was at heart very progressive. He was among the few Japanese advocating the adoption of Western knowledge and methods on a large scale. But it was too little, too late. In many respects, Japan was where Europe had been five hundred years ago. Five centuries could not be made up in the time Japan had before it would be overwhelmed. By the turn of the twentieth century, a little more than three decades hence, Japan, like the rest of the Oriental world, would be under the heel of a Western power. The only matter in doubt was which. With the right administration in Washington, it could be the United States. And why not? Who was to say that the imperatives of Manifest Destiny ceased at the western edge of the North American continent? The Mediterranean had been a Roman lake in the age of the Caesars. Why should the Pacific not be an American lake in the present one? There was no reason that Smith could see.

The samurai led him along a newly constructed walkway into the inner garden of the palace. There he was surprised to see Genji sitting on a chair in the main room, which, he noticed with even sharper surprise, had been entirely converted into a reception room in the Western style. Genji was dressed as usual in traditional samurai garb, except on this occasion he wore English riding boots instead of the traditional sandals.

"Why, Lord Genji," Smith said, "I see you have decided at last to begin your conversion to Western ways."

Genji laughed. "I would not call it a conversion. It is more like a sampling." He gestured at the room. "Does this meet with your approval?"

"How could it not? It looks very much like my own living room in Honolulu."

Genji smiled. "It should. I used your description as a guide. From what you said, I take it that the climate in Hawaii is not unlike that of Japan in the milder seasons."

"Yes, that's true. Winter is another story, however."

"In winter," Genji said, "perhaps I will redecorate following Lieutenant Farrington's description of his home in Ohio."

Smith's good cheer evaporated instantly upon the mention of Farrington.

"That sounds like more trouble than it's worth," he said. "You would be better advised to pick one scheme and stay with it."

Smith was affected the way he was because he suspected Emily preferred Farrington to him. He had never observed anything intimate or romantically conspiratorial passing between them in the brief moments he had seen them together. But her reaction to Smith himself was not particularly warm. Since she had made it clear to both of them that she would decide between them, the conclusion was obvious to Smith. He had not withdrawn his suit, because he was not a quitter. As long as the decision had not yet been announced, there was always a chance.

Smith held out for that chance, not because he loved Emily, but because he desired her more than he had ever desired anything in his life. She was, without question, the most beautiful woman he had ever seen in life or in portraiture, or had even dared to imagine. That he did not love Emily bothered him not in the least. Love was something for women and children, not men. Women were dependent and sympathetic, while men were powerful and dominating. This, too, followed Darwin. A healthy, dynamic man—like a healthy, dynamic nation—constantly strove for greater power and increased possessions.

"That is something I don't understand about Western architecture," Genji said.

"Which is?" Smith said.

"Its inflexibility. A room serves only one purpose. Furnishings, once placed, remain. Do you find this logical?"

"Yes, I do," Smith said. "Our rooms remain as they are because we have an abundance of furnishings and strong, solid walls. Your rooms alter depending upon the occasion because you have few furnishings, and instead of walls, you have removable screens."

"I see the logic of each. What I meant to ask is, do you find your way more logical than ours?"

"If I may be honest without giving offense," Smith said, and paused.

"I am never offended by honesty," Genji said. He smiled and added, "Indeed, I do my best not to be offended by intentional insult, either."

"I beg your pardon, sir, but it has been my understanding that samurai are always ready to answer the least insult with their swords."

"Yes, and a foolish waste of time, energy, and life it is. It is as if you gave control of the trigger of your pistol to anyone who cared to pull it. Would you do that?"

"No, of course I would not."

"I, too, prefer not to." Genji bowed slightly. "Please continue."

"Western rooms are more logical than Japanese ones because tables and chairs are more logical than their absence. Furniture of the Western type allows the human body to assume a healthier, more natural posture in repose, rather than the cramping of muscles and reduction of blood circulation required by sitting on the floor. Similarly, walls of solid construction are far more effective at protecting against turbulent weather, insects, and vermin, and also provide much greater security than walls of movable paper screens. I would think this last aspect would particularly appeal to you, since you are a samurai."

"Security does not come from the solidity of walls," Genji said, "but from the loyalty of retainers. Without them, walls of impenetrable steel could not protect me."

"My lord." Hidé, Lord Genji's chief bodyguard and senior general, appeared in the courtyard. With him was Lieutenant Robert Farrington, the American naval attaché and Smith's rival for the hand of Emily Gibson.

"I'm sorry to intrude," Farrington said. He shot a hostile glare at Smith. "I must have misunderstood your invitation."

"Not at all," Genji said. "Please come in."

"Forgive me, Lord Genji, but I have a strong preference to be elsewhere than in company with your present guest."

"Elsewhere is precisely where we are going. Please. Join us."

Smith stood, bowed to Genji, and returned Farrington's glare.

"Don't inconvenience yourself, Admiral. I am always ready to yield to Union war heroes." The way Smith spit the words out expressed his meaning far more eloquently than what he said.

Genji saw Hidé move slightly to allow himself a better angle to draw his sword and cut Farrington down in a single motion. The two samurai sitting in the corridor outside the room had their attention fixed intently on Smith. Both Americans were armed with revolvers. Since Genji considered them friends, he did not require them to disarm before entering his presence, against the advice, and much to the dismay, of his retainers. Whenever Farrington or Smith were visiting, his men were ready to strike. A little too ready for comfort. Americans shifted about more than Japanese, and moved their arms frequently in gestures large and small. These unpredictable movements often had his bodyguards reaching for their swords. If Genji had it to do over again, he would ask his American acquaintances to leave the guns at the entrance, for their sake rather than his own.

Genji said, "Well, I suppose if one of you were to decline to ride with me, it would simplify things for Emily. However, is that truly a good thing? Don't American women greatly value the ability to choose for themselves?" As he expected they would, his words surprised both men. They now looked at him instead of at each other.

"How is Emily involved in this matter?" Smith said.

"She is the heart of our involvement," Genji said. "I as her friend, and you as her suitors."

Farrington said, "Forgive the contradiction, Lord Genji, but I don't see how the question of whether or not Mr. Smith and I choose to ride together arises in that connection. We are both your friends, and we are both seeking Emily's hand. It does not follow that he and I must be in each other's society beyond absolute necessity."

"For once, sir, we are in agreement," Smith said, "and absolute necessity requires only that we are gentlemanly in our adieus should we find ourselves in the unfortunate happenstance of being in one and the same place."

Farrington made a shallow bow of the Western kind to Smith.

He said, "Since your arrival preceded mine, sir, I will not further interrupt your interview with Lord Genji."

"On the contrary," Smith said, making an identical bow to his rival, "since I have already had an opportunity to speak with him, it is clear that it is I who must yield to you."

"I beg to differ, sir," Farrington said.

Genji sighed. He had lost their attention once again. He was a patient man, but the endless squabbling of these two exceeded his limits. How different Americans were from Japanese. If they had been samurai, they would have dueled many weeks ago, and their dilemma would have been solved. Yet here they were, still exchanging meaningless words. Of course, no sensible samurai would have expended so much energy over a mere woman in the first place, certainly not one like Emily without rank, wealth, or political connections of any kind.

Genji said, "You may differ and yield as much as you wish, for as long as you wish, when and wherever you wish. I will excuse myself, however, and be on my way. May I convey to Emily your regrets for your absence?"

"Excuse me, Lord Genji," Farrington said, "but it was my understanding that Emily is not presently in the city."

"That is so."

Smith laughed. "Ah, now I see your plan, my lord. We are to ride to meet her."

Genji bowed in assent.

"And on the way," Smith said, looking at Farrington, "we will settle the matter of who is to win Emily's hand."

Again, Genji bowed. It was the only solution he could see. Emily was no closer to making a decision than she had been six months ago, when she first met the two men. It was imperative that she choose one of them and leave Japan as soon as possible.

"Have you forgotten Emily's admonition?" Farrington said. "If we indulge in violence of any kind, she will have nothing to do with either of us."

"If she is not there, how will she know?" Smith said.

"The permanent absence of one of us will be a telling fact, will it not?"

Smith shrugged. "It will be up to the survivor to weave a convincing tale."

"Are you suggesting that we lie to Emily?"

"Why not? How does it hurt her?"

Farrington said, "A lie, sir, is a lie. I will not utter it."

Smith smiled. "Rest assured, sir, you will not have to."

"Nor will you. I refuse to participate in any such deception."

Smith sneered. "How convenient, Admiral. As you have in the past not hesitated to shoot helpless women, I should not be so surprised to find you willing to hide behind their words."

"You are always accusing us of being illogical," Genji said, before

Farrington could answer. "If your present behavior is an example of Western logic, I must admit I do not see it. Mr. Smith had defined what seems to me to be the appropriate, and logical, solution."

"What is logical is not always ethical," Farrington said. "Yes, Emily's choice is made without further action on her part if one of us shoots the other dead. But she has trusted us not to do so. Ethics therefore requires us to conform to her trust. Yet even this is not entirely satisfactory. I love Emily very much. I know Mr. Smith does not, and I know therefore that he cannot make her happy, because he cannot treat her as she needs to be treated, that is, with love. Yet I fear she will not see this, and will be swayed by what is superficially attractive about him. His good looks, his wealth, his easy charm. Logically, therefore, I should accept his offer of a duel, for I have no doubt that I will triumph. I would save Emily from a lifetime of unhappiness with the wrong man. But I cannot, for I have promised not to. I am at a loss, sir. I admit it."

Smith's own face had grown progressively redder as he had listened to Farrington.

He said, "How can you speak of my innermost feelings? How can you presume to know anything of them?"

"You are not difficult to know," Farrington said. "A man who would lie so easily for a good reason would lie without difficulty for a bad one. And a liar is not a fit husband for Emily."

"Gentlemen," Genji said, interrupting what gave every indication of being an endless argument, "let us ride. If it will not bring us closer to a mutually acceptable solution, it will at least bring us closer to Emily."

Despite Farrington's disinclination to accept Smith's offer of a duel, it seemed to Genji that if he could get both men on the road to Mushindo, it was very likely that violence would solve the dilemma. They could barely contain themselves when they were in each other's presence for a few minutes. How could they both survive two days together? He did not think they could.

· · · · ·

Farrington lay back and looked up at the darkness between the stars. During the war, he had spent many nights ashore, encamped alone, under the unobstructed vault of the sky. He could not, in those days, stand being long within any building. Perhaps he had seen too many charred corpses in the ruins of the Southern towns and cities he had helped to blockade and bombard. When the war ended, so did his phobia. Perhaps the end of violence had lifted an inchoate fear from his heart. Perhaps. He did not know and never would.

Genji and Smith and the rest of the traveling party were somewhere behind him. They had probably taken shelter in one of the farmhouses of the village he had passed that day. He imagined Smith's discomfort at the fact that he was on the road ahead of them. He could not help but smile. He had made it a condition of the journey that he travel alone, apart from Smith. Smith, of course, had objected strenuously.

Smith said, Once out of our sight, what guarantee do we have that you will not speed ahead in an effort to gain advantage by arriving first?

Farrington said, You have my word that I will not do so.

Your word? Smith said.

Your word is sufficient, Genji said.

Smith said, Lord Genji, at least send your general Hidé with him so that he does not, shall we say, lose his way.

I have been to Mushindo before, Farrington said, and the way is not complicated. To Genji he said, Is it convenient for us to meet in the clearing immediately east of the monastery?

It is, Genji said.

Until then, Farrington said, saluted Genji, and rode off. He half expected Smith to shoot him in the back. There was little to separate a liar from a coward, and a coward would do anything to achieve his ends. He heard Smith's angry voice raised in protest. But no shot came.

It was not only to avoid Smith that Farrington wanted to ride alone. He needed solitude to order his thoughts, which were much confused. He had no doubts about his feelings for Emily. He was in love with her. That should have made his course of action clear, but it had not, for nearly everything else was questionable in a situation where there was a distinct paucity of certain answers.

The most pressing of the myriad uncertainties was the nature of the relationship between Emily and Genji. Even the first rumors he had heard had consistency only in the barest facts. Everyone began by telling him, rather breathlessly and too eagerly, that a beautiful young missionary named Emily Gibson was living in the palace of Lord Genji, one of the most dissolute warlords in Japan. There agreement ended.

They were brazenly flouting the laws of God and man against religious and racial miscegenation.

They were pious Christians, one the converter, the other the converted, living as nun and monk.

She was a desperate addict of the satanic poppy, and he, her conscienceless supplier.

He was a sexual deviant who had seduced her to his nefarious Oriental ways, ways to which she had become no more than a pathetic and degraded slave.

She was not a missionary at all, but a secret political agent of France, Russia, England, Holland, the United States, or the Papacy, plotting for or against the Shogun or the Emperor, with the ultimate aim of delivering control of the country into the hands of France, Russia, England, Holland, the United States, or the Papacy.

He was not only decadent, but insane, believing himself to be a prophet and devising a scheme, a scheme in which the fallen woman was deeply involved, to set himself up as Pontiff of a new religion, one that would enable him to displace Emperor, Shogun, Buddha, and the ancient gods of Japan, and become supreme ruler of a nation of fanatical believers in himself alone.

The wild rumors that had flown about among sailors and soldiers during the war were nothing compared to what Farrington heard within a week of his arrival in Edo. If the tantalizing fact of a Western woman ensconced in the palace of an Eastern lord were not enough, speculation of the most limitless kind was further encouraged by the scandal surrounding the Light of the True Word of the Prophets of Christ, that sect being the one for which Emily had arrived in Japan as a missionary. The True Word church had collapsed three years earlier amidst accusations of deviancy so extreme they strained credulity. Even the muted official findings had contained suggestions of perverse and outrageous carnality that would have well complemented the seraglios of Sodom and Gomorrah.

Farrington had neither given the rumors credence nor dismissed them outright. He had learned during the war that the unbelievable was unfortunately sometimes all too true. By degrees imperceptible even to themselves, it was possible for men to sink to a level more bestial than that of the beasts of an African jungle. Those savage creatures were constrained by the limits of natural law. Men who lost their humanity had no such saving grace.

The rumors of opium addiction caused the deepest concern. He had not at the time met or even laid eyes on Emily Gibson or her warlord host, so he knew nothing of their character beyond the conflicting reports he had heard. But he had visited Hong Kong during a naval tour of Eastern ports, and there had observed the insidious corruptive power of the drug with his own eyes. If this Miss Gibson was addicted, there was nothing she would not do to maintain her supply. In the opium dens and brothels of Hong Kong, he had seen women in various states of drugged compliance offered for the perverted pleasure of any who would pay the price. It shocked and saddened him that a countrywoman, and a Christian missionary at that, could have sunk to the same depths.

But he had felt no emotional engagement beyond that natural for a gentleman upon hearing of the misfortunes of a lady. This world was truly a vale of tears. He could not hope to alleviate the suffering of every unfortunate whose path crossed his own. He had learned this lesson repeatedly during the war. Thus, he had sympathy, but no inclination toward personal involvement.

Then he saw her.

It was at an embassy reception intended to bring together members of the growing American business community with influential Japanese nobles. Anti-foreign sentiment had made it necessary to surround the embassy grounds with a fully armed contingent of United States Marines.

"Unfortunate," the ambassador had said to him. "They somewhat diminish the welcoming atmosphere conducive to our purposes."

"Perhaps not, Mr. Ambassador," Farrington had replied. "Our military display may well be viewed in a more celebratory light than we imagine. The Shogun's troops patrol all roads leading here, and every warlord will undoubtedly arrive surrounded by his own regiment. Unlike the Chinese, the Japanese seem to find armed troops not unpleasant to behold."

"Let us hope you are right," the ambassador said. Then, as one of the invited warlords arrived, he said, "Good God. How brazen. He's brought *her*."

"Sir?"

"That worthy is Lord Genji, an influential member of the Shogun's inner council. I have mentioned him before."

"Forgive me, sir. I have heard so many Japanese names during the week I have been here, it has been difficult to keep them properly sorted. I cannot say that I remember what you said about him."

"Well, you do recall the so-called missionary I told you about? Emily Gibson?"

"Yes, that I do. Such a sad and unusual story."

"She is the woman with Lord Genji."

He saw her hair first, shimmering filaments of spun gold among the dark heads. Then he caught a glimpse of her form, surprisingly shapely in a rather prim and unstylish dress at least a decade out of date.

"There's no escaping it," the ambassador said. "We cannot afford to give offense to Lord Genji." He led Farrington toward the recent arrivals.

"Good evening, Ambassador Van Valkenburgh," Genji said. "Thank you for your kind invitation."

Genji was not the grim warlord Farrington had expected. He smiled most readily. Furthermore, his entire demeanor was distinctly unmartial, perhaps even to the extent of slight effeminacy. Most surprising, he spoke English nearly without an accent.

"The pleasure is entirely mine, Lord Genji," the ambassador said. He made a polite bow to Genji's companion. "Miss Gibson, how nice to see you once again. It has been too long."

"Thank you, sir," Emily said.

"Lord Genji, Miss Gibson, this is Lieutenant Robert Farrington, my newly assigned naval attaché."

More polite words were exchanged. Farrington hardly knew what he heard and forgot what he said nearly as soon as he had spoken. Had his eyes ever beheld such a vision of feminine perfection? He could honestly say that they had not. But it was not her beauty that captivated him, or at least, not her beauty alone. He saw within her open gaze and her tentative smile signs of a sadness hidden deep within. At once, that hidden injury, its cause unknown, touched him. From that moment, even before any significant words had passed between them, he began to care.

He had since then had occasion to contemplate the event. Would he have cared about her welfare and her salvation had her physical attributes not been as they were? What if she had been deformed, or even merely homely? What then? Would her fate have mattered so much? In truth, would his motivation bear close scrutiny? Were his feelings of love really more noble than the mere desire for possession he attributed to his rival Smith?

Always, he was able to answer yes, because he knew it was that sadness that made her beauty so compelling to him. He was vain enough to think he could cure her of it by the simple act of loving her faithfully and completely. Love was the last great hope that remained to him. He had lost his belief in everything else during the war.

He expected Genji to obstruct his suit, but the warlord did not. On the contrary, he encouraged it from the very start. He was, at the same time, also encouraging Charles Smith, though Farrington didn't know it at the time. In any case, both actions strongly suggested that Genji did not have an attachment to Emily. It did not necessarily indicate that their relationship was entirely proper, however. Once he had gotten to know Emily, he knew she would never knowingly engage in immoral behavior. But that did not mean she could not be victimized in some way without her knowledge. Genji was an Oriental potentate with absolute power in his own domain and among his own clansmen. His palace and his castle were undoubtedly riddled with secret passages, chambers, and observation sites. He was no Christian. This was plain to Farrington despite Emily's insistence that she had converted him to the true faith. In many conversations over the past months, Genji had made it clear that he was a follower of an ancient and obscure sect of Buddhism that embodied no laws of morality, ethics, or propriety, but focused instead on a mystical liberation from the laws of man and God. Such a man was capable of anything.

Farrington rolled to his side and closed his eyes. He should sleep. It did no good to stare at the night and review thoughts he had reviewed so many times in the past. Tomorrow they would reach the monastery, they would see Emily, and everything would be settled. He was not confident it would be settled as it should, in his favor. But even if she chose Smith, at least she would be taken away from Genji. Farrington feared she favored Smith rather than him. She must, because she showed him no signs of affection. All he received was the politeness of a proper lady for any gentleman of her acquaintance. If she felt nothing for him, then her affections must belong to Smith. But if so, why was she taking so long to make her decision known? He knew she was a very gentle soul. She was perhaps loath to hurt his feelings by rejecting him and hoped that somehow rejection would become unnecessary. She was not hoping for a duel, of course, but perhaps simply that he would see the futility of his suit and withdraw on his own, without the necessity of her having to say anything at all.

There was another possibility, which occurred to him now as he dropped into sleep, and which, it being so repugnant, he forgot before he awoke the following morning.

. . . . .

"The naval officer is alone, five minutes' gallop ahead of Lord Genji and the other outsider," Lord Saemon's scout said. "Lord Hidé and twenty-four samurai ride with Lord Genji."

Twenty-four men. Saemon wondered why. Genji always traveled with a minimal escort. Why would he have such a sizable contingent with him this time? The ride from Edo to Mushindo Monastery was neither long nor hazardous. Did he suspect something? Of course, no matter what he suspected, he could not possibly suspect what Saemon had planned. He himself was accompanied by only ten retainers. Not even they were necessary. He needed no one's assistance to realize his intentions. Since he was popular among both anti-foreign samurai and those who favored accommodation with the Western powers, as well as with those for and against the Shogun and the Emperor, he also needed no corps of bodyguards to protect him. They were there simply for the sake of propriety. A Great Lord could not travel through the countryside alone.

Saemon knew why Farrington and Smith were not riding together. Since the two had begun courting Emily Gibson, they had become bitter enemies. He found this highly amusing. The officer should be concentrating on his military career and the businessman on accumulating greater profits. Yet here they were, wasting irrecoverable time and precious energy on securing a wife who not only lacked connections but was viewed with disdain by her countrymen. Truly, how inscrutable.

"Were you seen?"

"No, lord. I am certain I was not."

Saemon was tempted to admonish the scout, but restrained himself. What good would it do? As much as two hundred years of peace had eroded the skills of samurai, so had it somehow increased their arrogance. How could the man be certain he was not seen? He could not. Yet he did not hesitate to make the claim. Genji was far more attentive than he seemed, and so was Hidé. They were both among the few contemporary samurai to have experienced actual combat. His scout probably had been seen, but Genji was clever enough not to let it be known.

Saemon said, "Let us join Lord Genji. Ride ahead and ask his permission."

· · · · ·

Genji said to Smith, "I am not insulted by rumors. It is the nature of rumors to be scandalous."

"I agree," Smith said, "and it is only natural to wonder what you and Emily have been doing the past six years."

"That is true," Genji said. He smiled but did not elaborate.

Smith laughed. "And what have you been doing? As Emily's potential groom, I feel it is not out of place for me to ask."

Hidé listened to the conversation as they rode leisurely toward Mushindo, more leisurely than he would have preferred. The spy he had spotted in the previous valley was likely Saemon's man. It was in expectation of an ambush that he had insisted on bringing a guard of twenty-four men.

Genji had said, Saemon is not going to ambush me on the way to Mushindo.

I wish I shared your belief, lord, Hidé had replied.

A hundred men are far too many, Genji said.

Not if Saemon has two hundred, Hidé said.

If we turn a casual visit into a procession, Genji said, which a hundred men will do, we will attract much attention, increasing danger rather than diminishing it.

Fifty, then, Hidé said, armed with rifles.

Twenty-five, Genji said, counting yourself, and bows and arrows will be sufficient.

Twenty-five, with rifles, Hidé said.

Genji let out an exasperated sigh. All right, twenty-five with rifles, then.

Now that an attack was imminent, Hidé was glad he had given up numbers and gained rifles. He looked at his men. They had been watching him. Without being told, they were prepared for an attack. Smith had not noticed anything. He rode along as casually as ever.

"Men and women," Smith said, "will behave as men and women were intended to behave by nature, not by the rules created by man."

"Is that a Christian belief?" Genji said.

"That is a fact, which I have observed my entire life in the Hawaiian Islands."

"Emily and I have been busy with our own separate work. She with propagating the Christian faith, and I with political crises."

"For six years?"

"The last six years have been extremely eventful," Genji said.

"Lord," Hidé said. He spurred his horse alongside Genji's. A lone horseman approached from the east.

It was a messenger from Lord Saemon.

· · · · ·

"Those two seem less than fond of each other," Saemon said, indicating Farrington and Smith, who rode side by side in complete silence and with intent interest in every direction except where the other was.

"They favored opposite sides in the recent American conflict," Genji said.

"I wonder if their animosity will last two hundred and sixty years, as Japan's has."

"Americans look to the future rather than to the past. It is likely they will avoid our folly."

"That can happen only if both make strenuous efforts to that end," Saemon said.

"I cannot but agree," Genji said, "and hope that such will be the case."

"I add my hope to yours," Saemon said.

Hidé looked away in order to hide his frown. The casual bantering allusions to the opposing loyalties of their ancestors irritated him. Genji was too much at ease. That Saemon the Slippery was in their midst did not mean, as his lord apparently thought it did, that an attack was no longer possible. All it did was change the varieties of available treachery. A pair of Genji's bodyguards watched each of Saemon's men. Hidé himself was more than ready to cut Saemon down at the first provocation.

Saemon said, "I understand there is also some rivalry between them with respect to your houseguest, Miss Gibson."

"You are well informed, Lord Saemon."

"Not particularly, Lord Genji. There is much talk about them, and Miss Gibson."

"And me?"

Saemon bowed. "Inevitably, yes. As your friend and ally, I must advise you to disassociate yourself from the lady as soon as possible. The political situation is highly unstable. She loses you valuable support you might otherwise have."

Hidé could not quite suppress a harsh laugh. Saemon, Genji's friend and ally?

Genji said, "Did you have something to add, Hidé?"

"No, lord. I coughed, nothing more. I inhaled some dust from the road."

To Saemon, Genji said, "Any support that is withheld because of Miss Gibson's presence is support that lacks a core, and I do not regret its absence. She is soon to be betrothed in any case, and will shortly thereafter leave Japan."

"Is that so?" That was a surprising revelation, and one Saemon was not sure he believed. He knew that Farrington and Smith were going through the motions of courting Emily. He had assumed—and still did, and would, until proof stronger than Genji's words appeared—that it was all a charade to allow the four to plot together. He had not been able to uncover the nature of the plot as of yet, but no plot involving so many people could be kept secret for long. That was why, whenever possible, his own plots were known only to himself.

He did not believe there was any real animosity between the two men, and as for the woman, well, no one could be as naive and as blind as she pretended to be. It was all too obvious to him that she was deeply involved in what was going on, whatever it was. She was likely an agent of the American government itself. The Americans could pick no one less likely to arouse suspicion or better situated to gather intelligence. They knew how little serious attention the Japanese paid to women. No one—except himself—had any real interest in Emily's activities, which gave every appearance of being innocuous to the point of complete futility. (According to his informants within Genji's household, she had ceased even the little Christian proselytizing she had formerly engaged in, and was now completely absorbed in translating the inner history of the Okumichi clan into English. That she would even attempt to perpetrate such a preposterous subterfuge showed how insultingly little she thought of the Japanese. A history that could not be revealed except to those of the lord's lineage would hardly be exposed to outsiders in their own language.) At the same time, she was an intimate associate of a politically important Great Lord, and was alternately resident in his palace in Edo, the Shogun's capital, and his castle in Akaoka Domain on the western island of Shikoku, a hotbed of anti-Shogunal activity. It was extremely clever. Farrington was a naval officer, Smith a merchant, so both had easy access to overseas communications. It was a simple task for Emily to slip messages to them when they pretended to come courting. Was Genji actively involved? If so, it would be treason of the worst kind. In India, certain Great Lords, there called rajahs, had turned their domains over to the British under the guise of asking for their protection. Might Genji do the same in Japan with the Americans?

"Which one does Miss Gibson favor?" Saemon asked.

"She hasn't yet decided," Genji said.

She hadn't yet decided! More cleverness. An excellent ruse to cover endless delays. How could Saemon fail to admire Genji's superb management of every aspect of the complex conspiracy. He was a formidable schemer of the first rank. No wonder he had defeated Saemon's father, Lord Kawakami, even though his father had enjoyed control of the Shogun's secret police. And even though he had apparently uncovered a vital secret about Genji, possibly touching on the missing geisha, Heiko. In this matter, if in no other, Saemon followed in his father's footsteps. Whatever his father had discovered, Saemon would, too. He expected a report from California any day now.

"Women are by nature reluctant to diminish their choices," Saemon said, "often preferring to forgo choosing altogether."

"Sometimes, it certainly seems that way."

The lead rider suddenly spurred his horse forward. Someone was approaching on foot from the direction of Mushindo Monastery. It was a woman whose head tilted away sharply to the right at a precarious angle. As she ran toward them, it bounced up and down so violently, it seemed her neck might snap at any moment.

MUSHINDO MONASTERY

"Stop dodging about like fools," Taro said. "Use your bows. You—shoot down that stone-throwing idiot. And the brat. You—kill the outsider woman. Take care not to hit Lady Hanako by mistake."

"Lord," the two men said. Their first arrows hit no one. All their targets dropped down into the high grass as the arrows flew harmlessly overhead. They nocked a second set of arrows, but no one reappeared.

"Find them," Taro said. He and his men moved forward with their swords ready. "Take Lady Hanako alive. Kill the others." Hanako alone might have eluded them. But she was burdened with the need to protect Emily. They could not have gone far.

It was a windless day. He focused his attention on gaps in the grass, which could indicate either a person's passage or presence, and watched for movement in the stalks.

There.

His concern for Hanako prevented him from stabbing blindly into the swaying grass. He approached with caution. The foliage had been pressed down by someone who was no longer there. A thin stick protruded into the space from the right. His eyes followed the stick. A girl's hand held it and pushed at the grass to make it move. The brat. He stabbed at her and missed, the tip of his sword going into the dirt. She moved with the speed and wiliness of a hungry rat.

"Lord Taro!"

His men had found Hanako. She stood encircled by them, shifting from side to side to keep them in view as much as she could. Emily was not in sight. She must be in the grass at Hanako's feet.

Taro lowered his sword as he neared her.

"Lady Hanako," he said, "we mean you no harm. Please step out of the way."

"Traitor!"

When she lunged at him, one of his men rushed at her from behind to seize her. This, of course, was what she wanted. She twirled deftly around and slashed. The man went down instantly, blood spraying from his severed carotid artery. Without pause, she went after the next closest samurai, forcing him back.

Taro jumped toward her, but as he did, the giant idiot rose from the grass and, standing nearly toe-to-toe with him, hurled a stone into his forehead with all his strength. Taro heard a crack like bone breaking. His entire body went numb. Reeling on the verge of unconsciousness and nearly blinded by the flow of blood from this newest wound, Taro fought back reflexively when he saw the flash of sunlight on a blade coming in his direction. He cut someone, he didn't know whom, and stumbled backward, wiping the blood from his eyes. He thought the shaking of the ground beneath his feet was another consequence of the stoning, until one of his men called out.

"Lord Saemon!"

Indeed, it was Saemon, along with a company of samurai, approaching at a gallop. That could only mean that the plan had succeeded. Somewhere behind him on the road from Edo, Saemon had ambushed Genji and killed him.

Taro had sacrificed personal loyalty for principle. In order to preserve the way of the samurai, he had betrayed the man he most admired and respected and conspired with a man he detested. Taro could not help but feel he had reached the pinnacle of the ridiculous. To sacrifice a tangible, venerated, and historic attachment for an abstract principle—was this not the essence of the way of the outsiders, to whom ideas meant so much more than people and traditions? Their thinking had infected everyone, including those who most opposed them. Could it therefore not be said that they had already conquered Japan? Where thinking goes, actions inevitably follow. Perhaps Genji had been prescient after all.

A woman screamed in front of him. The giant idiot was gone. Where he had been, Emily stood, her hands to her mouth, her eyes wide with horror.

Taro stepped back. Saemon was here. Let him finish the dirty work.

· · · ·

Genji and Saemon rode at the head of the column, with Hidé close behind them. The woman with the bent neck had barely been coherent. Exhausted by her run, intimidated by the presence of Great Lords, her voice partially strangled by her deformity, words had come from her mouth in disjointed spurts.

"Lord— Lady Hanako— Danger, great danger— Treason— Please— Now!"

Hidé watched Saemon closely as they sped toward Mushindo. The woman was almost certainly a device put into play by Saemon to draw their attention away from him. Hanako and Emily were guarded by Taro, Hidé's best friend and most trusted comrade. Treason could not come from a more unlikely source. So unlikely was it that Hidé was convinced the danger came from Saemon, as he had suspected all along, and that whatever treachery he had planned was now about to take place. That Saemon had so few men with him indicated only that many more were hidden elsewhere. His father, Lord Kawakami, had ambushed Genji at Mushindo and failed. How satisfying it would be for the son to avenge the father in the very same spot. Genji had brushed aside Hidé's counsel of caution, and rushed ahead. If Hidé could not protect his lord, he could at least die with him, and make sure the scheming Saemon did not survive to enjoy his treachery.

All such thoughts vanished from Hidé's mind when he burst from the woods into the clearing beside the monastery. In a few swift moments, he saw several samurai arrayed in a circle around Hanako, saw her cut one down, saw another slash at her, saw a gout of red spray into the air, saw her fall.

"Hanako!"

While Hidé was distracted, Saemon pulled a hidden revolver from inside his jacket. Hidé caught this with his peripheral vision, but not before Saemon drew and fired. He turned to attack Saemon, but stopped when he saw that Genji had not been shot. Saemon had fired at the samurai who had struck Hanako and was about to attack Emily.

That samurai was Taro.

· · · · ·

Emily sat in the grass with Hanako cradled in her arms. Hanako's blood soaked both women's clothing. Her eyes were open, but they were sightless, and had already lost the brightness that distinguished the living from the dead. Emily was too stunned by the suddenness of her passing to close them—indeed, too stunned to accept that her only friend was gone without even a single, final word of farewell. Next to her, she heard the girl Kimi's childish voice raised in excited triumph.

"Lord Genji has come! I knew he would. I told the traitors he would, didn't I?"

"Kimi," Goro said. "Kimi, Kimi, Kimi—"

Galloping horses came to a halt very close by, and men leaped from the saddles. Emily did not look up. She desperately sought in her heart for a prayer and found *Whosoever believeth in Him should not perish, but have eternal life.* It was not the right prayer, for Hanako had not believed in Him, but

had during her whole life trusted in Amida Buddha, the bringer of boundless compassionate light, and believed not in the Heaven promised by Our
Lord and Savior, but in Sukhavati, the Pure Land reserved for Amida's
faithful. Now they were parted forever, without hope of meeting again in
the afterlife, for Heaven and Sukhavati could not both exist, nor Jesus
Christ and Amida Buddha. Were it not blasphemy, she would wish that the
latter were real rather than the former, for it would mean eternal life in paradise for Hanako, and who deserved it more? Emily had never known anyone more fully embodying goodness, charity, and the highest Christian
virtues than she.

Genji had arrived. Emily knew this because Kimi and Goro dropped to
their knees and pressed their heads against the earth. She felt his hand
lightly touch her shoulder.

"Emily," he said.

During the years of her residence in Japan, her sense of time had
changed, gradually, almost imperceptibly, to such an extent that it now
bore little similarity to her former perspective. She no longer thought in
terms of the passage of days, weeks, months, years, but only of moments,
cast seemingly at random across the calendar of the past, gathered together in her memory to provide revelations that would otherwise have
passed unnoticed. These gathered moments, harvested like a rare and precious crop, formed her entire knowledge of those closest to her—Heiko,
Hanako, and Genji. Were these relationships real or utterly imaginary?
Heiko she had last seen six years ago. Hanako was dead. And Genji—did
he feel what she thought he felt, what she half feared, half hoped he felt?

"Emily," Genji said.

She felt his hand on her shoulder, and at last she began to weep.

Genji nodded to Hidé.

He took Hanako's body from Emily's arms. He did it as gently as he
could. He must have been gentle enough, for she seemed not to notice.
Tears fell from her eyes, all the sadder for falling in complete silence. Her
chest moved up and down but not even the slightest sigh escaped her lips.
Hidé felt great sympathy for Emily. Hanako had been her only friend. Now
she was truly alone. His own feelings Hidé suppressed completely. He did
not think of his son, now bereft of his mother at such a young age. He did
not think of himself, who had lost the one person to whom he could without shame expose his weaknesses and his fears, the one whom he could

always trust to be at his side in adversity, the one upon whom he had counted to be his intimate companion until the end of his days. He took Hanako's body from Emily and bowed low to Genji.

"Lord," one of his men said. His voice was anguished.

"What are you staring at?" Hidé said harshly. This was no time to indulge in emotions. "Are our lord and Lady Emily sufficiently guarded?"

The man straightened himself into a more martial posture. "Yes, Lord Hidé. And several men are keeping close watch on Saemon."

Hidé grunted approval. "If any of the traitors are still alive, don't kill them. They must be questioned."

"Yes, lord, I have so ordered."

"Well? Why are you still here?"

"I thought, perhaps—" The man's eyes went to Hanako.

Hidé said, "I am fully capable of dealing with one corpse. Go."

The man bowed and departed.

Hidé closed Hanako's eyes. She was still warm. Though the sky was cloudless, it had begun to rain. He wiped the droplets from Hanako's face. His hand was so coarse, callused, and roughened by the life of a samurai. How often he had apologized for the harshness of his being. How often she had laughed, and taken his hand in hers, and said, How could I be gentle were you not harsh, soft were you not hard?

His lieutenant dashed back to his side. "Lord Taro still breathes."

· · · · · ·

Saemon stared down at Taro and willed him to die. His bullet had not instantly killed his erstwhile ally. Otherwise, his plan had thus far worked to perfection. By drawing Taro into a conspiracy, albeit a false one, he had deprived Genji of one of his most vital retainers, and sowed the seeds of further discontent and suspicion within his clan. It would have been sufficiently effective if Taro had killed Emily, and Genji had killed Taro. But the timing of their arrival had provided Saemon with another, better opportunity. By shooting Taro as he appeared about to strike Emily, he had gained Genji's gratitude, and perhaps an enhancement of his trust. This had been the essence of Saemon's plan. His father's mistake with Heiko had been in trying to put someone next to Genji and have that someone do what was necessary. Saemon had learned from that mistake. The only person he could count on completely was himself, so it must be himself that

242 · *Takashi Matsuoka*

he placed as close to Genji as he could. Hanako's demise was an additional benefit, since it distracted and weakened her husband, Hidé, the most stalwart of Genji's retainers. All his success would evaporate, however, if Taro survived long enough to implicate him.

Hidé knelt down next to Taro.

"Who else?" he said.

For a moment, Saemon thought Taro's eyes would shift in his direction. That alone would be enough to condemn him. Hidé, already suspicious of him, would not wait for orders or permission. He would simply draw his sword and decapitate him on the spot. But Taro did not move his gaze from Hidé. When he spoke, he said only one word.

"Samurai."

"I am a samurai," Hidé said. "You are a traitor. Mitigate your crime. Tell me who else."

"Samurai," Taro said again, and died.

"Take his head," Hidé said to his men. "Leave his body for the peasants to burn." Six years ago, near this very spot, he and Taro had fought together against hundreds of Kawakami the Sticky Eye's samurai, and triumphed. Now Taro was dead, a traitor, shot down by Saemon, Kawakami's son. It did not feel right. It did not feel right at all.

Saemon said, "I regret we did not arrive in time to save Lady Hanako."

"We were in time to save Lady Emily," Hidé said, "and put an end to treason. That is sufficient." He bowed and walked away. Saemon was involved in this. He knew it. But if he was a secret anti-foreign zealot, why did he protect Emily? And if he was part of the plot with Taro, why did he shoot him? Hidé didn't know. He did know Saemon was a schemer who enjoyed complexities. Nothing he ever did was straightforward. Genji was still in danger.

. . . . .

Saemon was not disturbed in the least by Hidé's unconcealed suspicion. As the chief lieutenant of a Great Lord, it was among his principal duties to be suspicious, especially of his lord's closest associates. By definition, betrayals were always perpetrated by those one trusted. It was for precisely that reason that Saemon himself trusted no one but himself. He was among the lesser of the Great Lords, but among them all, he was the only one immune to betrayal.

Genji was making great efforts to effect a reconciliation between the Shogun, who favored accommodation with the outsiders, and the Imperial Court, which favored their immediate and complete expulsion. In this effort, Saemon was Genji's secret ally. He was also a secret ally of the Men of Virtue, who were zealously dedicated to expelling the outsiders and destroying all those who cooperated with them, be they commoners or lords. These were, of course, contradictory movements that could not both succeed. Saemon intended to be on the winning side, and he intended for Genji to be among the losers, no matter which side won. If that was the Virtuous, then Genji was doomed in any case. If the conciliators won, then Genji could still be undermined in the long run if he were seen by traditionalists to take a leading role in the suppression of the Virtuous. Since he was already despised by many for his incomprehensible determination to lift the sanctions against the outcasts, that would not be difficult to do.

Saemon was a patient man. There was no need for haste. Those who rushed toward their goals often did no more than hurry themselves to their own doom.

· · · · ·

Genji left Emily in the care of two of the young women who resided at Mushindo. They would help her bathe and change out of her bloodied clothing. When he stepped out into the courtyard, Farrington and Smith were waiting for him.

"How is she?" Farrington said.

"She is uninjured," Genji said, "but I would not say she is well. She has just seen her dearest friend killed before her eyes."

"Wasn't the murderer one of your samurai?" Smith said. "Taro was his name, wasn't it?"

"Yes, Taro."

Farrington said, "Lord Taro was your cavalry commander, was he not?"

"Yes."

"Why would he want to kill Lady Hanako?" Smith said. He suspected a love affair gone awry. Much as these samurai pretended disdain for women and an unyielding martial discipline, they were men after all, and subject to the passions and follies of all men. He did not exempt himself from his unspoken indictment. His desire for Emily distracted him from the pursuit of cattle, acreage, and trade commodities that would multiply his wealth. In possessing Emily, he would gain no more than that very possession. It was not rational. With women, men were not, more often than they were.

"He didn't," Genji said. "He was trying to kill Emily. Hanako prevented it."

"Emily?" Farrington said. "Why Emily?"

"Anti-foreign sentiment is very high," Genji said. "It has affected even those among my most trusted retainers."

Farrington could not accept the explanation. Since the opening of Japan by Commodore Perry more than a dozen years ago, there had been numerous attacks and assassinations suffered by the Western community. Not a single one had been directed against a woman. The warrior conceit of the samurai made such an act even more deplorable to them than to Westerners. That a samurai of the exalted rank of lord and general would stoop to the slaughter of a defenseless Western woman for political reasons was simply inconceivable. And Emily was not just any Western woman, she was one who enjoyed the patronage and protection of Taro's own Great Lord. As terrible as Genji's given reason was, the truth was likely even uglier.

Only the direct order of his lord could have compelled Taro to commit a crime so rife with dishonor. The entire journey to Cloud of Sparrows Castle must have been part of the subterfuge designed to bring Emily here, away from any possible Western observation, and murder her. This led inexorably to the question of why Genji would wish such an end. To even contemplate potential causes was abhorrent in the extreme. Innocent as she was, and more helpless than she realized in the various abodes of her despotic host, the possibility of Emily's unwitting victimization could not be ignored. Was he already too late to save her from a fate worse than death? And if so, what was he to do now?

"Some in the West have insisted on viewing the samurai as the knights of Japan," Smith said. "If what you say is true, your code of chivalry is not as it should be."

Genji bowed. "It is difficult to disagree with your assessment."

The two women who had assisted Emily came out of the room where she now rested. They bowed to Genji and departed, carrying bloodstained clothing.

"May I ask you gentlemen to wait here for Emily? When she has recovered sufficiently to seek company, I think she will find the presence of her countrymen comforting."

"Of course, sir," Smith said.

Farrington silently bowed assent. His thoughts turned to uncovering Genji's motives for inviting Smith and him along. Had they been intended to be witnesses? If so, for what purpose? To testify that Genji had done his utmost to save Emily, though tragically he had failed? Hanako's brave defense of her friend had thwarted that plan. Did it mean that all three of them—Emily, Smith, and himself—were now at risk?

Smith said, "May we agree to a temporary truce?"

"Yes, we may." Farrington extended his hand and Smith took it. "Let us concentrate our efforts on easing Emily's suffering." He wondered whether he should share his concern about their possible danger, but decided against it. It would require too much explaining, and explanations could quickly lead into very discomforting speculation.

Genji went looking for Kimi. He found her in the garden with Goro, turning soil for a new planting. As they worked, they were having, not quite a conversation in the usual sense, but an exchange of words that served to connect them as a conversation might connect others, or as singing united celebrants at a festival.

"Kimi."

"Goro."

"Kimi."

"Goro."

So rapt were they in their work, they didn't notice his arrival.

"Kimi."

"Goro."

"Kimi," Genji said.

"Lord Genji," Kimi said.

She dropped to her knees and pressed her forehead against the dirt. Goro followed her example exactly, except that instead of saying his name, he said hers.

"Kimi."

"Sshhh!"

What a wondrous land Japan was, that even an idiot did his best to behave as he should in the presence of a Great Lord. Genji didn't know whether to laugh or weep.

"You and Goro have performed a great service for me. I am grateful to you."

At the mention of his name, Goro raised his head enough from the dirt to peer up at Genji.

He said, "Kimi."

Kimi reached over, roughly took both of Goro's hands in hers, and pressed them against his mouth.

"Keep them there and be quiet," she said. Bowing again to Genji, she said, "I'm sorry, sir lord. He tries, but it's difficult for him."

"It is easy to overlook a minor breach of etiquette in one who has helped save the life of a friend."

"Thank you, sir lord."

"I know why he did so. You told him to. But why did you decide to risk your life?"

Kimi kept her head down and remained silent.

"Please. I will not be upset no matter what your reason."

Reluctantly, Kimi said, "People say you can see the future, sir lord."

"And you believe them?"

In a tiny voice, she said, "Is it permitted?"

Japan was a country with many levels to everything, including beliefs. Just as peasants could not even dream of entering the presence of the Shogun or the Emperor, so certain beliefs were not to be contemplated by them. Many, like everyone in Yamanaka Village, followed the teachings of Honen and Shinran, who explained in simple terms the way of Amida Buddha and the path to Sukhavati, the Pure Land. Lords like Genji followed the Zen Patriarchs, who pointed wordlessly to a way beyond the Buddhas, a way incomprehensible to simple farmers and townsfolk. Perhaps believing in Lord Genji's prophetic powers was allowed only for samurai and nobles. She tried not to tremble, with little success.

Genji laughed. It was not a derisive laugh, or a cruel one. It sounded very merry.

"Your head is your own, Kimi. You can believe whatever you wish to believe. I warn you, however, there are better things to believe in than my prophetic power. Seeing the future is not quite what people seem to think it is."

So he did have the power! He had as much as said so. Kimi was so excited she wanted to jump up and down. How lucky they were. With uncertainties all around, their lord could see what was to come. Well, Lord Genji wasn't exactly their lord. Lord Hiromitsu ruled Yamakawa Domain. But Mushindo Monastery had been a hereditary outpost of Lord Genji's clan for almost six hundred years, and Lord Hiromitsu deferred to Lord Genji in everything, so Lord Genji really was their lord in fact, if not quite in name.

"Thank you, sir lord," Kimi said.

"Your thanks are premature. I have not yet granted you a reward. And it is not necessary to address me as both 'sir' and 'lord.' One or the other will do."

"Yes, lord. Thank you, but a reward is not necessary."

"Nevertheless, you will receive it."

"Yes, lord. Thank you."

"So what will it be?"

"Lord?"

"Your reward. It is already granted. All that is left is that you name it."

Once again, Kimi began to tremble. Name her own reward! How could she dare such a thing? Yet how could she refuse? To do one was to display an acquisitiveness that would surely and deservedly bring harsh punishment down on her head. Who was she to take greedy advantage of the generosity of a Great Lord?

To do the other was to disobey his command, an act of brazen defiance meriting death—not only hers, but that of every one of her relatives, perhaps even her entire village.

What if she asked for just a small reward? That could easily have the same result—death! Asking for too little was an insult to the dignity of the lord. Did she think him incapable of rewarding her magnificently?

The shivering of her body became so violent it threatened to choke off her breath. What a terrible fate it was to be born a peasant. How much worse to be one who attracted the attention of a lord. Whether one pleased him or angered him, the result was the same. Doom. She began reciting the *nembutsu* in her heart so that when she was decapitated, Amida Buddha would take her instantly to the Pure Land. She didn't realize she was vocalizing her prayer until Lord Genji spoke.

"*Namu Amida Butsu,*" he said, repeating her words. "Are you asking Amida Buddha for guidance?"

"Lord" was all Kimi could say.

"We may be waiting for some time. It has been my experience that gods and Buddhas are rarely in a hurry to answer supplicants. Are you of a religious nature?"

"Lord."

"Of course," Genji said, "or you would not have taken it upon yourself to restore this monastery."

He was quiet for so long, Kimi was finally emboldened to lift her head from the ground. He was looking thoughtfully at the restored residential wing.

"May I make a suggestion?" Genji said. "Accept appointment as Abbess of this establishment. I will see to it that you receive the necessary funds and workers to speed up the restoration. Henceforth, Mushindo will be an abbey instead of a monastery."

"Would that be proper, lord?" Kimi feared contradicting him, but she also feared the wrath of the mystical protectors of the hall. "Does it not require the act of the Chief Abbot of the Mushindo Order to make such a change?"

Genji smiled. "I am the Chief Abbot, by inheritance through successive generations, from the original foundation of this place. And in the beginning, it was an abbey, not a monastery. Old Abbot Zengen made the change. I hereby change it back, Reverend Abbess."

"Lord, I know nothing of the Mushindo teachings."

"I am not at all sure there is that much to know. It has always been an obscure and variant sect. When Head Monk Tokuken comes down from the mountains, you may ask him for tutelage. Until then, I authorize you to practice nembutsu, or whatever else seems appropriate."

"If Mushindo becomes an abbey," Kimi said, "will it be only for women?"

"Yes." He looked at Goro. "Ah, I see. A caretaker's hut will be built just outside the walls, so your assistant can continue in that capacity."

"Thank you, Lord Genji," Kimi said, a great weight lifted from her. Surely he read minds as well as saw the future. Now Goro and Kimi and the other runaway girls truly had a home to call their own. No one would bother them. They were protected by the Great Lord of Akaoka.

"You are most welcome, Reverend Abbess," Genji said, going to his knees and bowing low to her, as if she were a real abbess. "Remember to consult the sacred texts and find an appropriate clerical name for yourself. When one enters the Buddha's Way, one must be reborn."

"Yes, lord. I will."

"Good."

Kimi kept bowing for a long time. When she looked up, Lord Genji was gone. In the excitement of the moment, she had forgotten to tell him about the scroll.

Two weeks ago, while searching for bullets in the field outside the walls, she had chanced upon a large, loose stone. It was one of four that had formed the foundation for an old building long gone. The scroll was under that stone, in a waxed box that had withstood the weather for many years, perhaps even centuries. She had looked in the box and found the scroll, but hadn't looked at the scroll itself. She was curious, but she was also illiterate, so there really was no point in opening it. She had intended to give it to Lady Hanako, but Lady Hanako was dead. She couldn't give it to Lord Genji earlier because that other lord was here then, a lord she had never seen before. She hesitated to show anything in front of him. There was something about his manner, the movement of his eyes, the quality of his smile, that reminded her of the toads that hid in the mud during the rainy season, only their eyes showing as they lurked for bugs.

It was too late to give it to Lord Genji now. He was back with his samurai and they would ask her what she wanted, and it might not be good to tell them what she had. It might be something secret only Lord Genji should know about. If Lord Taro could betray him, who knew about the other samurai? Now that she was abbess, she had to act prudently. She would wait for the right moment and give the scroll to Lord Genji then.

She heard a muffled voice at her side. Goro still had both his hands across his mouth where she had put them.

"You can put your hands down now, Goro."

"Kimi," Goro said.

"Goro," Kimi said.

"Kimi."

"Goro."

"Kimi."

SAN FRANCISCO

The Japanese community in the city was very small, barely more than a handful, so when two new shipborne arrivals turned out to be countrymen, everyone knew. They were not merchants, scholars, or farmers. Their samurai nature was quite obvious by their demeanor despite their efforts to affect Westernized clothing and the lack of the characteristic two swords, which they could not openly display in America anyway.

It was duly reported to Mr. Stark, the representative in San Francisco of Lord Genji of Akaoka, that two Japanese men had recently arrived, were clearly samurai, and were asking many questions about Lady Heiko, the young boy, Makoto, and Mr. Stark. The report was not made directly to Mr. Stark, of course, since he did not speak Japanese. As usual, Mrs. Stark received the information. She thanked her informants and pressed a reward on them despite their protestations that such was unnecessary. They were happy to be of service to Lord Genji, who while not exactly present, was the closest Great Lord in their proximity. America was not Japan, and here in California they did not owe allegiance to any lord anywhere. It seemed prudent, however, to follow the traditional forms of behavior until it was incontrovertibly clear that they were no longer necessary. Everyone knew of someone who had prematurely believed a new era had dawned, failed to render proper respect, and gotten separated from his head. While nothing like this had happened in America, why take foolish risks?

Within a week, the new arrivals were gone. All assumed they had moved on across the continent via the newly finished transcontinental railroad, or had gone north or south by ship, to Canada, or Mexico, or points beyond.

Coincidentally, two bodies washed onto the shores of San Francisco Bay about the same time. Or rather, what appeared to be the remains of two bodies. What the sharks had not eaten had deteriorated in the sea, and separation of the various parts made it impossible to determine identity or cause of death. The undertaker employed by the city for such tasks was able to say that there were most likely two bodies, since the arms and the one leg did not match the partial torso, unless it had been an individual disproportionate enough to be employed in a circus sideshow. He was also able to say with some assurance that they were both male, if they were indeed two, or in the alternative, women of very masculine appearance. Beyond that, he could only speculate. He guessed that they were either Mexican, Chinese, Indian, or possibly Irish, Negro, or German, but definitely not Hawaiian. The undertaker had a single experience with a Hawaiian, who had been brutally murdered by numerous bullets, multiple stab wounds and ferocious bludgeoning in a hotel room in the city some six years earlier, and assumed all Hawaiians were similar, meaning of exceptional size. The present remains were not nearly big enough to be Hawaiian. Of this he was certain, though of nothing else.

Given the condition of the parts, and the usual inebriated state of the undertaker, it was impossible to be more precise.

1882, MUSHINDO ABBEY

"Goro," the Reverend Abbess Jintoku said.

Her eyes opened. She had been roused from meditation, not by the striking of a temple bell, but by her own voice speaking out of a distant memory.

The other nuns in the hall continued in stillness and silence. They knew for themselves that surrendering to Buddha's compassionate guidance allowed imprisoned experiences and emotions to percolate to the surface. Random words sometimes sprang spontaneously out of meditation, as well as the occasional sobs, laughter, and even snores—the last from those who had allowed their attention to lapse. If any action was required, the monitor on duty, armed with a stick, would see to consciousness being refocused where it belonged.

The Abbess bowed respectfully toward the altar, then to her companions on the Way. She silently thanked Buddha and the guardian deities of the temple for granting her the peace in meditation that she had experienced. She left the hall and stepped outside. The night had passed. Early morning light came from the east. The Abbess bowed in deep gratitude for the blessing of another day.

Mushindo Abbey, Lady Emily had said so many years ago, when it was only a ruined monastery, and an abbey Mushindo had once again become. How swiftly the years passed.

One breath and it was then.

The next breath and it was now.

As the Reverend Abbess crossed the courtyard, it began to rain.

TOKYO

Makoto Stark sat on the windowsill of his room and rolled a cigarette. He was on the fourth and highest floor of the hotel, a large and mostly empty new building in the Tsukiji district, an area reserved for foreigners. He could see heavy gray clouds settling over the mountains at the north-western edge of the Kanto Plain. If his sense of direction served him prop-erly, it was raining at Mushindo Abbey and would soon be raining in Tokyo. The cigarette rolled, he put it in his mouth and let it dangle the way he imagined it dangled from the lips of the gunfighters he had read about in the dime novels of his boyhood.

What had he expected by going to Mushindo? He had hoped for some-thing other than what he got, which was more disappointment and confu-sion. It may have been a little thing that the battle story Matthew Stark and his mother had told him did not match what the nuns at the abbey said. But any and every discrepancy now took on disproportionate importance. He had come to Japan looking for a single truth—his parentage—and now feared that one truth would fall far short of what he needed.

Cigarette still casually on his lip, he left the hotel and went walking out into Tsukiji. It was difficult to believe that only a little more than a dozen years ago, when the Imperial capital of Tokyo was still the Shogun's Edo, this area was home to the great palaces of the *daimyo*—the samurai war-lords who ruled Japan for a thousand years. Those palaces were now all gone, replaced by this hotel and various shops and establishments cater-ing to foreigners. Or so the intention had been. Foreigners had not flocked here as the new government had hoped. They had continued to prefer the fuller amenities and livelier society of the port of Yokohama, twenty miles to the west. Tsukiji was virtually empty, an eerie condition in the other-wise teeming city. The policeman at the gate, dressed in a Western-style uniform, bowed to him as he left the district. He was not there to prevent the entry of ordinary Japanese into Tsukiji, but his presence there certainly did nothing to encourage free intercourse.

During his passage across the Pacific, Makoto's thoughts at first cen-tered entirely on Genji Okumichi and the matter of paternity and aban-donment. Rapid as the steamship was, the trip was still to be measured in weeks. Anger and bitterness could fuel only so much singular concentra-tion. Time was a benefactor. So were the free sea air, the cleansing alterna-tion of sunshine and rain, the vastness of the oceanic view, with its unbroken and unobstructed horizon, the buoyant rhythm of the ship it-self. He was surprised to find himself growing increasingly optimistic. Not about the reaction he expected from Genji. He had rejected Makoto twenty years ago, and had continued to reject him since then. There was little reason to believe his mere arrival would change any of this.

His rising hope attached, not to Genji, but to Japan itself.

Makoto could not remember a time when he did not enjoy the abundant benefits bestowed by his family's wealth and political power. He had never been without the protection of dedicated bodyguards and the care of attentive servants. In every establishment he ever entered, he was treated with the utmost deference. His social circle consisted exclusively of those with similar backgrounds and, of course, the children of the household staff. In these ways, he was like all of the select few who belonged to the elite of San Francisco. When he was a child, he had thought that he was exactly like them. That this was not so became apparent only after his passage out of childhood into youth, when the gatherings which he attended transformed themselves seemingly overnight from childish games to dances and flirtations. Reserve and distance now characterized his relationships, particularly with his female friends, even those whom he had known all his life. He understood the reason without being told. He did not, after all, have to look very far. It was in every mirror.

He thought he did not dwell on it. Yet awareness was never very distant. This became violently clear during his brief, exciting, and ultimately tragic tenure as the Chinatown Bandit. He felt a strange and joyous thrill every time he uttered mock Chinese imprecations, brandished the Chinese meat cleaver, and saw the fear in the eyes of those who took him for what he was not—a violent, unpredictable, opium-crazed coolie. These were the very same people who preferred to minimize his existence because they could not accept what he really was. Fine. Then let them fear what he pretended to be without them ever knowing that what they feared did not exist.

Satisfaction arising from such twisted emotions could not endure. The crude blend of jest and revenge emphasized rather than diminished his isolation. Besides, no matter how much of an entertaining distraction it was for him, he could not be the Chinatown Bandit forever. Makoto had arrived at no solution when Matthew Stark uncovered his criminal farce and brought it to an immediate conclusion. His subsequent presence aboard a Japan-bound steamer was entirely fortuitous. He had intended to go to Mexico—young women there often took him for a wealthy mestizo and did not disdain him—but the SS *Hawaiian Cane* was departing just as he arrived at the harbor. Haste was more important than destination.

During the voyage, horror at the deaths behind him lost their immediacy, and anger directed toward a man he didn't know grew vague. He began to recall the stories he had heard about Japan all his life from Matthew Stark, his mother, the household servants, visitors from Akaoka Domain and Tokyo. They described a society founded on ancient tradition, loyalty, order, and, most prominent of all, an established and unshakable hierarchy in which each and every person knew his place. He began to believe that if he was not truly at home in California, perhaps it was because it was not his true home. When the ship finally docked at Yokohama, his hope had metamorphosed into expectation.

What he subsequently found in Tokyo reminded him of the trip he had made to Montana the previous year. At Matthew Stark's insistence, he had gone to visit the Red Hill Company's Canadian mines. Being in the vicinity, he decided to visit the Sioux and Cheyenne reservations just south of the border. The danger thrilled him. He had been reading Wild West novels which glorified gunfighters and Indian fighters. Custer's Last Stand against Crazy Horse and Sitting Bull at the Little Bighorn had taken place only six years earlier. So his disappointment was keen when he saw unarmed, poorly dressed, and often sick Indians shuffling around dusty reservations. No war ponies, war paint, feathered headdresses. No ferocity. He couldn't picture these people destroying the famed Seventh Cavalry. They were the ones who had so recently had all America in an uproar?

He felt the same disappointment here. No one wore topknots, no one was armed with the emblematic two swords. The only swords were the Western-style sabers in the scabbards of military officers, who themselves wore Western-style uniforms. Most people wore kimonos, elaborate ones in some cases, particularly among the women. But almost everyone also wore one or more articles of Western clothing, most commonly, hats, boots, shoes, belts, or gloves. Many women carried parasols. The combination was utterly bizarre. If he did not know who he really was, he was not much different from everyone else here. The whole country didn't seem to know who it was anymore. At least, they dressed as if they didn't. The Japan he had heard about all of his life was as unreal as the Wild West of the dime novels.

Makoto turned abruptly and walked back to the hotel. Genji had replaced Quiet Crane Palace with a new one on the banks of the Tama River outside of Tokyo. He would delay no more. He asked the desk clerk for directions there.

"Lord Genji's estate is not easily accessible," the clerk said, "and there isn't really much to see out there. Why not visit the Imperial Palace? You can't go in, of course, but the view of the exterior is quite magnificent."

"*Lord* Genji?" Makoto said. "I thought all the domains were abolished, and along with them, their lords."

"The domains have been abolished, but some Great Lords have become Peers of the Realm, and are still entitled to the honorific. Some also have been appointed provincial governors of their former domains. Lord Genji, of course, is one of them, because of the important role he played in the Restoration of His Imperial Majesty."

"There are no Great Lords anymore," Makoto said, "and the domains have been abolished. But Lord Genji is still a lord, and he still rules his domain, but now it is called a province."

"Yes," the clerk said. "Japan is modernizing very quickly. At this rate, we will have caught up completely with the outsiders by the turn of the century."

"No doubt," Makoto said. "I want to go to the estate not for sightseeing but to meet with Lord Genji."

The clerk gave Makoto a doubtful look. "That may be difficult. And anyway, he is not at his Tama River estate but at Cloud of Sparrows Castle in Muroto Province."

"I take it Muroto Province is the new name for Akaoka Domain."

"Yes."

"Cloud of Sparrows Castle is still called Cloud of Sparrows Castle?"

"Yes."

"How comforting," Makoto said, "to know that some things don't change."

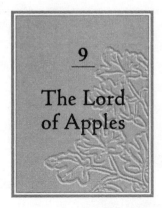

9

The Lord
of Apples

The young lord asked, "Where will I find words to say what I feel in my heart?"

"The deepest feelings are impossible to express in words. They can only be hinted at."

"Then it is hopeless," the young lord said. "No one will understand me, and I will understand no one."

"That is not so. Those who are closest to you will know you best by what you do not say, and you will know them in the same way."

AKI-NO-HASHI

(1311)

1867, CLOUD OF SPARROWS CASTLE

S mith rode out of the castle at an easy canter, reins loosely held, no particular destination in mind. His horse took him to the shore and paused, nose pointed southeast across the ocean in the exact direction of Hawaii. Smith noted the coincidence but his thoughts did not alight on any remembrance of home. They were too involved in another, more pressing matter. After a time, he encouraged his mount into movement with a light tap of his heels. It turned away from the water, trotted inland, up a rise, and, sniffing the air, halted rather abruptly.

Smith also caught the scent. It was an unfamiliar one. Growing up in the fecund tropics, he had learned to distinguish the bouquet of different fruit, especially mango, guava, and papaya, for which he had a particular fondness. This was not any of those, but it was a fruit. Smith could tell that much, not from the acuity of his nose, but from the sight of the well-ordered stand of perhaps one hundred trees in the small valley below. He rode down for a closer look.

Apples. He had sampled one while in Virginia, a gift hand-carried from a New England orchard by a cousin he had never met before.

New Yorkers claim theirs are the best, the cousin said, but I aver Vermont's are second to none. Go on, Cousin Charles. Have at it.

He did, and it required his entire store of self-control to maintain a pleased expression upon his face and the bite of apple within his mouth. This was not the soft, wet, yielding succulence to which he was accustomed with the fruit of Hawaii. His cousin had promised him the apple would be sweet and juicy. Sour was a more accurate description of its flavor, and it was not juicy in the dripping sense that a ripe mango was juicy, but juicy only as compared to desiccated. While he may have succeeded in concealing his dismay, he was unable to display a pretense of actual enthusiasm.

You have been too long in the pagan tropics, his cousin said. It is just as well you have come to William and Mary, before your taste and judgment suffered permanent degeneration.

Smith was back in Hawaii before Christmas. He told his parents he could not withstand the cold and dreary winter of Virginia. In truth, what exceeded his toleration was all the idle talk and irrelevant thinking that went on so endlessly at the college. His grandfather had survived and prospered under the first King Kamehameha, though they had been religious adversaries. His father, God rest his soul, had helped the fourth Kamehameha preserve the integrity of the kingdom from the depredations of the European imperialists. How could the grandson and son of such men of action spend valuable years of his young manhood in distant Williamsburg talking and thinking instead of doing?

While there, he had read—at least the better parts of—*Oliver Twist, A Tale of Two Cities,* and *Great Expectations,* because Dickens was said to be the greatest living writer in the English language. Smith thought him entertaining; he had experienced no noticeable expansion of his mind, his taste, or even his facility in letter-writing, however. Nor did he consider the Englishman particularly insightful. That honor he gave to Austen, though he could not publicly say that a woman had exceeded a man in any endeavor. Indeed, he had never even admitted reading her to anyone until he had said so to Lord Genji.

Women understand the duel between us better than men, Genji had said. Our first novelist was a woman. I believe no man has yet equaled her observations in that area.

Smith had said, Japan is the last place I would have expected a man to yield first place to a woman. Do you not rule absolutely and without question? Is not the word of a man law?

Rule and merit are not the same, Genji had said. Men rule Japan by virtue of their swords, not by virtue of their virtue.

Smith had read—more accurately, he had skimmed—the key chapters of Gibbon's *Decline and Fall*. The history of the barbarian invasions was intriguing, and that of the Empress Theodora usefully cautionary; women were not to be underestimated, nor was the vigor of their vengeance to be ignored. The relevance of Rome's destruction to his own life, however, he did not see at all.

He had read neither Aristotle nor Plato in Greek and had no intention of ever doing so. Indeed, even if the intention had existed, the facility in Greek most certainly did not. He had no intention of reading them in English, either. Was he to pretend, like the others, to be some kind of American Athenian? He refused to indulge in such idiocy.

His final evening on campus, he had listened to ignorant undergraduates engaged in a pretentious discussion of De Quincey's *Confessions*, and had decided then and there to abandon his useless college tenure. The world offered both opportunities and dangers in great plenitude. He would not waste another day risking the loss of the former or being shielded from the latter.

Thinking of those days, Smith always felt a certain odd emotion combining relief with regret. A little more than a year after his departure, South Carolina began the Secession, and the following summer, the Union Army invaded Virginia. Had he remained at college, he would not have missed the opportunity to serve. Once back in Hawaii, his parents adamantly refused him permission to return. He was the only son among five daughters. He would risk not only his life but his entire lineage. So he remained at home and missed what would surely be the greatest adventure of his time. He had also missed the slaughter of six hundred thousand of his fellow human beings, one of whom he might have been. It was a present irony that had he enlisted, he would have fought under the same banner as Lieutenant Farrington. Smith's family was originally Georgian, but they were also staunch abolitionists. In God's eyes, all of His children were equal. How could one of them own another?

Of course, Smith would never tell Farrington this. The pretense of complete opposition better suited their rivalry for Emily Gibson's hand. And it was thoughts of the strange turn this rivalry had taken that now weighed so heavily on Smith.

Farrington's behavior toward Emily had changed, not in any outward form, but in its essence. Though he still went through the motions, he was no longer in earnest pursuit of Emily. If this was not apparent to anyone else—and it seemed not to be—it was very apparent to Smith. Since the incident at Mushindo Monastery, Farrington's ardor had evaporated.

Why?

One aspect of the incident seemed to make a particular impact on Farrington. Smith remembered his expression of horror when Lord Genji had pronounced with complete certainty that Emily, not General Hidé's wife, Hanako, had been the assassin's target. That the assassin had been one of Lord Genji's most trusted subordinates also seemed to inspire great consternation. From this combination of fact and supposition, what conclusion had Farrington drawn that had caused his former affection to disappear so instantaneously?

It was not fear. Smith knew enough about Farrington's character to discount that possibility, his jibes about the War notwithstanding. If it was not a matter of courage, then it could only be one of honor. There were no other serious concerns for a gentleman. In other circumstances, Emily's lack of either family or inheritance could have been a deficiency, since she would come to her bridegroom without a dowry. This did not matter to Smith. It might have mattered to Farrington. But because her lordly patron was sure to gift the wedding couple most generously, the deficiency was conceptual rather than actual.

What matter of honor was so apparent to Farrington that Smith himself failed to see?

The answer must lie in the path of Farrington's thoughts.

The assassin's target was Emily.

The assassin was General Taro, Lord Genji's hitherto most loyal cavalry commander.

Therefore—

Therefore what?

Smith could not follow Farrington's reasoning further. Even if Emily had been Taro's target, how would that drive Farrington away? If anything, his protective instincts, especially prominent in a military man, should have come to the forefront.

The treachery of a warlord's loyal subject was likewise not a reasonable cause. Assassinations had grown unfortunately common of late, and the assassins were more often than not close retainers of the victim. Loyalties in Japan had become dangerously confused.

It was most disconcerting. To best Farrington was one thing. To have him retreat voluntarily was quite another. They would lunch together. Perhaps careful observation would prove revealing.

Smith turned his horse's head back toward the castle.

· · · · ·

Emily stood at the eastern window of the high tower and gazed out at the Pacific. Today it was as gentle as its name. At least, on its surface. Who knew what storms and currents tore at its depths? This very island, and all the other islands of Japan, were no more than the tips of oceanic volcanoes. They were quiescent now, but the earthquakes that constantly shook the chain were a stern warning against complacency. Stability was an illusion. A peaceful sea could gather itself up into a monstrous tidal wave at any moment, a mountain could explode into molten rock, the very earth beneath this mighty castle could tremble and collapse, and everyone and all their works within it could be cast down to destruction. Nothing was as it seemed, nothing could be trusted. Of all follies, was there any greater than believing in the permanence of anything?

No, no. What was she thinking? Blasphemy. Was it not said, *The grass withereth, and the flower thereof falleth away; But the word of the Lord endureth forever*? Yes, so it was said. Amen.

But the promise brought her no comfort.

She had lost her best friend.

She was about to leave the man she loved.

Soon she would be alone. Worse than alone. She would be living a lie, betrothed, then married to a man for whom she felt respect and nothing more, whether the groom was Charles Smith or Robert Farrington. She reminded herself that her actions were motivated by love, by a determination to relieve Genji of the danger created by her presence. It did not lessen her anguish. Rather than feeling joy in the sacrifice, she felt only pain in the loss. How selfish she was. What would Zephaniah say?

She had not thought about her former fiancé much since his death, and not at all in recent years. Surely he came to mind now only because of the grievous circumstances in which she found herself. What would he say to her? Something about her doom and damnation, surely. Hellfire was his specialty as a preacher.

Think of others before yourself, Emily.

Yes, sir, she would answer.

"Sir" is too distant an appellation for one who is to be your husband, Emily. You should call me by my given name, as I do you.

Yes, Zephaniah.

Wide is the gate, and broad is the way, that leadeth to destruction.

Amen.

She said amen always after each of his quotations from the Bible. He cited the Book often, so she said amen often.

He that believeth not shall be damned.

Amen.

As his enthusiasm grew, his voice increased in volume and sonority, the veins of his forehead popped dangerously, as if they were near to bursting, and his eyes widened and bulged from their sockets with the passion of his emotions.

Ye serpents! Ye generations of vipers! How can ye escape the damnation of hell?

Amen!

But Zephaniah was six years dead. He would not appear to unleash visions of divine retribution upon her. How she would welcome it now, if only to drive other, more dangerous thoughts from her hopes and her imagination. If he had lived, she would be Mrs. Zephaniah Cromwell, she would not be in this castle, she would not be in love with the wrong man, she would not be doomed to unhappiness no matter what she did.

Fear had brought her to the tower, and hope. She had imagined a ghost at Mushindo Monastery—or, more properly now, Mushindo Abbey. She had to have imagined it, for if she truly saw what she thought she saw, then the *Autumn Bridge* scrolls she had read were, impossibly, a portrait of her destiny. She was in the tower, the reputed favorite haunt of the ghost, as a challenge. If ghost there was, then let her show herself. Or itself, for demons have no true gender, only illusions of masculinity or femininity. She was certain there was no ghost, so had not considered what she would do if it appeared. That lack of preparation—though what preparation could there be?—frightened her now. She had an uneasy feeling of being watched, and hesitated to turn too quickly, lest she see what she feared. But each time she turned, there was nothing there but a wall, a window, a door, the columbarium with the urns full of the ashes of Genji's ancestors.

There was no one there. If she could not see it, it could not see her. Surely that was the case, was it not? A chill swept over her. How terrible if she could be watched without being able to see the watcher. Perhaps it had not been such a good idea to come here after all. She had just about made up her mind to leave when she thought she heard something in the stairwell, perhaps the faint, fading echo of a footstep. Whose footstep? Or the soft moaning of wind moving up toward the top of the tower. But the air outside was utterly still. There was no wind. There was no way in or out of the tower except by the stairwell.

She backed away. It couldn't be—

And it wasn't. Charles Smith appeared in the doorway.

"I hope I'm not disturbing you," Smith said.

"You are not," Emily said, somewhat more warmly than she had intended. "I am very happy to see you, Charles."

"The preparations are complete. We may proceed at any time."

"Preparations?"

"For the picnic."

"Ah, yes."

"If you are not up to it, we can leave it for another day."

"Oh, no, we can't. This is perfect weather for a picnic." It had been her idea. Charles and Robert had both been so worried about her emotional state, she felt she must do something to relieve their concern. They had to believe they were doing it for her, rather than the other way around, or it would do no good. So she had maneuvered Charles into making the suggestion. "Let me just gather up my things."

Smith glanced at the urns in the columbarium. "A strange place for study, even the study of ancient scrolls."

"The scrolls are here, but I am not studying. I came here in the hope that helpful thoughts would arise."

"If your thoughts arise more clearly in the presence of earthly remains, you may be better suited for life of a monastic nature than for marriage."

"I know I am not capable of the one. I fear I may also lack the necessary qualities for the other."

"Few people are truly suited to the wholly spiritual life, including those who have embarked upon it. A former inmate of the monastery at Monte Cassino told me the place was more riven with jealousies and politics than his previous abode, which had been the city of Rome itself."

"How did you happen to meet such a remarkable person?"

"I was visiting Honolulu when he passed through on his way to Cochin China."

"As a missionary?"

Smith smiled and shook his head. "As an arms merchant. He said that if he could not successfully save his own soul in a monastery, then he may as well help, in some small way, other souls find their way to their Maker."

Emily frowned, completely unamused. "That's a terrible story, Charles. I hope you will never repeat it again."

"I fear I must," Smith said, feigning a somber expression, "as it is entirely true, and may prove salutary to some." If this beautiful woman had a flaw, it was her limited sense of humor. Perversely, the fact amused him, which he was careful not to show.

"I fail to see any helpful moral."

Her disapproval was still vividly apparent. The color that rose to her cheeks and eyelids highlighted the smooth and snowy whiteness of her skin. The visible blood in the translucent flesh caused a sudden excitement in his loins. In a more barbaric age, or in a less inhibited one, he would respond to his instincts, without hesitation, and seek the consecration of marriage at another more convenient time. Or perhaps that justifying thought arose only because he had lately reread his favorite chapters of *Decline and Fall*, the two relating the conquests and exploits of Attila. How free a man the barbarian Hun had been, and how unfree were he and all civilized men. Civilization itself had suppressed their natural instincts and powers. The present ideal was the knightly gentleman, not the Hun. At times such as these, when he looked upon Emily's excruciating beauty, all the more seductive for its innocence and lack of intentional provocation, he truly regretted the era, place, and destiny he usually regarded as great blessings.

Snared in the lustful reactions of his bodily self, Smith's eyes lingered a moment too long in a carnal stare, and were met by a startled look in Emily's as she raised them. He spoke quickly and trusted his words to disguise his emotions.

"You see no moral in the story because you are not among those in need of it. 'They that be whole need not a physician, but they that are sick.' "

"Amen," she said, but she still looked at him doubtfully.

He hoped it was the applicability of his claimed moral that she questioned, and not the expression she had caught on his face.

· · · · ·

A large tent, usually employed by lords on hunts to provide a modicum of comfort, had been pressed into service for Emily's picnic. Genji, Smith, Farrington, and Emily rode their horses at a leisurely walk. A troop of servants followed on foot with the necessities.

"There," Emily said. "That's just the place." She pointed to a pleasant meadow not far from the shore. The projection into the sea of nearby Cape Muroto shielded it from the wind.

Genji could not bring himself to disappoint her by telling her where they were. She had experienced enough slaughter and tragedy firsthand. She did not need to know of more. Indeed, the shock of knowing could set back the excellent progress she had made in recent weeks.

This meadow had been the site of a massacre of his clan's enemies. That had been nearly six hundred years ago, true, but unpleasant mementos of the event still surfaced occasionally. He hoped no one—and especially Emily—would encounter anything of the sort today. He had not needed to tell the servants anything, of course. When Emily had pointed to the meadow, no expression on their faces betrayed their knowledge. As soon as their lord confirmed her choice, they quickly and unobtrusively examined the area before pitching the tent and laying out the furnishings for the meal. Respect for the dead would have compelled another location. For Genji, respect for the living took precedence. Besides, he could not think of a single meadow, knoll, or stretch of beach within a day's ride of his castle suitable for a picnic that was not also an ancient killing ground. At least this one had witnessed a victory.

"This is indeed a most pleasant location," Smith said as they waited for the servants to complete their tasks. "I am surprised you do not use it more."

"Lord Genji's is a race of warriors," Farrington said. "Picnics and such light entertainments are not their highest priority."

"In truth," Genji said, "our free time is abundant. There has been no war in Japan for more than two hundred fifty years. However, thanks to the Alternate Residency Law, we have been compelled to spend our idle hours in Edo. We have wasted much time indoors there." He looked around at the meadow and smiled. "It would have been nice to enjoy the benefits of nature more."

"No war," Farrington said, "but neither has peace reigned."

"Unfortunately true," Genji said. "We give swords to a million men and burden them with an exaggerated sense of history, honor, and duty. We demand that they be ready to kill and die in the next instant. Then we tell them to be quiet and behave themselves. Not quite the perfect formula for harmony."

"Must we talk of violence?" Emily said.

"We need not," Smith said to her. "Come, let us help the servants arrange the furnishings and let the soldiers trade war stories."

It was an accepted aphorism among the samurai that the outsiders were easily understood because they displayed their innermost thoughts so blatantly on their faces, unlike, presumably, samurai. Genji thought about how shallow a prejudice that was as he watched Smith and Farrington engage in luncheon conversation with Emily. Something was definitely occurring beneath the surface with both men, well below the surface, and he had no idea what it was. It did not involve their usual suggestions of criminality and immorality relating to the late American Civil War. This was something else, neither addressed nor alluded to, but there nonetheless.

Only Emily, as always, was entirely herself, without guile or dissemblance. She seemed to have recovered from the shock of Hanako's death, if not the loss. There was no recovery from such a loss. There was only acceptance or denial.

One of his earliest memories of his grandfather was of their meeting moments after his mother's death. He was very aware of Lord Kiyori's reputation as a fierce warrior, and so did his best to behave as a warrior, too. He kept his posture erect, and fought back his tears. He thought he was doing quite well.

His grandfather said, Why aren't you crying?

Samurai don't cry, Genji said.

His grandfather frowned. He said, Villains don't cry. Heroes cry. Do you know why?

Genji shook his head.

It is because villains' hearts are full of what they have gained. Heroes' hearts are full of what they have lost.

And Lord Kiyori surprised Genji by falling heavily to his knees. Tears flowed from his eyes in great profusion. His nose ran in a most undignified manner. Audible sobs racked his body with convulsions. Genji ran to comfort him, and his grandfather said, Thank you. They held each other and wept shamelessly. Genji remembered thinking, I must be a hero, for I am crying, and my heart is full of loss.

He had not cried as much as he should have since then. Perhaps that meant he was not quite the hero he liked to think he was.

Looking at Emily, he hoped that her present sorrow would later vivify her memories with joy.

She saw him looking in her direction and smiled. At the very moment he returned her smile with one of his own, a mysterious drama between Smith and Farrington commenced and compressed its entirety into the span of less than ten heartbeats.

It began with Farrington. An odd expression, perhaps combining anger and distress, tightened the muscles of his face as he glanced in Genji's direction, eyes rather too bright for friendliness.

Smith, catching the look, gave the appearance of momentary confusion, his brow bunching, his mouth turning down in a slight frown.

Farrington, turning away from Genji, looked at Emily, and his gaze softened into a profound sadness.

Smith, who had continued to watch Farrington, was now seen by Farrington to be doing so, and Farrington's reaction was unexpected. He blushed and looked down.

This apparently caused Smith to experience a sudden and shocking epiphany, for his eyes grew extremely wide and his mouth dropped open.

"You—" he said, and that was all he could or was willing to say, before he came out of his seat and launched himself at Farrington with intentions that were clearly violent.

Two of Genji's bodyguards restrained him before he could do anything. It was not clear to Genji whether Smith had been about to strike Farrington with his fists or was about to draw his revolver and shoot him. It was clear that, in either case, Farrington had not planned resistance or defense of any kind.

"Unhand me," Smith said.

"Give me your word that you will behave peacefully," Genji said.

"You have it."

Smith apologized to Genji and Emily without explanation for his outburst, and turned his attention away from Farrington. Though Farrington attempted to resume his conversation with Emily, she was far too shocked by the outburst to respond. The picnic was effectively at an end.

What had occurred? Genji had not the slightest idea. The supposedly scrutable nature of the outsiders was just that: supposition, not reality.

Smith stood first, bowed abruptly, and strode off across the meadow to where his horse was tied. Halfway there, he stepped on something that made a loud crunching sound. Two servants looked toward Genji with horrified expressions, and bowed apologetically, as if it were their fault. Smith, still distracted by the recent incident, paid no attention.

When Genji looked down where Smith had trod, he saw the right orbit and cheekbone of a skull, sitting amidst the whitened fragments that Smith's boot heel had created of its matching remnant.

· · · · ·

Smith avoided Farrington as completely as he could thereafter. It was not difficult, for Farrington avoided him in an identical manner. Smith's embarrassment was acute. He wished he had not discerned Farrington's thoughts about Emily and Genji. He wished even more fervently that he had not attacked him. Not only was that a disgraceful lapse of gentlemanly self-discipline, it also served to confirm his suspicions, since Farrington made not even the slightest effort to defend himself. Only someone ashamed of his own thoughts would act in that way.

It was now all very clear to Smith.

Farrington believed Taro, ever the loyal vassal, had attacked Emily on Genji's orders, and had done so because Emily's condition, not yet apparent, would soon render her a dangerous liability to him. That condition was the result—indeed, could only be the result—of an immoral, completely unacceptable intimacy. This was true whether the intimacy resulted from Emily's consent or from force or deception on Genji's part. Lord Saemon's unexpected and, for Genji, untimely intervention had saved her life. But only for the time being. Her condition made it imperative that she perish, and soon. Because of this, Farrington remained in attendance upon Emily. Though he no longer wished her to be his bride, as an officer and a gentleman he felt compelled to protect her from further assassination attempts by her host.

Such was Farrington's reasoning.

It was so tortured and ridiculous, Smith would have been unable to restrain his laughter had he heard Farrington enunciate these thoughts instead of discovering them by his own sudden inspiration. Emily's innocence was obvious and undeniable. No such pretense could be maintained for so long. Even more than her religion, her character would never allow her to descend from the highest morality. As for Genji, Farrington credited him with a degree of lustful deviousness and ungovernable passion that would only exist, if at all, in the Forbidden City of the Manchus or the seraglio of the Turkish Sultan, not in this martial land.

Smith's own feelings about Emily were unaffected by Farrington's delusions. But knowing them had caused Smith to look at her in another light, and in that light, he thought he had seen something, and it shocked him even more than Farrington's contorted imaginings. Had he glimpsed the truth or only a delusion of his own?

. . . . .

Smith found Emily in a room adjacent to the rose garden. The doors were open to allow the passage of the mild breeze and to permit a view of the flowers. Several scrolls of Japanese writing were open in front of her. She looked at neither the scrolls nor the flowers, but gazed thoughtfully up at the tower on the other side of the garden.

Smith said, "Even when you are not among the urns, your thoughts seem to be there. Are you so sure you are not suited for a life of religious contemplation?"

"If my prospects continue to evaporate as they have of late, that may indeed be my best choice."

"What do you mean?"

"Robert has returned to Edo."

"Recalled by the ambassador, no doubt."

"So he said."

"What other reason would there be? He is devoted to you, as I am."

"Do you really think so?"

"He stayed by your side for three weeks, to insure that you were well recovered from your recent loss. Only official duties would take him away."

"I felt less care than observation in his presence. He seemed to be watching me rather closely."

"A righteous man sometimes joins a too-brittle sense of propriety to an overactive imagination."

"I fail to see anything in my behavior that would warrant such exertion. And I am not sure I would call Robert righteous. Being quick to pass judgment does not make one righteous."

"If he has been hasty, then I am sure it is only because of his concern for your well-being." Smith smiled. "I find it highly ironical that I am justifying Lieutenant Farrington's actions to you on his behalf."

"So do I. Especially since you were ready to assault him only two days ago."

"A terrible lapse, for which I once again apologize."

"It was more than a lapse, Charles. That afternoon, something passed quite wordlessly between Robert and yourself. The result was violent outrage on your part, and acute embarrassment on his. What was the cause?"

Smith chose his words with care. He said, "His thoughts, and my sudden apprehension of them."

"I had gathered as much on my own."

"To go further would exceed the bounds of proper conversation between a lady and a gentleman."

Emily frowned. "You and Robert have shared a thought, presumably about me, a thought sufficiently volatile to cause you to attack him. Yet you cannot properly enunciate it in my presence? You will excuse me if I am not comforted."

Smith bowed, conceding the point. "Nevertheless, there we must leave it."

"That is most unsatisfying to both my curiosity and my feelings."

"Once you are betrothed, Emily, it will not matter anyway, so it should not matter now."

"Once I am betrothed. I am sorry to have delayed matters so long. I assure you, it has nothing to do with either Robert or yourself, and entirely with my own flaws."

Smith said, "I would not call being in love a flaw."

Crimson instantly suffused Emily's cheeks. He knew by this that his surmise had been correct. Her inherent honesty betrayed her even when she did not speak. She did her best to cover the truth, but he had already seen it.

She said, "It would be simple indeed were I in love with you or Robert. But while my admiration is great and equal, that is not yet the case. That is what makes the decision so difficult."

"There is difficulty," Smith said. "But not in the decision. It is already made. You are in love." Now that he knew, his sympathies were aroused. The road ahead of her was fraught with peril of a kind and degree she could not even imagine. Taro's attempt on her life—for Smith saw now that Farrington had been right about that, if nothing else—was certain to be only the first of many. "You must follow your heart. What else is there to do? The only question is, are his feelings consonant with yours? If they are not, love can only bring suffering, not joy. In that case, you would be well advised to choose admiration over love."

"I think perhaps we are not speaking of the same thing," Emily said.

"You are in love with Lord Genji," Smith said.

Had she not been sitting, she would surely have fallen.

"God help me," she said. "Is it so obvious?"

"No," Smith said. "I wasn't certain until now. So far as I know, I am the only one who even suspects."

"Robert doesn't?"

"His suspicions are of a different nature."

He was grateful that she did not pursue that line of thought. Instead, she bowed her head and buried her face in her hands.

She said, "What am I to do?"

"Be patient," he said. "When Lieutenant Farrington and I have gone, it is not unlikely that Lord Genji will deduce the truth. Then he will come forward, or he will not, and you will have your answer."

When she looked up, her eyes were wet, but she smiled and said, "Thank you, Charles. You are a very good and kind friend."

Smith bowed. "Should your best hopes not be realized, I stand ready to be good and kind and more than a friend. Business will keep me in Edo for another month. I will visit you again before I leave Japan."

"I have not deserved such consideration."

"Nevertheless, you have it." Smith smiled. "But be cautious. Your relationship with Lord Genji has already been the cause of malicious gossip within the Western community. Things highly damaging to your reputation have been said."

"It is written, *We can do nothing against the truth, but for the truth.* I will trust in that."

"Amen," Smith said, "but remember, it is also written, *The poison of asps is under their lips, and the sting of the asp is deadly.*"

"Amen," Emily said. "I have done nothing wrong. Nor has Lord Genji."

"I have never thought it of either of you," Smith said. He did not add, Unlike Lieutenant Farrington.

. . . . .

"First Lieutenant Farrington," Genji said, "and now you, Mr. Smith. How regrettable. I had hoped for a resolution. Nothing is amiss, I hope. Lieutenant Farrington seemed more morose than usual."

"He has let himself get caught up in wrong thinking," Smith said. "He will come out of it eventually."

"Wrong thinking?"

"It means faulty reasoning leading to the wrong conclusions."

"I understand the idiom," Genji said. "I don't understand the reference."

"Is that possible? Miss Gibson, an exceptionally beautiful young woman of marriageable age, has been your houseguest without chaperone, relative, or companion for several years. It is not difficult to reach the wrong conclusion about your relationship."

Genji said, "Emily has not been without watchful companions the entire time she has been my guest. She has also spent much of that time on expeditions of her own. In this castle and the palace in Edo, she has quarters entirely separate—and, may I add, distant—from mine. Days and weeks have passed without either of us even seeing the other in passing. I understood lords in other countries have accommodated guests on a similar basis."

"Her companions have not been from among her own people," Smith said. "They have been your vassals and servants. Anyone who has been in this country for a single hour knows that the command of a lord is obeyed without question. They are no real protection for her. And guests who visit lords in such places as England always have servants and chaperones of their own."

Genji nodded. "How foolish of me. I should have relied on an advisor other than Emily. Her innocence sometimes prevents her from seeing things as others might. May I assume Lieutenant Farrington believes I have somehow taken advantage of her?"

"In a word, yes."

"And you?"

Smith smiled.

"Lieutenant Farrington has a habit of suppressing his instinctive feelings and natural thoughts as if they were traitorous rebels. He refuses to acknowledge them as his own, and instead imputes them to others. I do not suffer from that habit. Besides, my lord, if you want something, you would take it openly, the consequences be damned. That is the way of the samurai, is it not?"

"That is the way as we like to think it is, and how we would like others to see it," Genji said. "In fact, we are so concerned with consequences and appearances, we frequently are capable of nothing at all. We rely so much on what is not said, we frequently do not stop to consider that nothing at all has been communicated, that there is only the wish in our own heads. We are often the opposite of decisive, I am sorry to say."

"Then let me relieve you of some of the burden by speaking plainly," Smith said, "and being as decisive as I can. I will return at the end of next month before departing for home. If Emily remains unbetrothed, I will renew my suit. I hope she is, yet I know her hope is the opposite, so I pray most sincerely that she finds happiness, wherever it is best found."

" 'Her hope is the opposite.' Do you mean she has a preference for Lieutenant Farrington?"

"Her preference is not for Lieutenant Farrington. And her feelings are quite beyond preference altogether. She is in love, and has been, I believe, for some time. Furthermore, I believe you have known it all along."

Smith wondered how Genji would react. Outrage? Surprise? Contempt? Laughter? Perhaps he had gone too far.

Genji's expression did not change. The small smile that was habitually on his lips remained, and he spoke in his usual tone.

"I have often wondered whether she is as transparent to her own people as she is to us," he said. "Apparently, she has not been, or neither you nor Lieutenant Farrington would have gone as far as you have. Sometimes, those on the outside can see what those on the inside cannot. May I ask what has led you to your new awareness?"

"Pure accident, sir." Smith was relieved by Genji's mild response. "A confluence of observation, remarks, oddities of behavior. All came together of a sudden, and I was able to make sense of it. You must remember, there has always been much talk amongst her own people, none of it flattering. Speculation has tended to be of an extremely salacious nature."

"But she is so prim and proper."

"She is also extremely beautiful."

"So I understand."

"You understand. You do not see it for yourself?"

"Frankly, no. Our ideals of beauty are so different, it is almost as if beauty and ugliness are reversed for us."

Now it was Smith who was surprised.

"You find Emily ugly?"

"Well, ugly is a harsh word. Unattractive would be the better choice."

Smith exhaled as if he had been holding his breath.

He said, "That is a great relief to me, sir. If you returned her love, then the situation would be dangerous to you both, in every way imaginable. Neither of our nations looks with favor on the mixing of races. Furthermore, you are in need of an heir, and it is certain Emily would never accept being a concubine. To her, that would only be a form of harlotry."

"You spoke of renewing your offer of marriage to her."

"As I said, I will, as soon as I return."

"Why wait? Do it now."

"A woman in love with one man needs time to open her heart to another. We must proceed with patience. For now, tell her we have spoken—of my suit, not of your knowledge of her feelings—and say that you approve wholeheartedly. Your enthusiasm will speak volumes. And she will then have a month to prepare for my return."

"Thank you, Mr. Smith, for your wise counsel."

Genji remained alone after Smith left. He could speak to Emily in the way Smith had advised. It would require a certain amount of lying, which was not a problem, since he was a much better liar than she was. He had concealed his feelings from her and everyone else for a long time. Another month would not present a problem. But there was a better way than speaking, and it would make whatever he eventually said more believable. The outsiders had an appropriate saying.

Actions speak louder than words.

· · · · ·

There was much excitement among the household staff of the castle. At last, their lord was taking decisive steps to insure the continuation of his lineage.

"Have you heard?" one maid said to another as they carried trays of tea to other rooms.

"Of course! Everyone knows."

"Who will they be?"

"I heard he hasn't decided yet."

A third maid passing in the opposite direction said, "Court ladies."

"The Emperor's or the Shogun's?"

"Both, of course!"

"Politics and sex," the first maid said.

The second maid nodded. "Is it not always so?"

"Not for us," the first maid said, and they both stifled their giggles. They would have laughed out loud if they were not so close to the quarters of lordly men.

· · · · ·

The week after Charles Smith's departure, two ladies with a connection to the Shogun's court in Edo arrived and were welcomed in a ceremony to which Emily was not invited. Masami, her maid, told her one was a relative of Lord Genji's ally, Lord Hiromitsu of Yamanaka. The other was distantly related to Lord Saemon.

"They will both be concubines for now," Masami said. "He may decide to marry one, later, especially if she gives birth to the heir. But it's more likely the lord will preserve that honor for an even higher-born lady with the best political connections. If one of the concubines does bear an heir, the child will then be adopted by his wife. I think a wife, whoever she is, will come with the blessings of the Emperor rather than the Shogun. The Emperor's fortunes are rising, and the Shogun's are sinking."

Masami prattled on and on as she worked. Emily smiled and nodded and said nothing. If anyone had noticed, they would have seen an unusual brightness in her eyes. But, of course, no one noticed.

· · · · ·

Genji knew he would have to speak with Emily, and he was not looking forward to it. He knew there would be many tears shed by her, amidst silent accusations. Silent, because she would never say anything openly. What was there to say? She didn't know how he felt about her, nor did she know Smith had communicated his own knowledge of her feelings to him. There was nothing to say. Yet, it would be excruciating. He could offer no solace, for that could come only by an admission of his affection for her, an admission he could not make. If he told her, she would remain in Japan, and if she did, she would die. His vision promised that. He did not want her to die, so he would send her away.

Life was more important than love.

· · · · ·

One month quickly passed. Genji had promised to talk to Emily, and he had not yet done so. He should have invited Emily to the welcoming ceremonies for Lady Fusae and Lady Chiyo. That would have made the point vividly. But he couldn't bring himself to do it. It would have been too cruel. He didn't want to hurt her more than necessary. Perhaps it would not be necessary to say very much more, or even to see her again until the day she left with Charles Smith, which day would be soon. When Smith returned, he would propose, and Emily would surely accept. It was both painful and amusing to Genji that his own actions verified what he had said to Smith about samurai indecisiveness.

He rode out to Apple Valley alone, as he often did when he mulled over difficulties. There was something calming about being among the trees his mother had planted so many years ago. Answers did not always come to him there, but an inner quietude always did, even if the problems remained unresolved. His bodyguards were under strict orders from Hidé never to let him go anywhere without protection, even here in the heart of his domain within sight of his castle walls. In Hidé's view, assassinations had become too frequent to permit relaxation anywhere. Genji had vainly pointed out that his visions of the future included a foretelling of his own death, so he knew when and where he would die, and it was neither here nor now. Hidé remained adamant. Who knew, he said, what intervening disasters could occur before then if they failed to be vigilant? Did Lord Genji's visions give him a view of everything that was to come? Genji had to admit they did not.

So to gain the solitude he needed, he had become skillful at evading his own men. Eventually, they always found him. But in the meantime, he was alone. To make himself harder to find, he entered the valley not from the direction of the castle, as usual, but over the narrow path that wound into the valley over the inland hills.

These trees always reminded him of his mother, yet with every passing year, he could recall less and less of her, and was forced to invent more. He had not yet reached the age of four when she died in childbirth. Twenty-seven years had passed since then. It was a long time to miss someone he did not truly remember.

There was a sudden rustling of leaves high in the branches of the tree above him. His thought, even before he spurred his horse into motion, was that Hidé had been right after all. There were too many assassins everywhere to permit relaxation anywhere. He drew his sword as his horse bolted forward, and looked up, expecting a leaping assassin or an arrow or a bullet to strike him at any moment. He saw nothing of the kind. Instead, he caught a glimpse of gingham fabric.

He brought his horse to a halt and cantered back under the tree.

Emily looked down at him and said, "You would never even have known I was here had I not lost my balance."

From that height, she could easily suffer mortal injury. Genji knew it was against her religion to commit suicide. It was not against her religion to fall accidentally. She stood precariously on two thin branches near the top of the tree. One hand held the trunk, which was not much more than a thick stalk at that point. Her other hand held her skirt close together in a ladylike fashion, if being in a tree at all could be called ladylike.

"Emily, what are you doing?"

"Climbing a tree. It seemed exactly the right kind of day for it."

"Please come down."

She laughed and said, "No. You come up."

Genji looked at her carefully. Her good cheer seemed genuine, her smile unforced, the sparkle in her eyes the sparkle of health and not of sorrowful derangement.

"I think it would be better if you came down."

She shook her head and laughed again.

"I see we cannot agree. So we must each follow our own inclinations and allow the other the same freedom."

"Such an approach leads only to anarchy," he said. "We must negotiate. I will climb up, if you will agree to then climb down with me."

"I agree, but only if you climb as high as I am."

"That would be reckless. Those branches are only just supporting you. They would not bear my additional weight."

"Then stay where you are and leave me where I am."

There was nothing else to do. He couldn't leave her there. Genji reached up and pulled himself out of his saddle and into the tree. He climbed quickly to the branch just below her and negotiated again.

"As you can plainly see, those branches will snap if I climb on them."

She said, "Perhaps."

"Not perhaps. It is certain."

"Very well, I will consider your obligation fulfilled if you will answer one question."

Ah, here it was. Now that they were both in the treetop, she would have her emotional breakdown. How could he prevent her from falling without falling himself? He could not. If she lost her balance, he would have to grab her and try to control the manner of their landing. From twenty feet above the ground, that would require a degree of martial ability he wasn't sure he possessed. Wasn't it just like a woman to make things unnecessarily difficult? It was a feminine quality that transcended cultural differences.

"Ask it after we are on the ground," he said. He didn't think it would work and it didn't.

She said very simply, "No."

He could not force her down. There was nothing to do but say, "What is your question?"

"Your English-Japanese dictionary is very complete," she said, "with one notable exception. You have not made an entry for the word *love* in either language. Why?"

It was not quite the question he expected, but he saw where it would lead.

He said, "Everyone knows the meaning of the word. Beyond giving the equivalent terms in both languages, further definition is not needed. Now, let us descend."

She shook her head. "Your answer is unsatisfactory. You say everyone knows the definition. Then tell me. What is love?"

"I object. You asked your one question and I answered it. Now you must keep your part of the bargain."

"Spoken like a merchant, not a samurai," she said. But she climbed down with him. When they were on the ground, she said, "I don't believe you know, Lord Genji."

"Of course I do. To put it into a dictionary definition is quite another matter."

The expression on Emily's face was as close to a smirk as Genji had ever seen.

"That is exactly the answer of one who doesn't know," she said.

1830, WHITE STONES CASTLE IN SHIROISHI DOMAIN

Lord Kiyori was happy to see his old friend Lord Nao, but he was not happy about what had brought him to this far northern domain.

"How can this not be a happy occasion?" Lord Nao said. "You have asked me to give my daughter as wife to your eldest son. This will join our families together forever. Splendid! Emi, take away the tea and bring sake."

"Wait," Kiyori said. "I have not told you everything."

"What more is there to tell?" Nao said. "My daughter will be the wife of the future Great Lord of Akaoka. My grandson—may heaven provide one soon—will be Great Lord in his turn. Emi, where is the sake?"

"She has just gone to get it, my lord," another maid said.

"Well, don't just sit there. Go help her."

"Nao, listen to me," Kiyori said, his face unremittingly grim. "I have asked you to give your daughter to Yorimasa in marriage, but I must also advise you, as a friend, to refuse."

"What? You are talking nonsense. How can you ask with one breath, and advise refusal with the next?"

"I have had a vision," Kiyori said.

"Ah," Nao said, and sat back to listen. He had known Kiyori for more than thirty years. In that time, Kiyori had told him of many visions, and all had come true. Others may doubt the Great Lord of Akaoka's prescience. He never would.

"The marriage will produce an heir," Kiyori said, "the only heir of either of our clans to survive a great change to come. Your daughter will not fully recover from the difficulty of his birth. The birth of her second child will kill her."

Nao looked down. He took several deep breaths and neither spoke nor looked up.

Kiyori said, "It need not be. Refuse the marriage, and let another bear the burden."

"How can it be avoided? You have seen it in a vision."

"I believe my visions are of what may be," Kiyori said, "not what must be."

"Have they ever failed to materialize?"

"No."

"Then what makes you think this one will be any different?"

"Always, in the past, I have followed what I have seen. What if we do not follow? Then surely our actions, and not the vision, will determine what is to come."

"You are certain of this?"

"No," Kiyori said, "that is precisely the point. If we act in contradiction to the vision, then we can be certain of nothing, including the deaths I have foreseen."

Nao shook his head. "We will also lose the certainty of your vision that our grandson will survive to carry on our bloodlines. The continuation of our clans is more important than individual lives, especially if both our clans are embodied in one future lord."

"You will let your daughter marry, knowing that the marriage itself will result in her death?"

"We will all die," Nao said. "That is our fate. If she dies to preserve our clans, then she dies as befits a samurai's daughter. Neither she nor we should have any regrets."

Kiyori nodded. "I thought you would say as much."

Nao laughed. "Then why did you bother to raise the objection?"

"Lord," the maids said, entering with trays of sake. Nao took a cup. At his urging, Kiyori took one also, though with clear reluctance.

Kiyori said, "Because it is only one reason to refuse the marriage."

"Astonishing. You mean there is another?"

"Yes, and together with the first, the weight of the argument against is great indeed."

Nao waited for Kiyori to go on, but he did not. He remained silent and grew ever grimmer. Nao drank his sake and waited patiently. If Kiyori was silent, Nao was confident there was a good reason. He had begun to think Kiyori had decided against sharing the second reason, when he spoke at last.

"My son, Yorimasa, is not a worthy man. He is a drunk, a womanizer, and a wastrel."

"Marriage will change him, as it changes everyone."

"When I said he was a drunk, a womanizer, and a wastrel," Kiyori said, "I was not speaking plainly enough. He is worse than that. Far worse. If he were my retainer instead of my son, I would have ordered his suicide long ago. It is a sign of my weakness as a father that I have not done so."

"What has he done?"

"Things that shame me to think of in silence, much less confess aloud," Kiyori said.

· · · · ·

Yorimasa long looked forward to two events. His ascension to the lordship of Akaoka Domain, and his first prophetic vision. Because he was the eldest son of Great Lord Kiyori, he felt assured of the first. His unshakable conviction that a special destiny was his promised him the second. From earliest childhood, his character was shaped by these expectations, despite repeated warnings from his father that life was uncertain and the devolution of prophetic power more uncertain still. Yorimasa had a strong stubborn streak. He would say, Yes, Father, but he did not mean it.

Because Yorimasa's confidence was so great, those around him had confidence in him, too. This was especially so because he was the first grandson on both sides of his family. The hopes of his relatives naturally rested on him. Fortunately, these hopes seemed well founded. He was a bright and cheerful child who spoke in complete sentences during his first year. He wrote an excellent hand by his third birthday. He wielded his little sword with notable skill, fired well-aimed arrows with his little boy's bow, and controlled his pony fearlessly, all before he was five. The household servants would have pampered him in any case. His attributes, including his good looks, encouraged even more attention than usual.

The birth of his brother, Shigeru, did not diminish his stature. Shigeru was quieter, shyer, and far less handsome than Yorimasa. It seemed to everyone, when they searched their memories, that everything Shigeru did while growing up, Yorimasa had done earlier, better, and with more flair. If he had any advantage at all, it was in his physical power. He was a very strong little boy. Mere strength, however, did not count as much among men as it did among oxen. In any case, by the governing principles of primogeniture, the second son was always so much less important than the first. How much more so when the first was so extraordinary. Relatives, retainers, and servants could not help but remark to each other on their good fortune in having such a gifted young lord. The future of the clan would surely rest in good hands, especially since every sign indicated that Yorimasa was the one in his generation destined to possess the prophetic power.

Such a young lord, having every gift that natural inheritance and family fortune can bestow, inevitably attracts a following among his peers. Yorimasa was no exception. Particularly because of the unsettled conditions of the time—unrest within, the increased presence of foreign navies without, disturbing political developments on the Asian mainland—the possibility of prophetic power drew even more young lords into his circle than would otherwise have been the case. This might not have occurred had Yorimasa not also been in every other way a sterling example of a lordly samurai. Living such a life, how could he take his father's warnings seriously?

So it was that his disappointment, when it came, was unutterably great.

On the eve of his twenty-second birthday, his father said, "You will not become Great Lord after me."

Shocked, all he could say was "Why?"

"Why does not enter into it."

"I am your eldest son. I will not yield to my younger brother."

"Shigeru will not become Great Lord either."

In his pain, he laughed. "If neither Shigeru nor I are to be your heir, then you must be thinking of siring another. Or have you already done so in secret?"

"Stop talking like a fool. I am telling you the truth. Accept it."

"Is this prophecy?"

"Call it what you will, or give it no name at all," his father said. "Acknowledge it or ignore it. It changes nothing."

"Who will be the next Great Lord of our domain?"

"One not yet born."

"Then you intend to take another wife, or a concubine." Yorimasa's initial shock began to simmer into rage. Some manipulative woman had turned his head. In his dazed infatuation, the old fool had promised to make her child the next lord. Who was she? "Are you so sure you will produce an heir? You are no longer young, Father."

His father's expression had a strange quality to it. The sternness on the surface seemed exaggerated. Was it to conceal another emotion beneath it? If one was hidden there, Yorimasa could not read it.

"The decision is made," Kiyori said. "There is nothing more to discuss."

There was nothing more to discuss, but there was much to do. First, Yorimasa would discover who this woman was, and where his father had hidden her, and the child if one already existed. Then he would dispose of them. This was not a matter of prophecy. Kiyori had spoken of a decision being made. He would not have spoken of a vision in that way. The future was therefore not yet set. Yorimasa did not intend to remain passive while his patrimony was stolen from him.

At first, his most strenuous investigations uncovered nothing. He questioned every servant and every retainer. No one had seen Lord Kiyori visiting any woman. No one knew of any child. Yorimasa assigned his most trusted friends to follow his father. They learned nothing. He himself followed Kiyori, with the same result. Nothing. There was no woman, no child. So what had led Kiyori to his strange decision? No one had any idea.

Then, shortly after Kiyori made his announcement to Yorimasa, his behavior took another strange turn. He began to spend many hours of every day on the seventh floor of the high tower. When he was there, his standing order was that no one could enter the tower beyond the third floor. This was at a time when the navies of outsider nations were becoming ever more frequent in Japanese waters. Their warships had even entered the bay outside Cloud of Sparrows on several occasions. It was highly inappropriate to withdraw in this strange way.

Yorimasa wondered if his father had gone insane. Tragic though it would be, it would also be convenient. If his father was mad, the chief retainers would all support his removal. There were ample precedents. Madness had not been an uncommon clan malady. It seemed to be caused by the same mysterious workings that brought prescience into the bloodline. The secret disinheritance of his only two sons and his newfound preference for life in the tower seemed to point in that direction.

Whispers of a regency headed by Yorimasa began to circulate among the vassals. To Yorimasa's great satisfaction, he had nothing to do with it. The idea sprang up spontaneously. Even his father's closest retainers—Lord Saiki, Lord Tanaka, and Lord Kudo—expressed their concern to Yorimasa. He was pleased to find that they, like all the other vassals, had already begun to treat him with greater deference. His father was energetically working his own undoing. All Yorimasa had to do, it seemed, was exercise patience.

But he was not quite patient enough.

His father's solitary periods in the tower piqued his curiosity. At last, he could resist no longer, and decided to discover for himself exactly what Kiyori was doing there for so many hours, day after day.

Entering the tower undetected was easy. Kiyori had stationed no guards at the entrance, within the stairwell, or on any of the intervening floors between the third and the seventh. He relied entirely on the strength of his command. It was enough to keep everyone out. Except Yorimasa.

Even before his eyes were level with the landing of the highest floor, he could hear his father's voice in conversation. Whoever was there with him spoke very softly, for Yorimasa could hear no one else.

· · · · ·

"You should have told him long ago," Shizuka said.

"As you advised," Kiyori said.

"What does it matter who advised it? To leave such an important matter until so late is error, my lord." She bowed to the floor. "Forgive me for speaking so bluntly."

"Well, now he knows. He will not be Great Lord."

"But you have not told him why."

"No."

"Nor have you told him that he will not be the one to receive the visions in his generation."

"No. I hope that when he sees how much suffering comes with the visions, he will not too strongly regret his lack of them."

Shizuka smiled. "He has not seen you exhibit any signs of suffering, my lord."

"Because, my lady, I have not actually had visions, have I? You are the one who has had them. You are the one who has told me everything I know of what is to come."

"Since you believe I myself am a vision, then my telling you of the future is the same as you seeing it yourself." She paused and pretended to ponder the thought. "But you sometimes believe I am not a vision but a ghost. In that case, are my words still visions for you? I suppose they are, for what else would they be?"

Kiyori frowned. "I will never be able to think my way through it. All I know is that everything you have told me has been true, without trickery or hidden meanings. Whether you are who you say you are or not, you are the way my visions come to me. With Shigeru, it will be different. You have said so."

"Yes, it will be different."

"He will suffer."

"Yes."

"He will understand nothing."

"Yes."

"When Yorimasa sees that, his regret will be diminished."

"You may hope so."

"Can you not tell me? Surely you know."

The door slid violently open and slammed hard against its stop. Yorimasa stood in the doorway, sword in hand. His face was white, his eyes red.

"What are you doing?" Kiyori said. He leaped to his feet, but did not touch his own sword.

Yorimasa saw a sake setting for two. His father's cup was empty. The lady's cup was full. But she was nowhere to be seen.

"Where is she?" Yorimasa screamed.

"Put down your sword and withdraw!" Kiyori stepped fearlessly toward his son. "You forget your place."

Yorimasa ignored him.

He said, "How long have you been a woman's slave? Don't glare so fiercely. I heard you admit it. You are a liar and false prophet. She is a sorceress. She must be, to make you abandon both of your sons for her. Where is she?"

His eyes scanned the room for the entrance to the secret passageway. The walls revealed nothing. He looked carefully at the mats on the floor. None of them showed signs of recent movement. She had not gone past him. She would not have gone out of a window, for in daylight, she would be seen from below. The secret entry had to be in the ceiling. His eyes went up.

When they did, Kiyori stepped forward and, in one smooth and economical motion, twisted the sword out of his son's grasp and threw him head over heels hard against the far wall. Before Yorimasa could rise or draw his other sword, Kiyori struck him in the temple with the hilt of the sword he had taken from him.

· · · · ·

Yorimasa recovered consciousness in his own quarters, with Dr. Ozawa in attendance. The right side of his head ached, but he was not seriously injured. There were no guards posted. His swords were where they should be, in a stand nearby. He took them and left the room. No one tried to stop him.

He did not seek out his father. He knew Kiyori would explain nothing. The woman, whoever she was, was gone, back into hiding. If he had not found her before, he certainly would not find her now. There was someone else he needed to see. If everything he had heard was true, then there was little of value left in life for him.

He found Shigeru in the practice yard, spinning and striking at targets behind him.

Shigeru noticed the bruised temple. "What happened to you?"

Yorimasa ignored the question.

He said, "Did Father ever speak to you about visions?"

"You know he has. He has always shared his visions with both of us at the same time."

"I meant your visions, not his."

Shigeru did not betray himself by any facial reaction, but his failure to answer immediately was verification enough. So it was true. Shigeru, not he, would have the visions, and Shigeru knew it.

"So Father finally told you," Shigeru said.

Again, Yorimasa ignored the question, and asked one of his own.

"Have the visions begun?"

"No. Father said they would not, for many more years."

"How long have you known?"

"Twelve years."

"Since you were a child?"

"Yes."

"Yet you said nothing to me." Why had no one told him? Why had they let him go on believing he would be the one? Worse than disappointment was the shame. How hollow and foolish all these years of his confidence and pride had been!

"I am not lord of this domain," Shigeru said, "our father is. He gives the orders. He tells what he wants to tell, and keeps the rest to himself. That is what it means to be lord. You should know it."

"Why should I? I will never be lord," Yorimasa said.

"Of course you will. You are the eldest son. Visions have nothing to do with who will follow Father."

"I will not be lord. Father told me I would not be lord."

Shigeru frowned. "What can that mean?"

"He has a woman we know nothing about. I heard them talking in the tower. Who knows how long they have been together. Perhaps we have an elder brother we have yet to meet."

"Impossible."

"Nothing is impossible," Yorimasa said.

He left Shigeru and went to the stable. He would not stay in the castle another hour. He would go to the palace in Edo and try to think of something.

"Yorimasa." His father stepped out of the shadows.

"Ah, you have come to bid me good-bye. Or will you forbid me to leave?"

"It is not what you think," Kiyori said.

"Oh? Then what is it?"

"There is no woman. I do not have another child who will become my heir. There is no other child. Not yet. And when there is, he will be your son, not mine."

"Is that prophecy, my lord?"

"It is."

Yorimasa bowed low. "Then I yield to the inevitable, and to my son yet to be born. Who will be my bride, and when?"

"That has not yet been revealed to me."

Yorimasa leaped into the saddle of his horse. He bowed again.

"Please let me know. Every word you speak is to me a command." He bowed yet again, laughed harshly, and spurred his horse into a gallop.

Everything he had dreamed of was lost. He would not be Great Lord of Akaoka Domain. He would speak no prophecies. The respect bordering on awe with which he had been treated would be replaced by ridicule. He wanted to die. But to take his life now was the act of a coward. He was not a coward. He would endure. But he did not have to endure grimly.

Yorimasa had spent the first twenty-two years of his life preparing to rule. He had read the classics. He had trained in single combat. He had studied the strategies of controlling armies. He had sat in *zazen* for several hours every day, letting go of everything, then letting go of letting go. These were the arts necessary for one destined for war and command. They were no longer of the slightest use to him. He abandoned them now and forever. Where once he had dedicated every moment to improving himself as a samurai, he now dedicated himself to complete indulgence of his every sensual whim. What else could life give him?

There was alcohol, opium, absinthe, and a wide variety of other concoctions to alter perception and mood in any way he wished. Of course, there were negative side effects. But there were always other solutions, powders, pills, and fumes to cure those ills.

He used them all, and every cure and antidote. He used so much, he could almost ignore the laughter behind his back.

Yorimasa expected his father to intervene, so when he did, he was not surprised. But Kiyori never held him in confinement for longer than necessary to effect the cure for the ill of the moment. Then he was released.

He soon understood why. If he were confined, he would have absolutely no reason to go on. Confinement was therefore impossible, since

Kiyori could not have him killing himself. His vision said Yorimasa must live to have a son.

That also guaranteed to Yorimasa that no matter what he did, he would not accidentally die. The inevitability of his doom was also the inevitability of his survival. Was this not a most amusing dilemma?

The drugs that brought relief also poisoned him. His body suffered; even more, his thoughts. Soon hallucinations and mood alterations were not satisfying. He turned his attention to women. One day, his father would command him to marry, and he would obey. He would service her like the reliable breeding animal that he was. In the meantime, there were so many women in Edo.

At first, he was attracted to beauty. But beauty of a merely physical kind, day after day, becomes the same as plainness. One no longer sees anything worthy of notice.

His fascination shifted to the different bodily parts. Their shape, their texture, their odor, their taste. There were fascinating variations, even on a single body, and when many bodies were considered, how much more variety there was.

When he tired of that, his attention went to his own body. He had experienced the many realms of pleasure. What remained was pain. He could not discover external pain equal to the pain he felt within. He did what he could. He was a samurai. He endured.

From his own pain, he turned inevitably to the pain of others. There, at last, he found the perfect joining of every element. Hallucinations, sensory enhancements, beauty, ugliness, and, most of all, pain.

Sometimes he went too far, and a woman was ruined. Then he had to pay a hefty bonus to the geisha house, and a special consolatory fee to the woman's family. It was only money.

He developed a fascination with those perverse sexual practices that caused pain to him, and even more pain to them. There was a special flavor to their tears, and a special music in their voices. Certain concoctions enhanced his pleasure. Certain fumes magnified their agony. He used them all.

He found his excitement was greatest when he knew he was destroying their best attributes. In the beginning, he thought this was their beauty; he did not have to scar the outside; if he scarred the inside, it was done. But he came to realize the physically visible aspects were not truly important; in every one of them, no matter how much they had done, no matter how much they had seen, a certain unspoiled secret heart remained deep within; in it was a precious sense of themselves they had managed to preserve. He became expert at finding it. Then the sound of their screams was so loud, it almost drowned out the laughter behind his back.

· · · · ·

"If your daughter were not important to you, I would not be so concerned," Kiyori said, "but I know you love her very much."

Nao said, "Midori is just a girl. She is not important. The son she will bear, he is important."

"Do not give your consent so easily, Nao. Let me tell you the kind of man Yorimasa has become."

"No. It doesn't matter." Nao bowed. "We are honored that you have chosen our clan. Midori will marry Yorimasa."

· · · · ·

Time passed quickly and slowly at the same time. Sometimes, Yorimasa couldn't say whether a week had passed, or a month, or the better part of his lifetime. Being lost in this way was the closest he could approach to what had been happiness.

"Yorimasa."

Through a haze of opium fumes, he saw Shigeru's face.

"Why, little brother. Don't be so timid. Breathe. It won't kill you."

Shigeru pulled him roughly to his feet. The establishment's guards, usually so forceful, stayed a respectful distance away. Shigeru's reputation as a duelist, born when he was fifteen, had grown increasingly fearsome over the years.

"I came to take you back to Cloud of Sparrows. Father has found you a bride."

"What year is it?"

Shigeru stared at him in disgust before answering.

"The fourteenth year."

"Of what Emperor?"

"The Ninkō Emperor continues to ennoble the world with his august presence."

Yorimasa let himself be half dragged, half carried out. Amazing. Only one year had passed. Perhaps less.

"And what month, little brother?"

. . . . .

For three weeks, his father forced him to train with the vassals as if war were coming. Yorimasa did not spend a single hour indoors, instead living day and night in a war camp in the mountains north of Cloud of Sparrows. Every dawn, he rode with the other cavalrymen down to the shore, dismounted, and ran in full armor from the Muroto Woods to the Cape. If he fell and tried to rest, Shigeru pulled him to his feet. If he did not run, he was dragged. When he threw up, the three clan generals—Lord Saiki, Lord Tanaka, and Lord Kudo—laughed uproariously, as if they had never seen a funnier sight. At night, vassals playing the part of enemy assassins raided the camp and struck mercilessly with bamboo staves at those who were too slow to rise. No provisions were provided. Only those who trapped game, shot birds, or found edible plants ate. The others went hungry. By the fourth day, he was reduced to eating the least repulsive insects he could catch. By the sixth, he was seriously considering butchering his horse. On the seventh day, the camp was moved to the shore, and fishermen from Kageshima Village delivered a small supply of dried cod and unpolished rice. It was the most delicious meal Yorimasa had ever eaten.

When three weeks had passed, sobriety had been restored to Yorimasa. It was temporary and meaningless. The man he had become could easily survive a period of deprivation. He would do what he was required to do, then he would rededicate his energy in a manner less offensive to him. Let his father raise the heir. He had no interest in a succession that passed over him. What would such a son be except another cause for ridicule? Yorimasa already hated him. He was not even born, not even conceived, and he hated him more than anyone he would ever hate.

And his bride-to-be. Whoever she was, he hated her, too.

. . . . .

"Lord Nao's daughter?" Yorimasa thought he was beyond shock, but he was wrong. "Lord Nao of Shiroishi Domain?"

"Do you know another Lord Nao?" Kiyori said.

"The Lord of Apples," Yorimasa said. What a fool. He had thought he could suffer no more humiliation. He should have known worse was always possible.

"He is to be your father-in-law," Kiyori said. "Do not insult him with such an epithet."

"Why not? The Lord of Apples. That is his title from one end of Japan to the other. You have betrothed me to the daughter of the most ridiculous Great Lord in the realm. Why?"

Yorimasa's shame and anger were so great, tears sprang to his eyes. Only his rage kept them from falling.

"Lord Nao's realm is small—" Kiyori began.

"Small, insignificant, poor, weak, and so far out of the way, one would have to live in the wretched Ainu villages of Yezo to be farther north!"

"Lord Nao's realm is small," Kiyori said again, "but soundly managed. His reserves of rice allowed him, like us, to survive the most recent famine without the uprisings that disrupted so many other domains. His army—"

"You call his handful of country bumpkins an army?"

"His army, accustomed to harsh winters, is one of the few capable of waging an aggressive campaign in that season."

"Because it is always winter there!"

"And his orchards, which you denigrate, produce the finest apples in the realm—"

"Who eats apples but horses?"

"—renowned for their beauty and flavor. Lord Nao himself is a worthy samurai of the old school. We fought our first battles together when we were barely more than boys."

"You and he crushed starving peasants for the Shogun. Now you elevate those slaughters to 'battles'?"

"Enough! We leave tomorrow for Shiroishi Domain. You will marry Lord Nao's daughter. Prepare yourself."

Yorimasa did as he was told. He prepared himself for marriage.

He fed his hatred and his anger, his disgust and his shame, with the memory of every slight and insult and humiliation he had received and imagined, every disparaging remark and snigger he had heard behind his back during the past, most miserable year of his life. He promised the demons of the ten thousand hells the pain he had suffered and the pain he had inflicted were nothing compared to the pain to come.

Lord Nao's precious daughter would soon envy even the hungry ghosts clinging miserably to the charnel mists.

. . . . .

"Well?" Lady Chiemi had glared at her husband all evening, and he had ignored her. Finally, she could keep silent no longer.

"Well, what?" Lord Nao said.

"When do you intend to tell me whatever it is you have gone out of your way not to tell me?"

"You are talking nonsense. If I have something I wish to tell you, I will tell you without hesitation."

Lady Chiemi said, "And if you have something you wish not to tell me, you will delay for as long as you can, then you will tell me when you think it is too late for my objection to have any effect. I know you too well, Lord Nao."

Indeed she did. Nao and Chiemi had been playmates as children, his father being the chief retainer of her father, then the Great Lord of Shiroishi. Because the lord had only daughters, he adopted Nao when the two were married, making him his heir. They were longtime friends, and almost brother and sister, in the best sense.

He said, "There is nothing to object to. It is already done. Midori is betrothed."

"To whom?"

"Lord Kiyori's son."

Lady Chiemi leaned suddenly to her left, as if stricken by dizziness, and held herself away from the floor with both hands.

"Shigeru?"

"Yorimasa."

"Oh, no. That cannot be. It cannot."

"The wedding will take place the week before the summer equinox."

"Please, my lord. I beg you to reconsider." She pressed her forehead against the floor in a full bow. "Yorimasa will destroy her."

"Nonsense. He is a samurai and a lord. He will be patient."

She looked up, her face wet.

"You cannot be ignorant of the reports about him."

"I do not listen to gossip."

"Yorimasa takes pleasure in hurting women—"

"You should not listen to gossip, either."

"He binds them, drugs them, tortures them—"

"Some geisha are said to play at those things. It is pretense, nothing more."

"He uses his organ as a weapon, to humiliate and injure. He forces entry with the severed appendages of beasts—"

"I refuse to dignify—"

Sobbing now, she said, "Several geisha can no longer work. One died of her injuries. Another killed herself. A third suffered such damage, she became completely incontinent, and went mad. When her brother came for her and saw how she was, he killed her, then he killed himself. Please—"

Lady Chiemi could not continue. She could only weep.

Lord Nao sat in silence, head bowed. When her tears stopped, and her breathing calmed, he said, "Lord Kiyori has shared a prophecy with me."

"Prophecy? No one believes he has such a power except ignorant peasants. And you. Are you really such a fool?"

"The year before the uprising, he told me—"

"The peasants were starving!" she screamed. "It did not take a prophet to see that they would riot!"

"Calm yourself, Chiemi."

"If you do not call off the wedding, I will kill myself. You have my word as the daughter of a samurai."

"Then you will rob Midori of an irreplaceable asset she will need in her marriage. She is rather young to be without her mother's counsel and comfort."

"If I kill myself, there will be no marriage. Such an evil omen will end it before it begins."

"No. Whether you live or die, Midori will marry Yorimasa, because Midori is to give birth to the heir of Akaoka Domain."

"That is the prophecy?"

Lord Nao nodded.

"But what of Yorimasa? Shigeru?"

"Neither will rule. That is for Midori's son. Kiyori has seen it in a vision."

"And has he seen the suffering his son will inflict on our daughter?"

"Do not think of such things. Accept what must be."

"My lord, Midori is your youngest child, and your only daughter. You love her very much. I know you do. How can you deliver her to such a fate?"

"Because it is her fate. To attempt to escape it can only lead to greater disaster."

"How can any disaster be greater?"

Lord Nao moved to his wife's side and held her close to him.

"Let us be happy together during the next weeks. It will be the last time she will be our child. After the equinox, she will go with her husband to Cloud of Sparrows."

· · · · ·

Kazu said, "Are you ready?" He was stripped down to his loincloth, his bare skin brown from the countless hours of peasant labor in the fields, a sheen of sweat upon it from his previous exertions.

"I am," Midori said. Her outer kimono was abandoned on the ground, along with the elaborate and heavy obi sash, her sandals, her fan, and the tanto knife that Father always made her carry for self-defense. To free her legs, she had hiked her kimono up between them and tucked it into her sash at the waist, forming makeshift pants, not unlike the hakama samurai wore in combat, though much shorter. It was not very graceful—indeed, it was extremely improper—and her parents, her mother especially, would be very vocal in her disapproval if she caught her this way. But what choice was there? She was sure she could beat that braggart Kazu, but not dressed like a little princess doll.

"Who do you think will win?" she heard someone in the crowd say. Work had come to a standstill. Everyone in the orchard had gathered to watch.

"Kazu's faster than anyone else in the village. He'll win, for sure."

"Midori's fast, too."

"She's fast for a girl. Girls can't beat boys."

"Midori can. She's beaten everyone she's ever faced, boys and girls."

"Oh, they just let her win because she's the lord's daughter."

Nothing anyone could have said could have made her angrier, or more determined to win.

She said, "Someone give the signal."

"I will," Michi said. She was the same age as Midori, and her best friend among the village children.

"No, I want to," someone else said.

"You always want to give the signal."

"Because I never get to, that's why."

"Stop arguing," Midori said. "Michi. You give the signal."

"Ha!"

"Aw!"

Kazu's eyes were focused on the tree in front of him.

Midori kept her gaze on Kazu. He was sixteen, strongly built, and handsome in a crude sort of way. For him, this was just another opportunity to show off, to display his strength and speed to the village girls, and perhaps to Midori as well. For Midori, it was far more serious. She was the daughter of the Great Lord of the domain. The blood of countless generations of samurai ran in her veins. Any match between two individuals was no different in essence from a duel to the death. She kept her gaze on Kazu. She didn't have to look at the tree. It was right in front of her. It wasn't going anywhere. Weapons were important, and so were weather, terrain, and time of day. But the real key to victory was to defeat your opponent even before combat began. She had heard her father say so many times as he trained her brothers in the arts of war. She continued to stare hard at Kazu. Finally, for an instant, he glanced in her direction. His eyes were caught by the deadly focus of hers. His lips parted slightly in surprise. Just then, Michi gave the signal.

"Go!"

Midori shot off the ground as fast as a fireworks rocket. She paid no attention to the shouts of the crowd, or to Kazu's progress in the neighboring tree. She no longer had any thoughts at all. She disappeared completely in the climbing, and there was no distinction between the wind and her breath, the leaves and branches and her hands and feet, the motion of her body and the stability of the tree trunk, the ground and the sky. She didn't even realize she had reached the treetop until she heard the shouts of the children below.

"She beat him!"

"Midori won!"

"I can't believe it!"

"See! Girls can beat boys!"

"Midori's the fastest!"

Above her were only the ocean-blue sky and the wave-foam white of the passing clouds. For a moment, she felt like she was underwater. She looked down at the suddenly quiet crowd and saw everyone on their hands and knees on the ground, bowing low, as if she were a princess of the Imperial Court.

Midori laughed happily.

"You don't have to be so formal. It was just a tree-climbing contest."

Then she saw why the peasants were bowing. They weren't bowing to her.

Three horsemen had arrived while the race was on. One of them was her father, and he was frowning most furiously at her. She recognized the second rider as her father's good friend and fellow Great Lord, Lord Kiyori. The third was the most handsome young man she had ever seen in her life.

His high arching brows, prominent eyelashes, and delicate features would have made him appear too girlish, were it not for a certain harshness in the line of his cheekbones, and the hard set of his jaw. Though he sat in his saddle in a rather indolent manner, his physique was obviously that of a samurai who had spent many years in serious training. He urged his horse forward so he could see her more clearly. He stopped directly under her and looked up through the branches. When he saw her, he laughed. He had a beautiful laugh.

Midori felt a blush spreading over her entire body.

· · · · ·

"Even knowing how foolish a girl you are," her mother said, "I can't believe you were climbing a tree on this day, of all days!"

They were in Lady Chiemi's bedroom. Her mother fixed Midori's hair while the servants struggled to help her into a new kimono at the same time.

"They were supposed to be here in the morning," Midori said. "They weren't, so I thought they wouldn't come until tomorrow."

"And naked, like a monkey!" Her mother put her face in her hands. "How mortifying! What will they think of us?"

"I wasn't naked, Mother."

"Did you have on your outer kimono?"

"No, but—"

"Were your legs bare for all the world to see?"

"Yes, but—"

"Then you were naked, you shameful child!"

"How can I win a tree-climbing race in a full kimono, with a gown clinging to my ankles?"

"You are the daughter of the lord of this domain, preparing to meet your betrothed," her mother said. "What were you doing climbing a tree in the first place?"

"Kazu said he's faster than I am. I know he isn't, so I proved it."

"What does it matter who's the fastest at such a silly thing?"

"You told me you were the fastest climber in the domain when you were a girl," Midori said. "I knew how to bind my kimono like hakama only because you told me how."

"Don't be impudent," her mother said, a flash of color rising to her cheeks. She turned away to hide her smile. But the smile fractured instantly and dissolved into sobs.

"I won't climb any trees after I'm married," Midori said.

She felt great shame for embarrassing her parents in front of Lord Kiyori and Lord Yorimasa. In truth, she wished she had made a better impression herself. What must Lord Yorimasa be thinking? His wife was an ignorant child so countrified and immature, she stripped to her underwear and raced up trees with peasants from the fields. How he must be lamenting his fate! He seemed so sophisticated, too. Could anyone have disappointed him more than she had?

She said, "I'll behave properly from now on."

Her words did not reassure her mother, for her sobbing grew worse. Soon the servants were crying, too. It did not seem at all like the joyous occasion it was. It was all her fault for acting so childishly. She would make up for it. She would be the best possible wife to Lord Yorimasa, and a dutiful daughter-in-law to Lord Kiyori. When her mother and father heard reports about her, they would hear only praise.

"Don't worry, Mother," Midori said. She struggled not to join in the weeping. Tears were contagious. "You'll be proud of me, I promise."

· · · · ·

Later, Yorimasa could not say with any certainty why he did what he did on his nuptial night. This inability to understand his own actions surprised him as much as what he did in that long hour before dawn. He thought he was beyond surprise when it came to what he could do with a woman and what he could force a woman to do with him. After all, had he not permanently erased the boundary between pleasure and pain? Had he not experienced everything possible? He thought he had, and yet, there was one thing he had missed without knowing it. The result was agony beyond his worst imagining.

He had devised no particular acts ahead of time. His only plans dealt with trifles designed to increase his amusement. Opium balls contained within the sweet paste of rice cakes. A flask of absinthe he kept on his person. A grotesque appendage fashioned out of sexual nightmares and various bestial organs by an anonymous lunatic artist, purchased from the same smuggler who supplied his opium. His father's attention was as complete as he expected, and neither rice cakes nor flask survived the search. As for the monstrosity, Yorimasa had never thought it would reach Shiroishi Domain. It was there entirely for effect. What would his father do when he found it? Would he continue to insist on the marriage? At the very least, Kiyori would bellow and rage, and probably strike him. Speculation on the matter was most entertaining.

The actual result was considerably less so.

Kiyori found it hidden among Yorimasa's clothing.

Leave the room, he said to the servants.

His voice was quiet, his expression bland. When they had complied, he wrapped the false organ in an undergarment from the luggage and removed it. He did not scream imprecations. He did not strike. Indeed, he never even looked in Yorimasa's direction. He said not a word as he departed. His eyes, Yorimasa noticed, were moist.

Recalling the incident now, Yorimasa felt a quick surge of anger. What right did his father have to feel sorrow, to feel shame, to feel anything at all? Was he the one who had lost everything? Was he the one who lived every moment with unendurable humiliation? Was he the son who was prevented by the father from ever truly becoming the man he should be? Kiyori was Great Lord, prophet, leader of loyal vassals. Those who did not respect him feared him.

Who respected Yorimasa? No one.

Who feared Yorimasa? Only women.

He would have liked sake, but even this harmless tradition had been

forbidden him. Anger became heat in his loins. If his father thought anyone but Yorimasa could determine his own behavior, he would soon learn
otherwise. Kiyori had found the drugs he had been meant to find. He had
not found the opium and absinthe secreted in the hilts of Yorimasa's
swords. What samurai would suspect another of stooping to such an
abominable desecration?

He walked leisurely to the bedchamber where Midori awaited him,
somewhat more leisurely and less steadily than he had intended. A month
of sobriety had diminished the amount needed for the desired effect, and
he had consumed too much. No matter. He was conscious enough.

He did not imagine the acts he would perform or force her to perform.
Preconceptions diminished the power of reality. The fact that the birth of
Midori's son was foreseen meant he could do anything he wished. No matter what he did, she would not be injured to the extent that conception and
birth were prevented. She could die after childbirth, of course, or during it.
That was unforeseen because it was unimportant. The production of the
heir was the only thing that mattered to Kiyori. In this knowledge—of his
own freedom and his father's pathetic dependence upon him, the discarded son—Yorimasa felt a great liberation. He could strangle her. She
would not die, she could not die, she could only suffer. Would she slip into
a coma? Could an unconscious woman carry a child to delivery? Perhaps
he would find out. The possibilities for the night were infinite.

They were afforded a measure of privacy in an isolated wing of White
Stones Castle. Still, they would be heard if she screamed loudly enough.
Could Lord Nao keep himself from intervening when he heard her agonized cries of pain? Could Kiyori? Perhaps Lord Nao and his vassals would
come to Midori's rescue, and his father and his vassals would try to prevent such a breach of clan honor. In that case, a bloody battle would certainly ensue, all the more tragic for being between good friends. That
would be a perfect outcome.

Midori would remain here with her family.

Kiyori and Yorimasa, if they survived the battle, would return to the
south.

A divorce would result.

Then, fulfilling the prophecy, the heir would be born at the opposite
end of the realm from his birthright.

No matter who lived and who died, grandfather and grandson would forever be estranged. Hatred and mistrust, not blood and name, would always be their only true bond.

For Yorimasa, no vengeance could be more perfect.

· · · · ·

Lord Kiyori and Lord Nao sat with their chief vassals in formal arrangement on opposite sides of the banquet hall. Samurai served as attendants. No women were present. No celebratory delicacies adorned the small trays before each man. No toasts were offered. Sake was consumed in grim silence. A guest arriving uninformed would never have guessed that this was a wedding festival.

Nao said, "As you requested, Lord Kiyori, I have sent my wife and her ladies-in-waiting to Kageyama Monastery." Because the one-castle rule imposed by the Shogun limited the number of fortifications in every domain, Nao was a great supporter of religious devotion. The monasteries that dotted his domain tended to be strategically positioned, strongly built, capable of withstanding heavy siege, and inhabited by monks rather more burly and warlike than one might expect. "It is an unusual request to make of a mother on her daughter's wedding night."

Kiyori bowed. "I apologize for the necessity of the request, Lord Nao. Please accept my deepest thanks."

"Neither apology nor thanks are necessary," Nao said. "But I cannot help noticing that this gathering, too, is extraordinary in character. Beyond every other remarkable fact—and there are many—one stands out most visibly. Lord Kiyori, why are you, Lord Tanaka, and Lord Kudo without your swords? And where are your own attendants?"

"They are in their quarters. I have ordered them to commit ritual suicide if I do not return by sunrise."

A murmur of shocked breathing rose from Lord Nao's men. He himself remained unmoved.

He said, "A strange way to celebrate a wedding. Why would you not return to your quarters?"

Kiyori said, "You did not permit me to tell you what you need to know about Yorimasa. If the night develops as I fear it will, the shock will be great indeed." He paused. Then he said, "Do you still trust me?"

"Always," Nao said.

"Then promise me this. Promise you will not intervene, no matter what you hear, nor will you permit your men to intervene. Do not go to the nuptial chamber until morning. Then, if circumstances warrant it, you have my permission to execute Yorimasa, and to discard his remains without benefit of any dignities or blessings."

"What?"

"Before you go there, you will execute me, Lord Tanaka, and Lord Kudo. This is inadequate, but it is the only apology I can offer. To avoid difficulties with the Shogun, you will report the deaths as accidental. I left Lord Saiki in Akaoka, for the heir will need a regent and a protector in his childhood and his youth. He expects to receive word of the 'accident.'"

"Lord Kiyori—"

"My younger son, Shigeru, will be the titular head of the clan until the heir comes of age. At that time, he will commit ritual suicide to further atone for his brother's actions. I have so instructed."

"Lord Kiyori, what do you expect to happen tonight?" Nao's voice was almost a whisper.

"Give me your word," Kiyori said, "or annul the marriage. It is still not too late."

"Have you foreseen this all?"

"No. My fears are based on my knowledge of my son."

Nao closed his eyes and sat silently for several breaths. When he opened his eyes, he said, "I promise to do as you ask."

Kiyori bowed low. "Thank you," he said. He contorted his face into a grimace to keep from sobbing. A few tears escaped, but no audible sorrow. "Sake," he said.

"Fear makes us imagine the worst," Nao said. "If you have not foreseen disaster, then it is only possible, not inevitable. Disaster is always neat, even in the best of circumstances. Let us toast the newlyweds, and wish them every happiness."

· · · · ·

Despite her promise to make her parents proud, Midori felt great apprehension as she listened to the rustle of her husband's kimono approaching the bedroom door.

She was so unprepared for marriage, even less so than the daughters of other lords. Most of them had spent considerable time in the Shogun's

302 · Takashi Matsuoka

capital of Edo, or the Imperial city of Kyoto, or in the bustling castle towns of the great domains. They knew of the subtleties in the relationships between men and women, because they had seen it played out before them in sophisticated society. Midori had lived her whole life in little Shiroishi Domain, in the far north of Japan, far from the centers of civilization. She was more like a farm girl than a Great Lord's daughter. How could she please an urbane and experienced young man like Lord Yorimasa? She didn't even know where to begin. Of course, she understood the crude outlines of sexual intercourse. She had peeked in on adults in the village, along with the most mischievous of the village children. But the behavior of peasants was no useful guide to the tastes and desires of a man like Yorimasa. She was sure to be a terrible disappointment to him.

Midori went to the door on her knees. She slid the door open as quietly and as gracefully as she could, and bowed to the floor. She was too shy to look up.

"My lord" was all she could manage to say before her nervousness made her throat too tight for words.

· · · · ·

Yorimasa looked down at the bowing woman. Her hair was already coming undone. Obviously, it was not a coiffure with which she was familiar. There would rarely be a need for such an elaborate arrangement this far from civilization. From the opening in her collar, the scent of a freshly washed body rose to meet him. Had she been a child, he would have called it the scent of innocence. As it was, all it did was remind him further of her ignorance and crudity. Even the least skillful woman of the city knew the importance of perfumes in the art of seduction. His father had married him to a peasant with a noble name.

He went to his knees and returned her bow. In a voice far more gentle than he felt, he said, "Let us stop bowing and go within. We can do nothing appropriate in the doorway, can we?"

· · · · ·

Lady Chiemi sat alone in the meditation hall of Kageyama Monastery. The rhythm of her breathing was greatly prolonged, with many heartbeats intervening between each inhalation and exhalation. It had been many years since she had engaged in meditation, and she was not doing so now. She was only using the breathing technique to impose a calm on her body she did not feel in her heart. She counted her breaths so she would not think of what was occurring in her daughter's nuptial bed.

She had no faith in Lord Kiyori's prophecies. That her husband believed them never failed to surprise her. He was an intelligent man who was not usually given to gullibility. The battles Kiyori and Nao had fought together as youths had apparently inflicted a permanent and unfortunate distortion on their relationship. Kiyori had saved Nao's life, and that was that.

He was a fool in this one thing, and it would cost them their daughter's life. Everything she had heard about Yorimasa convinced her Midori would not survive her wedding night, or if she did, she would be ruined, and not live long thereafter. When she inhaled, she felt the slight pressure of the tanto's scabbard against her abdomen. It was not proper to carry a weapon into Buddha's hall. It was not proper to shed blood there. She had done the first, and she would do the second as soon as she received the inevitable report she dreaded.

She had lost count of her breaths.

Lady Chiemi exhaled and began again.

· · · · ·

Midori had wondered if she should offer a rice cake to Yorimasa, or wait until after. There was tea, but there was no sake, which was an unforgivable lapse in etiquette. What were the maids thinking? When she had called for them, no one answered. It was as if the castle had suddenly been abandoned. How strange. She had considered going to her mother's wing, but thought better of it. What if Yorimasa came while she was gone? That would have been far worse than even the lack of sake.

Now he was here. They were together. Alone. She was already blushing most obviously and didn't think it was possible for her to blush more. She was mistaken. When she saw his smile, she felt another wave of blood flooding her skin.

"My lord," she said again. So far, these were the only words she had spoken to him. He must think her a fool. Of course he did, because she was a fool! What would a real lady say, or a sophisticated courtesan? A man like Yorimasa surely had much experience with both. How dull and immature she must seem in comparison. Should she do something, or wait for him to lead the way? And if she was supposed to do something, what was it she was supposed to do? She saw now that her mother had failed her terribly. She should have been told something, anything.

Yorimasa was still smiling at her when she looked up, and so caught her trying to sneak a peek at him.

"My lord," she said again. She could think of nothing else to say.

"You are an excellent tree climber," he said, "but not much of a conversationalist. Perhaps we should spend the night in the orchard."

Mortified, she could no longer restrain her tears.

It was the moment Yorimasa had been waiting for. Now she was at her weakest. She was unsophisticated, inexperienced, unsure. She needed comfort and reassurance. She had every reason to expect it of him. Instead, he would help her transcend such mundane considerations. He would reveal to her a precious truth she never expected to discover, on this night of all nights, especially. The meaning of life.

Pain.

The void.

There was nothing else.

Yorimasa placed a hand on Midori's shoulder and drew her to him. He did nothing crude or alarming. The experience of brutality had its subtleties, chief among them surprise and a sense of inevitability on the victim's part. Without perfect timing, the first was diminished. Without patience, the second could not be savored. He was the embodiment of gentleness itself.

After a moment, she let her head come to rest on his chest. She was beginning to trust him.

Either Lord Kiyori's prophecy would be realized no matter what happened here, or it would be denied by Yorimasa's actions. Whichever it was, he hoped one result would be the same.

His own death at the hands of others.

Let the survivors inherit nothing more than ruins.

Let them fulfill only prophecies cloaked in the stench of blood.

· · · · ·

No change of expression in his visage or increase of tension in his muscles indicated that Kiyori had heard the girl scream. He sat erect and impassive, as he had so far all night.

Nao flinched.

His vassals' hands went to the hilts of their swords.

"Hold," Nao said.

Again, they heard her scream, louder and more prolonged, and this time they could make out some of her words.

"Father! Help! Help!"

Nao's men looked at him for orders. His jaws and shoulders were tight, his hands were balled into fists against his thighs, but he did not move or speak.

"Lord Nao!" The youngest of the vassals leaned toward him, pleading in his face.

"Hold," Nao said again.

Midori's voice died away. The vassal who had spoken listened more carefully. Nothing. He bowed his head and wept.

Another vassal said, "My lord, we should investigate."

"No," Nao said. "I have given my word. We will wait until dawn."

"Lord Nao, it is inhumanly cruel to wait."

"I have given my word," Nao said. "Is the given word of a samurai subject to conditions?"

This vassal, too, bowed his head.

"Father! Father!"

Midori's voice was no longer distant. It was coming from a corridor adjacent to the banquet room.

With a sob, Kiyori said, "Help her! I release you from your promise! Go!"

Nao and his men bolted from the room, drawing their swords as they threw open the doors. Midori was at the far end of the corridor, her sash gone, her kimono open, the entire front of her underclothing from breast to thigh wet with blood.

"Midori!"

When she saw her father, she staggered forward a step, and collapsed in a motionless heap.

· · · · ·

Lady Chiemi heard the pounding hooves of a horse shatter the deep stillness of the hour before dawn. The messenger she dreaded was arriving. A small sob escaped her throat. Her torso contracted. The hilt of the tanto stabbed at her ribs.

In the silence of her grieving heart, Lady Chiemi called out to the Compassionate One, not for herself, but for the eternal peaceful repose of her beloved daughter.

Namu Amida Butsu, Namu Amida Butsu, Namu Amida Butsu.

Those few words, expressed with complete sincerity, assured Midori's rebirth in Sukhavati, the Pure Land.

Lady Chiemi was not sure she believed it. But she cherished the hope, for it was the only hope that remained for her in this life.

She removed the tanto from her sash. She held the scabbard with her left hand and the hilt of the knife with her right. She heard the horse slide to a hasty stop and, moments later, the rider's hurried footsteps on the wooden walkway outside the hall. She gripped the knife and prepared to draw it.

The door flew open.

"Lady Chiemi," the messenger gasped. Exhausted by the hard ride, his duty to report battled with his desperate need to breathe. His words came out in ragged spurts. Even before he finished, Lady Chiemi hurried from the meditation hall.

. . . . .

Until the moment Midori let her head come to rest against him, Yorimasa could see his future as clearly as if he were a prophet. Then, as his arm went around her in a false gesture of reassurance, he found himself embracing a kimono-clad body more childish in size and form than he had expected. He looked at her closely for the first time. Her makeup had been skillfully applied by her servants, or perhaps her mother. From a distance, it had been sufficient to disguise her immaturity, especially from someone who paid little attention to her. He should have listened when his father told him about her, for surely he had. But once he learned who she was—the daughter of the ridiculous Lord of Apples—everything else was a meaningless detail. Or so it seemed at the time.

"Midori?"

"Yes, my lord."

"In what year were you born?"

"My lord?" His question confused her. He must know. No one would agree to marry without a thorough astrological consultation. According to her father, Yorimasa's chart was favorable for her. Hers must be the same for him, otherwise no marriage could have taken place. But it was not for her to question her husband. She had to remember that. When he speaks, she obeys.

She said, "In the second year of the Ninkō Emperor."

"And the month?"

Midori blushed. To be born in *that* month and be caught by her husband climbing a tree! Could she possibly have done worse?

She spoke so quietly she hoped he wouldn't hear. "The month of the monkey, my lord."

Yorimasa looked at the girl's face beneath the makeup. No wonder she couldn't keep her hair properly coiffed. No wonder she raced farm boys up trees. It wasn't because she was mentally impaired, as he had assumed. It was because she was eleven years old.

Knowing what kind of man he had become and the brutality of which he was capable, his father had put a child into his hands. Kiyori cared only about an heir and the next generation's prophet. He didn't care who was sacrificed. His eldest son, this innocent child, they were equally nothing to him.

May the curse of the unforgiving gods fall on his father, and may the compassion and protection of the infinite Buddhas be denied him forever.

Yorimasa's arm fell away from Midori's shoulder.

He said, "I am not a monster."

"No, my lord." Yorimasa was beginning to frighten her. What was he talking about?

He rose to his feet, staggered, and almost fell. "I have done evil things, but I am not a monster."

Midori knew she was an inadequate bride for such a man. Had she disappointed him so severely that he would not even spend a few minutes of polite conversation with her? No, it was worse than that. Yorimasa knocked over the sword stand. He picked up his short sword, drew it, and threw the scabbard so violently it pierced a door's paper pane and flew out into the hallway. He was so insulted by her deficiencies, he was going to kill her!

Yorimasa screamed, "Let your prophecies explain this!"

Midori raised her arm. She shielded her face with the wide sleeve of her kimono. It would not protect her, but it would at least prevent her from seeing the descending blade. A splatter of blood struck the floor in front of her. A single drop fell on her cheek. She felt no pain, not even the slightest sensation of being cut.

It was not her blood!

Yorimasa had driven the blade into his own abdomen.

Midori screamed.

. . . . .

Had he eaten less opium, had he sipped less absinthe, had he not been weakened by his shame or made hasty by his anger, Yorimasa could have become the first person ever to prevent the fulfillment of an Okumichi lord's prophecy. But his bad habits frustrated his noble intention.

His sword, poorly grasped, went high and entered his stomach instead of his intestines. Because he had not prepared himself in the traditional manner, his blade had sliced in through several layers of clothing, and so, try as he might, he was unable to draw the blade in the proper crosscut and rip himself open. Even so, he would have succeeded in bleeding to death in short order, if not for one more unexpected occurrence.

Midori came to his rescue.

"My lord, what are you doing?"

Weeping tears of rage and frustration, Yorimasa tried to push the blade downward into his abdomen, but his bunched clothing allowed only a slight movement in that direction. With both hands, Midori grasped the outward-facing hilt of the sword and pulled with all her strength. Yorimasa's hands held the blade itself through the material of his kimono. His grip was less secure than hers. When she pulled, the sword and Midori both fell away to the floor.

Midori dropped the sword and quickly returned to Yorimasa's side. Yorimasa and the floor beneath him were soaked with blood. She could see it pulsating through the ugly gash in his belly. She pressed her hands against the wound, to no avail.

"Help! Help! Father! Father!"

She removed her obi, discarded the decorative bow, and pressed the sash as tightly as she could against the wound. Blood was everywhere. That he was still bleeding shocked her. Surely there was no more left in his body.

"Help!"

Where was everyone? She could wait no longer. If Yorimasa didn't get help right away, he would die.

She stumbled out of the room and went looking for her father.

. . . . .

"You should have let me die," Yorimasa said. "Now I will only have to try again. Disgusting, isn't it? A samurai who needs two tries to kill himself."

"I am proud of you," Kiyori said.

Yorimasa turned in his bed to look at his father. The effort made him wince.

"I know why you stabbed yourself," Kiyori said. "You wanted to keep from violating the girl."

"You know nothing," Yorimasa said. "I would not have touched her, never. I tried to kill myself because I was the nearest Okumichi. Had you been closer, I would have tried to kill you. Nothing matters to you but prophecy. You sent her to me like an animal to an outcast slaughterhouse."

"The prophecy will be fulfilled. You are married. You are alive. The heir will be born in due time. Of that, I have no doubt whatsoever."

"You have lost your mind at last, you old fool. After this disaster, Lord Nao will never permit the marriage to stand. Not even the Lord of Apples can stomach such a disgrace. By now, the story is spreading throughout the realm. As soon as I have recovered my strength, I will die."

"There is no story spreading," Kiyori said, "because nothing happened. The wedding went well. Bride and groom spent the early evening in conversation, then the bride returned to her mother's quarters, where she is preparing for her journey to Cloud of Sparrows. In the meantime, the groom and his father are enjoying Lord Nao's generous hospitality."

"Something this disgraceful cannot be kept secret."

Kiyori smiled. "You forget. Before you and Midori met for the night, Lord Nao sent all the women out of the castle. There is no one to spread any stories."

"I will not sleep with a child."

"I know you won't. I don't expect you to."

Now Yorimasa was confused. "Then how do you expect to get an heir?"

"He will arrive when he should. For now, you will protect Midori, and watch over her. In time, she will be a woman, and ready to consummate the marriage."

"Ridiculous. That happens only in fairy tales. As soon as I have recovered, I will complete what I began."

"Then kill Midori first," Kiyori said. "She thinks you tried to kill yourself because she disappointed you so terribly. Her shame is unendurable. She told her mother she will not live if you die."

"That is none of my concern," Yorimasa said, and closed his eyes.

Kiyori said nothing. But a smile appeared on his face and persisted for some time.

1867, CLOUD OF SPARROWS CASTLE

"My mother was seventeen when I was born," Genji said. "As my grandfather predicted, my father protected her and watched over her until she was ready."

"Such great changes in character," Emily said, "are usually the result of a religious awakening. Is that what happened with your father?"

"No," Genji said. "He was never a very religious man. It was something else entirely."

"And that was?"

"He changed because he discovered the meaning of love."

"Ah," Emily said, smiling. "That is very clever of you. You have come back round to it. I hope you will not again say it cannot be said."

"I didn't say it couldn't be said. I said it was not easily said. Now that I have told you of my mother and father, you will understand my definition."

"Yes?"

"My father was living a life of hatred because he could think of no one but himself. That could be said to be the very meaning of hatred itself. He changed because in my mother he found someone to care about more than he cared about himself. That is my definition of love." Genji looked at Emily. "What is yours?"

Emily willed the tears not to well, and when they did, she willed them not to fall. When they fell, she ignored them and said, "Mine is the same as yours, my lord."

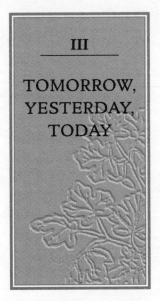

III

TOMORROW,
YESTERDAY,
TODAY

10
Views from the High Tower

Memory is treacherously seductive.

If you remember little, you strive in vain to remember more. If you remember much, you also strive to remember more. In each case, you will recall what flatters you and ignore what does not. Is it not amazing that your memory never fails you? Inevitably, you find what you seek.

And if you remember everything?

Then the secret is to forget with the same selfish attention.

AKI-NO-HASHI

(1311)

When they returned from Apple Valley, Emily retired to her room to rest. Genji went to the high tower. Everyone else avoided going there unless absolutely necessary. The rumors of ghosts, particularly the rumors about Lady Shizuka's ghost, did not encourage casual visits. Sometimes attendance was necessary. The ashes of the lords and ladies of the clan were contained in the columbarium on the seventh floor. On important dates, memorial services were conducted there. At other times, only monks and nuns climbed the stairs with regularity. Every morning, they placed flowers and incense on the altar, and recited sutras. Every evening, they returned to remove the flowers and the burned incense, and performed the formal ceremony closing the columbarium for the night.

Genji liked the quiet of the tower, and the views in four directions, and did not fear ghosts.

He knelt before the ashes of his ancestors and contemplated the ambiguous nature of his recent conversation with Emily. Why had he told her about his parents? He should not have felt any need to justify himself to her. Soon, Charles Smith would return and renew his proposal of marriage. Emily would be more inclined toward Smith if she believed Genji did not know the meaning of love. She would leave Japan. They would never see each other again. There was no reason for him to care how much, or how little, she thought of him. Yet he had told her about his mother and father. Worse, he had emphasized the details that tended to exaggerate the tragic aspects of his childhood, the excruciating depths to which his father had fallen, and the restorative and redemptive power of his child-bride mother's love. By doing so, he had brought tears to Emily's eyes, as he had known he would. A woman who would weep for you was a woman who could not help but love you. His words were therefore excellently suited for seduction. But seduction was the opposite of his purpose, was it not?

If he truly wanted her to leave, he should have told her nothing.

Or everything.

He looked at the two ceramic urns directly in front of him. The larger, squarish one in dark gray contained his father's ashes; the smaller, more softly curved one in a lighter, earthen hue held his mother's. Genji had come here to look at them for most of his life, at first out of duty and obligation, later in the hope that what remained of their earthly presence would inspire a guiding thought, or lift his spirits when he was discouraged. Even as a child, he had been aware of his status as a lord. He could not permit himself to show weakness in front of vassals and servants. In times of greatest need, only his parents could help him. Since they were dead, they never told him anything. But here they were. Somehow he felt reassured in the presence of their ashes. Why, he couldn't say.

Perhaps, after all, he was as superstitious as the next person and, instead of fearing the spirits of the departed, relied on them in some vague way.

Or perhaps it was as he told those who asked him why he spent so much time in the tower.

He liked the silence.

1840

Genji sat with his father before the ashes of his mother. He did his best to appear calm, though he was very excited. Next week, he would be five years old. Four was a borderline age. Many people, especially women, still treated him as if he were a baby. Five was not a baby. Five was a little boy. There was no doubt about that. If he became a little boy and not a baby, then next he would become a youth, and after that, not so very many years later, he would be a man. He was very eager to be a man. Then when vassals and servants said "Lord Genji," that touch of condescension and humor would be gone. They would say it the way they said his grandfather's name, or his uncle's. When anyone said "Lord Kiyori" or "Lord Shigeru," whether addressing them or mentioning them in their absence, it was always with a voice full of respect. He wanted very much to be the kind of samurai they were.

He didn't want to be like his father. People spoke of Lord Yorimasa with sorrow, or sympathy, or contempt, never with respect. What kind of samurai was that? Not the kind he wanted to be.

"Do you remember your mother?" Yorimasa said.

"Yes, Father," Genji said. His father always asked him the same question every time he saw him, which since his mother's death was not often.

"Good," Yorimasa said. "Always remember her. She was the kindest, loveliest woman in the world."

"Yes, Father." In truth, Genji's memory of her had faded substantially. A year might not be very long to adults, but for him, a year was a very long time. He remembered that she was very beautiful, and smelled wonderful, and smiled at him often, and never ever scolded him for anything he ever did wrong.

She would say, You must not do that again, Genji.

Yes, Mother, he would answer.

You are a good boy, she would say, and hug him.

He remembered these things, but her voice was faint, and when he pictured her, the light was weak, and her face was like a face seen in twilight.

"Before I knew her," Yorimasa said, "my life was full of bitterness. I was not to become lord of this domain. I was not to pronounce the prophecies of our clan. So I thought my life was utterly without meaning."

Genji hoped his father was not angry with him. Grandfather had told him he would follow him as lord, not his father, and not Uncle Shigeru. He hoped Uncle Shigeru wasn't mad at him, either. Uncle Shigeru was a great swordsman, the greatest since Miyamoto Mushashi, everyone said. If Uncle Shigeru decided to challenge him to a duel for the lordship of the domain, he was sure he would lose. A samurai was always supposed to be certain of his own victory, no matter what the odds. But Genji knew he had no chance against Uncle Shigeru. Against his father, it was not quite so hopeless, even though his father was a man and he was a little boy. His father was always intoxicated. An intoxicated samurai was not a complete samurai. His grandfather had said so many times.

But his father didn't seem angry. He was smiling and he kept talking about Genji's mother.

"The point of life," Yorimasa said, "is to love. I learned that from your mother. There is no need to be special beyond that."

When his father said such things, Genji felt great embarrassment. He was talking like a woman, not a samurai. Victory, honor, glorious death, these were what mattered to a samurai. Love? That was for women.

"I am not a strong man. For this, I apologize to you. All my life, I thought I was strong. Then I met your mother and discovered strength was not as strong as weakness. Love has many blessings. That is its one curse. Do you understand?"

"Yes, Father." Genji did not understand a word. How could weakness be stronger than strength? But if he said he didn't understand, his father would say more embarrassing things, and Genji didn't want that. He wanted his father to stop talking and go away.

"If she had lived : . ." Yorimasa's words faded away. He continued to smile. He said, "If we had not met, perhaps she would have lived—would be alive still. I would never have known her, never have loved her, never have been loved by her. My life would be the horror it was before we met. But I would have it that way if she could be alive, somewhere, and happy."

His father was making less and less sense the more he spoke. If he had never met her, what use would it be to him that she would be alive rather than dead? He would receive no benefit; he wouldn't even know she existed.

"Do you understand?"

"Yes, Father."

Yorimasa laughed. He put his hand on Genji's shoulder and squeezed it affectionately.

"You don't. How can you? But if you are very lucky, and very unlucky, one day you will."

There, he was doing it again. Talking nonsense.

"Yes, Father," Genji said. When would he leave?

Later, Genji always regretted wishing his father gone that day, because when he was gone, he was gone forever. The next month, he was found dead. With him was a gift for Genji, neatly wrapped in a silk cloth and accompanied by a short letter.

The letter said, *My dear son, forgive me for missing your birthday. Here is your belated present. I hope you will treasure it as I have.* There was no commemorative poem. A proper samurai would have written one.

The gift was a fine chain of silver strung with tiny white stones fashioned into perfectly shaped miniature apples. It had belonged to his mother. Genji remembered often seeing it attached to her sash.

Genji kept the letter and gift, not because he treasured them as the last mementos of his father—he did not—but because that was the proper thing to do. Samurai did what was proper, no matter what they felt. He put them away and forgot about them, as he promised himself he would forget his shameful failure of a father.

1867

Genji looked at the chain of tiny white apples he held in his hand.

Did they symbolize love, or death, or both? In his clan, at least, the two seemed inextricably entwined. In fulfillment of the prophecy that led to Genji's birth, his mother and his father had died. Far from saving them, love had doomed them both.

For years, he had disdained his father's weakness and cowardice. He understood his mother's death. Childbirth was a grave risk. But what kind of a samurai dies for love? Once, he thought he knew the answer. Now he was not so sure. Was it weakness that led to his father's death, or was it strength after all? The strength in weakness Genji the boy didn't understand made complete sense to Genji the man. Did his ability to understand mean he was strong, or weak?

Alone in the tower, Genji laughed out loud.

He looked at the tiny stone apples in his palm. With his other hand, he touched them. He had held them so long and clutched them so tightly, they were not cold, like stone, but as warm as his own flesh and blood.

Okumichi no kami Genji, Great Lord of Akaoka Domain, sat in the keep of Cloud of Sparrows Castle well into the night, alone with the ashes of his beloved mother and his revered father.

1860

Lord Kiyori felt a slight giddiness. He thought at first that he had drunk too much sake. Then he noticed his tongue growing numb, and his throat, and a tingling in the extremities of his hands and feet, and a brightening of his vision accompanied by a faint halo of light, as of a distant rainbow, appearing around Lady Shizuka. Because her image itself was transparent, the entire effect was doubly dizzying.

He said, "When you told me we would meet no more after tonight, I did not accurately take your meaning. You meant that I would die."

Lady Shizuka said, "No, my lord, I did not mean that. I meant no more than what I said, that after tonight we would not see each other again. I have never spoken to you in riddles, or with any intention to deceive."

"Do you deny that you knew I would be poisoned?" Kiyori looked at the empty soup bowl. "It was in the soup, wasn't it? Who is my assassin?"

"I know many things. I have shared only a small part of my knowledge with you. Would you rather I had told you of every event of your life to come, of your triumphs, tragedies, accomplishments, disappointments? Of the time, the place, and the manner of your demise?"

Kiyori shook his head. "You are right, as always. I have already known more than I have wanted to know. To know even more would have made a heavy burden unbearable."

"You have borne it well, Lord Kiyori. Nobly, with courage and with dignity."

"Have I?" He leaned heavily to one side. He still breathed without difficulty. His muscles, however, were beginning to weaken. He would not remain upright much longer. "Who has killed me? The Shogun's viper, Kawakami the Sticky Eye?"

Shizuka moved gracefully to his side without rising from her knees.

She made as if to rest her hands gently on his shoulder and arm. She could not really touch him, no more than he could touch her.

She said, "Do not trouble yourself. Be at peace. Follow the tide of your breathing."

"If it's Kawakami," Kiyori said, stubbornly staying on the subject, "then he has placed a traitor in our midst. Genji will be in danger. I must warn him." He could no longer rise to his feet. He crawled toward the alcove where paper, ink, and brush were kept.

"Kawakami is not involved," Shizuka said, "and Genji is not in danger. The one who has poisoned you will himself be struck down before the New Year grows old." She did not tell him his son Shigeru was responsible, or that he had gone mad and that Kiyori's death was only the first of many terrible murders he would commit this very night. The prophecy she had conveyed to him, which he had shared so many years ago with Lord Nao, would reach almost complete fulfillment. After this night's blood was spilled, the only Okumichi left alive would be Genji and Shigeru, and soon it would be Genji alone.

Kiyori had only crawled a few feet before he could go no farther. He rolled over on his back and stared at the ceiling. Even blinking was difficult.

Shizuka went to him and knelt by his side.

He looked up at her and said, "Genji will be safe—"

"Yes."

"The clan will endure—"

"Yes."

"We will overthrow the Tokugawa Shogun—"

"Yes."

"You are not just saying that to trick a dying man into happiness?"

"No, my lord. I would not do such a thing."

Kiyori began to gasp. The weight of his own body was starting to collapse the increasingly unresponsive muscles of his diaphragm.

"Tell me. The last thing. Who are you?"

"Your loyal friend, my lord, as you have been mine."

"I meant to ask—" Every breath he took was now a great victory. He could not say what he meant to ask.

She leaned close to him. If she could, she would cradle him in her arms and comfort him with a parting embrace.

He tried to speak, and could not. He exhaled, and did not inhale again.

Tears came to Shizuka's eyes. How foolish she was to weep for Lord Kiyori, a man whose death she had witnessed, but who would not be born for nearly five hundred years.

What else could she do? She was a woman who had seen the entire arc of a man's life. How could she not weep?

1308

Shizuka struggled to forget in the same way others struggled to remember. Born knowing everything at once, only by freeing herself of simultaneity and omniscience could she hope to make sense of her existence. Others had a tendency to remember too little. Hers was to forget too much. She had known there was a rose garden in the castle. She had forgotten when. No one had ever heard of Lord Narihira, who would plant it. He was as yet unborn. And now, in the tower, she was unable to ascend to the level she sought.

She came to a halt in the stairwell and stared at the ceiling above her.

"What is it?" Hironobu said.

"Nothing." As casually as she could, she went to the window facing south and looked out on the curve of the Shikoku coastline, forest dark against the ocean bright of the Pacific. Hironobu was already worried after her tearful reaction to the absence of the rose garden. He would only worry more if she asked him where the seventh floor was. She knew there would be one in her lifetime because that was where she would die, and where her daughter would be born.

This matter of remembering and forgetting was more complicated than she had thought. She had lived her life so far entirely in Mushindo Abbey, a single, small, enclosed place. Even within its confines, it had been no easy task to distinguish past from future or the present from either, or memory from vision, premonition from nightmare. How much more difficult it would be outside those walls, where there was vastly more to remember, and to forget, and very little of her lifetime left in which to accomplish it.

"Does the tower displease you in some way?"

"No, no, not at all, my lord."

Hironobu smiled and enfolded her in his arms. "When we are alone, you need not call me 'lord.' "

She glanced at the two bodyguards, who pretended not to notice his open display of affection.

"Leave us," he said.

"Lord." The men bowed and backed out of the room.

"If the castle is not grand enough, I will enlarge it for you. Tell me what you want and it is yours."

"Your castle is very grand. Nothing more is needed."

Hironobu must build the seventh floor, and soon. He must do so believing it is his own idea, however, because if he thinks it is hers, it will diminish his sense of self. She does not know why, but she knows it is so. Many of the disasters that will befall this clan will be due to that pernicious habit of imbuing one's own little existence with an exaggerated importance. It is a habit ingrained not only in her new husband but in all samurai. There is nothing she can do to prevent it. In her life, she perceives much, and changes nothing. She sees beyond her time, but she cannot act outside of it.

"I wonder," Hironobu said. He joined his gaze to hers and watched the waves advance and retreat against the shore. "My father built this tower." He said it with a slight edge of dissatisfaction in his voice. Was it because sons always strove to outdo their fathers?

Shizuka leaned against him. She felt the warmth of his body through their clothing. He was very warm. Before long, she would be very warm also, and the warmth of his body and the warmth of hers would not be separate.

1796

"Yes, Lord Kiyori," the architect said. "I understand your wishes completely."

"I hope you do," Kiyori said. Not even his servants took him seriously. He was only fifteen, and had become Great Lord of the domain only a month ago upon the sudden death of his father.

"I do, my lord."

"But?"

"You say you want to build another floor, a seventh, because you have discovered that in ancient times there was a seventh floor."

"Yes. And?"

"Your descriptions have been very clear, my lord. However, it would be very helpful if I could perhaps even just glance at the plan. As Master Kung said, 'A single picture may convey more than a thousand ideograms.' "

Kiyori's irritation began to rise into anger. "If I had the plan, don't you think I would have shown it to you by now?"

"You don't have it? I don't understand. Who does?"

"No one."

"But—" The architect stopped.

"Go on."

"I'm sorry, my lord, I must have misunderstood you. I thought you said you had seen the plan."

"No," Kiyori said. He could not speak the exact truth. It was far too embarrassing. "I said I had seen the seventh floor." The architect blinked, then his eyes widened with understanding.

"A vision?"

"Yes." He hoped he would not have to explain further.

The architect bowed all the way to the floor.

"May I offer my congratulations, Lord Kiyori, and the hope that we will have the benefit of many more visions."

"Thank you."

"I will proceed with construction—rather, the reconstruction—immediately."

"Good. When you are ready to lay the floor, inform me so I can observe."

"You wish to observe the laying of the floor?"

"Yes."

The wraith who had visited him the previous night told him that the floor must be precisely placed.

If there is the slightest error, she said, I will appear to you to be standing beneath the floor, and be cut off from my feet, or above the floor, and present myself as a floating apparition.

If you are my vision, then what does it matter? he asked.

The human mind can accept only so much that seems impossible, she said. Too much, and madness is the result.

"Very well, my lord." The architect bowed low once again. "It shall be done."

Word quickly spread that the young lord had inherited the gift from his sire. From that day, servants and vassals looked at him differently. When he spoke, they listened with care. When he commanded, they obeyed without hesitation. In other places, people might ridicule the prophetic abilities of the Okumichi lords. Not in Akaoka Domain. The ruling clan's power was founded on mystical foresight, and it was the foundation for the survival and prosperity of the domain.

Here, being prescient brought great authority, even if the prescient one was a boy of fifteen, and even if that prescience was not quite what everyone thought it was. No one would ever be the wiser.

That was Kiyori's hope. Surely, only he could see her?

1308, THE HIGH TOWER

Shizuka passed every night in her husband's quarters or, when he preferred to visit her, with him in her quarters. At other times during the first week after her arrival, she spent much of her time at the highest level of the tower.

"Why?" Hironobu asked. "You have ladies-in-waiting who will play games with you. Musicians, singers, poets, all are at your disposal. If you wish to ride, you have your choice of horses. Or a carriage, if you prefer."

"The view draws me here," Shizuka said. "I've lived all the sixteen years of my life on the ground, behind the walls of an abbey. To see so much of the world, and to be so far above it, this is a great marvel for me. I know this tower is a warrior's aerie. If I should not be here—" She smiled at him and bowed.

Hironobu laughed. "A warrior's aerie? Hardly. Okumichi samurai do not look for our enemies from afar. We do not wait to suffer siege. We do not wait at all. We are cavalrymen. The best in all the isles of Japan. In war, we ride to the attack. Our enemies must keep watch for us. And when they see us, it is already too late."

In the first conversation they had ever had, Hironobu had related the story of his conquest of a mighty Hojo army and his subsequent elevation to Great Lord status. Apparently, it was the custom among samurai to constantly boast of what they had done, and when they spoke of the future, they spoke as if the great feats they swore to perform were already as good as accomplished. Exaggeration, not fact, was the dominant element.

Shizuka bowed and said, "How fortunate are the people of this domain. They enjoy a security and tranquillity denied to so many others. War ravages the realm. But here, in Akaoka, there is peace."

"Yes," Hironobu said. "Security and tranquillity."

She could tell he savored those words. He would use them later in the history he was writing. When later generations read it, they would marvel at his accomplishments against seemingly impossible odds. They would wonder how it was that so successful a warlord—and one who was reputedly prescient as well—did not become Shogun, did not even manage to conquer the whole of Shikoku, the smallest of the three main islands of Japan.

"May I ask a question? Perhaps it is impolite."

"You are my wife," Hironobu said grandly. "You can ask me anything and it will never be impolite."

"Thank you, my lord. That is very generous of you."

Again, Hironobu laughed. He sat down next to her and put his arm around her shoulders.

"You called me 'lord.' We are alone now. Such formality is not required."

He put his face against her neck and shoulder and inhaled.

"You have a lovelier scent than any incense or perfume I have ever breathed, or even imagined."

Shizuka blushed. "Nobu-chan," she whispered, using a childish diminutive of his name.

His breath caught in his throat, and when he spoke, his voice had the harsh edge of sensual elevation.

"You," he said, and reached into the wide sleeve of her kimono.

Shizuka lay back on the floor. Hironobu's face above her was pale, except for the infusion of blood that flooded into his eyelids, his cheeks, and his lips. He looked like he was aflame. Behind him was the ceiling.

She knew that before very long, it would be the floor of the seventh level of the high tower.

. . . . .

After that, Hironobu no longer minded Shizuka's lengthy visits to the tower.

"Be here as much as you like," he said. "Had I lived so long imprisoned within the walls of a temple, I, too, would relish this perspective."

"You are very kind," Shizuka said. "Only the truly manly can be so kind."

She went there for the view, as she said, but not the one she had described.

She sat in meditation with her legs folded into the lotus posture, her hands at her abdomen in the zazen mudra, her eyelids hooded without being completely closed, her breathing so light and attenuated it was hardly breathing at all. She sat in meditation and concentrated her entire being on the opposite purpose. Instead of letting go, letting go of letting go, and letting go yet again, Shizuka grasped at this and that, discriminated one delusion from another, ventured meaningless opinions on useless matters, invaded every void of no-thought with conjecture, imagination, reasoning, hope, lust, and dread. She invited the sensory deluge of hunger, heat and cold, pain and pleasure, sweetness and bitterness, of scent, taste, touch, and sight, actual, imagined, and recalled. Inner silence and serenity were swept away by the uproar of ten thousand voices screaming demands at once.

She would let go later. Now it was imperative that she retrieve certain memories and premonitions she had wrongly abandoned in her zeal to understand the present. During her awakening, she had mistaken the limited confines of Mushindo Abbey for reality, and had purged her consciousness of knowledge she needed. To regain it, she had to revisit her madness.

A sudden warning chill emanated from her spine and spread out across her upper back, her shoulders, her neck, and her scalp. A conscious entity had entered the room behind her. No sound or movement of air from the stairwell had signaled anyone's approach. Was the gruesome apparition back to haunt her, or did stealth cloak a human danger?

Shizuka ceased her grasping and naming within, and turned her attention without. She recognized the arrival without turning to look. She could no longer see into the minds of others. Sanity could not coexist with such a faculty. But she retained one of its attributes, the ability to perceive intention. By his intention, she knew him.

She said, "If you do, Hironobu will know it was you."

Close behind her, she heard a short, quick intake of breath. Her words had stopped him just a few steps away.

Go said, "Let him know. Let him execute me. I will consider death a rich reward, for you, too, will be dead."

Shizuka spun around to face him. No weapon was in his hand. Had he thought to throw her from a window? Probably.

She smiled. "Are you so sure I cannot fly?"

"Witch." He hissed the word violently and drew his sword.

"My husband will not kill you immediately. He will torture you first, then he will crucify you."

"You think I fear pain? No more than I fear death, and I fear death not at all." He stepped toward her.

"For yourself, no," Shizuka said.

He stopped again.

"Surely, great general, you did not neglect to consider the full consequences of your treason? Hironobu will not crucify you alone. Your vassals, your servants, and your wife will accompany you to hell. And so will Chiaki."

The mention of his son's name depleted Go's body of all strength. He lowered his sword and staggered back.

"I *will* kill you," he said.

"Yes, you will," she said, "but not today."

"Soon enough."

"No, you will be too late."

"Too late for what?"

"That, too, you will discover too late," Shizuka said.

Go returned his sword to its scabbard.

"I will not be fooled by deceptive words and false prognostications. You don't know as much as you pretend to know. That is an old witch's trick." He spun on his heels and strode quickly to the doorway.

She said, "I know who I am."

He stopped and looked back at her.

"Everyone knows who they are except infants, idiots, and lunatics."

"I know who you are."

"Everyone knows who I am. This domain would not exist if not for me."

"I know who I am *because* I know who you are," Shizuka said. "How sad to be a father who wishes to murder his child rather than protect her."

"May you be damned for all time," Go said, "along with every witch who has ever come forth from that evil river of blood."

Shizuka listened to the receding sound of his footsteps in the stairwell. Her father would not enter the tower again until the last day of their lives.

· · · · ·

After exerting so much effort to forget, Shizuka was now doing her best to remember. She was driven to do so because of the ghoul who haunted the tower. Whatever she might have known of him in the days of her knowledge and madness, she had expunged.

Who was he?

She had to remember before the seventh floor was built. If he was a friend, then she no longer needed to hide from him. If he was a foe, she needed to know his nature so she could defend herself from him. The ghoul frightened her, and she was no longer used to being frightened.

She had seen him for the first time the day she arrived at the castle. She was sitting in the room on the sixth floor of the tower, nursing her disappointment at the absence of the seventh, when she heard someone coming up the stairwell. A young man she did not recognize appeared in the doorway. He was no more than fifteen or sixteen years of age. The full-size swords in his sash seemed too large for him. His face exhibited signs of sincerity more than intelligence, and determination more than handsomeness. She was about to call out to him when she realized why he seemed odd.

He was transparent.

He turned in her direction and seemed to stare directly at her.

Shizuka froze. Perhaps her lack of motion, combined with the lengthening shadows of twilight, prevented her from being seen. Perhaps she was as transparent to him as he was to her, and being in shadow she was more difficult to see. Perhaps he was no more than a hallucination.

The apparition walked past her as if she were not there. When he reached the far wall, he began to rise in the air, his legs making the motions of ascending steps that did not exist.

Shizuka choked back her scream. She bit her hand to keep from gasping. She feared making the slightest sound that might attract his attention.

Just before he reached the ceiling, the creature spoke.

"Lady Shizuka," he said. "May I enter?"

He apparently received permission from someone, for he bowed and, a moment later, disappeared into the ceiling.

Shizuka lacked the courage to move. She wanted desperately to get away from what was surely a demon, but just as desperately she did not want to attract his attention. She stayed where she was and listened. She heard nothing. For many long minutes, she was paralyzed by her fear.

Twilight gave way to night. The deep darkness of the new moon drenched the interior of the tower. Only the few stray rays of starlight that came through the clouds delineated one shadow from the next.

At last her fear of staying overcame her fear of moving. As quietly as she could, she shuffled toward the stairwell, clutching her kimono tightly so the layers of silk would not rustle against each other.

When she reached it and thought her escape as good as made, the second specter appeared. This one was a man in his early twenties. Swarthy, burly, with the confident swagger of a man who had killed other men, no doubt with the very two swords at his waist.

Like the first, he appeared out of the stairwell.

Like the first, he was transparent and ignored her presence.

But unlike the first, this one walked straight toward her. She backed away as quickly as she could, and just barely managed to get out of his way before he entered the room. He rose into the air in the same monstrous way as the first and, like him, paused and spoke a name that shocked her.

"Lady Shizuka. It is I."

This creature, too, then disappeared into the ceiling.

Shizuka pressed back against the wall. She was trapped. She could not risk descending the stairs. If she met another demon, what if it passed directly through her? She was not confident her mind was strong enough to experience that terror and still cohere. Yet if she did not leave, it was surely only a matter of time before one of them, or another yet to arrive, discovered her and—

And what? Uncertainty added to her fear.

She hoped Hironobu would come looking for her. But she knew he would not. Her clever little speech equating kindness with manliness would force him through pride to give her the freedom he thought she desired.

In the room, near the ceiling, she saw darkness moving within darkness, a faint shadow of a human form descending steps. It reached the floor of the room and moved toward the staircase, and her.

She could shrink back no farther. Which one was it? Of the two, she was uncertain which she feared more. The worst demons were said to take upon themselves a benign aspect, the better to deceive and horrify. The younger in appearance, then, the boy, was more dangerous than the man. As he neared, it seemed that it was indeed the worse of the two, for the outline of his spectral form was smaller than that of the warrior.

The creature paused before entering the stairwell and looked out the window. He was not two paces from where Shizuka cowered against the wall. He turned into the starlight. She saw the gaunt and wrinkled face of an old man.

Shizuka screamed in helpless terror and ran into the stairwell. Caution destroyed by the shock of what she had seen, she half ran, half fell toward the ground. A demonic wailing pursued her all the way down. Only when she ran into Hironobu's arms did she realize the wailing emanated from her own throat.

"Let none escape!" Hironobu ordered.

"Lord!" Samurai with drawn swords dashed into the tower.

Shizuka knew they would find no one, for no one was there, only ghosts.

Hirobonu held her firmly. "You are safe, Shizuka, you are safe."

She clung desperately to Hironobu, her body trembling uncontrollably. No, she was not safe. She would never be safe again.

The instant before she screamed, she had thought she was seeing a third demon. Then in the old man's face she recognized the boy, and the warrior. They were not three demons at all, but one and the same. He had caused his human aspect to age a lifetime in mere hours.

What would haunt her next? A rotting corpse?

A wave of bile surged up from her stomach. She locked her throat and held the bitter heat there for what seemed like a very long time before it seared the inside of her chest on the way back down.

Hironobu instantly fixed responsibility for the attack, which he supposed was by hired ninja, on a neighboring lord he had long disliked. Shizuka did not try to dissuade him. How could she? If she told him the attacker had been a demon and not a human being, and if he believed her, that would still not protect the enemy Hironobu had chosen. Once his suspicions were fixed, they always grew and grew until they attained the certainty of decisive evidence. A foul coward who would send a ninja would not hesitate to hire sorcerers to conjure up a demon. And if he did not believe her, if he doubted her sanity now, his responses could well be distorted when she shared her prophecies with him in the days to come. The outcomes she had foreseen would occur no matter what. But the surrounding consequences of those outcomes could be brutally different. She could not risk it. She had to let the innocent suffer and die.

That very night, Hironobu sent couriers to his chief vassals. Before the morning sun lifted the dew from the leaves, he and nine hundred mounted samurai rode off to the east to attack Lord Teruo. By then, the distress Shizuka had felt since the appearance of the demon had effloresced into high fever, chills, dizziness, and persistent nausea.

She retired to her quarters before sunset. She dismissed her ladies-in-waiting. They could do nothing to help her against any apparition. Like the nuns at the abbey, they would not have the slightest inkling of demonic presences. They would see only her behavior, and would simply think her mad. Guards remained in the corridor outside her bedroom. Since Hironobu had ordered them there, she could not send them away. She hoped she could restrain herself sufficiently that they would not hear too much.

If she had courage, she would not wait for the demon to come to her. She would go to the high tower and seek it out. But she was not that brave.

Alone, she was afraid to go and afraid to stay, afraid of sleep and afraid of wakefulness, afraid to meditate and afraid to give herself over to delusion. No place in the world nor any state of mind was a sanctuary.

When night came, her fever worsened. At last, overwhelmed by illness, fear, and exhaustion, she lay down. As soon as she did, she began to fade in and out of consciousness with deceptive subtlety. When she thought she was awake, she tried to move and found she could not. When she seemed to be asleep, she found herself thinking that she was asleep, which surely meant she was in fact awake. Yet, then, too, she could not move. The slightest shift of a little finger, the twitch of an eyelid, an alteration in her breathing, any change in the tension of her muscles—all were completely beyond her ability. As she struggled uselessly, she heard a distant, steady, high-pitched sound midway between a chirp and a whine. At first she took it for the singing of cicadas. But their characteristic cadence was absent. It was more like the dying peal of a temple gong, except instead of diminishing, it grew ever louder, ever more piercing. Was it a harbinger of the approaching demon? Again, she struggled to exert some control over her body, any control. Her external stillness belied the panic she felt, the terror caused more by fearful anticipation than by pain or paralysis. If only she could open her eyes, or clench a fist, or voice even a whisper—

Abruptly, the ringing ceased. In the same instant, she heard a voice outside her door.

"Why should I be afraid? It's just a room, like any other." It was a voice she did not recognize, the voice of a young man.

1796, THE FORBIDDEN WING OF CLOUD OF SPARROWS CASTLE

"Well, I am afraid," Lady Sadako whispered. "Let us go elsewhere."

"Coming here was your idea in the first place," Kiyori said.

"I've changed my mind," Lady Sadako said. She reached out and lightly placed her hands on his arm. She gently tugged at him and tried to draw him away before he opened the door. In the bright light of day, it was easy to laugh at the stories of evil, ghostly sorceresses. Here and now, with only distant stars and the slightest sliver of the waxing moon to light the world, ghosts and evil spirits did not seem so impossible.

"Please," she said.

He hesitated. In truth, he was afraid, too. He was the only Okumichi of his generation. That meant he must be the one who would receive prophetic visions. From his reading of the secret chronicles of the clan, he knew that such visions had come to his predecessors in many ways and in many forms, some so ghastly that madness had been the result. Was he not tempting fate by visiting the former quarters of Lady Shizuka, the very sorceress who had brought the power of prophecy into his bloodline? But his desire to impress Sadako was greater than his fear. Why was difficult to say. At fourteen, she was a year younger than he, and seemed even younger. She was far from being the prettiest girl he knew. Her family was barely of sufficient rank to allow her entry to the Great Lord's court. Yet, a mere character trait, her refreshing forthrightness, had won his affection as well as his admiration. Whenever she said something, he knew she meant it. Why that should attract him more than a beautiful face, a seductive manner, intimate skills, and clever words, he did not know. Perhaps there was something wrong with him.

"I have already said I would spend the night here," Kiyori said. "The word of a Great Lord, once given, must be kept." Because he had been Great Lord for all of three weeks, he was more emphatic about his status than he might otherwise have been.

"You didn't exactly give your word," Sadako said. "All you said was that you were not afraid to spend the night in the haunted part of the castle. And you only said it to me. And I believe you. Now, please, let's go."

"You may go," Kiyori said grandly. "I have given my word, so I must stay as I said I would."

He put his hand on the door and pushed. He hoped it was secured in some way that would prevent him from entering. But it slid open with ease. The room's reputation was such that it required no locks. Priests and nuns cleaned this part of the castle daily, so there were no cobwebs, dust, or musty odor.

Sadako gasped and stepped back from the open doorway.

Kiyori looked inside. He saw nothing. But the shadows in the room made it even darker than it was in the hallway where they stood.

"What do you see?" he asked.

"Darkness," she said, "an unnatural darkness. Please, I beg you, my lord, let us go."

Sadako never called him "my lord" except in the most formal situations where it was completely unavoidable. She really was afraid. That knowledge made him behave more boldly than he felt. He stepped into the room and began to close the door behind him. As he had hoped, Sadako stepped in before the door shut. One of her hands was on his arm and the other was on his shoulder. He could feel her trembling body pressed against him.

"Be calm, Sadako," Kiyori said, leading her deeper into the room. "Our eyes will adjust to the darkness. And the moon is rising. Soon, there will be more light."

"There will be more light sooner if you open the door," Sadako said, "or even if we stay near it."

"If I open the door, I may be thought afraid. If we stay by it, again there is the appearance of fear. Here. We will sit by the alcove."

"Isn't that where people say she placed her bed?" Sadako stopped abruptly. Since she was still holding on to him, he had to stop, too.

"So people say. People say all kinds of things. It is best to trust one's own judgment and not be influenced by the prattle of those who know nothing but speak much. Let us at least sit down."

"It seems a little brighter now," Sadako said, following his suggestion and seating herself. "But I still can't see much of anything."

"We forgot to bring bedding," Kiyori said with studied casualness. "We will have to sleep on the bare mats." Her reliance on him gave him a pleasing sense of confidence. He leaned back and began to stretch out on the floor.

And instantly plunged into impossibility. In one single moment, freezing cold and burning flames consumed him; the weight of the earth crushed him into a single infinitesimal point while the lightness of heaven pulled him apart into every direction of the cosmos; inconceivable pain racked his body and limitless ecstasy brought him liberation.

"Kiyori!" Sadako stared at him. The rising moon lit the fear in her face. "What's wrong?"

Kiyori could not answer. Even if he could, he would not have known what to say. He saw the present moment coexistent with the numberless worlds and the countless eons and the infinite myriads of beings that were and were not himself. He saw past and future stretching into the endless distance toward a beginningless beginning and an endless end that he could never perceive without disintegrating.

A shadowy female figure rose out of him like spirit separating from body. In an instant, he knew what had happened. She had come to him as he had come to her. Her long tresses spilled over her shoulders and onto him.

No, not quite onto him.

Into him.

She floated a hand's width above the mat in the usual manner of disembodied ghouls, and like a ghoul was partly inside him and partly outside. The fearful rumors of a ghostly presence were true, but it was nothing that he had imagined.

"Kiyori," Sadako said. She reached to touch him. Before she did, he spoke, and not to her.

He said, "Lady Shizuka."

"Lord Kiyori," Shizuka said, and pulled herself away and out of him.

When she did, he lost consciousness.

"Kiyori!" Sadako was too afraid to touch him. But something had to be done. She rose, threw open the door, and hurried away to find help. She had not gone five steps before she stopped. If anyone else saw him in this weakened state, in a possible condition of temporary madness—for he had spoken the ancient sorceress's name as if she had appeared before him—his still-unsteady hold on power could be lost. He was only fifteen, with many enemies and few friends.

Sadako looked back down the dark hallway toward the forbidden wing. Still trembling with fear, she started back to where Kiyori lay. She herself was the only one she could trust to keep silent. If Kiyori did not trust her, then he could put her to death and his secret would be completely safe. She did not want to die. But she knew her duty. Her father was of low rank, but he was a samurai, and she was a samurai's daughter.

Sadako held Kiyori in her arms until he awoke, finally, at dawn.

He said, "The high tower. The seventh floor."

"There is no seventh floor, Lord Kiyori," Sadako said. She purposely said his name in case he had forgotten who he was.

"I will have it built. That is where we will—"

He stopped and looked at Sadako. She had seen him in his time of greatest weakness. She had heard him babble to a ghost. Could he trust her to keep silent? There was only one way to be sure. Execute her.

Or—

There was an alternative.

Marry her.

Which was worse? he wondered. Every part of his body from his head to his toes ached. It took much effort to lift himself from Sadako's lap.

"Why do you laugh, my lord?"

"Oh, because our little adventure turned out so much worse, and so much better, than either of us could have expected."

1311

Shizuka smiled. Kiyori's face was peaceful though he had died by poison. He had not suffered much pain. She was glad of that.

For sixty-four of his seventy-nine years, Lord Kiyori had feared her. He feared her because she knew the future, he feared her because she was a ghost or an embodiment of his own insanity, he feared her because she appeared and disappeared without warning. But he feared her most because she was forever young.

He had never considered how frightening he was to her. That first night in the tower was only a premonition. In the next three years, Lord Kiyori deteriorated at horrific speed from youth to old age, as if a curse had been placed upon him by powerful and merciless gods. Perhaps it was true. A curse was as good an explanation as any.

Shizuka stayed with Lord Kiyori's ghostly corpse until the shadowy image dissipated for the last time.

Now there was only one ghost left in the high tower.

Before the sun rose again, there would be none.

1842

Lord Nao did not think he would ever return to this place. Perhaps if he were of a more religious nature, the ashes of his daughter would have some meaning for him. As it was, ashes were only ashes. He did not believe in immortality or reincarnation in any of its fabulously described forms. He did not believe evildoers were consigned to suffer in demonic realms, nor did he believe the good and the faithful were rewarded with an angelic existence in a heavenly paradise. He did not believe the spirits of the departed clung eternally to their earthly remains.

Life was life.

Death was death.

That was all.

Once, not so very long ago, Nao's existence was full of life, and the promise and possibilities that life contained. Then, in short order, death replaced life. Midori, so robust a tomboy as a child, was surprisingly fragile as a woman. As his friend Lord Kiyori had predicted, she never recovered from the birth of her first child, Genji. The birth of her second child, a daughter, killed her and the child both. Within a month of that, a plague brought ashore by Russian trappers swept through Nao's northern domain. He escaped without acquiring so much as a bad cough. His wife, sons, and grandchildren were not so fortunate.

His son-in-law, Yorimasa, had survived Midori by less than a year. His newly installed ashes were beside hers. That was a formality and an expression of sentiment that he hoped comforted someone, for it did nothing for him. Among some, there was doubt as to the cause of Yorimasa's death. Nao was not one of them. Yorimasa's sorrow drove him to return to the vices of opium, absinthe, and alcohol. He did not revert to his former violence. He simply could not endure the emptiness of a life without Midori. Nao understood. He felt the same sorrow and emptiness. That he still had one grandson who would carry on his bloodline was somehow inadequate. He no longer cared about his bloodline. It must have been the same for Yorimasa.

He was found by the side of the road, his neck broken, his horse grazing placidly nearby. All evidence suggested the obvious. He had intoxicated himself to the edge of unconsciousness, fallen, and died. That at least one person did not accept this view was confirmed by the subsequent deaths in short order of sixteen samurai, gamblers, and smugglers who would have been suspects had Yorimasa's death been the result of foul play. All sixteen were killed by a single sword stroke to the fronts of their bodies, a blow so powerful they were either decapitated or had their torsos cloven nearly in two. All had weapons in their hands, or their weapons had fallen nearby. None of the deaths was by ambush or stealth. Every rumor pointed to Shigeru, of course, but nothing could be proved. There were no witnesses. At least, none willing to come forth.

Nao heard the rustle of clothing in the doorway behind him.

He said, "If our lives had not been too long, perhaps theirs would not have been too brief."

Lord Kiyori sat next to him. "There is no connection between the two. If there were, all parents would sacrifice themselves for their children."

"Still, I cannot help but feel I have lived too long. When I was born, the Chien-lung Emperor was on the throne of China, and that empire was mighty beyond challenge. The British ambassador went to see him, and the Emperor said, You have nothing we desire, you may leave, and the British were summarily dismissed. Now the British come and go as they please, they sell drugs to the Chinese to steal their wealth and break their will. The Chinese and British fought a war, and the British won. It is hardly imaginable, but there it is. I am out of date."

"You and I were born in the same year," Kiyori said. "If you are out of date, then so am I."

"You can see the future," Nao said, "so you of all people can never be out of date."

"I have often wished I could not. What use is knowing of tragedy if it cannot be prevented?"

"You did not ask to be prescient. It is your burden to bear. Unlike you, I can lay my burdens down. I have written to the Shogun resigning my title and powers."

"I thought you might."

Nao said, "Remember, when we were young, we promised each other and our ancestors we would be the ones to avenge our clans and overthrow the Tokugawa Shogun? I think that is the only promise I have failed to keep."

Kiyori laughed. "That is the kind of foolish pledge young men make. We can be forgiven for not fulfilling it."

They sat for a time in silence.

Then Kiyori asked, "What will you do?"

"I will remember," Nao said. "Everyone I treasure now resides only in memory."

11

The Curse
of the
Witch's
Mother

*Men think it is they who rule the world. Do not make difficulties for
yourself. Keep silent and encourage this belief.*
   Knowing the truth is wisdom.
   Babbling about it is folly.

AKI-NO-HASHI

(1311)

1882, CLOUD OF SPARROWS CASTLE

Makoto spent much of the ocean voyage from Yokohama to Muroto
Province thinking of what he would do if Genji refused to see him.
He could have saved himself the trouble. He was admitted immediately.

The man who came to greet him in the large drawing room was approximately his own height and build. He was dressed similarly in a
double-breasted woolen frock coat, a white silk shirt with a black silk cravat, a silk vest, light woolen trousers, and low-cut dress boots with laces.
His clothing was in hues of dark gray, while Makoto's was black. That, and
the heavier riding boots that Makoto wore, were the only significant differences. It was a mild disappointment. Here in this ancient fortress, he had
looked forward to seeing a warlord in traditional regalia at last.

"I am happy to meet you, Makoto," Genji said, extending his hand.
Face-to-face, he appeared young enough to be Makoto's elder brother.

Genji's English was nearly flawless. If he had the slightest of accents, it was not the typical one of a native Japanese speaker, but one that Makoto recognized as that of New York, the middle Hudson River Valley, in the vicinity of Albany, if he was not mistaken. Makoto's linguistics studies had led him into the entertaining hobby of indentifying the birthplaces of speakers solely by their patterns of speech. Genji must have had a tutor from that region. He would have to ask him, if the appropriate opportunity arose.

"Thank you for seeing me on such short notice, Mr. Okumichi. I know you are very busy."

"I would not call twenty years short notice."

Makoto smiled. "You surprise me, sir. At the very least, I expected a certain degree of evasion, even outright denial. Indeed, even prior to denial, refusal to meet with me at all seemed the likeliest of all outcomes."

"Evasion is useless," Genji said, "and denial impossible. Look at you. Look at me. Our relationship is patently obvious."

"Is that so? Do you not see any of Matthew Stark in me?"

"In your boldness, yes, and in your calm in a difficult situation, I see much of Matthew. He has raised you, after all. How could you not be like him?"

Two maids appeared in the doorway and bowed before entering. They were dressed in traditional kimono instead of the Western clothing worn by the servants who had greeted him upon his arrival. Perhaps, like an Ottoman pasha, Genji affected modern ways to strangers while preferring the culture of his traditional despotism within his innermost chambers. Perhaps the warlord accoutrements that Makoto had not seen were then on display.

The maids placed their trays on the table.

"Shall the tea be poured, my lord?" one asked.

"Thank you, no," Genji said.

The maids bowed and departed. Their entry and exit had been most unobtrusive.

"Did my mother serve you that way?"

"She poured," Genji said, "because pouring can be a demonstration of grace, and a display of elegance and beauty. Since she possessed all three qualities in abundance, she naturally had that inclination. She was not particularly fond of carrying trays, however. She was not a servant, after all, so neither fondness nor necessity required it."

"She was not a servant? I understood that she was, sir. A maid or some such, in this castle, and the palace in Tokyo."

"Ah," Genji said. He walked to the window and looked toward the sea.

"Am I mistaken?"

"The mistake is mine," Genji said.

"You abandoned my mother, sir. No, please, I do not say it as an accusation or as a judgment upon your actions, simply as a factual statement. I would like to know why. I have not come to make any claim upon you, material or otherwise, nor do I propose that you announce our relationship to anyone, or acknowledge it in any way whatsoever. I want only one thing. The answer to 'Why?' "

"I admit that I did not acknowledge you as I should have," Genji said, "nor did I acknowledge your mother. I hope you will agree that, as much of a failing as it was, it is not to be equated with abandonment. Neither of you was abandoned. Your welfare was an important concern, and I believe I properly provided for your well-being."

"You will forgive me, sir, if I find a semantic discussion without interest," Makoto said. "The matter of why still remains, and it stands out rather prominently as the only matter of true importance."

Genji bowed at the waist in the manner of a Western gentleman conceding a point. Someone had tutored him well.

"I will try to explain," Genji said. "Our modernization is of recent vintage, and it is quite superficial as well. We are still bound by beliefs that are entirely medieval. Twenty years ago, at the time of your birth, the situation was even more backward. I think it will be impossible for you to imagine how backward."

Another person arrived in the doorway, this time a young girl about twelve years of age. Her child's kimono was not entirely compatible with her appearance, which reminded Makoto strongly of his sisters in San Francisco. Like them, it was obvious that only one of her parents was Japanese.

"Why are you wearing a kimono?" Genji asked in Japanese. "I thought you hated Japanese clothing."

The little girl strolled nonchalantly into the room.

She said, "That was yesterday. Today I hate Western clothing."

"I see," Genji said. "Come here for a moment. I want you to meet someone."

The girl resembled Makoto's sisters in her mixed lineage, but while they were merely pretty, she was astonishing. Her hair was light brown, with brilliant auburn highlights. Flecks of gold seemed to sparkle in her hazel eyes. Her face was as smooth as the finest ceramic without diminishing in any way the mobility and liveliness of her expressions. In the shape of her face, the size and angle of her eyes, the tilt of her nose, the rise of her cheekbones, a remarkable harmony between East and West was realized. Makoto also saw, especially in the shape of her mouth and the way it tended toward a constant, slight smile, a resemblance to her sire and to himself. She reminded him of his sisters because, quite obviously, she was one.

"Shizuka, this is Makoto," Genji said in English. "Makoto, my daughter, Shizuka."

Shizuka said in Japanese, "Why are you speaking English?"

"Your names are Japanese," Genji said, "so there wasn't much English in what I said."

"Stop it, Father," she said. "Your jokes are never very funny."

Makoto said, "Your father is speaking English because he is polite. I am his guest, and English is my primary language."

"You're not Japanese?" Shizuka said in English. Makoto's explanation had apparently been an acceptable one.

"I am Japanese by blood, but I was born in the United States and have lived my entire life there. This is my first trip to Japan."

Shizuka looked at him thoughtfully. "Ah," she said, "you're *that* Makoto. I recognize you now. I've seen many pictures of you. We're brother and sister."

Makoto looked at Genji.

Genji said, "I probably tell her more than I should. One of the classic sins of an indulgent father."

Shizuka said, "I guess we're really half brother and half sister. We had different mothers. We're half orphans, too. Our mothers both passed away in childbirth."

"I'm sorry about your mother, Shizuka. Mine is still alive."

"Heiko is still alive?" Shizuka looked thoroughly confused. She turned to her father.

So did Makoto.

"Who is Heiko?" he said.

1862, SAN FRANCISCO

Jiro and Shoji stood at the starboard railing of the *Star of Bethlehem* and looked across the water at San Francisco.

Jiro said, "Even from afar, it looks barbaric."

"How else could it possibly look?" Shoji said. In truth, this place reminded him more than a little of his mother's hometown of Kobe, in Western Japan, with the waters of the same ocean lapping at the very edge of the city, and green valleys visible in the near distance. He would never admit that to his friend, of course. And there were major differences. Here, buildings were built not only up to the hillsides but over and atop them. That would never happen in a civilized country like Japan, where everyone respected the mountaintops as the residence of the gods. "A land of barbarians will look like a land of barbarians."

A soft, musical voice drifted toward them. "Perhaps the time has come to adjust your thinking." The sound was pleasing, but the reprimand was clear.

Recognizing her voice, they said "Yes, Lady Heiko" before they saw her.

Her nearness caught them by surprise. Only moments ago, they had seen her on the other side of the ship, talking to Mr. Stark and the captain. Though her movements were always gentle, deliberate, and leisurely, it was obvious she could move very quickly, and very silently, when she chose to do so. The story of her ride through the mountains with Mr. Stark, her nighttime charge against the traitor Sohaku's barrier guards, and her dauntless ferocity at the battle of Mushindo Monastery were already legendary, though the events had taken place only last year.

Heiko said, "Both Mr. Stark and Lady Emily lived in this city before they came to Japan. To insult the place is to insult them."

"Yes, Lady Heiko." They continued to bow deeply, eyes properly averted and locked to the deck of the ship.

Protect Lady Heiko with your lives, Lord Genji had said, and honor her as you would honor me.

Jiro and Shoji, on their hands and knees, their heads pressed into the mats on the floor of Quiet Crane Palace, had said, Yes, Lord Genji.

Treat Matthew Stark as you would any lord in my service, and remember that he is my friend until we are parted by death.

Yes, lord.

In America, Mr. Stark and Lady Heiko will carry out plans designed to strengthen the clan. See that you do not fail to obey both of them without hesitation.

Yes, lord.

"Were you not sent here to provide protection for us?" Heiko said.

"Yes, Lady Heiko."

"And how can you accomplish that if you spend so much time staring at the ground?"

They looked up to see Heiko smiling at them. Despite the fact that they were being chastised, her smile was so beautiful and so warm, both men felt their spirits brightening.

"From now on, consider yourselves on a battlefield at all times, and shorten your bows accordingly. We do not know the conventions of this country. We must be cautious in the extreme."

"Yes, Lady Heiko."

Stark joined them at the starboard railing.

"Well, there it is. Jiro, Shoji, how do you like it? Your first American city."

"Very nice, sir," Jiro said.

"I believe it's grown considerably since I've been away. So much bigger in just a year."

"It mind me Kobe," Shoji said. "Same hills, same city at ocean."

Stark was impressed. Neither man had a particular facility with English, but both had studied hard during the past year. No matter how long he had stayed in Japan, he knew he would never have been able to master their language as these men had mastered his. Like the samurai that they were, they had approached the learning of English in the same way they learned swordsmanship, archery, and hand-to-hand combat—as a matter of life and death.

"Yes," Stark said to Shoji, "I can see the resemblance, now that you mention it. Except in Kobe, there are no buildings on the hilltops."

"Ah," Shoji said, "very right, Mr. Stark. Your observance acute."

"Until your usage is better, use simpler words," Heiko said in Japanese, "or you will seem pretentious and shame us all."

"Yes, Lady Heiko."

Within the hour, they were at the docks. Jiro and Shoji watched from the deck as groups of Chinese coolies, along with other groups of American laborers, unloaded the ship.

Jiro said, "The Chinese and the Americans don't seem to like each other."

"We don't like either of them," Shoji said, "and they don't like us. Of course they also don't like each other."

There seemed something illogical about what Shoji said. Before Jiro had time to reason it out sufficiently to reply, they were joined by Lady Heiko's maid, Sachiko. She had been busy below with the luggage. It was her first look at San Francisco.

"Why, it is more of a wilderness than a city," Sachiko said. "I thought this was an important seaport."

"It is," Shoji said. He had noticed before that Sachiko was very pretty. She seemed even more so now that she was the only Japanese woman he knew besides Lady Heiko within seven thousand miles.

Jiro was having much the same thoughts.

"It's nothing like Nagasaki or Yokohama," Sachiko said. "I expected more buildings, more people, more of everything. Isn't America a very powerful country?"

"Very powerful," Jiro said, "and very large. Twenty times the size of all Japan. Most of the population is far to the east."

"Is it as big as China?"

Sachiko was the same age as Lady Heiko, which would make her twenty. She should marry soon, while she was still young. Jiro wondered what Lord Genji had in mind when he'd sent the three of them here. There was Sachiko, and there was himself and Shoji. Someone would be left out. Unless Lord Genji did not intend for them to remain away from Japan for long.

"Bigger," Shoji said.

"Really? Bigger than China. How amazing."

Jiro struggled to remember more facts about America. He should have paid more attention to his studies. While it was likely that they would be returning to Japan after helping Mr. Stark establish an enterprise for Lord Genji, it was possible that their stay would be of longer duration. In that case, it would be good for him if he made a better impression on Sachiko than Shoji did. What else was notable?

Sachiko looked toward the gangplank, where Mr. Stark and Lady

Heiko were preparing to disembark. "I must go now. Later you will tell me more." She hurried away to help Lady Heiko.

Shoji said, "Look at the way Lady Heiko leans on Mr. Stark."

"Yes. She took ill almost as soon as the ship left Japan."

"She does not seem to be improving."

"Now that we have arrived at our destination, perhaps she will benefit from medical attention. They do have an understanding of medicine, do they not?"

"Yes," Shoji said. "I believe they learned the art from the Dutch, as we did."

In silence, they watched Stark, Heiko, and Sachiko depart from the ship. They moved slowly across the port toward a waiting carriage.

"Sachiko is very charming," Jiro said.

Shoji said, "Be careful."

"What do you mean?"

"I have heard rumors that she is a ninja."

"I have heard those rumors about Lady Heiko, but not about Sachiko."

"Don't be dull," Shoji said. "If Lady Heiko is a ninja, then wouldn't Sachiko also be a ninja?"

"I don't see how that necessarily follows," Jiro said.

"Look at us," Shoji said.

"What about us? We're certainly not ninjas."

"No, no, of course not. What I mean is, Lord Genji is a samurai, so his trusted servants are samurai, too. Would not Lady Heiko's situation be the same?"

They watched the three board the carriage, which then traveled in the direction of the city.

"She doesn't seem the violent type," Jiro said, a bit more hopefully than he felt.

"Does Lady Heiko?" Shoji asked.

"She doesn't, and that's why I doubt those rumors about her, too," Jiro said. "Remember, Lord Hidé overheard some of the men talking about it. He chastised them severely, and assigned them to a month's stable duty for talking nonsense."

"If the rumors were false, wouldn't he have just laughed it off," Shoji said, "and ridiculed them instead?"

Jiro wondered if Shoji really believed it, or was just saying it to discourage any romantic notions he might have about Sachiko, so that he would have a clear path himself. It was difficult to say. The best outcome for all concerned was a timely return to the homeland.

· · · · ·

"Here, lie down," Stark said, guiding Heiko to the nearest couch. Before they left Japan, he had arranged for the house to be built on a wooded hill outside the city. In the year he'd been gone, the city had come to it, though the hill itself was largely unoccupied.

"I'm not an invalid," she said.

"Indeed you are not. But there are no emergencies for you to deal with, and there are no battles to be fought at the moment. You should rest while you can."

"All I did aboard ship was rest."

"If I remember aright, you also did a fair amount of throwing up."

Heiko laughed. "I did, didn't I?"

"That seems to have passed."

"Three months," Heiko said. "About the usual time."

"When Lord Genji learns of this—"

"He will not learn of it," Heiko said. "Not yet."

"Why put it off? The sooner he knows, the better."

"There is no use bringing anything to his attention before we are sure."

"Sure of what? There is no doubt about your condition."

Heiko smiled. "We cannot be sure that the child will survive. Why bother him with something that may prove to be nothing at all?"

"I think he will want to know, Heiko, and I think he will want to know right away."

"We will wait until the child is born. If we tell him now, he may not be pleased. He may order an end to it."

Stark was shocked. "He would do that? Why?"

"He is a Great Lord," Heiko said. "Who knows what he would do? The circumstances are unusual, so it is difficult to predict what his feelings will be. What is certain is that the chances for the child are better once it is born. It is less likely that Lord Genji will order an execution than a termination of the pregnancy."

"I don't pretend to understand Japan any better now than I did a year ago," Stark said, "but I can't believe he would do something so barbarous, so completely without reason." Stark fought to bring his breathing back under control. "In any case, we are in America now. Even if he did order it, there is no one here to do such a horrific deed."

"Jiro and Shoji," she said.

"I'd kill them first."

Heiko smiled at Stark. As it always did, that soft and gentle expression made his breath catch in his throat.

"Would you kill *me*, Matthew?"

Stark looked at her for a long time without speaking. When he did, his voice was a harsh whisper, and his question one to which he already knew the answer.

"You would murder your own child?"

"I would follow my lord's command."

"I can't believe he would give such an order," Stark said again. "I don't see any reason for it."

"I am not saying he would do so," Heiko said. "Perhaps he would be happy. But he is a Great Lord. Great Lords have reasons ordinary men do not. It is better to avoid unnecessary risks, is it not?"

Stark's eyes were unfocused and he looked unwell.

Heiko felt much sympathy for him. She would explain it better to him if she could, but she herself was filled with uncertainty.

While professing to love her, Genji had sent her into distant exile. He didn't call it that, of course. He had given over into her charge a huge fortune in gold, and directed her to establish solid footing for the clan here in America. He had asked Matthew Stark, his trusted American friend, to protect her and guide her in his homeland. But the simple fact remained, and it was undeniable: An ocean's width now separated them from each other, and it did so only because Genji had commanded it.

She believed he did love her. The way he looked at her, the way he touched her, the tone of his voice, the expression on his face—even the rhythm of his breath when he was asleep beside her—all these things told her his love for her was as strong as hers was for him, and for her, there was nothing stronger in this life.

Yet she was here in this alien place and he was on the other side of the world. Why had he sent her away? Would she ever know? And when he learned that a child had been born, what would he do? Command her return? Order the child's death, and her own as well?

Heiko put her hand on the still-mild swelling of her abdomen. If the child survived—if it was male— But there was no use speculating. For now, the only thing to do was wait. Wait and take good care of herself. Time would resolve every question. Time and Genji.

She closed her eyes and, smiling, soon fell gently into sleep.

Stark didn't dare move. Heiko leaned against him as she slept. She was so small and delicate, and the voyage had been a hard one.

She was with child.

He could hardly believe it. She seemed still a child herself, far too young to face the mortal dangers posed by childbirth. Newborns died almost as often as they lived, and far too frequently they took their mothers with them. Added to the natural perils was the completely unexpected threat that Heiko said came from Genji.

Stark felt a blush of shame. He had asked her why, but he knew why. At least, one of the possibilities. He had not thought of falling in love with Heiko, and so had not been on guard against it. His concern in that direction was with Emily Gibson, his fellow missionary in Japan. She was an astonishing golden beauty of eighteen, just blossoming into womanhood. Her charms were so obvious, it was easy for Stark to keep his heart cold with her. His purpose in Japan was deadly. There was no room for the distractions of love. He had not guarded himself against Heiko, because the possibility had not even occurred to him. She was Japanese. She was a geisha. She was Lord Genji's lover. Ironically, his feelings for her arose, not because of her beauty, but because of her courage. Despite her diminutive stature and her apparent fragility, she had on two separate occasions cut down a total of two dozen heavily armed samurai with her own delicate little hands—and not with a gun but hand to hand, with a knife, a sword, and throwing blades called *shuriken*. By the time he realized his admiration had changed into something far more potent, it was too late to deny.

He loved her.

Did Heiko fear Genji's wrath because he knew how Stark felt about her? Did he wrongly suspect that those feelings had been translated into action? If he did, would he have sent her with Stark and asked him to watch over her?

There was no use wondering. Stark didn't understand the Japanese in general, and Genji in particular was even more confusing than most. Heiko was certainly right about one thing: The motives of a Great Lord were always complex and convoluted, and impossible to guess. He would have to wait and see.

Was it possible Genji would order the child's death once it was born? Stark knew him as a kind and gentle man, in manner and deed quite the opposite of the fierce warriors he commanded. If he didn't know better, he would never think him capable of any cruelties. But he had seen the most horrendous butchery carried out at Genji's command, and heard horrifying rumors of worse. Not many months earlier, Genji had led his men in the slaughter of an entire village of peasants. More than a hundred people—including women, children, and even suckling infants—had been brutally hacked to death, and the village burned to the ground. So the rumors went, and no one denied them. Why was it done? No one knew. It was ordered, and the order was obeyed. For samurai, that was enough.

Stark knew that if Genji gave the command, Jiro and Shoji would not hesitate. Nor would Heiko.

No, that would not happen. He would not let it happen. He had fought alongside the two samurai, but he would shoot them down like rabid vermin before he let them harm Heiko's child. And Heiko, what of her? If he simply took the child from her to prevent her from obeying Genji, she would kill herself for failing to carry out his command. He would have to find a way to save the child and Heiko both, if it came to that. How? He didn't know.

He felt Heiko resting warmly against his chest. His own breathing began to slow and match hers as she slept.

Half a year would pass before the child arrived. It was too early to worry, and maybe he was worrying about nothing anyway. Everything could work out right in the end.

It was easier to hope than believe, and it wasn't that easy to hope.

· · · · ·

In the first hour of labor, Heiko began to bleed.

The doctor said, "A certain amount of blood is quite natural. There is no cause for concern."

In the fifth hour, the flow became profuse, and the child had not yet crowned.

The doctor said to Stark, "I can do nothing to stanch the blood until the child leaves her womb."

In the fifteenth hour, Heiko had to struggle to stay awake. The sheets and towels under her turned dark crimson as soon as they were replaced.

The doctor said, "If she sleeps, we will lose them both."

In the twentieth hour, Heiko made the last push that sent her child into the world, and lost consciousness. The baby, healthy and strong, wailed with powerful new lungs.

The doctor said, "I will try to save her, Mr. Stark, but you must understand, she is a small woman and has lost much blood."

"She has the courage of ten men," Stark said.

"Yes, sir, no doubt," the doctor said. "But that tenfold courage is still contained within one tiny human being."

· · · · ·

"I will call him Makoto," Heiko said. She lay in bed with the boy wrapped in swaddling cloth and cradled in her arms. She had given Lord Genji a son and an heir. His order recalling them to Japan would come as soon as he knew. "*Makoto* means 'truth.' "

Heiko imagined the foliage in Japan now, turning orange to signal the approach of winter. She had always been fond of autumn, had never felt the melancholy of falling leaves and the withering away of summer flowers. After every winter was the rebirth of spring.

"Makoto is a good name," Stark said. For her sake, he fought back his tears.

I have stopped the bleeding, the doctor had said, but only because she has so little left to lose. It will begin again. I am sorry, Mr. Stark.

"He looks very much like Lord Genji, does he not?" Heiko asked.

"He is beautiful," Stark said, "like his mother."

Heiko smiled. Despite her weakness and her bloodless pallor, her smile was as radiant as dawn.

"Flatterer," she said. Then, worry creasing her brow, she moved the cloth away from Makoto's face. "It isn't true, is it? He doesn't look more like me, does he?"

"Why are you frowning?" Stark said. "He would be lucky to look like you. That would make him more handsome than those Kabuki heroes you women all love so much."

"He isn't going to be a Kabuki hero," Heiko said. "He is the next Great Lord of Akaoka. It will be much better for him to resemble his father. His official mother will be more likely to be loving to him."

"The boy's mother is the boy's mother," Stark said. "What does 'official' have to do with it?"

"I am not of noble birth," Heiko said. She nuzzled her son's soft, fat little cheek. He slept blissfully on. "Lord Genji must have a noblewoman as his wife. She will be Makoto's mother." She saw the expression on Stark's face and said, "Don't look so sad. I will see him often enough. Lord Genji will establish a separate residence for me. He may elevate me to concubine. And if not, it doesn't really matter. My son is his heir."

An hour later, the blood began to flow once again.

Heiko said, "I am dying."

"No," Stark said. "No."

"Bring Makoto."

Sachiko carried the sleeping baby to Heiko's bedside and offered him to her. Heiko shook her head.

She said, "You hold him, Sachiko. Don't let him feel the taint of death. Hold him and care for him until Lord Genji orders his return to his homeland."

Sachiko tried to answer, but she could not. Clutching the baby to her breast, she slowly collapsed to her knees, weeping uncontrollably.

Heiko said to Stark, "We are not afraid of death. You and I have been its messenger too many times to fear it."

"No," Stark said.

Heiko reached her hand out to him.

"Help me up," she said. "I want to see Japan."

· · · · ·

Heiko leaned against Stark in the seat of the carriage. They were stopped on the crest of a rise overlooking the bay, facing west across the Pacific.

Though it was a clear morning, Heiko said, "Mist. I have always loved mist. When I look into it, I can almost believe the most impossible dreams will come true."

"Heiko," Stark said.

But she was already gone.

When Stark walked back into his house, he felt dead.

Then he went into Heiko's room and saw Sachiko, still sitting on the floor, sobbing, with the baby held close against her.

He put his arms around them both.

The baby woke, and soon all three were in tears.

1882, CLOUD OF SPARROWS CASTLE

Makoto was so stunned by Genji's revelation, he barely noticed when Genji—that is to say, his father—excused himself and left the room. Not only was his father not the man he had grown up thinking was his father, neither was his mother the woman he had called by that name all his life. His attention returned to the present only when he found himself hand in hand with his little half sister. They were climbing a narrow staircase.

"Where are we going?"

"To meet Lady Shizuka," she said.

"I thought you were Lady Shizuka."

"I meant the first Lady Shizuka. My namesake. You don't seem to know anything at all about yourself or your family. That means you have to start at the beginning."

"Is there a beginning?" Makoto said. "If there is, I'll be very glad." The sequence of lies seemed to spiral endlessly backward.

"There are always beginnings," his sister said. "Without beginnings, how can there be endings? Of course, both are only temporary."

"Temporary? How can something in the past be temporary? It's over and done with."

"Just because there are beginnings and endings doesn't mean anything is really ever over and done with," Shizuka said. "Don't they teach you that in America?"

1308, MUSHINDO ABBEY

Sixteen years had passed since Lady Nowaki had come to the abbey with her damaged child. Often during those years, the Reverend Abbess Suku reflected on the events that caused the banishment. She received frequent inspiration to do so from the screams and moans emanating from

Shizuka's cell at all hours of the day and night. Although exempted by her rank from the menial tasks of the abbey, the Abbess herself often undertook the mad girl's cleaning and feeding. Her ability to touch the filthy body without hesitation and to endure the most disgusting sights and odors with no signs of distress brought much admiration from the other religious inmates. They all agreed the Abbess was a sterling exemplar of Buddha's compassionate way.

Shizuka's behavior did not change for sixteen years, and for sixteen years the Abbess's attention toward her continued with the same unvarying kindness. Though instability and unpredictability were universal laws, the Abbess came to believe that three things would be constant: Shizuka's madness, the incomprehensible nightmares that had afflicted the Abbess herself since Shizuka's arrival, and her own lifelong devotion to prayer.

Then one morning she awoke unusually refreshed, and realized she had passed the night without a single nightmare. She was still contemplating this blessed phenomenon when two nuns arrived, breathless from their rush to reach her.

"Reverend Abbess!"

"Yes?"

"Shizuka is awake, Reverend Abbess."

She knew immediately what the nun meant. There was no sound of mad lamentation coming from that wing of the abbey. Shizuka was quiet only when she was asleep, and not always even then. She was never quiet when she was awake.

The Abbess closed her eyes. She said a silent prayer expressing gratitude for the possibility of Shizuka's redemption from madness. She was about to rise when the coincidence struck her. Shizuka had attained silence on the same day in which she had realized her liberation from the nightmares. Were they related, and if so, might the connection be a sinister one? She closed her eyes again and added a second prayer beseeching the enhanced protection of the guardian deities should the madness have taken a quieter yet more evil form. Then she went with the nuns to Shizuka's cell.

The girl sat on the floor and quietly watched as they entered. Never before had the Abbess seen Shizuka's eyes so clearly focused, her demeanor so like that of a normal person.

"Good morning, Shizuka," the Abbess said.

Shizuka did not answer, but she continued to look at the Abbess with calm interest. The Abbess led the girl by her hand to the bath, cleaned her, and dressed her in fresh clothing. The recovery lasted only as long as the bleeding, then she plunged back into her former chaos.

The next month, when the blood flowed for a second time, she managed a longer respite. In the third month, her hold on reality was much firmer. At first, it was still necessary to change her clothing and bathe her several times each day, as she did not immediately understand the necessity of visiting the outhouse. But she learned before a week had passed. By autumn, a newcomer would have mistaken Shizuka for any other nun, except that she was younger than the others, utterly wordless, and given to observation rather than the usual inmate's daily labor. She had gone from noisy insanity to quiet dim-wittedness. She no longer screamed and cried and huddled in fear for no reason, though sometimes she drifted away as before and became very still, her eyes almost closed, as if she were elsewhere. Sometimes she seemed to understand what was said to her, and sometimes not. She was not quite as others were, though she was much improved. Some nights, the Abbess looked in on her and found her sitting on her bed, eyes open, staring at nothing.

The apparent connection between Shizuka's newfound sanity and the onset of her menstrual cycles worried the Abbess. She was not sure whether it was an appropriate concern, or one only called to mind because of the old superstition that women's blood and witchcraft were intimately linked.

It was soon the time of the year for Lady Kiyomi's annual fall visit. The widow of the late Great Lord of Akaoka and the mother of the present one, she was one of Mushindo Abbey's two principal patrons. The other, Lord Bandan, ruler of Kagami, never visited. The Reverend Abbess Suku especially looked forward to seeing Lady Kiyomi this time. She could witness the miraculous cure wrought by Buddha's infinite compassion, sixteen years of ceaseless prayer, and her generous support from afar.

But when she went to the gate of the abbey to greet the party from Akaoka Domain, she was disappointed not to see her noble patron. Lord Hironobu, her son, had made the journey without her.

"In truth, I have come in her stead," he said. "I regret to tell you my mother is mortally ill. The doctors say she will not survive the winter. I came only because she insisted. I will camp outside the wall overnight, and turn for home in the morning."

"We will recite sutras for her," the Abbess said.

Her sorrow was deep indeed. Fate had intervened with mercilessly cruel timing. Lady Kiyomi would never enjoy the fruits of her kindness to Shizuka. She would learn of it in the letter the Abbess would send back with her son. But she would not have the joy of seeing the miraculous recovery for herself.

She said, "The rules of the abbey do not permit men entry under any conditions. Please wait here. Let us share tea together in the gateway, you without, and I within."

One of the senior nuns leaned closer. She spoke softly so she would not be heard by any of the samurai.

"Is that advisable, Reverend Abbess? The sacred gateway defends Mushindo from visitation by evil. To pitch a canopy under it, to settle midway, is to deny its existence. Demons cannot fail to notice such a vulnerability."

"The canopy is small," the Abbess said, "the settling of brief duration."

She felt great sorrow for Lady Kiyomi's illness and great joy for Shizuka's recovery. In her heart, these emotions existed with impossible simultaneity. A tide cannot be in flow and in flux at the same time. It was this confusion that led her to insist on the invitation. She would come to regret her lapse for the rest of her life.

Nuns on one side and samurai on the other erected the canopy, served the tea, and waited in attendance. Their faces betrayed their unease. What the old nun had whispered, they all believed. Only the Reverend Abbess Suku and Lord Hironobu were comfortable where they were. They reminisced about the past, which seemed longer ago to him than it did to her, he being considerably the younger of the two. When Suku was appointed Abbess of the temple, Hironobu had been a boy of eight.

"I remember standing on that rock," Hironobu said, "and being chastised by Go for making myself a better target for assassins. I don't suppose you remember Go, my bodyguard. He came with Mother and me only that once, and I don't think he met you."

"You were a young boy," the Abbess said. She looked away, drifting into memory. "But you had already won two great victories. Lady Kiyomi was very proud of you."

"I remember— Well, do I remember what happened, or am I remembering something I imagined?" Hironobu laughed. "We are such unreliable witnesses of our own lives."

The Abbess turned back to Hironobu to reply. The movement of his hand holding the teacup halted halfway to his mouth and froze there. He looked past her shoulder into the front courtyard of the temple.

His eyes brightened.

A sudden tension in the muscles of his jaw tightened his visage.

His clenched teeth appeared behind slightly parting lips.

He inhaled sharply.

His breath remained in his lungs as if he were about to dive into deep waters.

The Abbess turned. She saw Shizuka walking toward them. She looked back at Hironobu, who remained transfixed. When she returned her attention yet again to Shizuka, she heard Hironobu exhale in a long, astonished sigh. She saw Shizuka then as Hironobu must have seen her.

In a nun's drab habit, a young woman moving with preternatural grace. Within the hood, a face pale yet vivid, like moonlight. The hands exposed at the ends of the sleeves, small, with long, tapered, feminine fingers not unlike those gracing representations of the Compassionate One. The eyes, too large to be called beautiful, too arresting to be called anything less. Her nose, perfectly shaped yet small enough to avoid excessive prominence. Her mouth, tiny and full, above a chin that perfectly completed the oval of her face.

Seeing her this way for the first time, the Abbess was too stunned to react as quickly as she should have. Before she could speak, before she could order a nun to take the girl away, Shizuka stood next to the canopy. She looked at Hironobu and brightened, as if recognizing him.

Shizuka smiled and said, "*Anata.*" You.

Nuns and samurai gasped. It was the first word Shizuka had ever spoken, but this was not the reason for their shock. "Anata" was far too familiar a way for a nun, or any woman, to address a man she had just met, much less a lord. Even worse, she had said it softly, with lengthened vowels and the slightest of feminine lisps, a manner reminiscent of its usage in the bedchamber, where in certain circumstances the one simple word was expressive of the utmost intimacy.

"Shizuka," the Abbess said. She stood, taking care to put herself between the two. "Return to the temple now." Without being bidden, two of the nuns came to her assistance, each firmly taking an arm on each side of the girl, and immediately leading her away. "I am sorry, my lord. The girl is not well. She doesn't know what she's saying."

"Shizuka," Hironobu said. "That was Shizuka?" He continued to watch her until she entered the temple and could not be seen.

"She is insane, my lord. Thus she has been here since her infancy, will always be here, will die here."

"When I was a boy, on every visit with Mother I schemed to find a way to see her. There were outrageous rumors. Some people even said she wasn't human, or not completely so, anyway. My friends and I speculated on the nature of her fur. Badger, bear, fox."

The Abbess said, "She might as well be part badger or fox. She cannot speak sensibly, or take care of herself, not even the most fundamental tasks of cleanliness. There are days when she is so unhinged, she must be confined in isolation. Then, she must be cleaned, for she fouls herself."

"How unfortunate," Hironobu said.

Reverend Abbess Suku hoped her discouraging words were discouraging enough.

They were not.

Hironobu left early the following morning as he had said he would. But his letter to the Abbess informing her of the death of his mother was shortly followed by Hironobu himself. His excuse for his return was Lady Kiyomi's ashes, which he brought with him.

"I ask that her ashes be kept in Mushindo temple for one hundred days," Hironobu said. "After that period of blessing, they will be returned to the columbarium of Cloud of Sparrows."

He bowed and placed the urn on the table before him. As before, they met in the open. This time, however, the canopy under which they sat was set up entirely outside the walls of the abbey, nowhere near the gate or any other place affording a view into the grounds.

"It will be done, my lord," the Abbess said, accepting the urn with a deep bow. "Sutras will be recited without pause for one hundred days. However, your saintly mother needs no such assistance to be insured a most beneficent rebirth. Her own good works during her lifetime guarantee it."

"Thank you, Reverend Abbess."

"When the hundred days have been accomplished, I will personally deliver her urn to you." The Abbess had not left the temple for more than a few hours at a time since her appointment. Her reluctance to enter the world was less, however, than her fear of Hironobu's return. The more often he was near Mushindo, the greater the danger that he and Shizuka would meet again somehow. The first meeting, though over in a few brief moments, seemed to her frighteningly portentous.

"For that kindness also, thank you, Reverend Abbess. But it won't be necessary for you to undertake such an arduous journey. I will remain here until the hundred days have elapsed."

"My lord?"

Hironobu gestured vaguely at the surrounding woods. "During my last visit, I found unexpected pleasure being in this untended wilderness. Surely it must be closer to what the gods created than the pruned and captive little forests of the south. So I have decided to build a small lodge and undertake a kind of bucolic retreat."

The Abbess said, "I have always understood the mountainous forests of Shikoku to be among the wildest in the realm. Have they not swallowed up whole armies of invaders? Can these little hills and sparse woodlands really compare?"

She spoke with a calmness that belied her complete absence of equanimity. It was no stand of pines, mountain stream, or valley prospect that had captured Hironobu's interest. His eyes did not wander periodically to the gateway as they spoke. He never looked that way even once. Only by constantly thinking of it could he so perfectly avoid it. To the Abbess, this was in itself proof of his true desires.

"Shikoku's wildness is exaggerated in the telling of it," Hironobu said.

"What of your domain? Won't your enemies make mischief during such a long absence?"

"Not with Go in charge. No one would dare."

"And what of Go himself?"

"He has protected me and guided me like a second father since my earliest childhood. If I cannot trust him, I cannot trust the sun and the moon to stay in the sky, or the earth to remain beneath my feet."

"Earthquakes frequently rend our land," the Abbess said. "Perhaps there is a lesson there."

Hironobu laughed. "Obviously I am no poet. My imagery doesn't quite match my meaning."

Since Hironobu would not leave, the Abbess did the only thing she could. She assigned nuns to keep constant guard on the gateway of the temple and the hallway leading to Shizuka's cell. Shizuka was never left alone. At night, she was locked into her cell.

The days passed without incident, then the weeks. The sound of chanted sutras never ceased. The Abbess began to think her suspicions had been excessive.

She met with Hironobu once a week outside the walls of the temple. They spoke only of Lady Kiyomi. Hironobu seemed much at ease. Perhaps the forests here were closer to the creation than those of the more populated parts of the realm. Perhaps the blessings of the gods would protect them all.

One night, she woke to find herself already sitting up in her bed. A freezing cold sweat soaked her clothes. Her body burned with fever. She had no memory of a nightmare, only a sense of dread that did not fade away. She rose quickly and, without changing her clothes, rushed to Shizuka's cell. The cold autumn night knifed through her wet kimono and her feverish flesh straight to the innermost marrow of her bones.

The nun on guard outside the cell sat in the lotus posture. But her head lolled off to one side, and a soft snoring marked the coming and going of her unconscious breaths.

The door to the cell was ajar.

Shizuka was not within.

The Abbess ran out of the temple, through the courtyard, out the gate, and straight to the lodge Hironobu had built in the densest part of the forest between Mushindo Abbey and the winter stream that was yet in this season no more than a fall of smooth rocks.

Hironobu was not there. Nor was Shizuka. Nor were any of the lord's samurai.

The Abbess looked in every direction. She saw no trails, no signs of recent passage. In despair, she threw back her head, and her sight went skyward.

The faint crescent of the new moon cast eerie beams her way.

· · · · ·

The Abbess saw nothing. All around her, she heard many voices.

"She will die," someone sobbed. "Then what will become of us?"

"We will continue on Buddha's Way."

"What are you saying? Without the Reverend Abbess Suku, there is no Way. Lord Hironobu and Lord Bandan will abandon us."

"She's right. Mushindo is far from their domains. It is only because of the Reverend Abbess that they have any interest in such a distant place."

She remembered looking up at the night. She opened her eyes. She was in her own room, with her nuns gathered around her bed. Many were in tears.

"Reverend Abbess!"

"Shizuka," the Abbess said.

"It is the middle of the night, Reverend Abbess. She is in her cell."

"Show me." She tried to rise and found it took more strength than she had. Two nuns practically carried her from her room to Shizuka's. The nun who had been asleep was wide awake.

"Let me see."

The nuns lifted her up to the tiny observation window. Shizuka was asleep on her side, facing the wall.

"Who brought me to my room?"

"Reverend Abbess?"

"From the woods. Who brought me back to the temple?"

The nuns looked at each other.

"Reverend Abbess, we heard you cry out in your room, so we came. You were feverish, halfway between consciousness and sleep, and could go in neither direction. We have been sitting with you for hours."

Here was trickery. Trickery, torture, and deceit. The nuns were innocent. They were not part of it. They were only being fooled. Hironobu had been bewitched. Shizuka was using her newfound dark powers to escape from this holy place and make mischief in the world. The Abbess was not taken in. She knew she had been in the forest. She had not imagined it. Under Shizuka's spell, Hironobu had carried the Abbess back to her room. Cloaked in the witch's invisibility, they were seen by no one. This was also why, when the Abbess went to Hironobu's camp, she had not seen Shizuka or Hironobu. They were hidden by a spell.

"She's dead," she heard a nun say.

"No, she's fainted again," another said.

"Is it the plague?"

"There are no signs of it. I think it is a brain fever. My cousin had it. He went mad and never recovered."

The Abbess saw nothing. She concentrated her attention on her hearing. She listened as the sound of distant sobs faded away into silence. She continued listening for a long, long time, but heard not so much as the beating of her own heart.

· · · · ·

Later that night—or had that night passed and another come?—the Abbess awoke. Instead of her previous agitation, she felt a great calm. The solution had come to her unbidden. There were two ways to insure that Shizuka did not escape. The first was to kill her. This the Abbess could not do. All disciples of the Compassionate One were sworn to abjure the taking of life, human or animal. She must follow the other course.

She slipped out of her room. She could not go to the meditation hall, for the sutras were still being read for Lady Kiyomi. She went to the kitchen and folded herself into the lotus posture. She sat in meditation until the first faint light signaled the imminent yielding of the hour of the rabbit to that of the dragon, then rose and went to Shizuka's cell. From the kitchen, she brought with her the long knife she used to slice vegetables.

The Abbess would save Shizuka from the curse. She would slash away her beauty, for without it, Hironobu would not want her, nor would any man. Shizuka would remain in the abbey where she belonged. The Abbess would cut out Shizuka's tongue, for she had begun to speak, and a witch can utter only lies. Shizuka would remain speechless, as she should. The Abbess would blind her, for sight had only brought her delusion. Blind, she would return to her former agony, but she would no longer be misled. The Abbess would take care of Shizuka as she always had, with patience and compassion, until the end of their days.

This was as it should be. The Abbess's heart was steady, without doubt, and so was the hand that gripped the knife.

"Reverend Abbess."

The nun on duty outside of Shizuka's cell looked at her fearfully as she approached. The nun's eyes flitted back and forth from the Abbess's face to the knife. She stood.

"Reverend Abbess," she said again.

The Abbess did not answer. She went past the nun, opened the door, and entered the cell. She strode into the darkness to the bed of the sleeping girl, knelt, and whipped away the coverlet.

Shizuka was already awake. She looked up at the Abbess and said the second word she ever spoke.

"Mother," Shizuka said.

The Abbess stumbled back. She felt hands gripping her. She heard exclamations. The knife fell from her grasp.

. . . . .

They were just outside the entry gate of Mushindo Abbey. All the nuns were there. So were Lord Hironobu, Shizuka, and many samurai mounted on fine warhorses. The Reverend Abbess sat quietly and listened to the conversation. Was she there or seeing it in a dream? She wasn't sure. So she kept silent and listened.

"It is fortunate that you were here when the tragedy occurred," said a nun.

"I am grateful I was," Hironobu said.

"So much has happened in a hundred days," the nun said. "So much to celebrate, so much to mourn. But is this not true of every step on Buddha's Way?"

"I'm glad she was well enough to attend the wedding," another nun said. "She seemed to enjoy it."

"I wonder if she will ever regain the power of speech," another said.

"How sad," the first nun said, "that she should lose it just as you gain it, Lady Shizuka."

"Yes," Shizuka said. "It is very sad indeed."

A nun raised a box wrapped in white cloth and offered it to Hironobu.

"May Lady Kiyomi forever enjoy the peace of the Compassionate One," she said.

The troop prepared to depart. Hironobu helped Shizuka into the saddle of a horse before mounting his own.

The nun said, "May you be blessed with health and prosperity and every treasure of family life, my lord, my lady." All the nuns bowed.

The Abbess rose to her feet.

She said, "May you and all your blood be cursed with beauty and genius forever."

"Reverend Abbess!"

Hironobu said to Shizuka, "I am sorry for her. If there were more we could do than secure her care, I would."

"Her curse—" Shizuka said.

"She's mad," Hironobu said. "Beauty and genius are blessings, not curses."

Shizuka said nothing. She looked at the Abbess and their eyes met. Neither looked away as the travelers departed. Hironobu may be ignorant, but the Abbess knew Shizuka understood the truth, because it had afflicted them both.

Beauty and genius were curses.

The Abbess no longer knew whether she was an old woman or a maiden, a dreamer or a lunatic, or whether any of these distinctions mattered. Questions without answers consumed her energy night and day. She never uttered another word.

The following spring, she died in her sleep. The Reverend Abbess Suku, who had been Lord Bandan's beautiful daughter, Lady Nowaki, had not attained her thirty-second year.

1882, GENJI'S ESTATE ON THE TAMA RIVER OUTSIDE TOKYO

As he waited to be received, Tsuda reflected on the enormous changes that had occurred in so short a time. This city was itself a prime example. When he was a young man, it was Edo, the capital of the Shogun whose clan, the Tokugawa, had ruled Japan for two and a half centuries. Then they had seemed likely to rule it forever. Now not only were the Tokugawas gone, so was the entire ancient office of Shogun, and Edo as well, replaced by Tokyo. It was more than a name change. Tokyo was the new capital of the Imperial family, which had resided in Kyoto for a millennium. The Emperor Mutsuhito was the first to reign from Tokyo, and the first to actually rule from anywhere for six hundred years.

Tsuda's own life was an equal example of change on a smaller, individual scale. He had been born a peasant in distant Akaoka Domain. His talent for constructing buildings of pleasing design had attracted the attention of the Great Lord of the domain, Lord Genji, and he had been awarded an important contract, the building of a Christian chapel. Tsuda's other talent, that of placing his structures in fortunate locations, was a credit to his serious, even religiously dedicated, practice of feng shui. It was the conjunction of the two that had led to his present elevated position as associate, advisor, and business partner of his former lord. In determining the location for the chapel he was to build, Tsuda had discovered a mysterious trunk decorated with a wild and barbaric depiction of blue mountains and a red dragon, and containing scrolls of an even more mysterious nature. He still did not know what the scrolls signified, though they were widely believed to be the legendary, prophetic, magical, long-lost *Autumn Bridge* writings. Whatever they were, the discovery had changed his life.

A maid entered and said, "Mr. Stark will see you now, Mr. Tsuda."

Makoto Stark was standing in the garden next to the arrangement of rocks and stones. Tsuda had expected to be received in a more formal manner, this being their first meeting. It was often said of Americans that they favored informality to a fault. This was apparently true. Keeping his disapproval from his face, Tsuda bowed.

"Mr. Stark, it is a pleasure to meet you at last."

"Thank you, Mr. Tsuda."

Makoto extended his hand. After the briefest of hesitations, Tsuda took it and shook it vigorously.

"Your father, the senior Mr. Stark, has spoken of you often. In that distant way, I almost feel that I know you."

"Then the advantage is definitely yours. The more I learn of myself, the less I know."

He said it as if it bothered him, not as the usual convention identifying self-discovery with the void. That caused Tsuda to refrain from replying with the conventional words about the liberating nature of Mushindo meditative practices. He didn't think Makoto was talking about meditation.

"It's so, yes?" Tsuda said, which was an even more conventional remark, applicable to virtually any situation, and meaning variously, Yes, No, Maybe, I agree, I disagree, I don't know what you're talking about, You have my sympathy, Please continue, Please stop. . . .Tone was important in setting the meaning; so, since he was unsure of what Makoto meant in the first place, Tsuda made his as vague as he could in order to obscure his own meaning, which in fact he did not have at all. Instinctively, he feared

Makoto would move the conversation onto dangerous ground. He hoped the young man would not be too American about it if he did—that is, too specific and too blunt. That hope was immediately shattered.

"Mr. Tsuda, how well do you know my parents?"

"Mr. Stark and I have been in business together—primarily import and export, and banking—for close to fifteen years. We meet once a year, usually in Honolulu in recent years. A convenient midway point for us. I have never had the honor of meeting Mrs. Stark."

"How about before she became Mrs. Stark?"

Tsuda was beginning to regret meeting Makoto at all. He said, "I was not then familiar with Mr. Stark or Lord Genji on a social basis. I had no occasion to meet the future Mrs. Stark."

"I see." Makoto noticed Tsuda's discomfort and mistook it for a physical one. "Oh, excuse me, Mr. Tsuda, let's go in. I forget that not everyone enjoys standing in gardens as much as I do."

The interior of the palace was almost entirely Western in design and furnishing. Makoto had not yet seen it in its entirety—he had been a guest here for only two days, and the palace was vast—but so far as he knew, there was only one small wing of traditional Japanese design. It said something about Genji that he spent most of his time in that part of the palace.

Tsuda accepted Scotch instead of sake, though it was rather early in the day for it. He had developed a preference for Western liquors.

Quite abruptly, Makoto said, "Did you know Heiko?"

"Heiko? Do you mean the famous geisha? I knew *of* her. Everyone did in those days."

"You were never her patron?"

"I?" Tsuda laughed. The Scotch was cheering him up quite rapidly. "Even if I could have afforded it—which I could not even if I sold everything I owned and stole everything belonging to everyone I knew—someone of her exalted stature would never have deigned to entertain someone like me. No, only lords enjoyed that privilege."

"Including Lord Genji?"

"Yes. They were lovers. That's no secret. Their romance was like a storybook adventure. I don't doubt that one day there will be a Kabuki play about it."

"Tsuda, what are you doing here?"

Lord Saemon paused at the doorway. The maid leading the way went to her knees to wait for him. Saemon was dressed, as was his habit these days, in an elegantly tailored English suit. His hair was closely trimmed, not unlike the style lately favored by the Emperor. He had no beard, but compensated for it with a luxuriant Bismarckian mustache.

"Lord Saemon," Tsuda said, getting to his feet and bowing. "I am here as a guest of Mr. Stark."

"Mr. Stark?"

"Mr. Makoto Stark," Tsuda said, "the senior Mr. Stark's son. He is visiting with Lord Genji."

"Ah." Saemon stepped into the room. "At last we meet. I have been looking forward to making your acquaintance for many years, Mr. Stark."

"Why?" Makoto said.

Saemon blinked. "I beg your pardon?"

Tsuda had never seen Saemon taken by surprise in all the years he had known him. This was a first. Not even such a wily son of a wily spy chief was prepared to deal with Americans. Tsuda suppressed his smile as best he could.

"Why have you been so interested in me? I am no one. Many years ago, I was even less."

"Well, naturally, I would be interested, Mr. Stark, since you are the child of—the son of—the only son of—a very important friend of Japan."

"A friend of Japan," Makoto said. "I have never heard him called that before, and I have heard him called many things. You know him well, then?"

"Better than most who can claim an acquaintance, but not as well as his close friends."

The maid who had led Saemon into the palace now knelt at the doorway.

She said, "Do you wish to wait here, Lord Saemon?"

"Yes, if Mr. Stark and Mr. Tsuda have no objection."

"Quite the opposite," Tsuda said. He drew a chair for Saemon and bowed. "In fact, you may be able to help Mr. Stark where I cannot. He was asking about Heiko. You and your father both knew her, I believe?"

"Heiko," Saemon said, and smiled. "My father knew her well, I only in passing."

Tsuda was glad he had introduced a subject that pleased Lord Saemon. He was a very powerful man, likely to be a minister in a future cabinet, perhaps even Minister of Finance. For a banker like Tsuda, the Minister of Finance was the closest thing to the earthly spokesman of the gods.

"What is your interest in Heiko, Mr. Stark?" Saemon declined Tsuda's offer of Scotch and accepted a cup of tea from the maid. "During her heyday as a geisha, you would have been—" He halted abruptly as if something had occurred to him. To cover the pause, he sipped his tea before continuing. "You would have been very young."

"More accurately, I would have been nonexistent. I was born in 1862. I understand her career ended a year prior, along with her residency in Japan."

"Yes, I recall," Saemon said. "She went to California, accompanied by your father. The circumstances surrounding her departure were rather mysterious."

"Those circumstances being?"

"I don't know that I should speak of them. I would be in the position of repeating rumors. Nothing was ever definitively established."

"I'm willing to settle for rumors."

"Very well. With your indulgence, then." Saemon bowed. "Heiko was thought to be an agent of the Shogun's secret police. That would explain her frequent contact with my father, since he was at the time the chief of that organization. It also goes a long way toward explaining her departure from Japan, since she would be less vulnerable to retaliation by those she might have injured in that capacity. However, it doesn't explain why she should have received your father's protection. The senior Mr. Stark was a close friend of Lord Genji, then as now, and Lord Genji and my father were mortal enemies."

"Were they? I understood you and Lord Genji to be friends."

"We Japanese have endless webs of vengeance stretching across the centuries. If we do not wipe them away, we will never catch up with the West. Lord Genji and I have left the past behind."

"How enlightened of you both," Makoto said.

To Tsuda, he did not sound sincere. But that might only have been the effect of the slight oddities in his Japanese speech. Tsuda refilled his glass and continued to listen. So far, he had not learned anything. But it seemed that important revelations might be made at any moment—revelations that could lead to profit.

"Please continue," Makoto said.

"Then there was the massacre shortly before Heiko left. An outcast village without any strategic value was burned to the ground and all its inhabitants slaughtered. They posed no threat to anyone, nor were they of any value, dead or alive. Very strange."

"Outcasts?"

"An evil of the Tokugawa era, now outlawed. There are no outcasts anymore. All Japanese have equal rights under the law, just as in any civilized country of the West."

This was utterly untrue, as Tsuda and every Japanese knew. The laws had been enacted, not with any intention of enforcement, but only to clothe a naked body whose attributes the Western powers found offensive. If they did not see, they were satisfied. It was not, to Tsuda's mind, wrong in any way. The purpose of politics was not the attainment of an impossible perfection, a perfection about which no two nations could ever agree in any case, but the smooth functioning of different interests through the wise balancing and meshing of hypocrisies. In this art, the two lords, Saemon and Genji, were masters, each in his own way. How fortunate he was to be in their service.

Makoto said, "Was Heiko an outcast?"

Saemon and Tsuda simultaneously said "What?"

"Excuse me, sirs," Tsuda said, bowing, red in the face. "I didn't mean to speak. I was only, that is to say—"

That is to say what? What could be said of such an outrageous, scandalous, insulting, and incredibly dangerous remark? Dangerous not only for the one who had uttered it, but also for those who had heard it. Especially for him! Saemon was a Great Lord—yes, there were officially no more Great Lords, but the prestige, power, connections, loyalties, and reach remained to many of them—he was a leader among veterans of the Restoration, he had powerful friends with similar characteristics, and he knew secrets he could use to pressure those who would otherwise do nothing to help him. Tsuda, in pathetic contrast, was no more than a counter and keeper of monies. Why had he come to see Makoto Stark? What a fool. Perhaps soon he would be a dead fool!

"Why are you surprised?" Makoto said. "The connection seems rather obvious."

"Not to us," Saemon said. He said nothing more, and continued to look at Makoto with a calm that seemed out of place in the circumstances.

. . . . .

"All right," Makoto said, "he's gone. Say what you have to say."

"What makes you think I have anything to say?" Saemon said. Tsuda had scurried away like a rat from a building about to ignite in flames. How could anyone who let his fear show so plainly think he could be the equal of men born samurai?

"Please, Lord Saemon. I don't mind being looked down on for being an American in a Japanese body. But I utterly resent being treated as if I am of diminished mental capacity. I assure you, I am not."

"No, Mr. Stark, you most certainly are not."

This was an opportunity of rare dimensions for Saemon. It was also a lethal trap that would take his head instead of his enemies' if he made the slightest error.

He said, "There is great danger here, Mr. Stark, for all concerned. The danger goes beyond mere truth and falsity. The suggestion that a nobleman of Lord Genji's rank would ever have touched an outcast is unacceptable. I must urge you never to repeat it."

"I don't understand. Ranks have been abolished, and you yourself told me there are no outcasts anymore. Who would care?"

"Everyone," Saemon said. "Lineage is of paramount importance here. If the lordly blood of the Okumichi clan had been polluted, it would be a stain from which no Okumichi could ever be cleansed. Lives would be ruined. Blood would run."

"Polluted, you say."

"That is how it would be viewed."

"Is that how you view it?"

"Of course not," Saemon said. "Destiny is in the hands of the individual, not in the dead grip of ancestors." He chose his words carefully. Whether lies were believed or not depended greatly upon their presentation. "We were born to create ourselves."

"Were we?" Makoto poured an inch of Scotch into a glass and held it up to the light. He put it down without drinking it. "So what do you advise, Lord Saemon?"

"Talk to your father." Saemon paused. The future turned on his words, and Makoto's reaction to them. "I have always found Matthew Stark to be honest to a fault."

Makoto said, "Matthew Stark is not my father."

Saemon felt such a surge of joy, his heart began to race. Every effort he had made to discover Genji's secret had been frustrated for fifteen years. He had suspected at the time that Makoto was Genji's child, not Stark's. But when Genji made no move to bring Makoto to Japan, Saemon had given up that line of thought. There was no reason he could think of that would permit Genji to leave his son in America. Heiko an outcast! The answer, as well as the tool to exploit it, had walked right into his hands. Exhibiting no sign of his excitement, he said, "I don't understand, Mr. Stark. How can that be?"

· · · · ·

Whenever he had been angry before, Makoto had felt his temperature rise. Now he was in a rage that made any previous anger seem like minor irritation, yet instead of heat, he felt cold. If anyone touched him, he was certain they would think they were touching ice.

Genji had told worse than a lie, struck a crueler blow than abandonment, taken more than his rightful name. He had stolen Makoto's entire life from him. All his memories, all his experiences, were false. They didn't belong to him. They belonged to someone who had never existed. At twenty years of age, he had been reborn as the son of an evil manipulator and a glorified prostitute. Even worse was in store, if Shizuka had told the truth. One of them would eventually evidence a hereditary affliction that was some form of seizure. She had spoken of it as a prophetic power, but that was obviously the result of comforting lies told to her by her father. By *his* father.

So who was Makoto?

He was the angel of vengeance. He would cleanse sin with blood. Genji was to speak with Imperial ministers this afternoon. Makoto would intercept him at the palace. It was the perfect venue. Let Genji's son, of whom he was so ashamed he had failed to acknowledge him for two decades, let this ignored son be the one to end his perfidy. Makoto took the revolver from his waistband and checked its chambers. The .32-caliber revolver, a gift from his father—or rather the man who had pretended to be his father—was fully loaded and ready to fire.

He stood to leave. As he turned toward the doorway, in front of a scroll painting in an alcove was a set of samurai swords, long and short, in a stand.

There was the final perfection.

He would kill Genji with this weapon, a sword from his own palace. With a blade that symbolized the supposedly stainless soul of the samurai, he would end the life of a man whose stance of honor was no more than a pose and a lie.

Makoto Okumichi took the shorter of the two swords from the stand, hid it under his coat, and left.

THE IMPERIAL PALACE, TOKYO

Genji's carriage slowed as it approached the bridge across the moat.

He still habitually thought of the great castle as the Shogun's Palace, in the same way the city resided in his mind as Edo rather than Tokyo. The overthrow of the Tokugawa Shogunate, the Restoration of the Emperor, the abolition of the samurai class, the dissolution of the domains, the unprecedented intrusion of foreigners into Japan, the destruction of the last heroic proponents of bushido—all these events had occurred in the span of less than ten years. Genji received more credit for these changes than he deserved, and more blame.

There had been seven attempts on his life since the Restoration. Each had failed because they were destined to fail. He would die by assassination, but not for many years. This he had foreseen. It would be at the Diet, which did not yet exist, and he would die in the arms of his daughter, Shizuka. In his vision, she was a young woman. Today, she was still a little girl. Many years remained guaranteed to him.

The carriage halted at the Sakurada Gate, the one through which Genji would enter the palace. Imperial guards came forward to verify his identity. In the few moments when they and his own guards were focused on each other, a young man in Western clothing suddenly rushed at the carriage, pulling a short sword from beneath his coat as he ran. He was only two paces away from Genji's window before the guards noticed him.

It was too late.

Genji saw the sword aimed directly at him.

In another instant, it would enter his chest.

The vision of his death, the one that had guided him for so many years, had been flawed. His assassination was not in the distant future. It was now.

He felt cheated. He was to receive three visions in his life. Only two had materialized, and one had been fatally defective.

Did he recognize his young assassin?

But the blade didn't reach Genji. Even as it plunged toward his heart, another young man stepped in front of the carriage with a sword of his own.

The two men impaled each other amidst their mingled cries of defiance and pain. Genji didn't recognize the failed assassin. But he did know his defender.

It was his recently arrived son, Makoto.

MUSHINDO ABBEY

The Reverend Abbess Jintoku peeked into the guest's room. Makoto Stark was still asleep. It was highly irregular to have a man resident in the abbey. In the old days—which for Japan was as recently as fifteen years ago, depending on which old days you were talking about—it would have been impossible. But Lord Genji had personally approved it. The serious nature of Makoto's injuries, combined with the valorous conditions under which he had sustained them, demanded an exception to the governing rule. So Lord Genji said. There was more to it than that. There was always more to everything than anyone said there was.

In this case, it was rather obvious.

The young man in question was the one who had made an enigmatic visit some weeks earlier. He had disputed the docent's version of the famous Battle of Mushindo in 1861. He knew, he said, because his parents had been there. When the Abbess asked who his parents were, he said that was a very good question, and departed.

His appearance also spoke volumes. During his earlier visit, he had reminded the Abbess of someone she could not quite place. Now the resemblance was so apparent to her, she marveled she had not known immediately. Of course, it was much easier to see when he was side by side with Lord Genji. The multitude of potential relationships was fascinating. He could be the lord's nephew, brother, or son. Of these, the most intriguing possibility was naturally the last.

If he was Lord Genji's son, who was the mother?

He had said his parents had been in the battle. Only three women had been in Lord Genji's party that day. One of them, Lady Emily, was not a possibility. She had given birth to only one child before her untimely demise, a daughter. That left Lady Hanako and Lady Heiko. It couldn't be the former. She had married Lord Hidé around the time of the battle, and had presented her husband with a child within the year. Lord Iwao, who had been that child, was close in age to Makoto, and bore no brotherly similarity to him whatsoever. That meant his mother must be Lady Heiko. Could it be? If she had been his mother, Lord Genji would have taken her into his household along with the child. He would have made her an official concubine—it was still the old days then—if he had not actually married her. He certainly wouldn't have sent both of them away to California and let his son adopt another man's name, even if that man was as good a friend as Matthew Stark.

So Makoto must be mistaken, or a liar. Or the Abbess was failing to see something vital. If there was truth to be discovered, she might learn it before Makoto left the abbey. That would be some considerable time in the future, since his injuries were serious. It was a wonder he had not died. It was fortunate for him that the sword had missed his heart. It was fortunate for Lord Genji that Makoto had been armed with a sword of his own, or the assassin might have accomplished his goal. The Abbess had to wonder, though, what Makoto was doing with a short sword concealed on his person near the entrance to the Imperial Palace. The assassin had done precisely the same.

On her way to Goro's garden, the Abbess met Lord Genji, who had just arrived.

Bowing deeply, she said, "My lord."

"How is Makoto today?"

"Better, I think. He's working in the garden with Goro."

"Have you been bothered again by reporters?"

"No, my lord. Not for more than two weeks. Perhaps interest is declining." The Abbess said this as a matter of politesse rather than of belief. Her interest had not declined. Why would anyone else's?

"I hope so," Genji said. He didn't seem to believe what she had said, either.

· · · · ·

"I went to the palace to kill you," Makoto said. He dug around the bush to loosen the soil.

"Had you just watched," Genji said, "the other would have done it for you." He stood nearby in the shade of a pine tree.

"Yes."

"Why did you protect me if you came to kill me?"

"I don't know," Makoto said. "When I saw him, I felt he was going to cheat me of my due, and I had been cheated enough. That doesn't make sense, does it? If anyone was going to take your life, it had to be me."

"Don't be so regretful," Genji said, smiling. "You will have other opportunities. Recover your health and plan anew."

Makoto laughed, briefly, then gasped and put his hand on his chest. "Yes, I will plan anew. Completely anew. When the sword went into my chest, I had a sudden realization, or, that is to say, I saw a face in my mind's eye. Do you know who?"

"Heiko."

"No, Lord Saemon. I realized in that instant that he had manipulated me, and very skillfully, too."

"You're not saying Saemon told you to kill me?"

"Quite the opposite. He said everything he could say to win my forgiveness and forbearance for you. I stress *said*. His meaning was not in harmony with his words. He's very good at that. Haven't you noticed?"

"Of course. I have always found Lord Saemon to be the opposite of a man of his word, not in the sense that he lies but in that if you rest yourself upon them, you inevitably slip."

"Yet you associate with him quite closely, and rely on his advice."

"It is appearance and performance rather than actual reliance," Genji said. "Since Lord Saemon knows this, there is yet another layer of truth and deception beneath that one, and so on and so on, and so on also for me."

"Everyone says you know the future before it happens," Makoto said, "but here you are, a prophet, talking like a complete idiot."

"Oh? Is it not prudent to keep your enemy where you can see him? For what reason do you disapprove?"

"You're outwitting yourself, and so is he. It is only a question of whose foolish cleverness will backfire first." Makoto dug out a weed and shook the dirt free from its roots before setting it aside.

Goro, hoe in hand, came into the garden, went to an edge, and began to more clearly define the divide between garden and walkway.

Makoto said, "Sometimes the blunt, direct route of the dullard is the best way to the destination." He looked at Genji. "Are you really prophetic?"

"One in every generation of us has been for six hundred years," Genji said, "but not in the way people imagine."

"Yes, so Shizuka told me. I suppose you put her up to it."

"I trusted that in her guileless and direct way, she would be better at explaining than I."

"Shouldn't I have been told earlier? The way she described it, it sounds more like a curse than a blessing."

"There are many things I should have said to you long ago. One thing unspoken led to another, and another, and another."

Makoto shrugged. "It doesn't really matter. Shizuka will be the prophetess. I have had no visions."

"Neither has she. The appearance of the facility is itself unpredictable. It often comes at puberty, especially for females. It may come much later. There's no way to tell which of you will have it."

"I don't suppose there's any way to prepare for it," Makoto said.

"Beyond accepting the possibility, none," Genji said.

He paused long enough that Makoto thought the conversation was over. He was about to move to another part of the garden when Genji spoke again.

He said, "In the matter of acknowledgment, I am ready to do so. I am also ready to declare you my heir in Shizuka's place."

Makoto laughed. He knew it was not polite, but he couldn't help it.

"There is no point in an acknowledgment, Lord Genji. I needed it twenty years ago. It is useless now. As for an heir, you have one, and she is entirely appropriate."

Makoto joined Goro and began helping him with the edging.

"Goro," Makoto said.

"Goro," Goro said, smiling.

"Makoto," Makoto said.

Still smiling, Goro said "Kimi" and returned his full attention to where the blade of the hoe intersected the earth.

Makoto smiled at Genji. "I am determined to get him to say my name before I leave."

"If he does, he will have named you his successor, and you won't be able to leave, ever."

Makoto and Genji looked at each other. Makoto laughed. Genji only smiled that small smile of his.

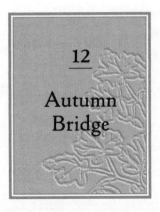

12

Autumn Bridge

Beauty, youth, and allure fade even as they first appear. In the earliest mists of Spring, we see the Autumn Bridge.

AKI-NO-HASHI

(1311)

1857, THE RUINS OF MUSHINDO MONASTERY

The children of Yamanaka Village often played in the ruins of an old temple on a hill above the valley. Most of them were afraid of the place. There were always strange sounds which, if they were not exactly like the groaning of tortured souls, or the howling of ghosts, or the cackling of demons, were close enough to make the children imagine all manner of terrifying possibilities. This was one of the reasons they went there, for like all children they dearly loved being frightened, so long as they could stop being frightened before it became too much to bear. The other reason they played in the ruins was because Kimi, the little girl who was the ringleader of the group, liked to play there. She liked to play there because, among them all, she was one of only two who were not afraid, even though she was one of the youngest and littlest. The other child who was not afraid was Goro. Goro wasn't afraid because he was a fool, like his mother, the village idiot woman. He didn't look like a child, because he was bigger than any man in the village, much bigger, and had the face of a man, rather than a child. In fact, he might have been a man, but he acted so childish, the children never questioned his presence among them.

One day, when they went there to play, one of the children pointed and screamed.

"Look! A ghost!"

A dim outline of a being was barely visible near the remnant of a stone wall that once might have encircled the temple. Several of the more timid children began to run away.

"It's not a ghost," Kimi said, "it's a man."

He was sitting so still, and his clothing was so dull and faded, he seemed to emerge like a shadow from the wall itself. He was old, with a shaved head, sunken cheeks, and bright eyes that maintained a very steady gaze. His tunic might once have been white, many years ago. On the ground next to him was a conical serge hat and a wooden staff.

"Who are you?" Kimi asked.

He said, "A renunciant and a pilgrim."

Kimi knew a renunciant was one who gave up the world. A pilgrim was one who traveled to seek enlightenment or perform penance. No one in the village had ever been either. There was nothing for poor farmers to give up. Everything they did and everything they had belonged to their lord. Poor farmers did not seek enlightenment, either, because exhausted people on the constant verge of starvation need sleep and food far more than wisdom. They did not have to travel afar to perform penance, even if they had time to travel, which they did not, because their every waking moment was a penance for sins they didn't even know they had committed, in some past life or another. If this old man was a renunciant, perhaps a visitation by a Buddha or god or demon had changed his life. He could have interesting tales to tell.

"What have you given up?" Kimi asked.

"Almost everything," the monk said.

"Where have you traveled?"

"Almost nowhere."

Well, this conversation wasn't going anywhere either. She decided to switch to easier questions. "What's your name?"

"Zengen," the old monk said.

"What does Zengen mean?"

"What does any name mean?"

"Well, my name means 'without equal,' " Kimi said. "His name is Goro, only it isn't really Goro, we just call him that, short for 'Gorotsuki,' which is "rascal." I don't know why. He doesn't do rascally things. So, what does Zengen mean?"

"What does any name mean?" Zengen said again.

"I told you what mine means. 'Without equal.' " Kimi was beginning to wonder whether the monk was a holy man or merely a lunatic. It was sometimes hard to tell the difference between the two, especially if he was a monk of one of the Zen sects, which his name led her to believe he was. But that could just be a crazy man being clever.

"And what does 'without equal' mean?"

"It means no one can match me, I guess."

"What does it mean that no one can match you?"

"What does anything mean?" Kimi said. "If you keep asking, you can keep asking forever and never really get an answer."

The old monk put his hands together in gassho, the Buddhist gesture of respect, and bowed. He said, "You're welcome."

"You're welcome? Am I supposed to thank you?"

"What you do or don't do is for you to decide," the old monk said.

"What am I supposed to thank you for?"

"If you keep asking, you can keep asking forever and never really get an answer."

"That's what I just told you."

"Thank you," Zengen said, and bowed in gassho again.

Kimi laughed. Then she returned his bow, putting her hands together the way he did. She still didn't know whether the old man was holy or crazy, but he was entertaining. No one in the village talked like he did.

"You're welcome," Kimi said.

"This was a temple," the old monk said.

"Yes, long ago. Long before I was born."

He smiled. "Long ago indeed. Do you know its name?"

"My mother said it was called Mu-something. She might have been joking." One meaning of *mu* was "nothing."

The old man blinked. He took his legs out of the lotus position in which he had placed them and rose to his feet.

"Can it be?" he said.

He looked at the wall, at the foundation stones in the grass, at the fallen beam of the main hall, now mostly rotted away.

"I am in Yamakawa Domain."

"Yes," Kimi said. "Our lord is Lord Hiromitsu. He is not a very great Great Lord, but he is allied with—"

"Lord Kiyori," the old monk said.

"Yes, the Great Lord of Akaoka," Kimi said, "a prophet who sees the future, and so can never be defeated in battle. If battles should occur once again, as everyone says they will."

"I am back," the old monk said. "I was abbot here, oh, was it twenty years ago? Or was it ten?" He chuckled. "I built a hut there. Not a very sturdy one. Neither I nor the hut was here for long."

Now Kimi was sure Zengen was demented. As far back as she could remember, this place had been a ruin. Of course, she was only six years old. It was possible. Unlikely, though.

"I will rebuild this temple," the old monk said, "in earnest this time, with my own two hands."

"I wouldn't do that," Kimi said. "To do anything anywhere in the domain without permission is a capital offense. You would need Lord Hiromitsu's approval, and also that of the chief abbot of this temple's sect. I'm not even sure which one it is, or even if it still exists."

"I will get the necessary permissions," the old monk said.

Though he smiled happily, tears rolled down his cheeks. This convinced Kimi he was indeed a follower of the Way of the Zen Patriarchs, for it was well known that such people, especially masters of that arcane religion, often laughed and cried at the same time. That didn't mean he couldn't also be demented.

"I have wandered so aimlessly for so many years," he said, "and without intention, I have found myself exactly back where I should be. My gratitude is immense." He went to his knees and performed a full prostration in the direction of the rotting beam.

Then he wrote a letter, which he gave to Kimi to deliver to Lord Hiromitsu's castle. Kimi entrusted it to Goro, who could run for miles without tiring. His sense of direction was extraordinarily poor, but the lord's castle was not so very far away, and it was directly at the end of the north road, so even Goro could find his way there without difficulty. She was afraid Zengen's letter would cause trouble and result in punishment for him instead of permission. But he insisted, even though she warned him. What more could she do?

Two weeks later, it seemed her worst fears were to be realized. A troop of twenty mounted samurai arrived and demanded the presence of the village elder. The leader of the samurai was a ferocious-looking man who seemed ready to kill everyone in sight.

He said to the groveling elder, "Where is Mushindo Monastery?"

The elder's eyes widened in shock and his mouth dropped open. He kept his head on the ground and said nothing.

The samurai leader turned to one of his men and said, "Taro, behead him. Perhaps his successor will be quicker to answer."

"Yes, Lord Saiki."

Kimi, at the back of the bowing crowd with the other children, looked up to see the samurai called Taro dismount and draw his sword.

"Wait, sir samurai," Kimi said. "I will show you the way." Lord Saiki glared angrily at her. She dropped her head back to the ground in fright. Why had she spoken up? She didn't even like Elder Buncho. He was always scolding and ordering people about. And she didn't know that the ruins of Mu-something was the Mushindo Monastery the lord was seeking. Now she would lose her head, too.

"You, girl," Lord Saiki said, "stand up!"

Her entire body quivering, Kimi did as she was told. She hoped she would not urinate in fear. It was one thing to die. It was quite another to be laughed at while dying. Next to her, Goro also stood, because he always followed her in everything she did.

"Idiot," Lord Saiki said, "why are you standing? I didn't tell you to rise!"

"Sir lord," Kimi said, "he *is* an idiot, so he doesn't know better."

One of the samurai among the troop laughed. He managed to choke it back, but not before Lord Saiki heard him.

"Hidé, you will remain on stable duty until notified otherwise."

"Yes, lord," Hidé said, no longer amused at all.

"Show us the way, girl," Lord Saiki said.

"Yes, sir lord." Kimi bowed and obeyed. A heartbeat behind her, Goro did the same.

If the samurai had come for Old Zengen, Kimi hoped they would only arrest him, not execute him. Imprisonment and torture were not as bad for Zen practitioners as they were for others, since their monasteries were like prisons anyway, or so Kimi had heard. There they were starved, beaten, deprived of sleep, and made to stare at the wall or the floor for days at a time. If they moved a muscle or made a sound, senior monks yelled at them and beat them with sticks. If they fell asleep, their eyelids were cut off. If they couldn't hold the lotus position, their legs were broken into place. Prison would be like going home for Zengen, wouldn't it? Kimi ran with Goro to the ruins and hoped for the best.

What actually happened shocked her more than anything she could have imagined.

Old Zengen was raking away some tall grass he had cut when the samurai arrived. He put down his tool and bowed in gassho.

The troop halted and all the samurai dismounted, including Lord Saiki, and all went to their knees and bowed with their heads to the ground.

"Lord Nao," Lord Saiki said, "Lord Kiyori, Lord Shigeru, and Lord Genji send their warmest regards to you. They ask that you inform them when you are ready to receive guests, and they will come immediately."

"Thank you, Lord Saiki," Old Zengen said, "but I am no lord, and he who was Nao is no more. I am Zengen, a follower of Buddha's Way, nothing more."

Lord Saiki looked up and smiled. "Well, perhaps a little more." He gestured, and Taro came forward with an elaborate silk scroll case and put it into Zengen's hands with a deep bow. "By order of the Chief Abbot of the Mushindo Sect, you are reappointed abbot of this monastery."

Zengen smiled. "My, my."

"We are to remain and assist you with the restoration, Reverend Abbot. Lord Hiromitsu has given his permission for us to employ as many of the villagers for the task as may be required."

"If the farmers are pulled from the fields during planting, their harvests will be reduced, and they will suffer for it. I do not require their help, or yours, Lord Saiki. I will restore Mushindo myself."

"At least permit us to bring the necessary supplies."

"That, too, will be unnecessary. I will use what I can find. What I cannot find, I will do without."

"Alone, and no supplies. It will be a daunting task. Mushindo has been in ruins for a century or more."

"I won't be alone," Old Abbot Zengen said. "Kimi will help me, won't you?"

"Yes, I will," Kimi said, "and so will Goro."

"A little girl, an idiot, and ruins. You have chosen a hard path, Reverend Abbot."

"Not at all, Lord Saiki. Once again, it is the path that has chosen me."

· · · · ·

Kimi and the other children came to visit Zengen often after that. It turned out that he had been to far more places than he'd said. Almost everywhere would have been closer to the truth than almost nowhere. He had visited all eighty-eight temples of the Shikoku pilgrimage, which was begun by the saint Kōbō Daishi over a thousand years ago. It was said that those who traveled that path in sincerity would find liberation from the eighty-eight delusions of the senses.

"Did you?" Kimi asked.

"I found tired muscles, sore feet, and sunburn," Zengen said.

Then he had crossed the Inland Sea to Honshu, and traveled to the holy mountain of Hiei. There he had listened to the sermons of the most celebrated Buddhist masters, and performed the rites and practices of the most esoteric and magical sects, seeking freedom from the pain and suffering of life.

"Did you?" Kimi asked.

"Only a fool believes in magic," Zengen said, "and only a bigger fool seeks to live and not suffer. In the midst of fire, how do you escape from the burning flames? In the midst of ice, how do you escape from the freezing cold?"

· · · · ·

The monastery Old Abbot Zengen built was less like other temples and much like those that he once had constructed in Shiroishi Domain, when he was one of the two hundred sixty Great Lords of the realm. It resembled a small fortress more than it did a religious retreat. This he regretted, since he no longer had any military thoughts in mind, but he only knew one way to build, and that was the way of the samurai he had been for so long.

· · · · ·

The ghostly, demonic sounds the children told him about were more than rumors. There were sounds, eerie and disturbing, but for him, who had lost everything and given up the world, they were only reminders of the inevitability of death and sorrow.

· · · · ·

In the course of time, a gentle calm suffused Zengen. One day, he found himself at peace. Not that the sorrow had gone, or even diminished, for it had not. But a kind of acceptance had changed everything.

Answers were overrated. Once, he had thought questions had greater value. Now he knew questions were quite useless, too.

· · · · ·

One day, a group of outsiders arrived. They had come, at the invitation of the Great Lord of Akaoka, to build a temple of their religion, for the worship of a Buddha-like being they called Jesus Christ. Zengen offered to let them use Mushindo for the purpose. Their holy day was Sunday. For Zengen, any day was the same as the next. The Christians—that is what they called themselves—declined, saying they would build their own temple. Before they could begin, a cholera epidemic struck them down, and all died but one. No one could pronounce his name, which sounded something like Jimbo. Somehow, in his illness, he learned the Japanese tongue. This was not unprecedented. Zengen knew of a shipwrecked fisherman who nearly drowned. He was rescued by Russian seamen, and was in a delirious fever for a month. When he came to, he spoke fluent Russian. Unexpected changes were sometimes brought about by the nearness of death.

"I wish to become your disciple," Jimbo said.

"You cannot," Zengen said. "I am not a holy man, I am only an ordinary man wearing a holy man's robe. What can you learn from an empty suit of clothes?"

Jimbo's eyes flashed with a sudden brightness of tears. He bowed and said, "Thank you, Reverend Abbot. I will meditate sincerely upon your words."

In this manner, without desire or intention, Zengen became a teacher of the Way.

· · · · ·

The old man sat in the posture of Zen meditation in the hut in the mountains two days away from Mushindo Monastery, where he had twice been abbot. Above him, through the sparse overlay of random branches that suggested a roof, the winter stars sparkled dimly. Mists drifted down toward the valley floor. He was in meditation posture, with his hands cupped in the Zen mudra, but he was not in fact meditating. He was dying, and, dying, had come out of meditation to find himself reflecting on how quickly his life had passed. There was no regret, only mild surprise.

Yesterday, he had been a Great Lord, with fierce samurai at his command, a loyal wife, two strong sons, a beautiful daughter, and laughing grandchildren. The day before that, he had been a frightened youth with his first set of full-size swords, sweating fearfully in his armor as his regiment attacked a desperate horde of starving peasants. And on the previous morning, he had been ten years old, kneeling at his father's deathbed, swearing through tears that he would fulfill the ancient mission of their clan: the overthrow and destruction of the Tokugawa Shogun.

And now he was dying.

Who knows? Perhaps he was already dead, no more than a lingering spirit hanging above a corpse the way incense smoke sometimes hung in the motionless air of a quiet room. The first strong wind and his spirit would dissipate.

His breathing, if he was still breathing, was so attenuated it was unnoticeable.

He saw his hands.

They had wielded swords, caressed women, comforted children.

They had killed, forgiven, loved.

Now they were very still. If he wished, could he move them?

He didn't wish, so he would never know—

1895, GENJI'S ESTATE ON THE TAMA RIVER
OUTSIDE TOKYO

Genji had prepared the speech he was to give at the Diet, though he knew he would die before he could deliver it. Today was the day he had envisioned long ago, the day of his assassination. For most of his life, he had known the time, place, and manner of his death. Had that knowledge been a blessing or a curse? A little of both, perhaps. It had sometimes made him complacent when he should have been attentive, and it had sometimes given him courage when he would otherwise have been paralyzed with fear.

Now his life was to end. Certainty had replaced every doubt except one. His grandfather, whose predictions had always come true, had told him he would have three visions in his life, and these three would suffice to guide him from beginning to end. Where was that third vision? Lord Kiyori had been a wily samurai of the old school. He might very well have lied about it to keep Genji alert. It seemed likely. There was little time left for a third vision. Even if it came, what good could it do?

Genji checked himself in the mirror. He looked ridiculous, with the mustache and beard of a French general, the morning coat of a British politician, and the face of a Japanese lord approaching the least attractive years of middle age. He recalled the way he looked that day so long ago when he had first met Emily Gibson. Then his hair had been in the complex array of the now extinct samurai. His face had been young, and beardless, and too obviously that of a man well satisfied with himself for no better reason than the fortunate circumstances of his noble birth.

Had he really been so arrogant?

Genji laughed.

Yes, he had, indeed, indeed.

He turned away from the mirror and—

·   ·   ·   ·   ·

Genji is three years old. He walks along the shores of White Stones Lake near White Stones Castle, the redoubt of his maternal grandfather, Lord Nao. He holds a small paper kite in his hands along with its anchoring string entwined around a stick. Upon its earthside face, the kite depicts a flock of sparrows in brilliant fantasy colors instead of in their drab reality.

A man is walking on one side of him, and a woman on the other. They are his mother and father.

Genji says, "White Stones Castle. White Stones Lake. White Stones Domain. Why is everything here called white stones when there aren't any?"

His mother says, "Because white stones were the original treasure of my father's domain. This lakeshore was famous for the white stones used in the game of *go*. They were preferred by connoisseurs over the best mother-of-pearl. It is said the great hero Yoshitsuné treasured his Shiroishi stones more than anything except honor, triumph in battle, and his lover."

"So where are the stones?"

"The supply was unlike mother-of-pearl. One day there were no more."

"Is that when Grandfather Nao planted his apple trees?"

"No, his ancestors did that generations ago. White Stones was the name of domain, lake, and castle long after the white stones were gone."

"That's confusing," little Genji says, loosening his kite string and preparing to run. "The names should be changed."

His father says, "A name is more than mere description. It is an emblem of constancy, no matter how different things become. Like your name. Genji."

Genji sees a look pass between his parents. They smile together.

The envisioning Genji remembers that look. It used to make him uncomfortable because it excluded him. He sees now that the exclusion was not intentional, only a consequence of so completely including the two. There was room for no one else.

"I don't like my name, either," Genji says, and runs off down the beach to loft his kite.

His name, Genji, was the name of the famous princely hero in Lady Murasaki's ancient novel. It was also an alternate name for the Minamoto clan of the great real-life hero Yoshitsuné, who won battles against impossible odds seven hundred years ago. Only a Minamoto could be Shogun. The present Shogun, a Tokugawa, claimed Minamoto descent. Genji had heard people whispering what a ridiculous and pretentious name Genji was to give to a son of a minor lord. What were they thinking? people said. That their little boy could ever be as handsome as the Shining Prince of legend? That he, a lowly Okumichi clansman, could be Shogun one day?

Now, as his three-year-old self runs down the beach with the kite bouncing flightlessly on the shore behind him, the fifty-eight-year-old Genji recalled why he has his name. His mother had married very young. She knew stories better than she knew life, and the story she loved best was Lady Murasaki's. She wanted a Genji of her own, even if he was her son, and not her lover. It was a measure of his father's love for her that he consented to the name, though it would multiply the ridicule he already received for being the son-in-law of the Lord of Apples. He must have had to stand against the furious opposition he surely received from both Lord Kiyori and Lord Nao. All that was in his name, and in the look his parents exchanged, along with the smile that belonged to only two.

The kite won't loft. Genji is growing very frustrated. He is thinking about ripping it up and throwing it into the lake when he hears his father call to him.

"Run toward us, Genji, into the wind!"

As he starts to do as his father suggests, the boy Genji looks back at the kite as it catches the wind and begins to rise. The Genji inhabiting his former self wants to look toward his mother. If he is three, then she is pregnant with his sister, the one whose birth will kill them both. These are the last happy days together for his mother, his father, and little Genji. He wants to look at his mother. He remembers her as being very beautiful. But all little boys think their mothers are beautiful. He is three and he is fifty-eight and his mother is twenty and will not see twenty-one. The kite flies high in the sky above the shore of White Stones Lake.

The boy looks up. His kite of fantastically colored sparrows stands out against the sky like a jeweled fragment of rainbow. He laughs, and hears the laughter of his mother and father grow closer as he runs toward them, as the kite rises higher and higher.

The man wants to see his mother, not the kite, and the man tries to will the boy's head to turn and—

·   ·   ·   ·   ·

"Lord Genji!"

He heard a voice, anxious, distant, faint.

When he opened his eyes, he saw Hidé, his most loyal retainer. But where was his topknot, his kimono, his swords? Genji revived further. He remembered that Hidé was dead, killed saving his life in one of the many failed assassination attempts his enemies had made against him over the years. The topknot, kimono, and sword had gone the way of the Shogun and the Great Lords and the samurai. They were gone forever. This young man who looked so much like Hidé was his son Iwao.

Iwao turned to the bodyguard behind him and said, "Inform the chairman Lord Genji has taken ill and will not make his speech to the Diet today."

"Wait." Genji sits up. "I will be ready to go in a moment." He knew this delay, caused by his third and final vision, would give his assassin precisely the time he needed to get into place. He could not help but be amused by the irony, though it would take his life. The very occurrence of his third vision will have enabled his first vision to come true. "Help me to the carriage."

Genji regretted that he had failed to fully utilize the vision, had failed to look as closely as he should have at his mother. Was she as beautiful as he remembered? He would die with the answer still mysterious.

Yet he had learned something, something precious. His vision of the past would not guide his future, because his remaining future could be measured in a few hundred heartbeats. Instead, he was given a vision of his happy childhood. Genji had always remembered it as full of shame and sorrow. He had forgotten those joyous days, when the three of them were perhaps the happiest little family in all the isles of Japan.

"My lord?"

They had arrived. Genji stepped from the carriage.

"Are you sure you are well enough to speak today, my lord?"

"Quite well enough."

The timing of his final vision assisted his assassin in another way. Genji's bodyguards, concerned about the seizure and his resultant unsteadiness on his feet, paid more attention to him than they should, and less to potential dangers lurking in the crowd.

Prediction and result were intertwined and inseparable. When he was a child, he had not understood this. He had wondered how Lady Shizuka could know so much of the future, and still be unable to prevent the treacheries that were known to her even before they were conceived. Now, at the end of his life, that mystery was cleared away.

Knowing the future was like knowing the past. Events could not be controlled or altered, only one's attitude toward them. Like the earth itself, the heart had directions. Bitterness, anguish, fear, and hatred lay one way; equanimity, gratitude, kindness, and love another.

This ability to choose the heart's direction was the true power of the prophet, which was no more than the only true power of every human being.

How fortunate he had been in the love he had given and the love he had received.

Loud voices of contention came from the Diet chamber. Iwao stepped to one side and opened the door for him.

Okumichi Genji, a Peer of the Realm, Minister without Portfolio in the government of His Imperial Majesty the Emperor Mutsuhito, former

Great Lord of Akaoka Domain, lover of geisha and missionary and help-less murderer of both, smiled that slight, self-mocking smile that was so often misunderstood, and walked calmly toward the fulfillment of his vision.

1867, CLOUD OF SPARROWS CASTLE

Emily's love for Genji was certain and unshakable. Her limbs, her senses, her life, her earthly happiness, her place in heaven, she would sac-rifice all for him without complaint. If to save his soul it were necessary to cast herself into the deepest pit of hell, she would plunge joyfully into the flames, for what greater happiness could there be than to insure the salva-tion of her beloved? In the innocence of her youth, she had imagined that such love once attained would thereafter unfailingly guide her every step. How naive a thought that had been.

Love, she had discovered, was not entirely a matter of the spirit.

She had lately begun experiencing certain disturbing physical symp-toms when she was in Genji's presence, particularly when they were alone together. Even worse, she did not find the resultant sensations wholly unpleasant. Her upbringing and her faith prevented her from fo-cusing too closely on them. Still, she could not help noticing that their ef-fects were powerful and intimate. There was no real danger as long as Genji found her repulsive. His lack of feelings for her were her best de-fense against her own for him. Lately, however, she thought she had caught him looking at her in the peculiarly intense way characteristic of men whose animal natures have temporarily overcome the restraints of morality and civilization. When she had seen that look, she was not em-barrassed or horrified, as she would have been in the past. Instead, she felt herself blushing, and her skin tingled most distressingly beneath her clothing. If he forgot himself, could she resist him? She did not think she possessed the will. This problem was easily resolved by her departure if her chief concern was her chastity. It was not. Genji's immortal soul was in the balance.

If she departed, she would keep from being an unintended instrument of carnal sin. But in thinking that way, was she not merely putting herself before him by cloaking her self-concern in righteousness? Genji had numerous opportunities for carnality apart from her. In addition to the ubiquitous geisha, there were now the two unfortunate young women who had recently entered a most degrading slavery in his household as concubines. Over the years, Emily felt she had made steady progress in turning him away from the iniquitous paths of his ancestors. But from such occurrences, it was easy to see that the work was perilously incomplete.

Far worse than these lapses into the temptations of the flesh was his continued blasphemous spiritual diffusion. He professed submission to the divine will and omnipotence of the Father, gratitude for the sacrifice and resurrection of the Son, solace in the forgiving and protective embrace of the Holy Spirit. Yet he would not admit that the myriad Buddhas and gods were superstition only. Further, he still practiced the worship of nothingness advocated by the mad Patriarchs of the Zen cult. He said it was not worship at all, but how else could it be characterized?

It is only letting go, he liked to say.

Was that not the very opposite of salvation, which was a holding on to the words and grace of Our Savior?

Genji suffered from the great affliction common to his countrymen: the ability to embrace many contradictory beliefs at the same time. He saw no problem in being Buddhist, Shinto, Christian, all at once. He could believe in free will, and just as firmly believe in predestination. He could accept the True Word and nothingness with the same amen.

Of all the ways in which he went astray, the most dangerous was his certainty of the prophetic gift supposedly vested in his bloodline. His grandfather, the late Lord Kiyori, had been so empowered, according to Genji, as well as his uncle, the patricide Shigeru. He no longer claimed it for himself, but that was only because he knew such a claim offended her most profound beliefs. Keeping silent about a heretical view to which one subscribed did not lead to divine forgiveness. Silence only compounded the sin.

Her departure would surely signal the end of his conversion from paganism to Christianity. Only if she stayed with him and continued to provide steady, gentle guidance would there be any hope of Genji completing his reformation, and thereby assuring his salvation.

Which brought her back to the physical dangers of continued proximity.

All her efforts at reasoning seemed trapped in this logical circularity.

Emily's dilemma was complicated further by the existence of the *Autumn Bridge* scrolls. They contained predictions that had seemingly come true. This was unsettling enough. Even more frightening, the narrative as a whole gave every indication of being addressed directly and specifically to Emily herself.

Lady Shizuka, the authoress of the scrolls, had died more than five hundred years before Emily was born.

There had to be another way to look at *Autumn Bridge*. Without Hanako to help her, she was linguistically hobbled. But if Emily looked with the eyes of a True Believer, and saw the words, not in a demonic light, but in the illumination of sincere Christian belief, would she not see the truth?

There was no alternative but to try.

She took up the last scroll, the twelfth, to look again at the final lines. She prayed she would interpret them afresh. She took a deep breath and opened the scroll.

Only faint, illegible marks remained, like vaporous wisps lingering over an extinguished fire. As Emily watched, these last remnants of Lady Shizuka's writing faded away completely.

She went to the Mongol trunk and examined the other eleven scrolls. They were as blank as parchment upon which nothing had ever been written.

· · · · ·

Emily leaned against the trunk of the apple tree. She had walked to the valley from the castle. The last time she had walked so far, she had been a girl leaving her parents' farm for the last time. Then flames had risen into the sky behind her, emblems of an arsonous cleansing by her mother to wipe away worse crimes. Now the flames were within her, invisible, and none the less searing for being unseen and so neatly contained.

Now she had only her memory of *Autumn Bridge* to guide her. Could she trust it?

Lord Narihira dreamed the arrival of American beauty would signal the final triumph of our clan. He was right. But when he lived, there was not yet your America, so he misunderstood his dream. You were not a flower to be named to suit his hopes.

Emily had been so shocked by this passage, she had tried to blot it from her memory. Now she desperately strove to recover it, and in doing so, was utterly unsure of her accuracy. The reference to *your America* was chilling enough. But that *Autumn Bridge* should say *You were not a flower to be named to suit his hopes* verged on the satanic. Could *you* be anyone other than Emily?

Your daughter's birth will clarify everything for him, but nothing for you. You will not long survive the nativity. She will hear much of you from her father. Since she will know you, let me tell of her, so you will know her as well. Her name will be the same as mine. You will insist on it with your dying breath. For this, I thank you.

Had she read what she thought she had read? A prediction of her union with Genji, and a prediction of her subsequent death in childbirth?

It couldn't be. No one could predict the future but Jesus Christ and the prophets of the Old Testament. If the scrolls pretended to do so, then they were blasphemous, deceptive, evil. To prove their falsity, she need do no more than accept, upon its certain proffer, Charles Smith's proposal of marriage. He would arrive within the week. Within the week, she could make lies of it all. But how would that help Genji? Her marriage to Charles would do nothing to turn Genji away from his belief in his own prophetic gift. This was the greatest danger to his immortal soul.

No matter how sincerely Genji proclaimed a belief in Jesus Christ as his Lord and Savior, it could not be made consistent with his belief in himself as a prophet. The collision of righteousness and blasphemy would separate him forever from the mercy and forgiveness of Christ, and would doom him to be excluded from the Resurrection. She thought she could stand separation from him in this life. The thought of eternal separation was more than she could bear. Perhaps her motives, even in this, were less than holy.

She saw a horseman crest the ridge above the valley. It was Genji. As he rode toward her, she remembered that day, years ago, when he lay bleeding to death in the snow. She had held him in her arms and sworn an oath to God that she would not hesitate to sacrifice herself to save him. For an instant, the past was more vivid than the present.

Remembrance brought her to a bold decision.

"I hope I am not disturbing you," Genji said.

"You are not," Emily said.

"I will leave you alone if you prefer. It is a fine day for solitude."

"I'm glad you have come to me," she said. "I was just about to go to you."

"Oh?" He dismounted and stood next to her. "For a specific purpose, or only because you've missed me?"

She felt herself blushing, but did not let her embarrassment deflect her from her purpose.

"I want to talk to you about the scrolls I have been reading," Emily said. She continued before she lost her courage. "They are not the *Cloud of Sparrows* chronicles."

"No?"

"They are, or they claim to be, Lady Shizuka's *Autumn Bridge*."

"Ah," Genji said, and waited for her to continue.

Emily was taken aback by the mildness of his reaction.

"You don't seem surprised," she said, "or even very curious."

"I am neither," Genji said. "Hanako told me about it as soon as she found out."

Emily stared at him in disbelief. "Hanako was my friend. She promised she would tell no one."

"You were her friend. But I was her lord. She could not be loyal to me and keep such a secret. In return—"

Genji stopped in mid-sentence and moved quickly to catch Emily as she put a hand to her face and lost her balance. She put her hand against the tree trunk and, leaning away from him, waved him off.

"No, please, I am quite capable of standing on my own."

"Are you sure?"

"I have not much choice in the matter. Nor have I ever, it seems. Even when I thought others were standing with me, they were not."

"Hanako did not betray you," Genji said. "How can you even think it? At Mushindo Abbey, she gave her life for you."

"She did," Emily said, beginning to weep. "But she said she would keep my secret, and she did not."

"She did not think it was your secret to keep," Genji said. "Since you thought it was, she made me swear not to interfere, or to speak of it until you spoke first. I have kept my word."

"It's purely chance that you did," Emily said. "You could not have been sure I would ever speak of it to you. If I did not, you would have asked me about it eventually. Your word to her was meaningless, as was hers to me."

"No, Emily, you are mistaken. I knew you would speak of it."

"Oh? Did you have a vision of me telling you of *Autumn Bridge*?" Only the hurt she felt caused her to use that word in a taunt.

"No," Genji said. He met the challenge in her look and voice with unaffected calm. "It was a different vision."

. . . . .

Genji, again a passenger in his own body, finds himself striding through the corridor. The man he is to be is impatient. Genji can tell by the hastiness of the stride. He is in the castle, walking toward his own quarters. From the far end of the corridor, he hears the cries of a newborn infant coming to him from the room to which he is hurrying. Servants kneel and bow as he passes.

When he enters the room, he sees a baby in a maid's arms.

"Lord Genji," she says, and holds the child for him to see. But he hardly gives it a glance. His concern is for someone else, the person in the innermost room. Before he can enter it, Dr. Ozawa steps out and closes the door behind him.

"How is she?" Genji's voice is anxious.

Dr. Ozawa says, "The birth was a difficult one."

"Is she out of danger?"

The doctor bows. He says, "I am sorry, my lord."

Genji drops to his knees. He feels grief fill his body.

"You are a father, Lord Genji," the doctor says, and places the infant in Genji's unresisting arms. Genji tries to look at the infant's face, hoping to see in it some indication of the mother's identity. But the Genji to be doesn't look at the baby. His entire attention is elsewhere, on a small piece of jewelry hanging from a silver chain around the infant's neck.

It is a small silver locket marked with a cross upon which is emblazoned a single stylized flower, a fleur-de-lis.

. . . . .

"It is the very locket you wear," Genji said.

"That proves nothing," Emily said. "Even if you saw what you thought you saw, it proves nothing." Genji's revelation had shaken her, but she could not admit it. To do so would be to admit the possibility that he had indeed seen a vision. "The strangest hallucinations occur regularly in dreams. It is the very nature of dreams. You have seen my locket. Hanako told you of Lady Shizuka's predictions. Your sleeping self assembled them in this bizarre manner. It is no more than that."

Genji said, "I had this dream, as you call it, six years ago, in the rose garden of the castle. I do not want it to be true any more than you do."

Emily turned away from him. She reached into the neck of her blouse and undid the latch of the silver chain. She turned back to Genji, took his hand in hers, and put the chain and the locket with the fleur-de-lis in his palm. It was her most precious possession. She had thought she would not part with it until death. That had been yet another false hope.

"Here, it is yours. You may give it to your wife, or mistress, or concubine, whichever first gives birth, and she can give it to the child. Your dream will come true, and it will prove itself not to be a vision of any weight at all."

Genji looked at the locket and shook his head.

"My grandfather told me it was futile to try to avoid the fulfillment of visions, that they would occur no matter what, and perhaps with more dangerous consequences if avoidance was attempted. But I have tried nonetheless. I have distanced myself from you as much as I could. I have spent time I did not wish to spend with geisha. I have brought concubines into my household. I have promoted your own relationships with Charles Smith and Robert Farrington. If a child is born to a geisha or concubine, I could perhaps convince myself that what I saw was no vision, but only a dream, as you say. Or if you marry Smith or Farrington and return to America, perhaps then I will believe it is as you say."

Genji took Emily's hand and placed the locket in it.

"Your marriage is our best hope, Emily. If we are not together, the vision cannot be fulfilled. It will be utterly impossible."

Emily held on to Genji's hand when he tried to withdraw it. She looked at him without expression for a long time. Then a smile slowly brightened her face, and as it did, she began to weep anew. She wept in silence, smiling, and never took her eyes from Genji's face.

"What is it?"

"I have loved you for a very long time." She stopped, took a deep breath, and said, "I didn't know until this moment that you loved me."

"If I have somehow given you that impression, I regret it," he said. Christians considered lying a sin. That was because they believed, quite erroneously, that the truth was always best. "It is not so," Genji lied. "I'm sorry."

"You have been a skillful deceiver for six years. But I see through you now."

He laughed to make light of it. "How have I given myself away?" He said it as if it were all a joke.

"You believe in your visions," Emily said, "and in the visions your ancestors have seen for six centuries. You believe that any attempt to evade them will fail, and will result in greater disaster as well. All this you believe, yet you would send me away in the hope of preventing its fulfillment."

"Just because I am not as good a Christian as you would like me to be, it doesn't mean I am totally lacking in Christian virtue. I am your friend. I do not wish to see you suffer. I certainly do not wish to see you die before your time."

"Liar," Emily said, and smiled.

The way she said the word reminded him of how Heiko had said it, the last time he had seen her. But Heiko had not smiled.

Emily said, "You are risking yourself, the future of your clan, and the safety, perhaps even the very existence, of your heir. Why? To protect me."

She released his hand, which she had been holding fast all the while.

"You care more about me than about yourself," she said. "Was that not your definition of love?"

Genji looked down at his hand. Emily had left her locket there.

If he wanted her to go, all he had to do was keep it, and deny her words. Then she would go. She would marry Smith, or Farrington, or another American, and leave Japan and Genji behind. Not because she believed he did not love her, but because she would never force herself on him, even to save him. By the tenets of her faith, so entangled as they were with her ideas of romantic love, free will played a crucial part.

Free will.

Genji didn't know what those words really meant. In his world, they made no sense. The will was the means by which one properly fulfilled one's fate. Free? No one was free. That was a delusion fostered by demons, and believed in only by fools and lunatics.

And which was he? Lunatic? Fool? Demon? Perhaps all three.

Genji held the locket by its chain. It glittered as brightly as it had in his vision. He reached around Emily. His hands lightly brushed her neck as he closed the clasp.

Free will, or fate?

"Genji," Emily said, and softened slowly into his embrace.

. . . . .

Emily had little time to marvel at the unexpected denouement. Once Genji made his decision, he planned and executed subsequent events with the speed and precision of a samurai general on campaign. In less than three weeks, the chapel on the hill above Apple Valley, the one they had talked about for so long, became a reality. The construction foreman, Tsuda— the very one who had discovered *Autumn Bridge* and then had it delivered to Emily—worked seemingly without sleep, as if his life depended on the timely completion. The castle maids sewed a wedding dress from a French pattern that was so elaborate, it might have originated before the Revolution. Yards and yards of the finest Chinese silk, Irish linen, and French lace went into it. She overheard a maid say that the cost of the intricately embroidered bodice alone approached the annual income of some of the smaller domains. Emily was terribly embarrassed by the extravagance. She doubted Queen Victoria had been as finely attired at her own wedding. But she said nothing to Genji. She knew he was putting on a grand show for very good reasons. A lord of one of the realm's most ancient lineages was to marry an outsider of no name, no political connections, and no fortune. He was combating the inevitable slanderous gossip with a grand display of pride. Perhaps it was strategically similar to a military campaign after all.

She could not quite believe it. Emily Gibson, a farm girl from the upper Hudson River Valley, was to be the bride of a pagan Japanese warlord.

. . . . .

Hidé stood at the edge of the water and stared at the ship anchored offshore. The sight of it filled him with such hatred, it took all his hard-earned martial discipline to keep his breathing calm and inaudible. Was it not a maxim of the samurai that a man whose breathing could be heard by his opponent was a defeated man? It would not do to set a bad example.

"I count only four cannons," Iwao said. "Our lord's ship, the SS *Cape Muroto*, has twenty. We are stronger than the Americans." He was happy when his father picked him up and held him in his arms. He was hoping for this, but he did not ask. A samurai never asked for favors, even if he was only five years old.

"We are not," Hidé said, "not yet. Our lord's warship is made of wood. That one is clad in iron. The shots from all twenty of the *Muroto*'s cannons would bounce right off those metal plates. And look at the size of those four guns, Iwao. See how they are placed in turrets? They can swivel and fire in any direction, no matter which way the ship is going."

Iwao did not like to hear about how strong outsiders were. He said, "*Hampton Roads.* Am I reading the ship's name right, Father?"

"Yes."

"That's a silly name. *Cape Muroto* is a much finer name."

Hidé smiled at his son to keep from laughing. "We are not the only ones with a sense of history. Hampton Roads is where ironclad warships fought each other for the first time."

"Really? Who won?"

"Neither ship could hurt the other. There was no winner."

The boy said, "If we can't sink it in battle, we will take it as it sits at anchor. Look, Father. The deck sentries aren't paying any attention at all. They're sitting and laughing and smoking pipes. I think they're drunk!"

"How would you do it?"

Iwao scowled in concentration.

He said, "At night. Longboats may be seen, even with no moon. I would lead swimmers from the east. The lights from the town to the west will blind the sentries."

"The water will disable your firearms," Hidé said.

"We won't need guns," Iwao said. "Short swords and knives. Gunfire would only alert the enemy. Blades are silent. We will take the *Hampton Roads* while most of the crew sleeps. Twenty men can do it, if they are the bravest twenty."

"Excuse me, my lords." A maid knelt on the sand behind them. "The ceremony is about to commence."

"Thank you," Hidé said. He put Iwao down and the two followed the maid back to Cloud of Sparrows.

"I'm glad Lady Emily is getting married," Iwao said.

"Oh?" Hidé looked at his son. "And why is that?"

"She won't be lonely anymore," the little boy said.

· · · · ·

"This isn't quite the wedding I had envisioned," Charles Smith said.

"Nor I," Robert Farrington said. Apart from the two Americans, the guests all were local despots and their vassals.

"I must admit, I am surprised to see you here," Smith said.

"The *Hampton Roads* has no set patrol," Farrington said, "and the captain and I are old comrades-in-arms. Travel here was not difficult."

"I was thinking of social barriers rather than geography."

"I see no reason to avoid the wedding of a woman for whom I have the highest regard," Farrington said, "even if I do not approve of her choice of groom."

The two men lapsed into silence. Neither knew what the other was thinking. But both could have guessed.

Farrington grimaced and tried not to dwell on it.

Smith, smiling, rather enjoyed the scenes that played in his imagination.

It was not every day a beautiful American virgin sacrificed herself on the altar of bushido.

. . . . .

The bridal chamber was furnished and decorated so perfectly in the American fashion, Emily could easily have imagined herself in Albany instead of Akaoka. Most prominent, perhaps only because of her state of mind, was the large four-poster bed, with the fluffy quilts and pillows, and sheets of pure white silk.

Emily stood before the mirror next to the dresser. She saw without pride or false modesty that the reflection in the glass was all elegance and beauty. Had she been gazing upon a stranger, she would have been so astonished by the perfection of the display, she would have had to remind herself that all is vanity, that every work of man and man himself passes quickly away. Because it was herself she looked at, she needed no such reminder. Beneath the apparent calm of the face in the mirror, she saw utter bewilderment.

The ceremony itself had been—amazing. There was really no other way to describe it. Charles and Robert had both been there, which had surprised her, and they had been more than civil to each other, which surprised her even more. Their congratulations seemed quite sincere. Robert's emotions were muted, as usual, while Charles was near to exuberant, as if he himself had been the groom. The nuptials had been performed by a Dutch minister of the Calvinist faith. He and his predecessors had been acquainted with the lords of the Akaoka for many generations.

Emily considered it a clear sign of the will of God that none of Genji's family had become Calvinists during all that time, and that Genji himself had been baptized in the True Word a week prior to the wedding. It had not had any visible effect upon his relations with his peers. Every Great Lord of Western Japan opposed to the Tokugawa Shogun had been in attendance, as well as a high-ranking emissary of the Shogun himself, and each had been respectful to her and jovial during the celebration.

In truth, she remembered only those few details. Ceremony and celebration had both passed in a haze. She had been far too worried about what would follow.

And now that time had come. In minutes—in a very few minutes—Genji would come to her with expectations of her obedient submission. She would trust in God, she would do her best, she would not let bodily anguish or emotional distress deny him his conjugal rights. But she was afraid. She could not deny it.

What would he desire?

Christians, even bad Christians, understood that marriage existed for the sake of procreation, not as an avenue for sexual license. So there was for them a barrier of conscience that served as some defense against the worst bestial inclinations. No such barrier existed for Genji. He was, first of all, Japanese, and the natives of this land seemed not to recognize any act as forbidden, so long as it was consensual. Indeed, once a woman was a man's partner in intimacy, consent to every subsequent act was implied, and those acts included a multitude that would be thought of as perversions, atrocities, and capital crimes under the laws and morals of any Western nation.

She had not sought these awful truths. Living in this country for six years, it had been impossible for her not to discover them. The first intimations came from remarks overheard among the ladies and maids of the household. Their comments about their relationships suggested behavior completely devoid of morality. This was followed by an incident in the castle library, where she came upon a collection of books and scrolls that had previously escaped her notice. The first one she chanced to open contained lavish illustrations of intimate behavior of the most repugnant kind, made worse by the depiction of male and female genitalia exaggerated in size and coloration. Horrified, she closed it almost in the same instant she had opened it. Yet that brief glance was certain to forever scar her memory. Another hour passed before she found her courage and opened the volume next to it. She did so, not out of any prurient curiosity, but in an attempt to increase her understanding of the people among whom she lived. To know weakness was the first step in finding its cure.

The second book contained plain ink sketches, little more than line drawings, but what they depicted was even worse. Women were shown bound naked in grotesque, painful, obscene positions. Emily's Japanese was far from fluent, but she could read well enough to know that it was a book of detailed instruction in sexual torture.

She left the books where they were and busied herself elsewhere in her study. When Hanako arrived to assist her, Emily tried to broach the subject. But how did a virtuous woman begin to speak of such things, even with her most trusted friend? Several times Emily tried and, tongue-tied, could only blush. She ended up saying not a word on the subject.

Then Hanako was gone, and there was no one else to whom Emily could turn. She was on her own.

She would trust in God to show her the way. But standing there before the mirror, so dazzling in her wedding gown, she saw no way, no way at all.

She began undressing.

The worst she had to face was not any physical act but a confessional one. She had been committing fraud ever since her arrival in Japan, with her show of purity and sanctity. She was not what she pretended to be.

She was not a virgin.

Though the circumstances of her defilement were not of her choosing, she could not justify having kept that fact from Genji. It had happened when she was barely more than a child, and her compliance had been brutally forced. But that did not change the fact, nor mitigate the shame. She should have told him before their marriage. She wanted to, she had intended to—but somehow, the right occasion had never arisen. Now she had to tell him, before he found out for himself.

Would he greet the news with quiet disappointment, or with rage?

She had seen Genji angry only once.

On that occasion, he had beheaded the person who had aroused his disapproval.

· · · · ·

Genji walked toward the nuptial chamber, his heart filled with apprehension. He was no longer concerned about the vision that equated Emily's doom with the birth of their child. They had decided together to go forward. They would live and die with the consequences of their decision. It bore no further thought. His anxiety was not caused by an event in the distant future but by one looming imminently: the consummation of their marriage.

From his first experience, at age twelve, his partners had been almost exclusively women possessing a high degree of expertise in the intimate arts. When they were virgins, as were the two concubines he had recently acquired, they were young women who had been extensively trained and prepared to please and be pleased. Their chastity had been a requirement of their station in life—the potential mother of a lord's heir—not a result of disinclination, ignorance, or lack of opportunity. His reputation as a skilled lover, while perhaps not entirely unwarranted, had been achieved through mutual mock seductions, pretenses following a pattern of long-standing tradition in noble romance. The excellence of his performance was the only goal of the women with whom he slept. If he was not excellent, then they were at fault, for the bedroom was their realm, and their intimate skills were their arsenal. Of course, Genji had paid attention. He had learned many lessons from the best experts in the land, and he had learned them well. Though there was never any way of being absolutely certain of a woman's feelings, he was reasonably confident that his abilities were not lacking.

It was only as he left the festivities to join his bride that the implications had struck him full force.

He did not have the slightest idea of how to behave with a woman who knew neither how to lead nor how to follow. In contrast to that stark and frightening reality, that she was an American and a Christian missionary faded away into utter insignificance.

. . . . .

Emily heard a knock at the door. Genji was the only one who ever knocked. Everyone else followed the established custom of announcing their presence by voice. He knocked in deference to her.

In her heightened emotional state, this simple realization brought tears to her eyes. It was a moment before she was in sufficient control of herself to say, "Come in."

Genji saw that Emily was already in bed, the quilt pulled up to her neck and tucked under her chin. He hoped she was not naked. Charles Smith had told him that Western women preferred to make love completely un-hindered by clothing. Genji didn't believe him, of course. Smith was a nat-ural jester, and often said things to shock his listeners rather than to accurately inform them. The only woman who had regularly been naked with him was Heiko. Such adventurous disregard for propriety had been part of her charm. Other women made love in traditional seductive disar-ray and dishabille. There was art to that. There was no art at all in nudity.

Or was there? Was it not likely that this was yet another aspect of life outsiders perceived in an entirely different way? There was no nudity in Japanese art, and precious little of it even in explicit sexual renderings, while in the West, nudity proliferated in statuary and paintings that adorned even the official buildings of their capital cities. Or was he con-fusing the ancient West with the modern, the Greeks and the Romans with the British and the Americans?

Genji sat on his side of the bed—Emily was noticeably positioned en-tirely on one half of it—and removed his outer kimono. For the wedding, he had dressed as usual in the Japanese fashion. Emily had asked if she should wear the wedding kimono that came in the Mongol trunk, but Genji had said no. He knew she would not be comfortable in it. And he was doubtful of how she would look in a kimono. Her configuration—protuberant in the extreme at breast and hip, constricted in equally dra-matic measure at her waist—was too extravagant to provide the proper structure over which a kimono should flow. She had looked perfectly right in her wedding dress, as he knew she would. It was one thing to adapt. It was quite another to attempt to be what one was not. This was a lesson he and his countrymen would do well to remember in the time to come.

He was about to slip beneath the quilt when he remembered another thing Smith had told him. Western women, he had said, preferred inti-macy in darkness.

Darkness? Genji said. You mean night rather than day?

Smith said, I mean darkness. At night, with no illumination.

Genji said, With no illumination other than moonlight or starlight.

No, Smith said. In a closed room, with pulled shades and curtains to shut out the heavens, and without generated light of any kind.

But it is impossible to see anything in such conditions, Genji said.

Exactly the point, Smith said.

Genji did not believe him, but he had learned that the unbelievable was not always to be ruled out with outsiders.

He said to Emily, "I will snuff the candle."

Emily had been thinking about this as Genji undressed. Thank God, he had not undressed completely. She longed for the cover of darkness, yet she feared it as well. Without any visual anchor, subject to who knew what physical invasion and abuse, she could easily become disoriented and panic.

"Please," she said, "let it burn." She would look at his face, and find what comfort she could there. The man she adored was certain to disappear from view as his animal nature triumphed over his better self. But until then, she would look into his eyes, and she would see the goodness within him.

Genji lay on his side of the bed, propped up on an elbow. Emily stared at him like a condemned prisoner awaiting her executioner's blow. Surely love was a jest of the gods, that it could make two people who loved each other so afraid.

Emily had undone her hair. It pooled on the pillow under her like an abundance of the gold filaments used in the best embroidery. The white silk bedding complemented her fine, pale skin. Her dramatic features were balanced by the innocence of their presentation; she used no cosmetic enhancements at all. Those eyes, which had once dizzied him with their strangeness, he now saw were nearly magical reflections of the boundless sky, and the ocean in its brightest days. How had he ever thought her any less than beautiful? He had been blind.

Genji pulled the edge of the quilt gently away from her chin. Her shoulders tightened briefly, then relaxed when he stopped without uncovering her completely. She had worn a sleeping kimono to bed. The pale blue silk, the color of her eyes, rose and fell at her breast as she breathed.

Genji slowly drew a line with his fingers from her throat to her waist along the skin at the inner edge of her kimono, opening it slightly. Her flesh was soft and fever hot. Blood rouged her cheeks and eyelids.

Her breath quickened. She turned her face away.

Genji touched her cheek and she faced him once again.

He said, "May I kiss you?"

That he would ask, that he would say it so shyly, it was more than she could bear. Tears welled and fell. "Yes," she said, and closed her eyes.

His kiss was so light and subtle, it was little more than a warm breath upon her lips, yet it made her shiver.

She had to tell him. She had to tell him now, before silence became a lie.

"I am not a virgin," she said.

"Neither am I," Genji said, and kissed her again.

1953, MUSHINDO ABBEY

Sometimes, when she first woke up in the morning, Old Abbess Jintoku did not wake up when she should, in the twenty-seventh year of the Shōwa Emperor, but in Meiji 15, or Taisho 6, or, most often these days, Komei 21. Meiji 15 was the year Makoto Stark first came to the temple. Taisho 6 was memorable because Japan became a full-fledged power then, as one of the victors in the Great War. She thought she awoke so frequently in Komei 21 because that was when the second battle of Mushindo occurred, the one that took Lady Hanako's life, made Jintoku abbess, and—and what was the other thing? There was one more. Old Abbess Jintoku had been thinking about it just as she woke this morning, then promptly forgot it. Ah, well, it would come to her. Or it would not. It mattered little either way.

She sat patiently on her cushion as her attendant nun and three guests busied themselves around her in the small living room of her cottage. Such a crowd for so small a space. Especially since the guests had brought several large pieces of equipment with them, including what looked like a movie camera.

"Are you ready, Reverend Abbess?" the young nun said.

"I am always ready. Is there anything in particular you would like me to be ready for?"

"That's great," the man in the flashy Western suit said. "Let's get her to say that on camera. Hey, Yas, set the camera up here right away."

His hair was cut in a manner that had become popular with the American Occupation, rather long and greasy, gangsterish and somewhat effeminate at the same time. She didn't know him, and she didn't like him. Not because of his clothes or his hair, but because of the way his eyes glittered and shifted about. That was the way young men's eyes had been during the war—not the Great War, which had ended thirty-five years ago, but the Great East Asia War, which everyone now had to call the Great Pacific War, or World War II, by command of the Americans. Young men's eyes had been that way because before they went off to die in airplanes or ships, they were given little white pills, which made sleep and food unnecessary, and made them eager to crash into American ships in suicide attacks.

"That will be difficult," the nun said.

"Why?" a young woman asked.

She was dressed in a style similar to the man Jintoku didn't like. Her clothes were of the American type, particularly gaudy in her case, with a skirt that exposed the better part of rather fat and unshapely calves. She wore an abundance of makeup that would have suited a Ginza whore. Her hair was an elaborate mass of immobile curls called a perm. Jintoku didn't dislike the young woman the way she did the young man. She felt sorry for her instead. Her grotesque distortion was no doubt due to the man, if not this one, then another. Women always did what men wanted, even when what they wanted was bizarre and harmful. How sad.

The nun said, "The Reverend Abbess never repeats herself."

"We'll just ask her the same question," the man said.

"She never answers a question with the same answer," the nun said.

"What a character," the man said, as if Jintoku were not there. "That's great, too. We'll have terrific footage for the program."

Jintoku said, "What program?"

The nun said, "Remember, Reverend Abbess? Today, the reporters from NHK Television are here to interview you. You're going to be on their special program, *The Centenarians of Japan*. It's part of a celebration of the first anniversary of the end of the American Occupation."

"Yes, Reverend Abbess," the reporter said, "Japan is free again."

"Japan was never free in the first place," Jintoku said. "Great Lords ruled before and they rule now."

"I got that," the camera operator said.

"Great," the reporter said, "but we can't use it. It sounds too much like a militaristic reference."

"Doesn't she know feudalism ended a century ago?" the woman made up like a whore said.

"The Reverend Abbess was speaking metaphorically," the nun said. It wasn't the same nun who had been assigned to her last month. Jintoku wore her out. This one was still fresh. She was also young. Perhaps she would outlast the others.

"Anyway, let's get on safer ground," the reporter said. He looked at his notes, refreshed his memory, and spoke as if reciting. "Reverend Abbess, you are one of the most prominent one-hundred-year-old citizens in our country. As Founding Abbess of Mushindo Abbey, you are a vital link with our valued traditions. Japan has more centenarians per capita than any other country in the world. Do you think this is a result of the deep spiritual interest that so many Japanese have?"

"I think it is a kind of curse," Jintoku said. "We Japanese are slow learners. We keep making the same mistakes over and over again, war after war, killing everyone in sight. So the gods and Buddhas have condemned us to long life, to contemplate at greater length the error of our ways."

"I got that," the camera operator said, "but I guess we can't use it, either."

"No, maybe we can," the reporter said. "It's antimilitarism and properly penitent. It could go."

"No one should live so long," Jintoku said. "Everyone I knew when I was young has been dead for thirty years. And there are too many years to keep in their proper place."

The camera operator shot the reporter a questioning look. The reporter moved his finger in a circular movement, and the camera operator kept his camera rolling.

"Surely, you have found religion to be a solace, to others as well as yourself?"

"I don't know anything about religion."

"You're too modest, Reverend Abbess. For most of a century, you have been a much respected religious leader. Many thousands have come to their beliefs through your guidance."

"Don't blame me for what anyone believes," Jintoku said. "The Mushindo sect teaches liberation from delusion. It has nothing to do with belief, just practice. You do or you don't. Very simple. In the meantime, you can believe or disbelieve whatever you wish. Belief has nothing to do with reality."

"Well, that's a novel view, Reverend Abbess. Certainly different from what the abbots of the great temples and shrines of Japan would say."

"Not really," Jintoku said. "One of the Zen Patriarchs of ancient times—or was it a Kegon master?—put it quite succinctly. A famous saying around the time of the Opium War, when the British forced the Chinese to buy opium. He said, 'Religion is the opiate of the masses.' "

The reporter drew his hand across his throat in a cutting gesture.

The camera operator looked up. He said, "I'd already stopped when she called the British drug dealers."

"Amazing," the reporter said. "She managed to insult our British allies, defame the Zen and Kegon churches, and spout outlawed Communist propaganda all in three sentences."

"Ask her about the books," said the woman with the helmet-hard curls and the blood-gash lipstick. "Everybody loves those books."

"That's right," the camera operator said. "And it's a real link with our nation's hallowed traditions."

"All right," the reporter said. He looked doubtful. "Fumi, show her some of the books. She might need them to revive her memory."

The garishly made-up woman, whose face was quite pretty beneath it all, put a colorfully illustrated children's book into Jintoku's hands. It was the fairy tale about Peach Boy, a superhuman cherub born in a peach. The pictures were bright and cheerful. Even the demons looked friendly.

"I like it very much," Jintoku said. "Thank you."

"No, no," the reporter said. "You wrote the book, along with all of these." He put a stack of a dozen similar books on the table between them. "They were very popular during the Meiji era. Now that the Occupation is over, they have become very popular again. I think they mean the good old days to people."

"I wrote these books?" She looked at another. This one was about a Turtle Princess. "I didn't know I could draw so well. How sad. I have lost the talent so completely, I don't remember ever having had it."

"You wrote the stories. That is, you wrote the retelling of them. These are all old fairy tales. You didn't make the illustrations. The caretaker of this temple did." He turned to the camera operator. "Too bad we can't talk to him. It would make a great story."

"Not if he said the same kind of things she does," the camera operator said.

"Goro illustrated these books?"

The reporter turned to the woman. "Who's Goro?"

She looked at her notes and shook her head. "I don't know. He's not on the list."

"Find out." The reporter turned back to Jintoku. "You don't remember the caretaker of the temple? He was an American, Makoto Stark."

"Makoto? Makoto is the caretaker?"

"He was, Reverend Abbess. He passed away many years ago."

"Poor boy." Tears came to Jintoku's eyes. Had he never recovered from his wound? He seemed to be doing so well the last time she saw him. As far as she could remember, that had been in the fifteenth year of the Meiji Emperor, seventy-one years ago. If he illustrated these books, as the flashy man said, he must have recovered from the wound and died later, of some other cause. Still, it was sad. She remembered the young man, so in her heart, the young man was the one she mourned.

"Well, we might as well pack up," the reporter said.

"Total loss?" the camera operator asked.

"No such thing," the reporter said. "I'm a master of the cut and splice. We'll put together all the smiling footage, the cute stuff. No direct talk from her. We'll have Fumi do a voice-over. By the time I'm done, she'll be positively adorable." He bowed to Jintoku. "Thank you very much, Reverend Abbess. We'll be sure to let you know when the show airs so you can see yourself on television."

"I see myself in person every day," Jintoku said. "I don't need television to do it."

The nun said, "Thank you very much for coming to talk with the Reverend Abbess. She doesn't mean to be impolite. Her way is the direct way, that's all. I understand she was very direct even as a child."

As she watched the television crew leave, Jintoku remembered what she had been thinking of when she woke this morning. In the early autumn of the fourteenth year of the Komei Emperor, when she was perhaps fourteen years old, she had discovered a scroll hidden under an old foundation stone. She had intended to give it to Lady Hanako, but then Lady Hanako had been killed, so she had decided to hold it until she could give it directly to Lord Genji. For reasons she could no longer remember, she had kept the scroll until this very day. Had she opened it and read it? If so, she didn't remember. But she remembered exactly where she had hidden it. Or had she moved it?

Old Abbess Jintoku rose laboriously to her feet and proceeded toward her bedroom at the back of the temple annex. Halfway there, someone called to her from the front door.

"Granny! Granny! We're here!"

It was a little boy's eager voice. He must have slipped right past the departing television crew. Now, who could it be? She should know his voice. Perhaps not. There were so many of them. After the Meiji government decreed that all Buddhist temple keepers must marry or quit the religious life, Jintoku had married. It wasn't her fondest wish, but if she hadn't, she would have lost control of the temple, and the temple was her life.

"Granny! Where are you?"

It was yet another voice, a girl's this time. She couldn't place this one, either. There were so many of them. Grandchildren, great-grandchildren, great-great-grandchildren. Were there even great-great-great-grandchildren? Ah, she couldn't remember. Her memory wasn't what it once was. But, then, had it ever been?

"I'm coming," she said.

Old Abbess Jintoku, who had once been Kimi, the brightest little girl in Yamanaka Village, turned herself around and, with a surprisingly lively step for a centenarian, went to greet her progeny.

What was it that seemed so important a moment ago? Never mind.

Nothing was so important it couldn't be forgotten.

1311, THE HIGH TOWER OF CLOUD OF SPARROWS CASTLE

Shizuka awaited Go's arrival.

She thought of the way the world was, so full of sorrow, because men were fools, and the worst fools among them were samurai, and samurai would always rule this tragic land of Yamato. The things that were important to them were poison mistaken for treasure.

Power, over man and bird and beast, over wives and children and lovers, over household, castle, domain, and empire.

Wealth, in gold, vassals, concubines, rice fields, pastures, mountain passes, and rivers, trade in rarities from exotic and distant lands, objects and artifacts of no value in themselves beyond their rarity and exoticism.

Fame, among those nearby, so every encounter resulted in demonstrations of respect from those below; among those far away, so stories of their greatness grew ever greater in the telling, and they could imagine the fear and admiration of those they would never see.

Victory in battle.

Courage in death.

A glorious name that lasted beyond one lifetime.

The easy pathos of moonlight and falling blossoms.

The music of swords unsheathing, of arrows flying, of the hooves of charging warhorses tearing the earth in angry attack, of battle cries, of the screams of the maimed and dying, of the weeping of the mothers and wives and daughters of slaughtered foes, of blood, always the music of blood.

And most important, fear.

The fear that inflamed hatred in the hearts of enemies.

The fear that commanded obedience from unruly vassals.

The fear that bred compliance and chastity in women.

Shizuka listened to the fighting in the stairwell. Her ladies-in-waiting were brave and loyal. They were far too young to die, but they would, except one. Giving up their lives, they would delay her assassin almost long enough.

The door opened, not with the burst she expected, but gradually, almost gently. Go stood in the doorway, bloody. His wounds were superficial. The blood on him was the blood of her defenders. He glanced up at the ceiling of the room and laughed.

"Very clever. You had your slave build it high, so you could wield your witch's spear within the tower. I had forgotten that. No matter. You are outmatched. My sword will take your life." He continued to push the door open with the tip of his sword and entered the room.

Shizuka watched his eyes directly and, with her peripheral vision, caught the movements of his sword, his feet, his shoulders. She held the blade of her naginata long-bladed spear low, to invite attack. She knew he would not fall for such an easy trick. But perhaps he would feint in an effort to make her think he would. Then there would be an opening. She could not die too quickly or all would be lost.

"What of your famous prescience now, false prophet?" Go said. "Do you see your death approaching?"

"It is the end," Shizuka said.

"Yes, and the end was born in the beginning. You don't have to be a prophet to see that."

"And the beginning will be born in the end," Shizuka said.

"Don't comfort yourself with that false hope, witch." Go pointed the tip of his sword at her swollen belly. "The child dies first."

He lunged at her stomach. She moved to deflect the blow. That was Go's first feint, and it was effective. He knew she would have to protect the unborn child. When she moved her spear to do so, he cut upward and caught her in her throat. At the instant before the blade reached her, she managed to tilt her head to the side. Otherwise, her jugular would have been opened instead of just her skin.

Go smiled.

"I will burn your body and scatter the ashes in the offal pit. Your head I will put in an iron casket, smother it with lye, and cast it into the northern marshes of White Stones Lake. You will not return to life this time."

"Such a fool, from beginning to end," Shizuka said. She ignored the blood dripping from her neck. "So blind to the truth, unable to see the fate so clearly in store for you."

Go shifted to the right.

Shizuka moved her blade as if to meet him, then, as he shifted left, she struck him hard in the unprotected back of the knee with the staff end of her spear. Go went down. Shizuka slashed at his thigh, and cut it. But Go had been in motion and her strike was like his—superficial. He was back on his feet in the next instant.

There was a slight sound behind her. She turned and saw one of Go's men entering through the window. He had climbed the tower. Before she could turn her attention fully back to Go, he struck again. His blade sliced deeply into Shizuka's left shoulder. She felt the muscles and tendons separate from the bones. Her naginata's point dropped. It took all the strength of her right arm to raise it up again.

"You didn't foresee this, did you, witch?"

Shizuka backed away from Go and his man. She could not retreat too far, or the wall would impede the motions of her spear. Yet without the wall, and without the use of her left arm, and with her strength fading with the outflow of her blood, she was vulnerable to one when she defended herself from the other.

Shizuka looked into Go's eyes as deeply as she could.

She said, "Your granddaughter will pray for the peaceful repose of your soul."

Her stare froze him for a moment. In that moment, his man, shocked by her words, looked away from Shizuka and to Go. She struck the man under his chin with an upward sweep of her blade and cut his face in two. With a short, last scream, he went down. But her stare had not held Go long enough. Before she could recover from her attack, he attacked her. She felt the blade cut across her back, felt her ribs open up as they should not.

Shizuka went to her knees. She would never rise again. She could hear rain within the room. It was the heavy rain of her blood drops.

Her naginata's blade rested on the floor. She had no strength to raise something so heavy. The shaft resting against her chest was all that kept her from falling.

Go moved toward her with his sword raised for the beheading stroke.

"No!"

Ayamé's blade sliced into Go's right armpit as he turned to meet her attack. Behind Ayamé was Chiaki, his son, bloody sword in hand.

"Father! What are you doing?"

"Stay back!" Go said. He turned once more to Shizuka.

"Die!"

His sword began its sudden descent toward her neck.

And halted just as suddenly.

The blade of Chiaki's sword entered Go's back and burst from the center of his chest. An explosion of blood splattered the floor, Shizuka, and the wall behind her.

Chiaki drew his blade from his father's standing corpse and, in a swift continuation of the same movement, struck off his head.

"Traitor!"

Chiaki picked up the head and flung it violently from the nearest window.

"Traitor!" he screamed again.

"My lady!" Ayamé caught Shizuka as she collapsed. Her blood soaked them both. "My lady!"

Chiaki's vassals stormed through the door.

"Lord Chiaki, the traitors have retreated. But not for long."

Chiaki, weeping, fell to his knees beside Shizuka and Ayamé.

"My lady," he said. "Shizuka." His words were so enwrapped in sobs, they were barely distinguishable.

"You must do it," Shizuka said to Ayamé. "I have not the strength left."

"No," Ayamé said. "You can do it, my lady. You must."

"Have courage, Ayamé, as you have always had. If you don't help me, Sen and I will both die." Shizuka pulled the knife from her sash and put it into the palm of her friend's hand.

Ayamé's shoulders trembled, her eyes lost their focus, her body swayed. But she did not fall.

She said to Chiaki, "You and the others must leave the room. Men cannot be present at the birthing."

"Under normal conditions, yes, but you cannot do this alone."

"I can. I will."

"Do as she says," Shizuka said. Her lungs were growing heavy. Soon, very soon, she would lack the strength to fill them even once more.

She heard men say, "Yes, Lady Shizuka, we hear and obey."

Ayamé drew the knife from the scabbard.

Shizuka felt neither the opening of her kimono and her undergowns, nor the entry of the blade, nor the increased flow of her blood, nor the departure of her daughter from her womb into the world. Sight remained to her, dimly, and sound, as from a distance. Every other sense was already gone.

She heard a newborn's first cry. Even from afar, as she was, the infant's vigor was obvious. Shizuka smiled.

"Your daughter, my lady." Ayamé placed something against her chest and held it there. It was warm, it moved, it cried, it was very heavy.

Shizuka felt a rhythm not her own, insistent, faint, reminiscent of the earliest warning tremors of an imminent earthquake.

It was the rapid beating of a new heart.

Shizuka could no longer move her arms. There was no embrace, no first, no last. She thought she could feel the heat coming from the tiny body, but she knew it was her imagination. There was no feeling left in her body at all.

"Sen," Shizuka said.

. . . . .

They were a troop of thirty-one, thirty samurai and one former lady-in-waiting, moving northwest around Cape Muroto, into the hidden mountain passes of Shikoku island. Behind them—a burning castle called Cloud of Sparrows, pursuers in their thousands, the ashes of their lord and lady, the headless corpses of the traitors who murdered them.

Ayamé sat in the saddle like a samurai. She could not be ladylike and ride as hard as she must. In her arms, she held Lady Sen. She would tell Chiaki of Lady Shizuka's prediction, that Ayamé's own child would be a son, and that he was adopted before he was born, before he was conceived, into the Okumichi clan. He would be Great Lord, Shizuka said, and he would marry Sen.

Ayamé will tell Chiaki all this, but later. Now she saw that his mourning was too heavy for him to bear anything else. He mourned his father, whom he loved, who was a traitor. He mourned his lord, a great leader who might have been Shogun.

But most of all, he mourned Lady Shizuka, as Ayamé did.

After the next rise, they would descend onto a valley pathway. Ayamé turned for a last look.

She could not see Cloud of Sparrows. It was too far away. She could not even see the smoke from its flames.

It did not take long for so small a troop to pass.

Soon it was as it had been before they appeared.

The green pines of Muroto.

The sky above.

The earth below.